Under The Magic

By: Terri Talley Venters

A Collection of six novellas

Sulfur Springs
Europium Gem Mine
Noah's Nickel
Manganese Magic
Platinum Princess
Plutonium Princess

Elements of Mystery Books
By:
Terri Talley Venters

<u>Carbon Copy Saga</u>
Carbon Copy
Tin Roof
Silver Lining
Luke's Lithium

<u>Cauldron Series</u>
Copper Cauldron
Cobalt Cauldron
Calcium Cauldron
Chromium Cauldron
Zirconium Cauldron

<u>Under The Magic Adventures</u>
Sulfur Springs
Europium Gem Mine
Noah's Nickel
Manganese Magic
Platinum Princess
Plutonium Princess

<u>Stand Alone Novels</u>
Iron Curtains
Body Of Gold
Elements of Mystery
Hidden Helium

To the happiest place on Earth

Part One
Sulfur Springs

Sulfur Springs
THE FOUNTAIN OF YOUTH
AN ELEMENTS OF MYSTERY-
UNDER THE MAGIC ADVENTURE

TERRI TALLEY VENTERS

Prologue

Excerpt from *Silver Lining*

"You wanted to see me, Grier?" Tommy Garrison walked through the door of his cousin's study at Castle Garrison in Scotland. Wearing Levis, a plaid flannel shirt and hiking boots, his rugged appearance never surprised anyone. His archaeology tools, nestled in his work belt, hung loosely around his waist. His straight, sandy blond hair was parted to the side. The sea-green of his eyes, a Garrison family trait, stood out against a tanned complexion.

"Hey, Tommy, I've gotta surprise for ya. Let's take a walk, shall we?" Grier led Tommy outside Castle Garrison. They stood on the terrace overlooking the sparsely landscaped lawn in front of the castle. Grier looked up at the sky and held his hand over his brow to block the noonday sun.

"What are we looking at?" Tommy asked, looking at his watch like he had somewhere else more important to be—digging in the ground somewhere.

"My helicopter, it's due to arrive any moment now from Edinburgh." Grier kept his gaze on the horizon. He moved his hand behind his ear and cocked his head to the side to listen for the loud noise of the rotating chopper blades.

"That's nice, but what's this got to do with me?" Tommy's tone rang with his impatience, another Garrison family trait.

"Lilly is picking up one of her girlfriends from the airport. I'm surprised I can't see the bird yet."

Tommy shook his head, took a step back and held up his hands in reluctance. "Oh, no, please don't tell me you're setting me up with someone."

Grier turned and smiled devilishly. "Trust me on this one."

Tommy threw his hands up in the air and retreated. "Uh, uh, no way, I'm outta here."

Grier grabbed him and pulled him into a headlock. He treated Tommy like the little brother he never had growing up.

"Dude, let go, you piece of crap. I don't have time for relationships. My work is my life. No woman can put up with me being gone for six months at a time. Believe me, I've tried." Tommy sighed.

Grier released him. "She's an archaeologist, too."

Tommy's eyes lit up.

"Oh, and she looks like Megan Fox." Grier winked.

Tommy grabbed his chest over his heart like it just stopped beating.

"You had me at archaeologist." Tommy smiled.

"Look, there she is." He pointed towards the small spec on the horizon. "Come on, let's go meet her."

"You don't have to tell me twice." Tommy followed Grier down a flight of stone steps off the terrace to the lawn.

The helicopter grew bigger and bigger, and the noise from the chopper's blades grew louder and louder. Tommy covered his ears. The wind from the blades blew through his hair, and the helicopter hovered over the lawn before setting down. When the blades finally slowed to a stop, two women, Lilly and Victoria, emerged from the helicopter.

Both striking, the women were complete opposites. Lilly with her long, blonde hair, and Victoria with her long, brunette locks. Lilly wore a fitted suit, and Victoria dressed exactly like Tommy.

"I think I'm in love," Tommy said.

Chapter One

"Hi, mom, I'm home." Victoria Ventures entered her parents' tiny house in her hometown of Charleston, South Carolina and dropped her duffel bag on the terrazzo floor.

"Oh, Vicky, you're home early. I'll be out in a minute, just putting my face on." Victoria's mother hollered from the guest bathroom, knowing full well that her daughter hated being called "Vicky" since she was a teenager.

"Fox News Update with Brit Hume." The television blared from the corner of the living room.

The bright light of the blaring television drew Victoria like a zombie to a human. Slowly stepping, she meandered through the maze of recliners and end tables to stand in front of her parents' ancient, tiny television.

"Another sinkhole in Central Florida claims its next victim. No human casualties, but this two-story home in Kissimmee, Florida collapsed into the newest sinkhole." Brit Hume's face disappeared to reveal aerial footage of the brick home sucked into the earth in a giant hole. "This is the third sinkhole this month. The massive draught in the area lowered water levels to a record low. The absence of water in Florida's underground caverns weakened the cave ceilings. Without the underground water to support it, the cave ceilings collapsed to create a sinkhole."

"Isn't it awful?" Anne, Victoria's mother, walked out of the bathroom. Her long, black hair, pulled into a tight bun, stretched the pale skin back on her face, now caked with make-up. Her beautiful, ice-blue eyes, like Victoria's, still stood out under layers of eyeshadow, eyeliner and mascara. A faded, floral print house dress, also known as a mumu, covered her petite frame.

"Hi, mom." Victoria bent down to hug her. She'd inherited her six-foot height from her father, but her blue eyes and raven hair came from her mother. Releasing the hug, she turned to the television. "Isn't is awful? At least no one was hurt."

"Seems like there's a new one every week. It ain't rained down der in months." Anne's southern drawl made Victoria feel at home again.

"I hope Disney World doesn't fall into the Earth." Victoria always wanted to go back to the 'Happiest place on Earth.'

"Is that another crack about us not taking you to Disney as a child?" Anne grabbed her pack of Pall Malls and a lighter. The skin between her eyebrows wrinkled as she lit her cigarette and drew in her first drag.

"No, mom. I know you and dad couldn't afford it." Victoria referred to her parents' riches to rags story, thanks to the collapse of the real estate market in eighties.

"At least I let you go down to Disney with Lilly for her and Luke's tenth birthday party." She stepped out onto the screened-in porch and blew her smoke out.

Victoria followed her mom outside and sat on the worn wicker loveseat. She'd given up getting her mom to quit smoking, but prayed she'd kick the habit on her own one day.

"Speaking of Lilly, the wedding was beautiful. You should've come. I'd've paid for your plane ticket." Victoria referred to her healthy, yet hard earned savings account.

"I can't take your money. I know how hard you work for it. Besides, I couldn't go eight hours on a plane to Scotland without a smoke. I'd go nuts."

"You could've met Tommy." Victoria grinned just saying his name.

"Huh? Who's Tommy?" Anne flicked her ashes into the overfilled ashtray.

"Tommy Garrison, he's the Scottish cousin of Lilly's husband, Grier Garrison."

"You met someone? At the wedding? Tell me all about it." Anne crushed her cigarette butt into the ashtray and leaned forward, obviously excited to hear news about Victoria's new man.

"He's dreamy." Victoria closed her eyes, leaned back in the loveseat and sighed.

"You said he was Scottish? As in, he lives in Scotland?" Anne's thin, drawn-on eyebrows arched inquisitively.

"Well, kinda sorta, but not really."

"Huh?"

"His home is in Scotland, Castle Garrison actually, but he travels a lot."

"Oh, then that'll never work, not as much as you travel, too."

"But not if we work in the same field."

"You mean? He's an..."

"An archaeologist, too." Victoria finished her mother's sentence.

"Well that's convenient. Ya'll can dig around in the dirt together. You didn't sleep with him already, did you? You know how I always tell you not be 'fast.'" Anne referred to the old-fashion saying about promiscuous girls.

"No, mom. We just danced at the wedding and talked shop all evening. He didn't even give me a real kiss yet, just a peck on the cheek goodnight."

"What? Is he gay or something?"

"I hope not. He said he wanted to take me on a real date."

Ring, ring, ring.

Victoria pulled her cell phone out of the back pocket of her skinny jeans. The name Tommy illuminated her iPhone. "Speak of the devil. I'd better get this."

"I'll give you some privacy. Besides, I was just fixin' to go to Walmart." Anne stood up and left the porch.

Chapter Two

"Hello, handsome." Victoria answered the phone and leaned back into the love seat with the corners of her lips turned up. Hoping her boldness didn't scare him off, she lifted her feet onto the ottoman to get comfy.

"Hello, beautiful." Tommy's compliment with his Scottish accent hypnotized her.

"Perfect timing, I just got home."

"Good, I'm glad you made it home safe. That's one of the reasons I called."

"Oh, yeah? What's the other?"

"I wanted to tell you how much I enjoyed meeting you and talking to you at the wedding," he said.

"Me, too. It's refreshing to get to talk about my passion without boring the other person." Twirling her hair, she was dying to bring up seeing him again. Since he seemed like an old-fashioned gentleman, she'd let him broach the subject. His calling her right away told her that he'd felt a strong, romantic connection, too.

"You're preaching to the choir. In our line of work with constant traveling, it makes dating impractical."

"Not impossible I hope."

"No, not with you. Which is why I want to ask you out on a date."

Yes! Raising her arms over her head like a referee signally a touchdown, she tried not to excessively celebrate her victory. "I'd love to."

"Fantastic," he sighed, obviously relieved.

"How's it going over there? Are you swamped with the silver mine?" She referred to the recent discovery of a silver mine beneath Castle Garrison.

"It's insane here with all of these people. And the silver mine is boring, nothing of any archaeological significance, so far."

"Are you able to get away anytime soon?" Victoria already worried about their geography problem.

"Yes, as a matter of fact, I can. I just finished a three-year dig in Africa, and I have nothing in the pipelines yet. But something always seems to come up. I'm often asked to consult so I can write about it in our professional journals."

"I love reading your articles. Attaching your name to a dig is highly coveted here in the States. Your name brings lots of clout, and more importantly, funding."

"Thank you. It means a lot that you read my articles."

"You're welcome. But back to our first date. What time frame were you thinking?"

"This weekend if you'll have me. I can't wait to see you again. How about I come to the States? We can meet somewhere. Where would you like our first official date to be?"

Although a little disappointed that he didn't want to plan their first date, she forgave him. After all, he offered to fly across the Atlantic Ocean to see her. And his giving her what she wanted thrilled her. Not wanting to do something traditional for their first date, she knew exactly where they'd go. "Disney World."

Chapter Three

Flight just landed. Can't wait to see you.

Reading Tommy's text, anticipation filled Victoria. But she was nervous about spending the whole weekend together. Getting a hotel with a man assumes certain, physical things. But he swore he'd gotten a great deal on a two-bedroom suite at the Grand Floridian, only a quick monorail ride away from the Magic Kingdom.

I'm just outside of security

Texting back, she stepped closer to security. Trying not to appear too anxious, she watched arriving passengers walk by at Orlando International Airport. But when she spotted him, her aloofness faded.

Tommy's straight, sandy blond hair, feathered to the side, stood out on top of his six-foot, four-inch muscular frame. He looked and sounded like a younger Ewan McGregor. A smile formed while this handsome vision approached, and she waved eagerly.

Spotting her, he smiled a perfect set of teeth and ran towards her. Getting closer, his sea-green eyes beckoned her, and she ran towards the most handsome man she'd ever met. Picking her up in a bear hug, Tommy swung her around effortlessly, like a soldier coming home to his girlfriend after months apart. But for them it'd only been a few days.

"Oh, Victoria. You're more beautiful than I remember." Tommy set her back down on Earth and continued their embrace.

"It's great to see you, too, handsome." Victoria tilted her head up and smiled at him.

Grabbing her hand, he led her towards the baggage claim. "I just need to fetch my suitcase, and then we can head straight to Disney."

"How was your flight?" Grasping his big strong hand, she felt his calluses from digging in the dirt for a living. Relief swept through her knowing that he wouldn't mind her own rough hands.

"It flew by. I slept most of the way. I'm one of those lucky few who can sleep on airplanes."

"Me, too. Probably because I'm used to long flights. A big meal, a glass or two of wine, earplugs and a blanket and I'm out." She snapped her fingers.

"Ah, here it is." Picking up his suitcase effortlessly, he turned to her. "Where's your car?"

"This way. It was just easier for me to drive down from Charleston. Besides, I packed way too much stuff for a weekend away."

"Tell me about it. I'm worse than a girl. With so much to do at Disney, I packed for every possibility." His stride matched hers.

"I have a confession to make. I always travel with my tools. You never know what you'll find."

"Like silver in Scotland."

They laughed.

"Great minds think alike. I brought my favorite tools, too." Tommy nodded to his suitcase. "Blew the fifty-pound weight limit, but I feel naked without them."

The word 'naked' caught her attention. A sight she'd fantasized about since they'd met.

Stepping off the elevator in the parking garage, she spotted her car. "There it is." Pointing to her Gator blue Jeep Liberty, she knew there'd be plenty of room for his luggage.

"I think I'm in love. How practical to drive a Jeep in our line of work."

"I know. Plus, I have a surprise for you." Opening the back hatch, she waved her hands at two sets of golf clubs.

"It's official. I'm in love." He pecked her cheek.

"I remember your saying how much you love to golf. So I borrowed my friend's sets—his and hers Titleist."

Rubbing his hands along the driver, he studied the excellent quality of the clubs. "Thank you so much, Victoria. It's a Scottish thing. We love to golf. I've played many famous courses in Scotland. And I try to play whenever I travel. It's fun trying a new course, just to say I've played there. This weekend I can scratch Disney off my Bucket List."

"Well, unfortunately, I'm terrible. But I promise my bad shots will be entertaining. I brought plenty of balls for when I lose them in the woods."

"Perhaps we'll get lucky and stumble upon the archaeological find of the century." Tommy laughed.

Chapter Four

"Excellent choice for a first date," Tommy said.

They pulled up to the Grand Floridian Resort at Walt Disney World and were greeted with bellhops in white caps, blue and white striped shirts and white knickers. The white hotel and its red intricate roof with turrets, took them back in time to the Victorian Era. A refurbished horse-drawn carriage, minus the horses, was parked on the sidewalk of the covered driveway entrance to the hotel.

"I've always wanted to come back to Disney, ever since I was a kid." Stopping her Jeep, she waited for the eager bellhop to open her door.

"When was the last time you were here?" Tommy asked while the bellhops removed their luggage and stacked them onto a rolling luggage cart.

"I was ten years old. But I'm not saying how many years ago that was. It was for Lilly and Luke's birthday party. That's the only time I've been here," she confessed.

"That's some birthday party."

"Yeah. The best *ever*. I know I picked Disney for our first date. But I'm very inexperienced here. I've only been to the Magic Kingdom, but I understand there are three more theme parks here, plus two waterparks and Disney Springs, formerly known as Downtown Disney."

"Don't fret, my love. Grier gave me excellent tips. He says he takes Lilly here 'all the time.'" Using air quotes, Tommy mimicked Grier's sarcasm perfectly.

A monorail roared overheard, stopping to pick up its next batch of passengers and tote them to the Magic Kingdom, Transportation and Ticket Center, Contemporary Resort Hotel or the Polynesian Resort.

"How cool is that." Covering her ears, Victoria craned her neck back.

"Welcome to the Grand Floridian. Checking in?" a man in a dark suit and Disney name tag asked.

Nodding, Tommy grabbed Victoria's hand. "Thank you, yes."

"What the name on the reservation?"

"Garrison."

The man consulted his iPad. "Ah, I see. Checking in today for seven nights?"

"Yes." Tommy cringed, like he didn't want her to know he'd booked it for the whole week.

Victoria shot him a confused look, a little miffed at his presumption, but thrilled he had high expectations for their future.

Turning to her, he squeezed her hand. "Please forgive me for not telling you sooner, but they talked me into a package deal including meals, park tickets and this hotel for a week."

"Best first date *ever*." She kissed his cheek.

"Follow me. Are we celebrating anything?" the greeter asked.

"Yes, my first trip," Tommy confessed.

"No, get out." Victoria's tone oozed with incredulity.

"Scotland's pretty far away. And I never take vacations. When a dig or trip is finished, I just want to go home and see my father."

Walking into the grand lobby, Victoria gasped. The high ceilings, four stories tall, boasted an enormous chandelier. A wide staircase led to the second level restaurants and balcony overlooking the lobby. Twin birdcages, large enough for humans, decorated the lobby with exotic plants. Victorian furnishings scattered the lobby in cozy seating arrangements. But her favorite part of the lobby was the grand piano with its pianist playing Disney songs. She immediately recognized the Oscar winning tune—*When You Wish Upon a Star* from the movie *Pinocchio*.

"Right this way, Sandy will check you in." The suited man led them to the check-in desk. "Enjoy your stay. The bellhop will hold your luggage until after you check in."

"Welcome to the Grand Floridian. Is this your first time staying with us?" Sandy asked with a pleasant smile.

They nodded.

"Are we celebrating anything?" Sandy asked with a perky tone.

"It's our first date," Victoria blurted. *Please don't judge me.*

"And my first time at Disney," Tommy added.

"Ah, then ya'll need buttons." Sandy retrieved three buttons from her drawer. All boasting Disney characters, one button read, "First Time." And the other two read, "Special Occasion." On the blank space of the two special occasion buttons, she wrote with a Sharpie, "First Date," dotting the *i* with Mickey Mouse ears. "Ya'll can wear these on your shirts for your whole trip."

"Thank you." Victoria and Tommy eagerly pinned the buttons to their shirts, excited to act like kids together.

"Now, for the fun part. Let's see if we can upgrade your suite to a park view. It's not often I hear of Disney being a first date." Clicking the buttons, Sandy made faces at the computer screen. "Just bear with me, I'm not playing Tetris, I swear. Ah, here's a great suite with a view of the Magic Kingdom. You can even see the fireworks from your balcony."

"Wow. Sounds wonderful." Victoria smiled, hoping for fireworks with Tommy, too.

"Your Magic Bands arrived." Sandy retrieved a small rectangular box from the shelf behind her. Opening the box revealed two Magic Bands—one pink and one blue.

"What are these?" Victoria asked.

"These are Magic Bands. They are your room keys, park tickets and FastPasses, plus you can use them for charging, too," Sandy explained.

"Amazing technology." Victoria pulled her pink band from the box.

"Here, allow me." Tommy wrapped the pink bracelet with the Mickey Mouse emblem around her wrist, snapping it into place. "You have tiny wrists, my dear."

"Now just enter your own four-digit code into this machine. This will be your code to use for charging privileges with this band."

Tommy typed in four digits, showing Victoria his number selection.

"Now enter the code again to confirm."

Tommy typed the code again.

"You're all set. Now James will show you to your room. Enjoy your stay." Sandy waved goodbye.

Victoria and Tommy followed James out double glass doors onto a patio. "Now if you'll wait here one moment, I'll put your luggage in the golf cart and drive it around to pick you up and take you to your room."

Nodding, Victoria and Tommy stood hand in hand, enjoying the view of the resort. To the right was a pool with water slides and fountains, perfect for families. To the left was a quiet pool with two hot tubs and a bar. Beyond the pools was a white, sandy beach at the shore of the Seven Seas Lagoon.

Cabanas and lounge chairs lined the beach. Although too cold for sunbathing in January, it looked inviting for a place to relax. Across the lake to the right was the Polynesian Resort. The tropical paradise with palm trees and tiki huts contrasted the Grand Floridian's Victorian style.

"Our chariot awaits, milady." Tommy waved his arm towards the approaching golf cart with their luggage and golf bags.

Boarding the cart, Tommy slid in next to her. The bellhop drove them around the pool towards their building. "There are seven restaurants at the Grand Floridian."

"Which do you recommend?" Tommy asked.

"My two favorites are the Garden View Tea Room for a traditional English Tea with the all the trimmings."

"Just like home." Tommy pulled Victoria close.

"And my favorite restaurant in the world is...."

"In the world?" she asked.

"Victoria and Albert's, the epitome of fine dining. It's the only five-star restaurant in Orlando. Here we are." James stopped the golf cart and transferred the luggage to a rolling cart.

Exiting, Victoria and Tommy followed James into the building and up to the fourth floor. Entering their suite, a plush living room, dining room and kitchenette greeted them. To the left was a bedroom with an en-suite bathroom. A king size bed with gold and white linens beckoned them. To the right was another bedroom with two queen beds.

While James brought in their luggage and placed it on suitcase racks, Tommy pulled out a twenty-dollar bill. "Thank you, James."

"Thank you, sir. Have a magical day." James left the room twenty bucks richer.

Tommy and Victoria walked out onto a large, private balcony overlooking the lagoon. On the other side of the lagoon stood the Magic Kingdom with Space Mountain and the park's crowning glory—Cinderella's castle. Inspired by Schlöss Neuschwanstein in Germany, the beautiful blue and cream-colored castle provided the best view imaginable.

"I've wanted to do this since I met you. Looks like a great spot for a first kiss. Tommy looked into her eyes, slid his fingers behind her neck and kissed her.

Victoria returned the kiss. Then pulled apart slowly and said, "Now I see why they call this the 'Happiest place on Earth.'" Victoria kissed him again.

Chapter Five

"What are these FastPasses I keep hearing about?" Victoria asked. They walked down Main Street USA in the Magic Kingdom, and the shops beckoned them. But the magnificent view of Cinderella's Castle ahead kept them on a forward path.

"Instead of waiting in line for an hour or two for a popular ride, you can schedule your time in advance. Then just show up at your allotted time range and avoid the wait time." Tommy held her hand as they approached the castle.

"That's clever. What FastPasses did you get?" Victoria kept her gaze forward, admiring the castle and all its blue, glittering turrets.

"Space Mountain, Buzz Lightyear and Under the Sea: Journey of The Little Mermaid," he said.

"I love those movies—*The Little Mermaid* and *Toy Story*. I've watched all the Disney movies with my girlfriends, Lilly, Britta and Chelsea."

"So I chose wisely? I wasn't sure what to pick."

"Those sound great, but..."

"Uh, oh. But what?" Tommy faced her with a concerned expression.

"It's just that, one of my favorite rides when I was a kid was 20,000 Leagues Under the Sea. It's a submarine ride underwater."

"Are you a Vernian?"

"Huh?" She stared at him, confused.

"Vernian, an avid fan of Jules Verne, the author of *20,000 Leagues Under the Sea*."

"Oh, no, I just thought it was the coolest thing, but I guess everything's fascinating through a ten-year-old's eyes."

"Hmmm. I don't remember seeing it on the FastPass list. Maybe we'll just have to wait in line with the rest of the schmucks. We have time before we ride Space Mountain and shoot aliens on Buzz Lightyear. Let's see if I can find it on the map."

"I remember where it is—through the castle and to the right." Grabbing Tommy's arm, she dragged him up the ramp and into the castle.

Walking into Cinderella's Castle, Victoria stopped and admired the intricate mosaic tiles depicting various scenes from the movie *Cinderella*. Suffering from "Shiny object syndrome," she forgot all about the 20,000 Leagues Under the Sea ride. Touching the shiny colored glass, she followed the story from Cinderella scrubbing the floors, to marrying her Prince Charming. Fantasies of her and Tommy filled her, and she wished for her own "'Happily Ever After.'"

Sliding his arm around her waist, Tommy pulled her close. He looked into her eyes and kissed her, right in Cinderella's Castle.

Throwing her arms around Tommy's neck, Victoria kissed him back, ignoring all of the tourists and children walking by. Finally ending the kiss, she hugged him and said, "Sorry, I kinda got distracted."

"So did I." He hugged her back.

"Oh, we have to ride the carousel." She pointed at the merry-go-round on the other side of the castle. "Later, I guess."

"Let's take a picture. Turn your back to the castle." Tommy pointed. Spotting an eager Cast Member, he asked, "Do you mind taking our picture?"

"Of course not." Taking the camera, the Cast Member stepped back and framed the shot to include the back of the castle with its beautiful stained-glass windows.

Tommy stood beside her, put his arm around her and smiled for the camera.

"Say Mickey." The Cast Member took the picture.

"Thank you." Tommy retrieved his camera and viewed the picture on the display screen.

"We make a lovely couple," Victoria blurted. Cringing, she hoped she didn't scare him off for referring to them as a couple so early in the relationship. Cursing her "foot-in-mouth disease," she held her breath waiting for Tommy's reaction.

"Yes, we do." Then he rewarded her with a kiss on the cheek.

Phew.

"Mickey Mouse ears, we have to get them." Pointing at a family all sporting the black ears on a hat, Victoria enjoyed acting like a kid.

"Of course." Tommy led her into a store which displayed the mouse ear hats.

Each grabbing one, they tried them on and studied each other.

"How do I look?" she asked.

"Ridiculous and beautiful. We have to buy these." He carried the hats to a counter.

Noticing the sewing machine with gold thread, she pointed. "Look, we can get our names sewn on the back of the hats."

Tommy paid the cashier, and they watched the Cast Member sew their names on each hat in cursive with gold thread.

Donning the hats like excited five-year-old children, they left the store hand-in-hand.

Walking past the carousel, Victoria paused. "They've changed things. I remember that Snow White's Scary Adventure and Mr. Toad's Wild Ride were right here."

"Bummer, those sound like fun rides."

Turning to the right after the carousel, she walked the path which she remembered led to her favorite ride. A new castle stood near where the submarine ride was *supposed* to be.

"This is all different than what I remember. I don't recall another castle." She wandered aimlessly, hoping to find it. Staring at the castle in the New Fantasyland, she recognized it from Disney's animated version of *Beauty and the Beast*. Taking a second to admire its magnificence, she recognized the rock formation to the right of Belle's Castle.

Pointing, she said, "That's it. I remember those rocks. It's part of the cave which the submarine ride goes into." Grabbing Tommy's hand, Victoria excitedly hurried down the sloped sidewalk leading to the cave.

Passing tall rock formations along the way, she searched for the entrance to the ride. But instead of finding the steps up to the platform to ride 20,000 Leagues, she found disappointment. *Little Mermaid?* The Little Mermaid ride didn't disappoint her, but the absence of her favorite submarine ride did.

"Ah, the Little Mermaid ride. Now we know where to come back to after Space Mountain and Buzz Lightyear." Tommy placed his hand on her shoulder and pulled her in.

"But, where's my submarine ride?" She whined like a toddler. Remembering the park map, she retrieved it from her small backpack and consulted it. Starting with where the 20,000 leagues ride *should* be, she scanned the entire New Fantasyland. After finding nothing, she searched the list of attractions in Fantasyland: Under the Sea—Journey of the Little Mermaid, Seven Dwarfs Mine Train, Dumbo, Peter Pan's Flight, It's A Small World, Philharmonic, Winnie the Pooh, etc.

"Can I help you?" a cheerful Cast Member asked. The nice lady wore a medieval maiden costume. Her name tag read, "Janine" from "Orlando".

"Yes, please. I'm looking for 20,000 Leagues Under the Sea."

"Oh, I'm sorry. That attraction closed in 1994. It sat unused for the longest time, and then they incorporated its cave structure into the Little Mermaid ride when they built the New Fantasyland." Janine waved towards the new mermaid ride.

"Well, at least I was in the right place." Victoria forced a smile to mask her disappointment.

"I'm sorry, my dear." Tommy squeezed her hand with a sympathetic pout of his lips.

"Why did they close it? I loved that ride when I was a kid."

"Something about the water," Janine said.

Chapter Six

"Thanks again for bringing these golf clubs." Tommy drove the golf cart towards the first hole of the golf course near the Grand Floridian Resort.

"You're very welcome. But remember to forgive my golf skills, or lack thereof." Victoria winced just thinking how bad her game was.

"There's nobody behind us, so we have plenty of time." He stopped the cart at the first hole.

"Maybe you could give me a lesson." She thought of Tommy's arms around her under the ploy of improving her swing.

"Anything for you, my dear." Walking to the back of the cart, Tommy read the sign at the first hole. "Par three, 177 yards."

Knowing her horrible swing, she pulled the Florida Gator golf club protector off the driver and walked towards the ladies' tee.

Tommy pulled out a five iron and said, "Uh, my dear, you don't need a driver on this hole, especially from the ladies' tee."

"Oh, trust me, I do." Leaning over to tee her pink golf ball, Victoria slightly bent her knees and extended her club to the ball.

"I'll watch your technique on the first hole and then give you tips on the second." Leaning on the club with his right arm fully extended, he crossed his legs.

Nervous with him watching, she told herself, "It's just a game." She took two practice swings before she sliced the ball into the woods, barely half the distance to the green.

"Told you I'd never make it to the green." She banged her driver on the ground like a frustrated golf pro.

"It's okay. Here, let me help you." Tommy pulled a five iron from Victoria's pink golf bag.

Giving her the club, he stood behind her. The warmth of his body consumed her. His hot breath on her neck gave her goose bumps. "I warned you." She bent her knees to follow his stance.

"We'll improve your game," he whispered into her ear with a sexy, bedroom voice. Grasping her hands, he maneuvered her fingers. "Keep your fingers laced around the club, like this."

"Oh, I just kinda held it awkwardly, but this feels so much better."

"Keep your feet a shoulder-width apart, and then swing back." He kept his hands on hers when she swung the club up behind her.

"Now, keep both feet on the ground, and keep your eye on the ball. Then swing the club all the way around, like a pendulum."

"Oh, I just stopped once I hit the ball." Grimacing, she envisioned herself hitting the ball perfectly with his arms around her.

"I know. It's called 'following through,' You'll want to end your swing back up where you started—above your head." Tommy stepped back to watch her.

Holding the club above her, she kept her eye on the ball and swung the club all the way around.

Whoosh.

Holding her hand over her forehead, she lost sight of the ball in the setting sun. The ball dropped onto the green near the edge of the rough.

"Nice. That's our goal on a par three—first shot to the green, and then two putts to make par." Tommy gave her a high five.

"It was your excellent teaching." She stepped back with Tommy to the men's tee.

"Normally, furthest from the hole hits first, but I wanted to watch your swing. Now, watch my technique and try to keep this stance and posture."

Whoosh.

Tommy's white ball flew towards the sky and dropped onto the green. Rolling to the hole, the ball disappeared.

"Where did it go?" she asked.

"Oh my, gosh, I just got a hole in one." Grinning, he hugged Victoria, picked her up and swung her around.

"Wow! Congratulations. You made it look so easy." She pecked him on the lips while he set her back down.

"You're my good luck charm. That was my first hole-in-one." Tommy escorted her back to the cart.

"Everything's magical at Disney." Grabbing the rail of the golf cart, she slid in next to him. "What do they do for a hole in one?"

"I don't know. Each golf course is different. Some give trophies or plaques with the golf ball incorporated into the trophy. Some have a wall they add your name to. Surely Disney will do something nice." He drove the cart to the far side of the green, just before the second tee.

"Let's get your ball." Climbing out, she pulled her putter out of the bag and held it up. "I know this one is right."

Tommy laughed and walked towards the hole. Pulling out his camera, he took a snapshot of the ball in the hole.

"Do you mind?" After handing her the camera, he pulled the ball out of the hole and held it between his thumb and index finger.

"Oh, sure." Taking the camera, she stepped back a few feet and framed the shot, admiring the handsome man grinning like a kid at... "like a kid at Disney." Chuckling at the irony of the metaphor, she clicked the camera.

"Let's see you sink this one." Tommy pocketed his ball and stepped back.

Encouraged by his optimism, Victoria squatted to the ground and lined up her shot like a pro. Standing back up, she putted the pink ball and watched with enthusiasm as it rolled directly towards the hole and disappeared.

"Yippee!" She jumped up and down to celebrate her birdie shot, ignoring the first slice into the woods, of course.

"Nice shot, babe. I'm impressed. They say putting is eighty percent of the game. We'll just work on your swing, and you'll be good enough for the LPGA." Tommy high-fived her.

"My girlfriends and I played a lot of mini-golf." She admitted and walked towards the golf cart to trade in her putter for a driver. Turning to Tommy, she held up the club for his approval.

"Yes, you'll need a driver for this par five." He hit his ball first, dropping it halfway towards the second green.

"Nice drive." Victoria picked up on the golf lingo quickly.

"Do you see that large oak tree to the right?" Tommy pointed.

"The one before the half-empty pond?" She squinted towards the late afternoon sun.

"Yes, drop your ball just before that tree, and then you can cross the water on your second drive."

"Okey dokey." Trying to remember everything Tommy'd taught her, she placed her ball on the tee and bent her knees.

"Now remember, you tend to slice towards the right, so don't end up in the woods again," Tommy said.

"Yeah, yeah, yeah." Taking a practice swing, she tried to focus on this being fun, *not* frustrating. "Okay, here it goes, to the left, but not too much." She pulled the club back and up over her head with an awkward pause at the top. Then she swung the club like a pendulum.

Whoosh.

The ball sliced right into the woods, again. Dropping her head with disappointment because she'd tried so dang hard to do everything Tommy'd told her, she refrained from banging her driver on the ground, again.

"Must be a cursed club. Want a 'do over' with a three iron?" Using air quotes, Tommy laughed.

"No. I'll play it where it lies. Or else I'll run out of my pink balls. Something tells me I need to find this one." Sulking, she walked into the woods with her head down. She walked at least twenty yards into the woods, surprised the bright pink ball didn't stand out against the pine straw covered ground.

Turning back to Tommy, she couldn't see him through the trees which grew denser as she walked further in. *Don't get lost in the woods like Snow White.* Half expecting to find a cottage with seven little men, she plugged on. Finally, the bright pink ball lay on the ground ten feet away.

"Victoria? Any luck. I'm coming in to find you," Tommy hollered from the second fairway.

Picking up the ball, she paused. The ground changed drastically ahead. The tops of the pine trees were on the ground, not thirty feet above her like the rest.

"Victoria? Where are you?" His tone rang desperate this time.

"Tommy, you've got to see this," she hollered back. Continuing towards the anomaly in the forest, she picked up her pace with excitement. *I think I know what this is.* Stopping just short of the edge, she saw the pine trees which had fallen into a large hole. But *sunk* was a more accurate term to describe the nearly fifty-foot hole in the earth.

"Ah, there you are. I've been running everywhere trying to find you." Tommy jogged up to her and bent at the waist, slightly out of breath.

Turning to him, she nodded towards the big hole. "Check this out."

"What? Another shiny object?" Poking fun of her tendency for distractions, he stood upright. His eyes widened once he saw what Victoria meant.

"I'll say." She smiled, thrilled to find one of these on her own.

"What is it?" Looking perplexed, he tilted his head and raised his eyebrows.

"It's a sinkhole."

Chapter Seven

"No way!" Tommy stepped closer to the hole and placed his hands on his hips. "It's huge!"

"I know. I'm speechless." Victoria shook her head, incredulous at her find. Although there probably wasn't any archaeological significance to the sinkhole, her fascination with geology piqued her curiosity to explore.

"This is so cool. We don't get these in Scotland." Stepping carefully, Tommy walked along the perimeter of the hole.

"We don't get these in Charleston, either. Remember, Florida originally came from Africa before the tectonic plates shifted." Placing her hands on her hips, she followed Tommy around the circumference of the sinkhole. She estimated that the hole was at least one hundred feet in diameter, and fifty feet deep.

"One hundred feet across, at least." He pointed.

"I reckon." Cringing for letting her Southern slang slip out, she recalled the recent news stories about sinkholes in Florida.

"My mother said there have been a lot of sinkholes in the news, about two or three a month."

"The water table must be low." He walked around to the opposite side of the hole.

"I'll say. I wonder if Disney knows about this?"

"Probably not. They're lucky this didn't happen in one of the parks. We're so close to the Magic Kingdom." He waved his arm towards the direction of Cinderella's Castle.

"Should we tell someone?" She regretted the question because her curiosity made her want to jump right in and explore.

"Maybe, eventually, but I'm dying to explore this hole. You Americans with their bureaucratic red tape would keep us from exploring." Tommy pointed at her.

Phew. "Don't tell Jiminy Cricket."

He laughed. Stepping on a tree, which lay horizontal, Tommy tested his weight. "I think we can climb down. There's a bunch of uprooted trees that fell into the sinkhole." He extended his hand to hers.

"What about our golf cart and clubs?" She remembered how they got here in the first place, her sliced drive into the woods from the second tee.

"I booked the last tee time of the day. That's how I knew there was no one behind us."

"Oh, cool. We have time to explore." She took his hand and walked on the horizontal timber.

"At least until the sunlight runs out."

"It must've happened recently, because these pine needles are still green." Letting go of Tommy, she pointed to the tops of the trees.

"Easy there. I'd say don't look down, but we have to in order to climb down all of these trees."

"I've climbed worse heights than this." Looking down, she could almost see the bottom. "Besides, even if we fall, a tree branch would break our fall before we hit the bottom."

"I don't suppose you have a flashlight with you?" His expression pleaded.

"In the hotel, of course, but I think we can get down without one." She sat down on the limb, reached down to the next tree with her leg, and climbed one level down.

"Okay, I'll follow you then. It's your find, after all."

"*Our* find, *if* there's anything to find." She grabbed the next branch below and eased herself down another level.

"Hey, wait up, you little monkey." He followed her down the same route.

"I practically lived in trees growing up." Recalling her childhood summers in Charleston's gigantic oak trees, she descended two more levels with ease.

"We won't have much sunlight soon." He pointed to the rapidly setting sun.

"I know, but we can always come back tomorrow with our gear." Climbing her way to the center and then down again, she easily traversed the next three levels.

"What do you think is down there?" Tommy asked from two levels above.

"Caves." Her curiosity, and short time frame, aided her rapid descent to the bottom.

"Caves?"

"Underground caverns. Think back to Geology 101 in college. Sinkholes are caused by underground caverns filled with water. When the water level drops, the cavern system weakens and sometimes the ground above collapses in. The ground in central Florida is riddled with limestone caverns. The underground is like swiss cheese, filled with holes," she recited a section of her college geology textbook from memory.

"Ah, so you're hoping that this sinkhole will expose an entrance to an underground cave system."

Jumping down off the last tree trunk, she hit the soft pine needles covering the ground. Standing up, she surveyed the bottom of the hole. Exploring the bottom of the once water-filled cavern, she peered through the waning sunlight. A seven-foot hole in the cavern wall beckoned her.

She smiled. "I love being right!"

Chapter Eight

The sunlight evaporated, leaving Victoria and Tommy in the dark.

"Oh, no. It got dark quick." He turned on the flash light of his cell phone.

"I wanna explore so bad," she pleaded.

Tommy grasped her hands. "Let's do this, instead. We'll get cleaned up, buy some supplies and have a nice dinner to celebrate."

She got lost in Tommy's sea-green eyes and could've easily agreed to anything. "And come back tomorrow?" Holding her hands in prayer, she begged.

"Yes. We can come back tomorrow. I'll schedule an early tee time, and we can spend the whole day down here exploring." He kissed her hand.

"Yeah!" Throwing her arms around Tommy, she hugged him tight.

"You don't mind skipping Disney?" His eyebrows rose with his tone of voice.

"Not for cave exploring." Her giddy tone matched her enthusiasm.

He looked up the sinkhole through the tree trunks. "We better climb out of here right now, unless you want to spend the night down here."

"Race you to the top." Grabbing onto the nearest branch, she pulled herself up onto the lowest tree and started ascending. She flew up the trees like a monkey and reached the surface in less than a minute.

* * * *

"Mmmm. This is so good." Victoria hummed with the goodness dancing on her taste buds. The *Rigatoni con Funghi* at Il Mulino New York Trattoria tasted wonderful. The truffle oil accentuated the wild mushrooms and garlic over pasta.

After shopping for supplies at the nearby outlet malls, they drove to the Swan Hotel near Epcot to eat at this restaurant based on Grier's recommendation.

She wore a simple, yet low-cut red dress with a flowing skirt. Her straightened, long black hair hung nearly to her waist.

"It's the truffle oil." Tommy poured them more Chianti. His teal-green dress shirt accentuated his gorgeous eyes.

Patting her full belly, she said, "We'll have to walk off this pasta after dinner."

"You read my mind, but not because of the calories. After dinner, I planned a nice, romantic stroll along the Boardwalk. We can walk to Epcot from here and catch the Illuminations show and fireworks."

"You've thought of everything. I'm looking forward to tonight, but I can't wait until tomorrow." She sipped her wine.

"Me, too." He looked up like he contemplated tomorrow's logistics.

She read his mind and solved their dilemma. "We can stuff both golf bags full of supplies. And then lower them down into the sinkhole."

"You're both brilliant and beautiful, Victoria." Sitting back in his chair, he looked impressed.

Loving the sound of her name with his Scottish accent, she blushed. "Thank you. You're pretty brilliant and beautiful, too."

Tearing off a piece of bread from the bread basket, he dunked the bread into his mostly empty pasta bowl to soak up the remaining truffle infused olive oil. "Mmmm. I've gotta try to make this sometime."

She followed his example and tore off a piece of bread to sop up the oil in her pasta bowl. "I'm so glad you did that because I was dying to do the same thing."

"Be a shame to let this wonderful sauce go to waste." He took another bite of his bread dipped it into pasta sauce.

"Did I hear you say, you cook?" Her eyes widened with enthusiasm. *A male archaeologist who's sweet, handsome and cooks. Let's get married and make brilliant, beautiful babies together.*

"Yes, it's a Garrison family trait. All of the males love to cook. We're descended from Norwegian Vikings. The men had to cook when they were off on their expeditions."

"You mean off pillaging and what not," she quipped. Sipping the rest of her wine, she sat back in her chair.

The waiter removed their empty pasta bowls and asked, "Can I interest you in dessert this evening?"

Tommy looked at Victoria to ascertain her interest in dessert.

"No, thanks, I'm stuffed."

"No, thanks," Tommy said, then the waiter left them. "Speaking of pillaging, what are we going to do if we find anything?"

"We'll do the right thing, of course. I'm not in it for the money. I'm in it for the possible archaeological significance, if there is any."

"Good, me too, eventually. But I want to document everything first before we announce it. Because once we do, it'll turn into a circus. Assuming we find anything, of course."

The waiter appeared with a silver bucket on ice, two small wine glasses and a ladle.

"What's this?" she asked, adjusting the napkin in her lap.

"Limoncello. It's an Italian liqueur invented in Capri. It's complimentary." The waiter ladled out a sample into each dessert wine glass. "Enjoy." He stepped away.

"To tomorrow." Tommy raised his glass to hers and clinked it.

"To tomorrow." Raising the Limoncello to her lips, Victoria sipped it. The tart balanced with the sweet, and the chilled liqueur went down smooth. Happiness filled her with the thought of tomorrow and the future with Tommy Garrison.

Chapter Nine

"Do we have everything?" Tommy asked from the living room of their hotel suite. He shuffled through the empty bags from Gander Mountain, the camping/outdoor supply store where they'd shopped at the night before.

"I think so. I even fit my cave scanner in here." Victoria nodded to her overstuffed, pink golf cart.

"Who brings a cave scanner and cave-plotting software to Disney?" Tommy joked.

"I just happened to have it from the silver mine at Castle Garrison." Wheeling her golf cart towards Tommy, she walked through the door he held open. She pushed the down button on the elevator.

Ding.

"Awesome." He waved her into the elevator and filed in after her.

She rolled her cart out of the elevator and onto the first floor. After a quick drive in her Jeep, they arrived at the golf course.

"Back again, Doctor Garrison and Doctor Ventures?" the man at the golf course check-in desk asked.

"Yes, we are. Bright and early today," Tommy said.

"Do you need a golf cart?"

"No thanks. It's a beautiful morning. We're going to walk the course today. Oh, can you please put a couple of those breakfast sandwiches and waters on our bill."

"Certainly." He retrieved two wrapped sandwiches and waters. Placing them in a to-go bag he said, "'Have a magical day.'"

Walking towards the first tee, she winked at him. "'Walk the course?' Good one."

"Well, we couldn't leave the golf cart parked on the second hole all day. People would grow suspicious."

"And booking the first tee time for the rest of the week isn't suspicious?" She rolled her cart to the tee and pulled out her five iron to keep up appearances.

"Good, you remembered not to use the driver on the first hole." Tommy poked fun of her awful swing from the day before.

"Hey, my lousy drive found us that cave," she hollered.

"Shhh. Play through until we're out of sight." He pulled out his five iron, swung and landed the ball on the green.

"Ahh. So close." She stared down the fairway.

"No hole-in-one today." Stomping his foot, he added, "Oh, shoot. I forgot to tell them about my hole-in-one yesterday."

"Well, we kinda got distracted. Besides, we have all week to tell them." Victoria teed up her ball, bent her knees, swung, and watched her pink ball land on the green near Tommy's ball.

"Nice. You're great with an iron, just cursed with the driver." He wheeled his golf cart to the green.

"Thank goodness I stink with the driver." Winking, she followed him down the fairway.

They arrived at the first hole green and turned back towards the small golf building where they'd checked in. With the building hidden from the trees on the first hole fairway, they knew the coast was clear. Picking up their golf balls without putting, they scurried past the second tee and into the woods.

"Ugh. This golf bag doesn't roll very well on the pine straw." Victoria struggled with her heavy cart.

"Here, allow me, my dear." He grabbed her bag and pulled both behind him.

"Thank you." His effortlessness didn't surprise her after seeing his strong, arm muscles bulge with the extra load.

Twenty yards later, they arrived at the sinkhole. "Okay, let's get these carts down there." He opened his golf bag and pulled out one of several ropes. Lassoing one end around a thick pine branch, he tied the other end around the strap of the golf bag. He put on his golf gloves to reduce friction and lowered the bag into the sinkhole.

"Should I go in first to guide the bag down?" She'd already begun the descent before he answered.

"Sure, go ahead. Don't let me stop you." He laughed because she was nearly halfway down already.

Guiding the bag through the trees, Victoria found a path which led the golf bag straight down the rest of the way. When the golf bag hit the bottom, she jumped down next to it and untied the rope from the strap. "Okay, we're down. Go ahead and pull the rope up," she hollered up to Tommy.

The roped disappeared back up through the fallen tree trunks. She opened the bag, retrieved a flashlight, and waved the beam around the cave.

"Hey, don't forget we have another bag to lower down," he yelled.

Victoria chuckled because Tommy already knew her too well. *How could she not get distracted in this cool cave?* Sighing, she climbed back up to the halfway point to maneuver the second bag down.

Tommy and the second bag descended quickly, and they removed all of their equipment out of the golf bags and onto the cave floor. Tommy turned on the large lantern, and the cave lit up.

"Look, there's the hole we saw yesterday." Pointing excitedly, she walked towards what she hoped was a vast, undiscovered cave system.

"Ah, ah, patience. We must take safety precautions." Tommy pulled out the twine and tied it to the trunk of a sunken pine tree.

"I wanna see how far it goes."

"So do I, but let's at least pack our backpacks with supplies and equipment. We'll need water, food, camera, flashlights, batteries, cave scanner, a pick ax and twine."

"I know, you're right. I'm just excited that's all." She acquiesced. "Great idea about leaving a trail with the twine. We wouldn't want to get lost in here."

"No one knows we're down here. And no one would even know to look for us until we don't check out in four days." Tommy's expression turned serious.

"That's scary, we could die down here and no one would ever find us. Although, I guess there are worst places to die." She slid her backpack over her shoulders and turned on her headband light. "I'm going to send a text to my mother so someone knows where we are."

"Good idea."

Victoria typed away on her phone, hit send and asked, "Ready?"

"Ready." He pecked her on the cheek. "You look beautiful."

"In my work clothes and headgear?"

"Yes, my dear. Now, let's go exploring. I'll follow you."

Shining her flashlight, she walked towards the hole. Taking a few steps inside, she said, "It's a tunnel."

Chapter Ten

"Victoria, wait up!" Tommy hollered from behind. "I've got to unwind this twine so we can find our way back out of this cave."

"Okay." Slowing down, she silently fumed. The anticipation of what lay ahead consumed her. The dry limestone of the cave tunnel slowly descended in a meandering pattern. Dead crustaceans on the floor piqued her curiosity. *Could they be walking on a dried up, underground river bed?*

"Thank you." He caught up to her, slightly winded.

"Are you getting this?" She pointed towards the GoPro camera mounted on his head.

"Yes, look at the ground. It's smoother than the walls. Like water once ran through here." He studied the ground. "In fact, I'm sure it did, based on the tiny remains I see on the ground." He took several still photos with his digital camera.

"Let's see where it takes us." She followed the dry riverbed further into the cave system.

"Hold up a minute. I want to scan the tunnel to document this leg." He placed his backpack on the ground and retrieved the scanning device. "Can you please get behind me before I scan?"

Stepping back behind him, she exited the riverbed tunnel into the giant hole.

Tommy pointed the scanner into the tunnel and resembled a cop pointing a speed scanner at speeding drivers. The scanner's laser touched every surface of the tunnel and stored the image on the USB drive.

Marveling at the technology she asked, "Did you get it?"

"Yes, thanks. I like to scan each area as we go. We can map out what we've discovered in the hotel tonight with your laptop." Tommy placed the scanner back in his backpack and flung one strap over his shoulder.

Taking the lead again, Victoria's forward momentum quickened her pace because the ground sloped down about thirty degrees. "We're getting deeper into the cave. I'd say we just descended about twenty feet in the last hundred yards."

"Since we started fifty feet down at the bottom of the sinkhole, this puts us at least seventy feet down already.

"Below sea level?" she asked.

"Probably. I'm not familiar with Florida, but I recall the whole state is barely above sea level."

"You're right. In fact, most houses in Florida don't have basements, except for Hemmingway's home in Key West."

"Florida is screwed when the glaciers melt from global warming. It'll become the next Venice, or Russia's St. Petersburg."

"The tourists at Disney would need a gondola to get around." Her attention turned to the tunnel walls, now smooth to match the ground. Even the ceiling was smooth, like the once river went all the way to the top of the tunnel.

"Let's just hope it doesn't happen while we're down here." She brushed off the horrible notion. Her worst fear was drowning.

"How far have we walked? I feel like we've been in this tunnel forever."

"You're the gadget man, a mile maybe?"

"If this system is vast, we may want to camp down here for a night or two. Just so we don't waste time going back out of the cave."

"Brilliant idea. We wouldn't really need a tent, just some rollout pads, pillows, and blankets," she said.

"We could get our provisions down here in the golf bags again. We'd just have to leave some stuff here tonight to make room in our golf bags."

"We could even load up our suitcases and take them out here tonight after the golf course closes."

"We'd have to buy nonperishable food for a few days. And nothing we have to cook. We don't want to die of smoke inhalation by starting a fire in a confined cave," Tommy said.

"I hear that happens all the time. Sad that some people can be so stupid. I once went on a tour of Mammoth Cave in Kentucky. The Violet Lantern Tour includes the old tuberculosis camp inside the cave. Back in the late 1800s, doctors prescribed T.B. patients to live in the cave because of the cool, dry climate. They even built a small hospital for the patients. But everyone died of smoke inhalation from the camp fires used to cook their food," she said.

"Gross, can we please refrain from discussing *dying* in a cave? Especially while we're *in* a cave." Tommy shuddered.

"Sorry, I think we've gone a least another mile. What direction is this tunnel headed?"

"Northeast, I think. In fact, I need to stop and scan again." He pulled out the scanner and took another shot to map the latest leg of the tunnel.

"How much twine do we have left? Maybe we could do the math that way."

"We're almost out of twine, actually. But I think it's safe to say we can't get lost in this single tunnel." He held up the nearly empty bolt of twine.

"Use the other one?"

"This is the other one." He grabbed his stomach. "I'm starved, by the way."

"Me too, for some reason. It's only...." Her Mickey Mouse watch displayed the time. "Wow. It's one o'clock already?"

"Want to stop for a quick lunch?"

Dropping her backpack on the floor she said, "You don't have to ask me twice." She sat on the cold, hard floor and grabbed her sandwich from her backpack.

"Mmm. This is the best sandwich I ever had." He ate half of his turkey on whole wheat in two bites."

"Everything tastes great when you're starved." She finished the first half of her sandwich and took a sip of water. She didn't want to get dehydrated, but she didn't want to squat to pee in front of Tommy either.

"Let's look at this twine. This bolt says there's ten thousand feet of twine, and we went through almost two bolts." He looked up as if he did the math in his head.

"And there's 5280 feet in a mile. We walked almost four miles already." Proud that she did the math in her head before him, she envisioned what was above them on the surface.

"Yeah, that's what I got, too." He polished off the rest of his sandwich.

"I wonder if we're under the Magic Kingdom?" She finished her sandwich and put the trash in her backpack.

"It's possible. Hard to keep my bearings straight."

"But I've heard there's an underground Disney, almost twice as big as the park itself. Wouldn't we have seen that if we were under the park?"

"We're at least seventy feet down. Even underground Disney is above us.

"Are you ready to press on?" She stood up and put on her backpack.

"Yes and no. It took us five hours to get here. So it's at least another five hours to walk back. And don't forget, it's uphill going back." He pointed up the tunnel leading back to the entrance.

"Fine." She dropped her head. Her nose smelled something foul. "Did you have an egg salad sandwich?"

"No, turkey, why? We really should turn around soon. We've got to shop for more provisions if we want to camp here tomorrow night."

"I know. The smell is coming from over there." She walked ten more feet, but stopped when the horrid smell wafted into her nostrils.

"Argh! It smells like rotten eggs." Tommy stopped next to her and pinched his nose.

"It's sulfur. We must be near water, a sulfur spring."

Chapter Eleven

"I'm starving!" Victoria rubbed her flat abs at Epcot's Italy.

"According to Grier, Alfredo's restaurant should be right here." Tommy looked up from his cell phone and pointed.

"It says Tutta Italia."

"Huh? They must've closed Alfredo's and put in another restaurant. I was looking forward to this meal. The original Alfredo's is in Rome, and there is one in New York City, too. They serve the original and authentic Fettucine Alfredo."

"Well, this new place must be good because it is packed." She waved her arm at the crowded lobby.

A couple walked out shaking their heads in frustration. "Completely booked," the man mumbled.

"What's plan B?" Tommy studied the Disney app on his iPhone and searched for dining options.

Victoria admired the beautiful scenery of Epcot's Italian pavilion. She felt like she was in Italy, from the mini Trevi fountain and Tuscan winery, to the dominating brick tower and shops with Italian leather.

A hanging painted wooden sign caught her eye— Tutto Gusto Wine Cellar. Pointing, she asked, "What is that?"

"I don't know, but the word 'wine' appeals to me." Tommy grinned.

Victoria glanced at the small-bites menu hanging on the wall outside of the wine cellar. Once her eyes spotted the words "ravioli" and "lamb," she walked right up to the hostess' stand and asked, "Do you have a table for two?"

"Of course, follow me." The Cast Member grabbed two menus and escorted them inside which was decorated like a wine cellar with a low, arched brick ceiling, dimmed lighting, wine bottles and big oak wine barrels.

The hostess took them to an alcove with couches and coffee tables. She placed the menus on the table and said, "Have a magical meal."

Tommy promptly picked up the wine menu and flipped to the vast selection of red wines. Quickly making his selection, he ordered a bottle of chianti riserva.

Victoria went straight to the small-bites menu, found her ravioli and smiled.

"I'm going to get the Ragu d'Agnello," Tommy referred to the lamb dish with pasta. "But these small portions won't be enough for a meal. Would you like to share a platter of mini gorgonzola paninis to start?" Tommy asked.

Nodding, she said, "You just read my mind. I saw another customer get their ravioli, and the small portion won't be enough because I'm *starving*."

The waitress returned with their bottle of chianti, poured them each a glass, then took their order.

Tommy held up his glass to toast and said, "To our cave."

* * * *

Back at the room, Tommy and Victoria uploaded the cave scans from the USB drive to the cave-plotting software on her laptop. They held up the map of the entire Disney property and compared it to the new map of the cave.

Staring at the location, their mouths gaped in unison.

"We walked right under Cinderella's Castle today. And it looks like we stopped mapping between the

Seven Dwarfs Mine Train ride and the Little Mermaid ride." Tommy rubbed his evening stubble with his thumb and index finger, pensive in thought.

A light turned on in Victoria's mind. "We stopped about where the 20,000 Leagues Under the Sea ride *used* to be."

"Remember what the Cast Member said about *why* the ride closed down?"

Nodding, Victoria said, "Something to do with the water."

Chapter Twelve

The next morning, they returned to the cave with enough supplies to camp for three nights.

"You're brilliant, Tommy." Victoria rolled two suitcases through the downward slope of the old underground river bed.

"Thanks, you can tell me that anytime." A wink accompanied his smile. He rolled the two larger suitcases behind him.

"We should've marked the spot where we left off yesterday." Grimacing, she estimated that they were almost there. At least she, and her exhausted arms, hoped.

"I did. I left the empty twine bolt there."

"Ooooh, litter bug." Her loud scolding echoed through the cave.

"Hey, at least I left something to mark the spot," he defended.

"I'm sure we'll smell the sulfur once we get close."

"Speak of the devil. Here it is." Stopping, he picked up the empty twine bolt.

"Should we bring it with us?"

Shrugging, he waved his hand behind him. "Nah, we're pressed for luggage space enough as it is. We can always grab it on the way back."

"Wait for it, wait for it." Stopping, her nostrils inhaled the putrid smell of rotten eggs. "And there it is."

They both pinched their noses and grimaced.

Tommy pulled two nose clamps out of his pocket and handed one to Victoria. "Now it's time for me to applaud your brilliance. Genius idea to buy swimming nose clamps from the hotel gift shop."

They put the clamps over their noses, pointed at each other and laughed.

"Kids use them in the pool all the time with their goggles. It won't keep the smell completely away, but it will help." Her voice sounded like she had a cold.

"Ha, ha. You sound funny." He laughed at her.

"So do you," she defended with her sniffled voice.

"How are we going to sleep down here with this smell?"

"We'll get used to it. Or so I've heard. You know, sulfur springs were used medicinally for hundreds of years. Something about the sulfur produced a healing power. Many would flock to sulfur baths for medicinal reasons."

"Is that what some people thought was the Fountain of Youth?"

"Possibly. Ponce de León searched for it in the 1500s. What he thought was the Fountain of Youth could have just been the healing powers of a sulfur spring."

"That makes more sense than the real thing. Imagine finding an elixir water that causes eternal youth."

"Botox and plastic surgery would become obsolete."

"Even with these nose clamps, I can tell the smell is getting worse."

"Look." She pointed to the ground. "It's wet."

"This part of the tunnel must've recently been under water. We may have to get wet really soon."

"I hope the tunnel doesn't just dead end into water." She kept walking until her feet hit water. "Oh crap. I shouldn't have said that."

"It's all your fault then." He shined his flashlight, and the water level grew higher further down the tunnel.

"Does the water reach the tunnel's ceiling?" She peered down the tunnel.

"I don't think so. We can leave our stuff here and trudge through it, just to see how far we can go without scuba tanks."

"I'm game." Sitting down, she took off her boots and socks, then rolled her pant legs up to her knees.

"Are you sure taking off your boots is a good idea? We don't know what's under that water." Tommy's gaze bore his concern about her bare feet.

"I'll be fine. This ground has been smooth for the last few miles. If you're so worried about my precious tootsies, how about you go first?" she asked.

Dropping his head in defeat, he said, "Fair enough."

Tommy pulled the suitcases upright and set them aside on the dry tunnel ground. Taking a step, his Timberland hiking boots splashed into the shallow water.

Victoria stepped into the water. "Yikes, it's freezing." Chills ran up her legs, and goose bumps prickled her skin.

"There's nothing like a good 'I told you so.'" Tommy turned and grinned.

"I'll get used to it, I guess." She pursed her lips.

"You know, if it wasn't for this draught, we'd never have gotten as far down as we did." He nodded to the wet walls of the tunnel.

The water got deeper with each step. She trudged her legs along. The water swooshed around her feet and calves with each step. "I'm getting used to it now. It's refreshing."

"Whoooo, eeeeeeeh, that's cold. It's up to my calves now." Tommy grimaced.

"Your socks are going to take forever to dry out, especially without a fire. Mine are nice and dry back there with the rest of our stuff."

"I packed an extra pair, smarty pants," he teased.

"It doesn't seem to be getting any deeper. The water line and ground are leveling out." She pointed ahead.

"Maybe we're almost there."

"Almost where?" she asked.

"The next part."

"What's that up ahead? I think I see a light." Her tone rang with excitement.

"Probably just our flashlights reflecting off of the water."

"No, it's getting brighter, look."

"Huh? You're right. Maybe it's the bottom of another sinkhole and the sun is shining in."

Picking up their pace they rushed towards the source of the light.

"It doesn't look like sunlight, and I think it's coming from the ground, not the ceiling."

"It can't be from the sun. Remember when we mapped the tunnel last night? We are somewhere under the Magic Kingdom. We haven't walked far enough to be on the other side of the park, and I don't remember seeing any sinkholes by the new Fantasyland the other day."

Tommy stopped suddenly. Victoria stopped next to him. Their mouths gaped open at the enormous cavern. But more shocking than the lit cavern in front of them, was what it held.

"Someone's been here before."

Chapter Thirteen

"It's incredible," Victoria gasped. The top of the cavern soared fifty feet above. But it wasn't the enormity of the cavern that shocked them, it was the manmade temple inside.

The room was nearly a perfect cylinder with different levels. It reminded her of the cenotes found in Mexico and South America. She recalled from a college course that a cenote is a natural pit or sinkhole. It forms when limestone bedrock collapses and exposes groundwater underneath. Their tunnel ended towards the bottom of the well. If the water level was normal, they'd be underwater. That's why all the cool stuff was high above them.

Tears flowed down Victoria's cheek. She turned to Tommy who cried with happiness, too.

"It's the most beautiful thing I've ever seen." Stone columns were carved around the perimeter of the cylinder on two different levels above them. A ledge at the base of the column protruded out at each level. Small steps were carved into the ledge, leading down into where the water once was.

"It's like a Roman bath."

"But we're nowhere near Rome."

"They found one in Bath, England during the Victorian Era when someone had a leak in their basement." Victoria was fascinated with the era of her namesake.

"I remember the tale from Archaeology 101."

"Look, I see carvings on the columns." She pointed with an excited, high-pitched voice.

"I can't make them out from here. We'll have to climb up. Do you see the ledge to our left?" He nodded up.

"Yes, it looks wide enough to sleep on."

"You just read my mind. We can toss the suitcases up there and set up camp. Do you think you can carry your small suitcase above the water through the wet part of the tunnel?"

"Sure, it's not that far." She flexed her biceps.

"Great, let's get all of our gear and set up camp." Tommy led her back into the tunnel.

"I'm so glad we're spending two nights. We'll have all day tomorrow to explore the temple." Following him, she practically skipped with excitement. Luckily, they didn't have far to walk through the water with their stuff. Setting up camp was quick without tents. Rolling out their nap mats reminded her of preschool. The thermal blankets would warm them in the cold cave environment. The heaviest thing they brought was five gallons of water.

"Looks like we're all set." She walked to the ledge, looked down into the water and studied the source of light coming up through the sulfur springs.

"What do you think it is?" Tommy walked up behind her, wrapped his arms around her waist and held her close.

"Phosphorus?" She leaned back into him.

"I thought that at first, too. But phosphorus glows more neon and it's greenish yellow. Besides, I think phosphorus is found in salt water, not fresh water." Tommy nudged his cheek against her head and rocked her side-to-side.

"I don't know. Some sort of undiscovered, rare Earth element?" Her mind ran wild with possibilities—far-fetched ones she felt too embarrassed to bring up to another intellectual.

"It could be manmade." Tommy released his embrace and moved beside her.

They stared down into the abyss which glowed with a bright light, almost white, but with the faintest, light blue tinge.

"But by who? Man or... It's hard for me to even say what I'm thinking. Please forgive me if this sounds crazy. But could this be...." Pausing, she bit her lip, and then dropped her head.

"Ancient Aliens." Tommy laughed.

"Yes, Ancient Aliens. Have you ever watched the show?" Turning to face him, she searched his eyes to see if he was teasing her or not.

"I love that show. I'm a true believer that we're not the only ones in this universe. It's just too probable that there's other life out there besides mankind on Earth."

"Phew, I'm so glad you said that. I was terrified you'd think me ludicrous." Exhaling, relief washed through her.

"I'm starving. We skipped lunch you know."

Her Mickey Mouse watch read four o'clock. "Wow, I guess with all of the excitement, we forgot to eat."

"Come on, I've got a surprise for you." Tommy grabbed her hand and led her to their small campsite on the ledge. Pulling out a bottle of Dom Perignon, he handed it to her.

"Champagne?"

Nodding, he said, "Let's celebrate our find." He pulled two wine glasses, "borrowed" from the hotel, out of his suitcase and handed them to her. "Here, hold these, please."

After unwrapping the aluminum from the cork, he pressed his thumbs against the exposed cork and pushed up.

Pop.

The cork shot away from them, and some champagne escaped the confines of the bottle. He quickly poured the bubbling liquid into two glasses.

"To.... whatever, this is." Clinking her glass with his, he smiled.

"Yes, to this magical place." She clinked his glass and sipped the champagne.

Spreading out the blanket on the nap mats, Tommy placed a lantern in the center and said, "Your seat, mademoiselle."

"Wait, just let me rinse my dirty hands in the water." Walking over to the edge, she knelt down in front of the water.

"Me, too." He followed her.

Dipping her hands in the cool water, she rubbed them together. "Ahh, the water's so cool and refreshing." She cupped her hands together underneath the water and splashed the cool water onto her face.

"It's the smoothest water I've ever felt. And I can barely smell the sulfur now that we're at the source." He removed his nose clamp.

"I know." She removed her nose clamp, too, relieved to have her normal voice back.

"But we better not drink it. We have enough water for several days. I packed extra in case we got lost, or... trapped," he said.

"We should be fine. What's on the menu, Chef Garrison?" She plopped down on the blanket and lay on her side with her elbow propping up her upper body.

"Smoked salmon with capers, diced red onions and cream cheese."

"I thought we couldn't have perishables?" Her eyebrows arched inquisitively while she sipped her champagne.

"We can tonight, just not the rest of the trip, so eat up. I also have cheeses and crackers." He handed her a plate and sat down on the blanket.

She sat up, criss crossed her legs and took the plate. Biting into the salmon with cream cheese on a cracker, she closed her eyes with euphoria. "Mmmmm, this is so good. You're a genius. Better than any food I've ever had on a dig. And you didn't even need a campfire."

"Thank you, my dear." His gaze dropped to her bare feet. "Hey, you forgot to put your boots back on."

Shrugging, she said, "I guess I don't need them tonight." Taking another bite, she hummed.

"I hope you don't mind me saying this, but you have the most adorable feet. Your skin is flawless, like a newborn baby."

"Thank you." Studying her feet, bewilderment filled her. "That's odd?"

"What's odd?" His blond eyebrows rose.

"My feet, I can't explain it. But they somehow look...younger."

Chapter Fourteen

Victoria gasped. "Tommy, your face. Did you splash water on it?"

"Yeah, why? Oh, Victoria, your face, too."

She looked down at her hands, shocked at their youthful, smoothness. "My calluses are gone."

"You face, is absolutely breathtaking. Even more beautiful than before."

"Yours, too. I don't see the wrinkles on your forehead anymore." She leaned over to her backpack and rummaged through her toiletry kit. Retrieving her mirrored, powder compact, she flipped it open and studied her reflection. "It's amazing. It's me, but younger. All of the tiny wrinkles around my eyes are gone. Hurrah, no more crow's feet. Here." She handed him the mirror.

Tommy took the mirror and studied his reflection. "It's miraculous. I look ten years younger. And even the small scar on my chin is gone." Closing the mirror, he handed it back to her.

"What do you think it is?" She studied her reflection again, amazed at the quick transformation.

"Well, sulfur springs are known for their healing powers. But this..., this is more than that, much more."

"Anti aging, even reverse aging."

"It explains why there's a temple around it. Whoever found this wanted to worship it and hide it from mankind."

"The Fountain of Youth!" they shouted it in unison.

"Are you thinking what I'm thinking?" Her eyes pleaded with him.

"Of course, my dear. But it could be risky. We don't know what's in that water."

"If it was toxic, we'd be dead by now. If there's acid in there, we'd have been burned when we washed our hands and faces in it."

"True." Standing up, he slowly unbuttoned his blue flannel shirt. "I'm game if you are."

"Yippeee!" She jumped up and hugged him. "I, I love you, Tommy Garrison."

Taken aback at her words. He grabbed her by the waist and pulled her close. Looking lovingly into her eyes, he said, "I love you, too, Victoria." Then his lips touched hers.

Stepping back after the kiss, she covered her mouth with her hand. "Oh, sorry, please forgive my salmon and onion breath." She dropped her gaze and blushed with embarrassment.

"It's okay, my love, I have it, too." He took off his shirt, then bent at the knees and untied his boots.

"Race you in." She pulled off her pink flannel shirt and dropped her Khaki pants, grateful she didn't wear skinny jeans. She was down to her bra and panties before Tommy removed his hiking boots.

"Ah, no fair." Hurrying, he stripped down to just his boxers.

Their undergarments resembled bathing suits, so she didn't feel embarrassed. Marveling at Tommy's muscular chest and ripped abs, she held her shoulders back to show off her slender, yet curvy figure.

"I can tell the difference in your skin. Your hands, face and feet appear younger than the rest of you." He pointed to her arms.

Holding out her hands and arms in front of her, she noticed the difference. The skin on her hands appeared more youthful and flawless than the skin on her arms.

"We should take before and after pictures."

"Selfie."

They laughed.

"Seriously." He grabbed the digital camera and held it up to her. "Smile, my dear."

Posing, she sucked in her belly and smiled.

Click.

"Okay, now you take one of me. Do you see these scars?"

She nodded, held the camera, and framed the shot.

"Chicken pox scars from when I was a kid. I'd love for them to go away."

Click.

Examining the display of the digital camera, she nodded, gave him a thumbs up, and said, "It looks good."

"Okay, let's do this." Grabbing her hand, they walked to the edge.

"Ready on three, two, one." They jumped in holding hands.

Plunging into the water, she stayed underwater for several seconds, allowing the water to work its magic. Holding her breath while she remained submerged, she contemplated opening her eyes to admire the beautiful water and the mysterious source of light below. *What the heck? I'm past the point of no return now.*

The cold water chilled her, but she stayed under and opened her eyes. Tommy stared at her. He'd opened his eyes underwater, too.

Keeping his lips closed, he pointed up, signaling for them to surface.

She nodded and kicked up to the surface. "Wow, this feels incredible and rejuvenating." She treaded water next to him.

"The water is so clear." With his head down, he studied the clear blue water below.

"I wonder how deep it is?" Sticking her head in the water, she peered down below her feet. The pale blue light beckoned her, like the mythical Sirens singing to the sailors to lure them.

"I don't know. We can weigh down the twine with a rock and see how far it goes. Maybe even break out the scuba gear. But first thing tomorrow, I want to explore the temple." Pointing up, he floated on his back and did the backstroke across the length of the spring.

She followed him with a side stroke. And they swam together in the Fountain of Youth.

Chapter Fifteen

"Wanna dive down?" Victoria asked.

Tommy dropped his head into the water, looked down for several seconds, then came back up. "First, let's check the depth by weighing down the twine with a rock."

"Good idea." She swam back towards the camp.

Following her, he said, "I'll get it. No need for both of us to freeze getting out of the water."

"How valiant, thanks."

With his strong arms, he pulled himself up out of the water and onto the ledge. His back muscles flexed, and his wet boxers clung to his muscular butt.

Treading water, Victoria submerged herself again, hoping the rejuvenating water would work its magic on the rest of her body.

Tommy retrieved a new bolt of twine from his suitcase. Finding a large rock near the campsite, he tied the twine to it. "This should work. I think it's about twenty pounds."

"Feel like a wager?"

"Sure. Twenty bucks says it's more than a thousand feet. Here, hold the twine."

Taking the twine from him, she treaded water with only her legs. "You're on."

He jumped in the water with a large splash, spraying her. Holding the heavy rock under one arm, he side stroked to the center of the spring and dropped the rock.

The twine unwound from the bolt, and the rock sank quickly to the bottom. "That was fast. I think I'm twenty bucks richer."

"Huh?" He scratched his head with a bewildered expression.

"I'll hold the spot on the twine while you pull up the rock." Holding up her hand, she wrapped the twine around her wrist.

Treading water effortlessly with only his legs, Tommy pulled the twine and let the slack float around him. The rock ascended much slower than its drop. "Here we go." Grabbing the rock, he tossed it aside.

They climbed out of the water and stood on the ledge. Dripping wet, they briskly walked to the largest suitcase and pulled out two towels.

"It's freezing," she said through chattering teeth and shivering limbs. Wrapping herself up in the towel, she rubbed her arms with her hands and longed for a fire.

"How tall are you? About six feet?" He held the twine next to her body and measured a length of the twine to match her height.

"Yes. I see what you're thinking." She silently applauded his brilliance of using her body for a measuring stick.

"Here, hold out your hand." He handed her the end of the twine.

"Now that I know this part is six feet, we can count the number of six-foot lengths to measure the depth." He worked through the twine and measured the next twelve lengths until it ended at the piece tied to her other wrist.

"Eighty-six feet. Told you so." Elation filled her. She loved being right.

"We don't need the tanks. These tiny portable breathing air compressors hold five minutes of air each." Tossing through the suitcase, he grabbed four breathers and held them up.

"Perfect. Grab the fins while you're in there."

"Of course, we just dry off, and now we're going to get wet again." He handed her a pair of fins.

"Oh, I know." She sat down on the blanket and put the flippers on her feet. "We brought masks, too, didn't we?"

"Yes. Here you go. Who gets the GoPro?" He held it up.

"Oh, me, me, me." She raised her hand like an excited preschooler.

"I guess it's only fair, you guessed the depth. I was way off." Sighing, he strapped the GoPro onto her head above the mask.

"I wonder what's down there?" Standing up, she awkwardly walked with her fins to the edge.

"Something awesome I imagine." Sitting on the edge next to her, he tinkered with his dive watch. "In two and a half minutes, we'll have to head back up. When this alarm goes off, head to the surface immediately. Understand?"

Nodding, she said, "I understand. Don't get distracted by shiny objects."

"Exactly. At least while we're in the water. Ready in three, two, one." Hitting his dive watch, he slipped into the water.

They sank quickly, each holding a large rock for weight. The light grew brighter the closer they got to the bottom. The sides of the cenote were smooth and continued their perfect, cylinder shape all the way to the bottom.

Just before they reached the bottom, they dropped their rocks onto the glowing sphere below. The rocks landed, and Victoria and Tommy floated just above. Glowing bright white, the light source resembled a miniature moon.

Chapter Sixteen

Victoria shot upright at dawn. Forgetting her surroundings, she rubbed her eyes while her brain woke up. Everything flooded to the forefront of her mind when yesterday's discovery sank in. They'd found the Fountain of Youth, along with a strange, glowing miniature moon.

"Good morning, beautiful." Tommy lay beside her, tucked cozy into a thermal blanket.

"Morning, handsome." She pecked his lips. "This is real, not just some fantastical dream." She held out her arms and admired the fountain's effects on her limbs. The rejuvenated youth now encompassed her entire body, not just her hands, feet and face.

"I can't decide what's cooler—the elixir water, the miniature moon below the water, or the temple above." Tossing off the blanket, he sat up and put his boots on.

"I know. They're all super cool, but in entirely different ways." Cringing, she regretted using dated, high-school slang.

"It's like the moon shrunk and crashed down to Earth. Then the force of its crash created this perfectly shaped cylinder tunnel until it stopped, permanently wedged into the Earth's crust." He pulled out a bag of beef jerky and handed it to her.

"Then water flowed into the hole it created." Opening the bag, she bit into the chewy beef jerky, grateful for the protein to start her day.

"The geology makes sense. How else could this shape form naturally?" Opening a box of raisins, he took a handful and then handed her the box.

"What about the cenotes in Central and South America? Those have the same shape. Could there be miniature moons under those, too?" she asked.

"Perhaps. Maybe all the bodies and animals the Aztecs, Incans and Mayans sacrificed covered up a miniature moons' illumination." He poured water into their cups and said, "I'd kill for some tea, but water will just have to do."

"I'm a coffee drinker myself, but the adrenaline will keep me alert." She finished her unusual breakfast and drank most of the water from her canteen. Finding her toothbrush and toothpaste, she brushed her teeth and rinsed her mouth out with the remainder of her water. She laced up her boots and splashed water on her face. "Ready?"

"Absolutely. That was great camping last night. I think we should spend the entire day exploring the temple and documenting everything." Tommy grabbed the ropes and rock-climbing clips and secured them to his backpack.

"Any ideas on how to get up there?" Looking up she'd estimated the climb would only be about twenty feet to the lowest level of the temple.

"Yeah, I'll toss the rope up with a grappling hook and hope it catches. Then we'll climb up towards those stone steps." He unwound the rope and attached the four-pronged hook.

"At least if we fall, it's only water below. Except for the narrow ledge we're standing on."

Tommy swung the rope with the hook and tossed it up towards a column. The hook caught on the base of the column, and he tested its hold by hanging from it.

"Nice throw."

"Ladies first." He handed the rope to her. "I'll be right underneath to catch you if you fall."

Placing her right foot on the wall, she pulled her weight up and planted her left foot on the wall. Thankful for her upper body strength, she ascended quickly. Reaching the bottom step, she pulled herself up and onto the ledge next to the column.

"You made that look too easy. How secure is the rope?"

Tugging on it, the hook came loose from the crevasse. "Oops. I'll just tie the rope around the column. It should hold." She wrapped the rope around the column and tied it securely. The strange carvings caught her eye. She'd never seen anything like it before.

"You're good to go."

"Alright, I'm coming up," he hollered from below and climbed up almost as fast as she. Arriving at the lower level, he sat on the ledge, winded. "That's tougher than it looks."

"Check out these carvings. I've never seen anything like it. My GoPro is on video mode. Can you please take some pictures?"

"Absolutely." Snapping away with his digital camera, he looked pensive. "I've never seen anything like this before either. There are carvings all over these columns."

"It's like someone just made up a language and alphabet, then carved them into these columns."

"The Fountain of Youth, a miniature moon, an undiscovered language, what's next?"

"Oh, look, stairs." She pointed to stone steps carved into the wall. Running up the steps, she arrived at the top level of the temple which resembled the lower one.

"Hey, wait up," Tommy hollered from below. He arrived on the upper level and stood next to Victoria and her gaping mouth.

Above them, steel beams, placed about ten feet apart, stretched the length of the ceiling. Between the beams, a reddish-brown rock formation covered the ceiling. The same color as the rocks on the Little Mermaid ride.

A pile of rocks covered the upper level floor of the temple. Protruding from the pile of rocks was one of the Captain Nemo's *Nautilus* submarines from the 20,000 Leagues Under the Sea ride.

Chapter Seventeen

"Oh, for me?" Back in the hotel the following evening, Victoria removed the crown from the round velvet-lined box and admired it. The sparkling rhinestones reflected the light's rays. "It's beautiful."

"And so are you, my love." Kissing her lips, he took the tiara from her and raised it above her head. "Here, allow me." Balancing the tiara on her head, he stepped back.

She stood in front of the mirror and admired her reflection—a far cry from her normal skinny jeans, flannel shirt and hiking boots. The pink, sleeveless satin dress accentuated her long, black hair and ice-blue eyes.

Standing next to her in front of the mirror, Tommy wore a black suit, a light-blue dress shirt and a coordinating pink tie. "We could be Victoria and Albert dining at Buckingham Palace."

Slipping her arm into his, she said, "So tell me more about the Queen's room?"

"Better yet, I'll show you. We have much to celebrate."

They walked to dinner at Victoria & Albert's in the Grand Floridian. Walking into the restaurant, the maître de greeted them.

"Garrison, party of two," Tommy said.

Checking the list, his face lit up. "Ah, the Queen's room. Follow me."

He escorted them past an enormous bouquet of fresh flowers. The rose scent permeated the air, and Victoria stopped to inhale the delicate pink roses.

"Shiny object," Tommy whispered in her ear and tugged her away.

They passed a harpist stringing an instrumental version of *Once Upon a Dream* from the movie,

Sleeping Beauty. Leaving the main dining room, they entered a smaller room to the left with only four tables.

The maître de waved towards the table in front of the fireplace. Above the mantle hung a portrait of Queen Victoria and Prince Albert in their youth.

Holding out the chair for her, Tommy gestured for her to sit. She sat in the soft cushioned seat. Tommy pushed her in and sat down.

"For your handbag, mademoiselle." The maître de pushed a silk cushioned footstool next to her seat and gestured for her to place her handbag upon it.

Feeling like a princess, she placed her silver clutch on the stool and took the menu offered to her. Opening the menu, their names greeted her on the customized menu—*Victoria Ventures and Thomas Garrison.*

She studied the *prix fixe* menu before her, all eleven courses for only $210 per person. "Wow. Lobster, caviar, octopus, lamb, scallops, veal, fish, Kobe beef, assorted cheeses...."

"And three desserts." Tommy finished her sentence.

"How am I supposed to eat all of this? And they pair a wine with each course?"

"It's a three-hour meal with small portions."

The waiter poured them each a flute of champagne.

"To our fantastic first date." Tommy raised his glass to hers.

"And to many more." She clinked his glass. Sipping the bubbly goodness, she set her glass down next to the white plate with gold trim which read, "Victoria & Albert."

"We have much to discuss over the next three hours," he said.

"I know. Do you think Disney knows about the Fountain?"

He nodded and sipped his champagne.

"Who built the temple?"

"Ancient Aliens."

"Possibly. What if Disney discovered the Fountain of Youth when they broke ground for the Magic Kingdom? Bear with me, but what if they built the temple and invented a fake language to decorate the temple and turn it into an attraction."

"Interesting theory. That actually makes more sense than Ancient Aliens." Nodding, he took a bite of the amuse-bouche placed in front of each of them.

"Then they discovered the healing powers of the water and wanted to keep it hush, hush."

"So they build the 20,000 Leagues Under the Sea ride on top of the fountain to hide it from the rest of the world.

"Remember what the Cast Member told us the first day at the park. They closed the ride down because there was something wrong with the water." She bit into the lobster, and it slid down her throat.

He nodded. "So how did the submarine get down there?"

She finished her caviar and drank the remainder of her champagne. "The cave ceiling/bottom of the ride broke through, like a sinkhole. The submarine fell through, and they closed the ride for years until they decided what to do."

"And when they decided to build the new Fantasyland, they reinforced the bottom of the mermaid ride with steel beams so nothing would fall through again," he finished her train of thought.

"Now, the question is, what do we do about it?" she asked.

"You mean, besides bringing back five gallons of water from the Fountain of Youth." Tommy turned his head to see if anyone had overheard him. But the waiters were elsewhere, and the other tables remained vacant.

"First, we just enjoy this meal."

"And then?" he asked.

"Let's sleep on it."

Chapter Eighteen

"Let's take a walk to the 'Happiest place on Earth,'" Tommy said the next morning.

Holding hands walking down Main Street USA in the Magic Kingdom, they stopped in front of Cinderella's Castle, just in front of the bronze statues of Walter Elias Disney and Mickey Mouse, a.k.a. *Partners*.

"Do you think Walt discovered the Fountain of Youth?" Tommy asked.

"Possibly. Did he *really* buy all of this land in Central Florida to make room for his precious theme park to grow and flourish for decades?"

"I hear that's what he claimed. He regretted not buying enough land in California to expand his dynasty."

"Or did he *really* buy all this land to hide the biggest discovery of mankind?"

"But why would he hide such a remarkable discovery? Think of all the lives he could save. Not to mention the fortune to be made."

"It was never about the money. Yes, lives could be saved. But think of the corruption that could happen if the Fountain of Youth ever fell into the wrong hands. What's to keep terrorists from attacking on American soil and keeping the Fountain of Youth for themselves."

"You're right. Plus, if everyone lived forever, the world population would multiply exponentially. We'd run out of natural resources and all die."

"For the greater good, he kept it hidden and protected, during his lifetime and for generations to come. No one in their right minds would ever plow down Disney World."

"But you and I can use it, for ourselves and for our loved ones, right?"

"Of course, my love."

"Do you think Walt ever used the water from the fountain?"

"There've been rumors for years that he'd been frozen cryogenically until a cure could be found to bring him back."

"Maybe he'd already found the cure for eternal youth and immortality."

"But then, where is he? No one's seen him."

"Perhaps he's in disguise." Victoria studied the bronze statues of Walt and Mickey. Then the costumed characters, Mickey and Minnie Mouse, walked by hand-in-hand, surrounded by Cast Members escorting them to the next Character greet. *Anyone could be in those costumes.*

"What a great way to spend eternity, walking around the 'Happiest place on Earth' with someone you love."

"Sounds like a dream come true."

"Well that begs the question—now what?" Tommy stared into Victoria's eyes, begging for her to answer his question correctly.

Smiling, Victoria squeezed his hand and said, "Let's go see what's *under the magic* of the other Disney Parks. Besides, I've always wanted to go to Paris."

THE END

Part Two

Europium Gem Mine

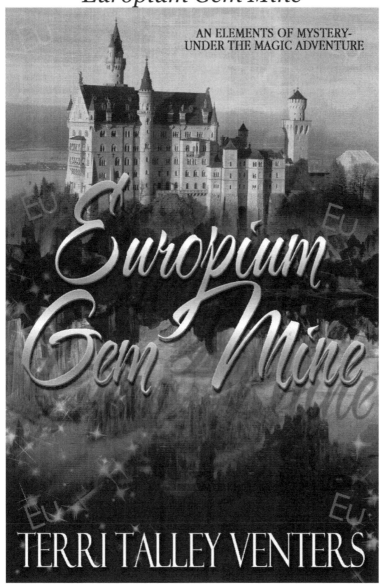

AN ELEMENTS OF MYSTERY-
UNDER THE MAGIC ADVENTURE

Europium Gem Mine

TERRI TALLEY VENTERS

Chapter One

Eiffel Tower
Paris, France

"Oh, my God! This is fabulous." Victoria hummed. The smoked salmon appetizer with capers, red onions and cream cheese melted on her tongue. Sipping her glass of Champagne, she turned to the fabulous view from 58 Tour Eiffel Restaurant. But to her, the view of Paris's nighttime skyline paled compared to her hot date for New Year's Eve—Tommy Garrison.

"We lucked out on a table, right next to the window." Tommy touched the glass and smiled. His sea-green eyes and straight, sandy-blond hair sparkled in the candlelight. Wearing a charcoal-grey suit with a cobalt-blue dress shirt and tie, he looked gorgeous. His handsome face and Scottish accent reminded her of Ewan McGregor.

"How long ago did you make these reservations?" Rubbing her bare arms, she warded off the chill. A strapless, red-satin dress may not have been the best choice in the winter, but her favorite frock accentuated her long, black hair, ice-blue eyes and tanned complexion.

"The day we met." Dropping his chin, he blushed.

"That was over a year ago, just before Lilly and Grier's wedding." Her tone rang with incredulity, and her heart burst with love. He'd obviously felt the same sparks she did when they first met.

"I know, but you need to book New Year's Eve at the Eiffel Tower a year in advance. I even prepaid for the meal." He referred to their *fixe prix* menu with a choice of appetizer, main course and dessert.

"Well, I'm touched. And I loved that you called me the second I returned home from the wedding." She referred to her hometown of Charleston, South Carolina. Although she grew up there, she never spent much time at home because she hopped from one dig to the next. Traveling the globe year-round had made it impossible to stay in a relationship, until she met Tommy. Now they finagled their schedules to dig in the dirt together.

"Love at first sight. Besides, the holidays are a great time to travel because all of the digs basically shut down for three weeks." Finishing his Champagne, he signaled the waiter for more.

"It's just an amazing coincidence. You planned to take me to Paris a year ago. You took me to Disney World for our first date. Then after our find in Florida, *I* decided I wanted to go to Disneyland Paris next."

"Must be fate. Perhaps we're destined to discover another, 'Find of the century.'" He referred to their finding the Fountain of Youth and an ancient, perhaps *alien*, temple in a cave deep beneath the Magic Kingdom. But they decided to suppress their discovery for the 'greater good.'

Raising her champagne flute, she toasted, "I'll drink to that. Here's to our next great find."

Chapter Two

"This had better be good." Tommy crossed his arms and scowled.

They waited in the long line for the Catacombs.

"Relax, I'm sure it'll go fast." Leaning into him, Victoria rubbed his arm and smiled.

"The line is around the block." Pouting, he shook his head.

"But this is the last big thing to see in Paris before we head to Disneyland tomorrow. We've done Versailles, the Louvre, Notre Dame, Arc de Triomphe, the Orsay and Eiffel Tower. How about I forage some espresso and pastries to cheer you up?"

"Think you can cheer me up with French food and caffeine?" he asked, arching his right eyebrow.

"Yes, I'll be right back." She pecked him on the cheek, then walked across the street, following the other tourists with presumably the same idea.

The aroma of freshly baked French baguettes filled her when she walked into the corner bakery. Although it was only ten a.m., her stomach rumbled. Studying the contents of the glass display cabinet, she spotted quiche and smiled. She quickly figured that if the line for the Catacombs was two hours, and then allotting two to three hours underground with dead people, she knew they'd miss lunch. Better get something substantial to tide them over for the next few hours because she and Tommy both grew cranky if they weren't fed in a timely manner.

"Yes?" The young French man asked, obviously spotting her as an American tourist.

Pointing to the items, she spoke perfect French. *"Deux Quiche Lorraine, deux espresso, une baguette, si vous plait."*

The young man appeared surprised, but pleasantly

so. Smiling, he said, *"Oui, Mademoiselle."* The cute, young Frenchman rewarded her perfect French by filling her order next, skipping the tourists in front of her.

Smiling, she took the espressos and bag of goodies he offered and said, *"Merci, au revoir."* Exiting the shop, elation filled her.

After crossing the street, she followed the queue in reverse around the block. Thank goodness Tommy had moved up substantially in the line. She just prayed that they'd have time to enjoy their French cuisine before they entered the Catacombs of Paris.

Spotting Tommy, her heart fluttered just looking at his striking form. His six-foot four, lean and tan muscular body still took her breath away. Combined with her own six-foot height, they made a striking couple.

He fiddled with his iPhone while he waited and periodically stepped forward as the line progressed.

She snuck up behind him, playfully smacked his perfect bottom, and asked, "Are we there yet?"

"We're getting closer, but according to Facebook, we're 'checked-in' to the Catacombs." Glancing up from his iPhone, he eyed the French baguette sticking out of the bag. "Oh, I love you."

"You're welcome." She sipped her espresso.

Taking the baguette, he tore off a chunk, shoved it into his mouth, and hummed. "Oh, my, God. It's so good." He offered her the bread.

"Oh, thank you. I also have quiche Lorraine." She held up the bag and tore off a chunk of French bread.

"Quiche what? They say, 'real men don't eat quiche.'" He sipped his espresso.

"Quiche Lorraine is filled with egg, cheese and ham. And your secret is safe with me. Besides, I happen to know firsthand that you're a 'real man.'"

Winking, she bit into the bread.

"Egg, cheese and ham in a pie—perfect for a second breakfast." Humming, he bit into the quiche.

A man in front of her spoke French to his companion.

His words caught her attention. She placed her right index finger on her lips, signaling for Tommy to be quiet so she could eavesdrop on the French conversation. What he said made sense, and her archaeological curiosity grew.

"What is it?" Tommy whispered before shoving more French bread into his mouth.

"These catacombs aren't the only ones in France. Urban Legend says there are miles of undiscovered catacombs beneath the outskirts of Paris."

Chapter Three

"Audio guides?" Victoria asked Tommy when they purchased their tickets at the entrance to the Catacombs.

"Yes, definitely." He handed the ticket salesman twenty Euros.

"Nerd." She coughed.

"That's not what you called me last night, baby." Winking, he grabbed the audio guides.

"Touché. Besides, you know I'm teasing. I love caves, too." She took the audio guide he offered and placed the headphones over her ears.

"Ladies first." He waved his arm towards the turnstile.

"Fraidy cat," she teased. Walking through the turnstile, she paused at the top of the steps and asked, "How many steps did the guidebook say again?"

"279"

"Gee, thanks." Grabbing the handrail, she descended the endless stairs, grateful for her toned physique.

Finally arriving at the bottom of the stairs, they were greeted by a cavern. The cave walls were covered with pictures and text showcasing the history of the Catacombs and their rediscovery in modern times.

"So where are all the dead people?" Tommy tucked his hands into his pockets, then teetered back-and-forth on his heels.

"Patience, my love." Victoria read every word of history, turned on her audio guide, and listened to the same spiel she'd just read.

"I guess this is a self-guided tour?" Tommy turned. Tourists walked out of the history area and down the main tunnel.

Nodding, she said, "I'm surprised. You'd think

people would get lost in here being left on their own."
She followed the crowd through the long tunnel. Its
square walls went on forever.

"Don't even think about it," he warned. "Besides, I
see lots of guards around. Probably for just that
reason."

"And to stop tourists from using flash
photography." She nodded to the signs posted
periodically.

"Ah, finally, dead people." He stopped in front of
the first display of bones.

"Wow, this is cool." Victoria grimly studied the
arrangement of bones. The femurs were neatly
stacked about four feet high. Skulls, lined up side-by-
side facing her, topped the stack. The rest of the bones
were just strewn behind the femur and skull wall.

Turning, she didn't see any guards. Defiantly, she
snapped a flash photo.

"Ohhhh, I'm telling," Tommy teased.

"Shhh. The picture is better with a flash. And
besides, they're dead."

"But the flash could fade the art."

"It's not like I'm taking a flash photo of the Mona
Lisa in the Louvre. It's just a skull." She handed him
the camera. "Here, take one of me with the skulls,
then I'll take one of you."

They snapped silly pictures of each other. Victoria
puckered her lips and pretended to air kiss the skull.
She couldn't wait to post these pictures on Facebook.

"Come on, let's continue on." He prodded her with
his arm.

"Okay, I guess there's more." She meandered
through the tunnel.

"Millions of bones to see."

Walking past more meticulously displayed stacks
of bones, she said, "They kind of all look alike after a

while."

"Ah, but this display is different." Tommy pointed to the skulls forming a cross within the stack.

After studying the room and finding no guide, she snapped another flash photo. "Come on, let's go." She scurried out of the chamber.

"I don't see anyone coming back this way. I wonder if the path just circles around?" His expression grew perplexed.

"It exits in a different location than the entrance. At the gift shop, of course. Or so the guide book says," Victoria explained.

They walked into a large cavern with a ceiling several feet taller than the main tunnel.

"Whoa, that's tall." Tommy titled his head back.

A guide stood in the corner and said in English, "This is where the Catacombs collapsed. The weight of the building above broke through the thin ceiling and fell through. Imagine enjoying an espresso in a café one minute, then falling into a hole the next."

"How awful." Another tourist grimaced.

"But what an amazing discovery." Victoria whispered to Tommy.

Chapter Four

"Here, this looks good," Victoria stopped in front of Le St. Martin's restaurant and studied the menu posted on the window.

"Yeah, roast beef special today. Sounds good to me." Tommy rubbed his belly, then opened the door.

A man with black hair, glasses, white shirt and black tie greeted them. "Welcome. Follow me please. We have a lovely table by the window." He grabbed two menus.

Victoria took the seat in the corner, and Tommy sat opposite her.

"My name is Walter. Can I start you with a drink?" he asked.

"Yes, can you recommend a bottle of red wine?" Tommy asked.

"Of course, may I suggest a bottle of our house wine? It's what all the locals drink." He gestured to the table of four elderly gentlemen with a bottle of red wine.

"Sounds great." Staring at the table next to theirs, Tommy's eyes grew bigger. "That's what I'm having." He pointed to the gigantic steak overflowing the plate.

"That's huge. How about we share?"

Tommy shot her an annoyed look.

"I'll just have a few bites, I promise. Instead of a main course, I'm going to have two starts—escargot and the cheese plate."

Walter returned with their bottle of red house wine. He poured a sample into Tommy's glass for him to taste.

Tommy swirled the wine around in his glass, sniffed, then sipped. "Mmm, this *is* good."

Walter poured Victoria's glass, then topped off Tommy's.

"*Santé*." Tommy lifted his glass.

Raising her glass to his, she said, "*Santé*."

"I'm so excited about tomorrow. I didn't know that Disneyland Paris had two parks." Victoria opened her guidebook.

"Good thing we're spending five nights there." He sipped his wine and studied the menu.

"I thought we're getting steak?"

"We are. I was just curious about what else they offered." Putting the menu down, he grabbed her hand from across the table.

"Didn't you say the hotel is right at the entrance to the park?" She squeezed his hand.

"Yes, in fact, some of the rooms actually overlook Main Street USA."

"There's a Main Street USA? In Paris? I'd figured they'd cater the park to the French. I was hoping for the Champs-Elysees. I wonder if there are differences. I'm looking forward to comparing this park to the one in Florida."

Tommy filled her wine glass, draining the bottle in the process. "More wine?"

Nodding, she sipped her wine.

Walter, quick on the job, asked, "Another bottle?"

"I'm not sure we need another bottle, but I would like wine with my steak."

"Our steak." She corrected, eating the last bites of camembert, blue and Romano cheese from her plate.

"May I suggest another bottle? And if you do not finish, you can take it with you," Walter offered. Although his English was slightly broken, it was pretty good for a second language.

"Yes, another bottle then." Tommy pointed to their empty wine bottle. "Your English is very good."

"Thank you. I'm actually from Portugal. Learning French was easy compared to learning English. And learning Italian was easy because it's similar to Spanish." Walter cleared her cheese plate.

Make that his fifth language.

"Is there anything to do other than the theme parks at Disneyland Paris?" She dunked her bread into the garlic sauce leftover from her escargot.

"Not much. But there's plenty to do at Disneyland with two parks. Plus, I think there's Downtown Disney between the train station and the parks."

"Oh, I was just curious. Maybe there's a little town or village nearby." She recalled what she'd heard today in the line for the Catacombs.

"I know that look, my dear. You're wondering if the urban legend about undiscovered catacombs beneath the outskirts of Paris is true." He arched his right eyebrow.

After draining her wine glass, she said, "Guilty. I'm always up for a good spelunking."

Chapter Five

"Why did we have to wake up so early?" Tommy yawned.

They stood on the platform waiting for the red line RER train to take them to Disneyland Paris.

"Because it's a forty-five-minute train ride, and I want to arrive *before* the park opens." Victoria sipped her espresso.

Rolling his eyes, he chided, "You're killing me." He sat on his suitcase while they waited for the train. They'd brought their luggage because they'd checked out of their hotel near the Eiffel Tower.

"Here, cranky butt. I was saving these croissants for the train, but..." She held out the bag to him.

Snatching it, he said, "The way to a man's heart." He removed a croissant from the bag and bit off half of it in one bite. Flakey crumbs fell onto his lap.

"Ah, here it comes." Pointing, she grabbed the handle of her suitcase and rolled it closer to the yellow boarding line painted on the cement platform.

The train slowed, and they adjusted their position on the platform in hopes of standing directly in front of a set of doors once the train stopped.

"Cool, a double decker." Tommy's face lit up with excitement, like a kid at....

They boarded the train, and Tommy raced up the stairs to the second level.

Victoria struggled with her suitcase on the stairs. Tommy carried it for her to the top level and easily tossed it on the chrome luggage rack above their heads. Sitting in one of the chairs, she exhaled with relief.

Tommy grabbed her hand, placed their combined hands into his lap, turned to her, and asked, "Are we there yet?"

Victoria smiled and turned to the window. Watching the other passengers board, she saw four dwarfs running to catch the train.

Tommy recited Jenny's famous line from *Forrest Gump* with an exaggerated Southern accent, "Run, Forrest, run."

Slapping him, she scolded, "Tommy Garrison, you're terrible."

"What time does the park open?" He checked his watch. His expression grew concerned, like he could've slept for another hour.

The train closed its doors and gained speed as it pulled out of the station.

"Oh, I don't know. I assumed it was nine. But I didn't think to check for magic hours, like they have at Walt Disney World." She referred to the extra hour in the park, offered only to guests staying on Disney property.

The four dwarfs climbed the stairs and sat across the aisle from them in four seats facing each other with a table in between. Without saying a word to each other, they pulled out their cell phones and tapped mindlessly away in a comfortable silence. All four sipped large coffees from Starbucks.

What's with the international obsession with American fast food and beverages? Victoria recalled the train station in Paris with the line, equipped with queuing rope and security guards, to get *into* Burger King. Shaking her head incredulously, she mentally patted herself on the back for preferring freshly baked French bread, croissants and espressos from a quaint French corner bakery instead of Burger King and Starbucks.

The dwarfs' attire reminded Victoria of her and Tommy's work clothes—jeans, flannel shirts, and Timberland hiking boots. The dwarfs wore beards and knit hats. They reminded her of the dwarfs on one of her favorite television shows, *Once Upon A Time*.

Tommy snapped his fingers and said, "Earth to Victoria, you and your shiny objects."

Shaking her head from her tangential trance, she said, "Oh, sorry. You were saying something?" Turning away from the dwarfs, she studied the window. The train left the underground of Paris, ascending to the surface. They passed dozens of buildings, mostly run-down apartment buildings with peeling paint and cracks in the walls. The quality of housing diminished the further away the train took them from the heart of Paris.

"Check the guidebook to see what time the park opens." Tommy pointed to her *Rick Steves' France*.

Shrugging her shoulders, she asked, "What does it matter, we're already up and on the train?"

Nodding to the four dwarfs sitting across the aisle from them, he whispered, "I think we're on the train with Disneyland Cast Members."

Victoria studied the passengers around them. Two beautiful, petite blondes sat ahead, facing them. Their big blue eyes and perfect ivory complexions screamed *Disney Princesses*: Cinderella, Aurora, Rapunzel, Elsa, or Anna, she speculated.

Across the aisle from the princesses sat two gorgeous, slim muscular men with square jaws and perfect hair. They held hands and fiddled with their cell phones. Disney Princes, probably Prince Eric from *The Little Mermaid* and Prince Charming from *Snow White and the Seven Dwarfs*.

Tommy's nudged. "Another shiny object?"

"Oh, sorry. But I think you're right." She nodded to the princes and princesses sitting in front of them on the train. Flipping the pages of her guidebook, she quickly found the Disneyland Paris section she'd earmarked.

"Did you find it?" he asked.

Nodding, she held up her finger and scanned the page to the section about park hours. "Oh, sorry."

"What? Don't tell me it's closed." Tommy slumped in his seat.

Pointing to the park hours during the months from October to March, she said, "It doesn't open until ten a.m."

Tommy glanced at the digital clock above the door of the train, shook his head, and said, "It's only eight a.m."

"I've always wanted to be the first in line at Disney."

* * * *

Twenty minutes later, the train slowed as it pulled into a small station. The presumed Disneyland Cast Members, along with most everyone, stood and held the chrome handrails.

Victoria turned to Tommy, who arched his eyebrows with a quizzical expression, and wondered if they should get off, too. Shrugging her shoulders, she studied the red line RER route painted above the train's windows. The route, dotted with large circles at the names of each stop, forked about two-thirds of the way to Disneyland Paris.

One of the standing dwarfs ogled her appreciatively. Then he studied Tommy with a jealous expression. Turning to the dwarf standing in front of him, he whispered in French.

After easily translating the dwarfs' conversation, Victoria stood, grabbed her suitcase from the chrome luggage rack and said, "Come on, we have to change trains here."

The trained stopped, and almost everyone exited.

Rushing, Tommy gathered his belongings and followed her off the train.

After stepping onto a cement platform, they followed the masses down a long flight of stairs, through a corridor, then up another long flight of stairs to a different platform.

Victoria studied the RER train schedule posted in a large, glass case. Running her fingers along the times, she quickly found the train to Disneyland. Once they were huddled together, she whispered, "Good thing I speak French. Those dwarfs were making fun of us and called us 'Stupid American tourists.'"

"I can't believe we had to change trains to get to Disneyland Paris. You'd think they'd offer a direct train. I can't imagine how many tourists miss the change and end up in the middle of the French countryside." Frustrated, he shook his head incredulously.

"Apparently, the earlier RER trains, like the ones for the Disneyland workers, are not as crowded so they have to change. During peak Disney train times, there are several direct trains to Disneyland," she explained.

Their new train pulled into the station, and everyone climbed aboard.

After stepping safely onto the train with Tommy and their luggage, Victoria studied the train's route painted above the window. The last stop was Disneyland Paris. Sighing with relief, she followed Tommy to two empty seats in the back.

As she rolled her suitcase down the narrow aisle, she spotted the same rude dwarf who'd called her a 'Stupid American.'"

With a surprised expression, the dwarf ogled her creepily.

Using perfect French, Victoria sarcastically thanked him for his kindness and predicted that Karma would properly repay him.

Chapter Six

"Oh, Tommy, the room is beautiful." Victoria immediately walked towards the window.

Tommy tipped the bellhop who'd brought their luggage to their room and said, "*Merci beaucoup.*"

Opening the sliding glass door, she walked out onto the tiny balcony overlooking Main Street USA. Two chairs with a small table in between greeted them. Placing her hand on the railing, she marveled at the lack of tourists, just Disneyland Cast Members preparing the park for the imminent onslaught of tourists.

Tommy walked out onto the balcony and placed his hands around her waist from behind. Resting his head on her shoulder, he nuzzled his lips against her neck and asked, "Remember our first kiss?" He referred to the balcony from their room overlooking the Magic Kingdom at the Grand Floridian Resort at Walt Disney World.

"How can I forget?" She turned and placed her hand on his cheek.

"Well, in keeping with tradition." He pulled her close and ran his fingers through her hair. His head dipped, and he bit her bottom lip playfully. Humming, his mouth crushed down on hers, and his tongue slid into her mouth.

* * * *

"It looks exactly like the park in Orlando." Victoria scanned Main Street USA and marveled at the replica of the park in Florida.

"The park itself is actually much smaller than the one in Orlando. It's modeled after the original Disneyland in Anaheim, California," Tommy explained.

"I can't wait to visit the one in California. In fact, we should make it our goal to visit *all six* Disney locations around the world." She leaned her head against his strong shoulder.

"Sounds like a great plan." He kissed her brow and wrapped his arm around her waist.

"Oh, it's Sleeping Beauty's Castle." Excitedly, she pointed past the shops to the pink castle which dominated the center of the park.

"What a great place to start. But let's ride Space Mountain first." Tommy hugged her to him.

"Oh, yeah, rollercoasters first." She followed him to the right.

They meandered into Tomorrowland, and familiar rides greeted them—Space Mountain and Buzz Lightyear.

"It's colorful, not white like the one in Florida." She pointed to the brightly colored Space Mountain ride.

"And part of the ride goes outside." Tommy pointed to the rollercoaster tracks on the outside of the mountain.

"No line, cool." Beaming, she pointed to the sign. "Let's ride this, then Buzz Lightyear. See, aren't you glad I woke you up early so we're the first ones here? No lines."

"Now I am. But not this morning when you woke me up at the crack of dawn."

They rode Space Mountain and Buzz Lightyear.

"That was so cool," she proclaimed as they exited the Buzz Lightyear ride.

"I like how you could hold your laser gun when you shoot, not just rotate it on the ride like in Florida." Tommy pretended to shoot a gun with his hand.

"Yeah, but I still beat you. I'm a Galactic Hero!"

She referred to the maximum level awarded for her uber high score.

Obviously defeated, he dropped his head in shame, "No need to rub it in. Having a girl outshoot me is bad enough."

"I was born and raised in the South. I could shoot before I could walk," she *slightly* exaggerated.

"Thanks, that makes me feel better, but a little scared, too." His expression grew worried.

"Ooh, what's that?" She pointed to the *Nautilus* submarine from *20,000 Leagues Under the Sea.*

"I think you know."

"Oh, my God. I can't believe it's here. Remember how bummed I was that they'd closed my favorite childhood ride at Disney World?"

"I do, let's go check it out." Grabbing her hand, he led her to the ride.

Climbing up the plank to the ride, she said, "But wait, I don't see much water. And there's only one *Nautilus.*"

Following her, he said, "Oh, it's not a ride."

They walked into the partially submerged submarine. The interior was decorated like the real *Nautilus* from the Jules Verne classic novel.

"It's not what I'd hoped, but this is really cool." She meandered through the submarine.

Like he sensed her slight disappointment, he pulled her close and said, "Remember what we discovered buried under the former 20,000 Leagues Under the Sea ride at Disney World?" Winking, he referred to discovering the Fountain of Youth almost a year ago.

"Well, who knows what lies underneath Disneyland Paris? If the Fountain of Youth is hidden under the Magic Kingdom in Walt Disney World, I wonder if anything is hidden under *this* park." Her imagination went wild with possibilities.

Chapter Seven

"I love this castle." Victoria tilted her head back to admire Sleeping Beauty's castle. The bottom half was made of stacked, blue-grey stone. The top half was pink with blue roofing on its many turrets.

Placing his arms around her waist, Tommy hugged her close and kissed her brow. "It's not as beautiful as you, my love."

Blushing she dropped her head. "It's much smaller than Cinderella's castle in Florida." Unfolding the park map, she studied it.

"What's our plan, Sacagawea?" Tommy asked, referring to the famous, female Native American explorer who helped the Lewis and Clark Expedition.

"This map shows that there are things to do inside the castle. We can actually go into it, not just through it like Cinderella's." Excitement filled her with something new to see at Disney.

Tommy looked down at her and asked, "You're loving this, aren't you?"

Nodding she said, "I feel like I'm five."

"You're young at heart, one of the many things I love about you." He squeezed her hand.

They entered the castle's foyer which had two levels. The ceiling boasted gothic arches. But instead of your typical Roman or Greek columns, these columns were shaped like trees supporting the upper balcony.

They took the stairs to the second level. Smaller than the first, it was a wrap-around balcony which led you around the inner perimeter of the castle. Starting at the top of the stairs, tapestries were hung on the walls. Next to the tapestries were stained glass windows. Each one depicted a scene from the animated film *Sleeping Beauty*.

Walking the perimeter, they enjoyed the various scenes from *Sleeping Beauty*. Near the end, they stopped in front of the famous scene when Prince Phillip kissed Aurora to awaken her from the sleeping curse.

Tommy turned Victoria to face him. Looking lovingly into her eyes, he brought her hands to his lips and kissed her fingers. "Remember the last time we were in a castle?"

"Yes."

Wrapping his arms around her waist, he pulled her close. "Well, in keeping with tradition." He closed his eyes and dipped his head. His lips touched hers.

"Oh, Tommy." She knew they were surrounded by tourists with kids. Otherwise, she'd continue their passionate kiss. But she'd have to wait until tonight in the room to continue expressing their deep love for one another.

He hugged her and asked, "What's next, Sacagawea?"

They walked back downstairs, and she studied the map. "Hmmm, there's *Snow White's Scary Adventure* nearby. I really want to ride that since they closed the one in Florida."

"Sounds great. What else?"

"There's a dragon cave underneath the castle. There's-"

"-Any good places to eat?" Tommy interrupted.

She smacked him and turned. "Oh, look a glass blower." Pointing, she dragged Tommy inside the gift shop.

"You and your shiny objects." Shaking his head, he smiled and followed her into the gift shop.

Glass display cases showcased Disney figurines. Behind a glass half-wall, a man stood wearing a protective mask. He held a blow torch in one hand

and a stick of glass in the other. Heating up the end of the glass, he used a tool to bend the molten glass into Mickey Mouse ears.

"This is so cool." Her eyes widened with fascination watching the man create something so beautiful.

He added a small emerald to the middle of the mouse ears and placed the completed piece down to cool.

Victoria admired several finished pieces locked in a display cabinet. They hung from silver chains. But instead of glass floating Mickeys, some were made of gold and silver.

"Oh, look, it's a floating Mickey pendant on a necklace. And it's my birthstone." She gave Tommy the 'pretty please, buy it for me' look.

Not missing the hint, he said, "Okay. I've been wanting to buy you a pretty piece of jewelry. And I can't think of anything more appropriate than a piece of Disney jewelry."

"Oh, Tommy." She hugged him. "And how special for us since our first date was at Disney."

Walking a few steps over to the cashier, he pointed to the locked glass cabinet and said, "We'd like to look at some of these, please."

Victoria was immediately drawn to the silver Mickey Mouse pendant with an emerald stone. She knew gold was more valuable than silver, but she had a new fondness for silver.

A year ago, she'd discovered a silver mine underneath Castle Garrison. Castle Garrison was where Tommy grew up. Tommy's cousin, Grier Garrison, married Victoria's best friend, Lilly Allen. It was just before the wedding at Castle Garrison when Lilly showed Victoria the cool pirate cave beneath the castle. Victoria's cave exploring skills led them to discover a silver mine.

"You already picked one out, didn't you?" Tommy asked.

Nodding, she beamed at the shiny object before her.

"Hmm, let me guess." He placed his thumb and index finger on his chin, pointed to her favorite, and said, "That one."

"You know me pretty well. But only if it's not too much." Her humble beginnings drove her frugal tendencies.

He gave her a dirty look and asked, "Why are you worried about money? You just earned a 10% finder's fee on the royalties from the silver mine. The rest was split amongst the Garrison clan."

Shrugging her shoulders, she confessed, "Humble beginnings."

"We'll take this one." He told the Disney Cast Member running the register.

"Would you like to try it on and wear it today?" the Cast Member asked.

Nodding, she beamed, "Yes, please."

"Excellent choice. And it comes with a certificate of authenticity for both the emerald and the silver."

"It's real?" Victoria and Tommy asked in unison.

"Yes, the stone is small, but real. That's why these pieces are locked up and the price is so high."

Tommy removed the pendant from the box and wrapped the chain around her neck.

Victoria lifted her hair out of the way to allow Tommy to wrap the chain around her neck and clasp it. A hand-held mirror appeared in front of her, courtesy of the Cast Member. The silver, floating Mickey Mouse with an emerald stone lay against her tan chest, falling just above her cleavage.

"We'll take it." Tommy pulled out his wallet and

retrieved his Disney Chase Visa.

"Oh, Tommy, thank you." She kissed his cheek.

"At least we're earning double Disney dollars in the park." Winking, he handed the card to the Cast Member.

"*Heigh, ho.*" One of the seven dwarfs sang as he entered the store. He was followed by two other dwarfs, all carrying pick axes on their shoulders.

Victoria presumed, based on their height, that they were the same dwarfs they saw on the train to Disneyland Paris this morning. Only now they were in costume which included an oversized head.

The dwarfs walked behind the counter and into a small room. Their pick axes were extremely realistic, and dirty, like they'd just been used to mine gems from a cave.

From her vantage point, Victoria watched the dwarfs meet with another Cast Member. One dwarf handed the Cast Member a small, velvet bag. The Cast Member emptied its contents onto a velvet cloth. A dozen small rubies, sapphires, emeralds and diamonds fell onto the cloth, and the Cast Member beamed. Opening up a safe, he placed the bag into the safe and locked it.

Chapter Eight

Tommy and Victoria turned to each other with gaping mouths. *What the hell was that?*

Quickly signing the credit card receipt, Tommy returned the card to his wallet. The dwarfs walked towards the exit of the store. Victoria and Tommy nodded towards them, silently indicating their intention to follow the costumed Cast Members.

The dwarfs exited the gift shop and continued singing their famous work song from *Snow White and the Seven Dwarfs*. They walked out of the castle and down the ramp which led to the dragon cave below the castle.

The black dragon lit up in the cave and moved its gigantic head towards the tourists.

Pointing, she said, "Oh, neat."

Tommy pulled her away from the dragon and whispered with an agitated tone, "Stop getting distracted."

"Fine, but we're coming back here later." She followed him quietly behind the dwarfs.

The dwarfs stopped in front of a door which read, 'Cast Members Only.' One of them waved a key card in front of the card reader, and the door opened. The dwarfs walked through the open door, and Victoria and Tommy snuck in behind them before the door closed.

They walked down a flight of stairs. The walls were part of a cave, similar to the dragon's cave they'd just seen. At the bottom of the stairs, the cave tunnel opened up into a giant cavern.

Beaming excitedly, she whispered, "It's Underground Disney."

Dozens of Cast Members walked about. Golf carts

and Segways whizzed by with various Disney characters in costume. Several mirrored vanities were sprinkled throughout the cavern. A blonde, Disney princess had her makeup and hair done at one of the vanities. Most of the characters in costume spoke on cell phones, texted and drank either Red Bull or Diet Coke.

"Kind of kills the magic, huh?" Tommy whispered.

"Ah, there you are. I've been looking for you two." A man in a pink, oxford button-down dress shirt said with a feminine voice.

Tommy and Victoria remained silent, clueless to what this man, whose nametag read 'Jacques,' wanted with them.

"Come on, we're late for the character meet and greet. The kids love Pocahontas and John Smith.

Victoria turned to Tommy and silently pleaded with her best 'lost-puppy dog' expression, *Please, please, please, let's just go with it and see what happens.*

Sighing, Tommy dropped his chin and reluctantly nodded his acquiescence.

Jacques led them to two mirrored vanities where makeup artists awaited. A Pocahontas and John Smith costume hung on a rolling dress rack. He gestured for them to take their seats and said, "You two are lucky today, since it's so cold, they're not making you stand outside in Frontierland. We've set up the character greet inside one of the gift shops. Otherwise you'd be a frozen Pocahontas in your skimpy costume." He winked at Victoria.

Removing her Disney windbreaker, she sat in the beautician's chair.

Two women pounced on her, one with a hair brush, and the other with a tray of makeup. One brushed her hair, while the other applied foundation to her face with a makeup sponge. The base color was slightly darker than her already tan complexion.

"I see why they cast you as Pocahontas. You have the perfect hair for it. Makes my job much easier when all I have to do is brush it. You have the most beautiful hair." The stylist spoke French.

"Oh, thank you. Any advice for my first day? I'm a little nervous." Victoria blushed.

"Just enjoy being a Disney Princess."

Glancing over to Tommy, who sat at the hair and makeup station next to her, she held back her laughter. He looked so uncomfortable getting makeup unnecessarily applied to his already handsome face. Grimacing, he gave her a phony smile. His evil eye appeared and silently questioned. *How far are we going to take this?*

Shrugging her shoulders, she turned to her reflection and smiled at the finished product in the mirror. She stood and slid behind a privacy curtain to slip into her skimpy, but not slutty, Pocahontas costume. After lacing up her animal-skin boots, she returned to the makeup station to find Tommy dressed in his John Smith costume. His tight pants, boots, and light-blue, old-fashioned shirt transformed him into his new character.

"Don't say a word." He shot her a dirty look and held out his elbow for her.

Slipping her arm into his offered elbow, she said, "What, no Facebook photo?"

"Oh, dear, God. Kill me now." He rolled his eyes.

"Ah, perfect. You two look *fabulous*." Jacques sang the last word.

They followed Jacques to a golf cart. Jacques slid into the driver's seat while Victoria and Tommy took the back seat.

"All aboard. We got kids waiting for pictures and

autographs. Hold on tight."

The cart accelerated surprisingly fast. Victoria and Tommy instinctively grabbed the hand rail to hold on. The cart whizzed past numerous Cast Members, not bothering to weave around them. Jacques honked the horn repeatedly to warn those to move out of the way. He didn't slow down for the slowpokes who took their time moving out of the way. A few curse words were sworn in French when Jacques nearly clipped Jack, the Pumpkin King and his ragdoll girlfriend, Sally, from the movie, *The Nightmare Before Christmas*.

Once they left the densely populated makeup area, they sped through a narrow corridor. Jacques slammed on the brakes and mouthed a few colorful words. Stopping them was a line of dwarfs crossing their path and entering a tunnel. But what they transported in a mining cart on tracks, shocked Victoria and Tommy.

Chapter Nine

After an hour of standing and posing for pictures as Pocahontas and John Smith, Victoria's face hurt from smiling so much. *Oh, the woes of a Disney Princess.*

Jacques stood nearby with another Cast Member to control the crowd still lining up to get their picture taken with Disney characters. Jacques's walkie-talkie spewed static sounds. He retrieved it from his belt and answered, *"Oui?"* Nodding his head several times, he shot Victoria and Tommy a disdaining scowl.

"Uh, oh, party's over," she whispered.

"What do you suggest we do? It's not like they're going to cuff us in front of a bunch of kids." Tommy asked.

Still talking out of the side of her mouth so the younglings couldn't hear her, she said, "I don't think we should run for it? Do you?"

Shaking his head, he said, "No. One, they'd catch up to us. And two, they might ban us from Disney."

"Great point. Here he comes now." Victoria posed for a picture with a young Chinese girl.

"I'm sorry ladies and gentlemen, boys and girls, but Pocahontas and John Smith need a quick break. They will be back in about ten minutes, but in the meantime, Chip and Dale will be here," Jacques said with his arms in the air.

Jacques whispered to Victoria and Tommy, "The party is over, you two. Don't make a scene. If you follow me quietly to return your costumes, we won't eject you from the park."

Nodding, they followed Jacques.

Chip and Dale arrived to take their place. Dale opened his arms to Victoria, signaling for a hug. She obliged, but he held her a little *too* long. *"Mon*

Cherie," he whispered in her ear with a sexy French accent.

She slid out of the hug, but Chip immediately took her into his arms, too. Rolling her eyes at Tommy, she mouthed, "Sorry."

Tommy's expression grew enraged, and his fist clenched.

Jacques witnessed the commotion and intervened. "Come on, Chip and Dale, the kiddies are waiting."

Chip released Victoria and blew her a kiss.

They followed Jacques through the door marked, 'Cast Members only.' They walked down two flights of stairs and listened to him rant in French. They reached the tunnel and climbed aboard the golf cart.

Jacques inhaled and exhaled deeply, as if he silently counted to ten to mitigate his anger. "It's partially my fault. I practically dragged you two to makeup and costume so we wouldn't be late for the character greet. I mean, who could blame me right?" he said in broken English.

"We're sorry. We just got caught up in everything and thought it might be fun," she confessed.

"And I just went along because of her. I mean, do you think I like wearing tights, makeup and hair spray?" Tommy laughed. Then he covered his mouth, the same one he'd just put his foot in.

Jacques shook his head, obviously offended.

They rode in silence through the tunnel. Another golf cart passed with the rightful Pocahontas and John Smith. Their dirty glares spoke volumes, "Shame, shame, shame for impersonating Disney characters."

The cart sped through the tunnel, then slowed as it crossed the train tracks leading from one side of the tunnel to the other. The tracks were blocked with a closed door which read, 'Dwarfs only.'

"What's down there?" she asked.

"Disney secret, sorry." Jacques shrugged his shoulders.

They arrived back at the makeup and hair station and jumped off the golf cart. Quickly changing out of their costumes, Tommy asked the makeup lady, "Do you mind removing this gunk from my face?"

Nodding, the Cast Member gestured for him to take a seat. After Tommy's makeup was removed, Victoria plopped into the chair and let the lady remove hers, too. Although the makeup looked stunning, it was a bit much for her typical attire of skinny jeans, flannel shirt and Timberlands.

"Here, let me just give you a little something so you don't feel naked." The makeup lady quickly sponged a lighter shade of foundation on Victoria's face. Then added loose powder, light blush, two strokes of mascara and pink lip gloss.

"Ahem." Jacques cleared his throat, impatiently waiting to escort the truant archaeologists out of Underground Disney.

They followed Jacques up the stairs which led outside. The warm sun and blue sky greeted them.

Jacques wiggled an angry finger at them, then returned to Underground Disney.

"Now what?" she asked.

Tommy's face lit up.

Turning, she saw what got Tommy's attention— Marionettes. The restaurant resembled Pinocchio's in the Magic Kingdom at Walt Disney World. The big sign boasted, 'Brats on pretzel bread.'

"We eat." He grinned.

Chapter Ten

Victoria woke up from her nap in their suite at the Disneyland Hotel. Her stomach, still stuffed from beer, pretzels and brats, bulged from the high carb lunch at Marionettes. Tommy's beautiful form still slept beside her. His muscular forearms hugged the pillow while he slept on his stomach.

Slipping out of bed, she donned on her baby blue, soft robe and walked to the bathroom. Stepping into the shower, the steam and hot water soothed her. Then she washed away the memory of getting into trouble at Disney.

She exited the bathroom and found Tommy sitting up in bed reading the Disney brochures they'd received in the welcome packet at check-in.

"Hey, Honey?" Tommy asked.

"Yeah?" She dried her hair and crunched it with gel to make it wavy.

"Did you know you can rent bikes here?" His tone rang with excitement.

"No, I didn't, that sounds like fun. We can work off lunch." Laughing, she struggled into her skinny jeans, hopping up and down until the stretchy denim snuggled her hips. Grabbing her new hot-pink Minnie Mouse t-shirt out of the plastic Disney shopping bag, she cut off the tags and pulled it over her head.

Rubbing his eight pack abs, he said, "What do you think about riding bikes into that little town we saw on the train ride in?"

"Sounds good to me. We may as well since the park closes at six o'clock and it's after five already.".

"And we can have dinner in town." He smiled.

Men, always thinking about food. "How can you be hungry?" Laughing, she hit him over the head with her pillow.

"I'm not *starving*, but I will be soon. Besides, we need to eat dinner *sometime*." He climbed out of bed and pulled his jeans over his narrow hips and muscular bottom.

"It's a shame we didn't get to see the entire park today. And I also want to see Walt Disney Studios next door."

Walking over to her, he kissed her lips and wrapped his arms around her waist. "Relax, my dear, we still have, like four days left." He looked up at the ceiling like he mentally calculated their remaining time in France.

"I know, you're right." She stepped into her hot-pink Converse sneakers and tied the laces.

Tommy pulled his black t-shirt with a white skull of Jack, the Pumpkin King over his head. "Ready?"

They grabbed their jackets and walked out the door.

After renting bikes downstairs, Tommy studied the map of the area which the concierge had given them. After getting his bearings, he peddled across the paved walkway away from the hotel.

She followed him, and they wove around the pedestrians exiting the parks. They rode through Downtown Disney which offered restaurants, shops, and a movie theater. Planet Hollywood's enormous Earth globe dominated their view.

After they turned right at the train station, the crowds vanished.

Tommy stopped, and she squeezed the handle brakes to stop next to him. Studying the map, he compared it to the street signs at the intersection in front of them. "Ah, here we are." He pointed to their location on the map.

"Where to?" she asked, not caring where they went, so long as they were together.

Moving his index finger along the map, he said, "Let's go straight, then just meander through the town and see what we find."

"You mean, a place to eat dinner," she quipped.

"Touché." Grinning, he slid his bottom back onto the bicycle seat and peddled across the street.

She peddled beside him because the streets were empty. The town appeared abandoned. The buildings were old and falling apart. The shops were all closed and 'out-of-business' signs appeared in most of the windows. Yellow tape blocked off the entrance to an apartment building. Hazard signs and 'do-not-enter' warnings hung on most of the doorways.

"I wonder what happened here?" She shook her head incredulously.

"I don't know. The whole town is deserted. You'd think that with Disney nearby, this town would thrive." He signaled for her to turn right at the next crosswalk.

Slowly peddling around the corner, she asked, "Where do the people live who work at Disney?"

"Paris probably. Remember the Disney workers we rode with on the train here?" Clearing his throat, he added, "When we arrived an *hour* before the park even opened."

"Yes, dear, but we got to ride Space Mountain and Buzz Lightyear without waiting in line."

They took another right turn and stopped, shocked at the sight before them. The apartment building rested two stories below the ground, like it'd fallen into a sinkhole.

Chapter Eleven

"What the...?" Victoria asked with her mouth gaped open.

"The buildings have fallen into the earth." Tommy stepped closer to the Sixties' style, green cement apartment building in front of them. "By about twenty feet, I'd wager."

"It can't be a sinkhole, not in France," she reasoned.

"You're right. No limestone caverns here. But what could it be?"

Victoria scanned the buildings on the block. The tiny ones remained above surface, but the larger ones sank twenty feet below the ground. Their tour of the Catacombs the day before in Paris flashed in her mind. Two memories swam in her brain—the Catacombs in Paris weakened the surface, causing buildings to collapse into the earth, and the Urban Legend that catacombs existed outside the city limits.

Tommy must've come to the same realization.

They turned to face one another and said in unison, "Catacombs."

Thrill filled her. The excitement of another archaeological find caused her to do a happy dance in the deserted street of a tiny town near Disneyland Paris.

Tommy wrapped his arms around her and said, "I gave you credit for finding the Fountain of Youth, but I think that *I* deserve credit for this one."

"Fine." She exhaled. Recognizing her defeat, she slumped her shoulders and said, "It was *your* idea to rent bicycles. And *you* navigated us here."

"But it was *your* idea to go to Paris and Disneyland." He referred to their decision to travel here, just after they'd discovered the Fountain of

Youth underneath the Magic Kingdom in Walt Disney World, Florida.

"Joint credit." She extended her hand for a shake.

He shook her hand and smiled. "Let's hold off celebrating, we haven't officially found anything yet."

"You're right. But what else could it be?" She stepped towards the third-floor window, broken from the collapse.

"Something's weakened the ground below." He stomped his feet. "Could the catacombs be a cave system?"

"Could be an abandoned mine?" She turned to him.

"No matter what, it seems we have some exploring to do."

Victoria opened her fuchsia cinch sack and pulled out two headbands with flashlights. Tossing one to Tommy, she said, "Here, put this on."

Shaking his head, he asked, "You brought head flashlights for a bike ride?"

Nodding, she pulled the elastic band over her head and said, "I'd've made a great Boy Scout, 'Be prepared.'"

"Thanks for bringing me one, too." He pulled the elastic band over his head.

Peering into the broken window, she turned to survey the room. "Is it breaking and entering if the window is already broken?" Without waiting for his response, she lifted her foot and kicked off the glass shards from the window sill, then stepped into the building.

Tommy quickly followed her into the third floor. "What a small apartment." He waved his arm towards the small bedroom. Books had fallen from the shelf, and the bed slid towards the center of the room.

They walked out of the bedroom and into a small

living room with a tiny kitchenette. They walked out the front door of the apartment and into a dark hallway.

"Watch out for squatters. Homeless people love abandoned buildings." Tommy picked up a two-by-four for a makeshift weapon.

"Okay, you can go first then, there's the stairs." She pointed. A poignant aroma wafted. "Argh, what's that horrible smell?" She covered her nose with the inside of her elbow, resembling a vampire.

Tightening his grip on the two-by-four, he gingerly descended the stairs, careful not to make any noise in case they weren't alone. Despite his efforts to be stealth, like a ninja, the hardwood floors creaked beneath his feet. Tommy turned the corner and froze. His flashlight shone on a person, a dead one.

Victoria screamed. The corpse's head was crushed from a cement block.

Chapter Twelve

Victoria immediately sought the comfort of Tommy's strong embrace. Crying, she shivered.

"It's okay. He's not going to hurt you." He cooed into her ear and stroked her hair.

Pulling back from his embrace, she snuffled her last sob. "Sorry to be such a big baby. Why is it that I'm fine with seeing thousands of skulls and bones, morbidly stacked for the amusement of tourists, but I can't handle the sight of one dead body?" She looked up to him for a soothing answer.

Rubbing her shoulders, he said, "Because you're human, that's why. Why don't we call it a night?"

"You're hungry, aren't you?"

"Not as much as I was before we found this guy." He pointed to the corpse. "But we do need to eat dinner. Let's come back tomorrow with gear, hardhats, and camping supplies."

Nodding, she said, "Okay."

* * * *

"Well, that was fast," Victoria said sarcastically. She referred to their *long* trip to the store this morning to procure supplies.

"But think of all the time we'll save if there's something to explore. We can stay down there for days," Tommy rationalized.

With an acquiescing tone, she sighed, "I know, you're right. We don't want to back track like we did in Florida. I wonder what we'll find."

"Anything's possible." They each pulled a large suitcase along the paved sidewalk of Downtown Disney. But instead of normal suitcase contents, theirs contained camping gear and supplies for their exploration beneath the collapsed apartment building.

Tommy hoisted the luggage into the same third story window they'd entered yesterday.

Victoria climbed in. "I wonder if the elevator works." Not wanting to go down the stairs, she dreaded the thought of facing the dead man.

"Probably not, the electricity is out, most likely from the collapse. Besides, I wouldn't want to risk getting stuck."

"Great point, who's around to hear us cry for help? No one even knows where we are."

"Should we tell someone?" Tommy asked.

"Who? The concierge at the hotel. 'Hey we're trespassing, and oh, by the way, we found a dead body.' I'll text Lilly to call in the Cavalry if she doesn't hear from us in a week."

"Sounds like a plan."

She Google mapped their precise location, took a screen shot with her cell phone, then texted the picture and message to Lilly.

We're off on another adventure. Here's where we entered the underground, near Disneyland Paris. xoxo

They let each suitcase slide down the stairs, mindful to not hit the dead guy. They arrived at the first floor and searched for an opening. Victoria kicked the door down to one of the first-floor apartments. Adrenaline rushed through her. Partly because she'd never done that before, just seen it in movies. And partly because she couldn't wait to find the cause of the cave in.

With her flashlight secured to her hard hat, she shone the light into the apartment until she located the window. Motioning for Tommy to bring the luggage in, she pointed through the window with the glass blown out of it.

"A cave tunnel. We'd hoped something like this was down here, but to see it. Wow." He beamed.

Chapter Thirteen

"Now what?" Victoria asked Tommy. "Should we see how far it goes before we lug all of these suitcases into the tunnel?"

Tommy opened his backpack and retrieved his cave scanner. "Let's map it first."

"I should have guessed."

He stepped through the broken window, careful not to get pricked with the remaining shards of glass along the sill.

"Careful," she warned, nodding towards the broken glass. Climbing through after him, she studied the tunnel. The ceiling barely accommodated their six-foot plus height. It was just wide enough for them to comfortably walk in tandem. Its nearly perfectly-square shape indicated that someone carved this tunnel out. *But why?*

Tommy held up his mapping gadget, which resembled a scanner used by policemen to entrap speeding drivers. He pushed the button and held it still. Blue laser beams scanned the interior walls which fed the image to the attached laptop.

"Okay. I think we can bring our stuff. It's just one suitcase and a backpack each."

"Yeah, good idea. I can manage. Don't forget the twine to mark our path in case the tunnel branches off." Victoria reminded him of their method to not get lost.

Nodding, he climbed back through the open window into the apartment. He easily lifted both suitcases through the window and into the cave tunnel. "I'll take the heavy one with the water."

"And the champagne."

"In case we have reason to celebrate." He grinned optimistically.

"Won't that jinx it?"

"Think positive, my love." He kissed her cheek.

"'Think happy thoughts,'" she quoted Peter Pan.

"Which way are we headed?" She spun around, already disoriented.

Tommy pulled out his iPhone with GPS. He showed her the pinpoint on Google maps and pointed their direction.

"We're going towards Disney, yet again." Anticipation filled her. She hoped to find something wonderful. And to share another adventure with the man she loved, made her heart burst with elation.

Taking out the roll of twine, he tied one end to an exposed pipe in the building. He left the twine on the roll and secured the spool to his backpack. All he had to do was walk forward, and the spool would unwind the twine while they hiked through the tunnel.

"Ready?" She took a big swig of water from her canteen.

Nodding, he turned towards the tunnel and wheeled the big suitcase.

She put on her backpack, grabbed the handle of her suitcase, and quickly caught up to Tommy.

Turning towards the ceiling and walls, he said, "Someone definitely carved this out, but why?"

"I don't see any veins of precious metal running through here. No signs of mining."

"Not yet. Perhaps it leads to a mine."

"Let's hope so. There's only one other reason someone would carve out a tunnel underground." His face grimaced.

"Like Napoleon hiding his army in underground tunnels?" Her mind envisioned soldiers here.

"Okay. I like your reason better."

"Why, what's your explanation?"

The tunnel curved. The flashlight strapped to her

forehead shone on something terrifying, and she screamed.

Chapter Fourteen

Victoria flew into Tommy's comforting embrace. Burying her head into his chest, she shivered.

Stroking her hair to soothe her, he said, "There, there. It's okay. I got you. He can't hurt you now. He's been dead for a while." Tommy referred to the skeleton morbidly arranged on the wall in front of them.

"Is this what you meant? The other reason for building a tunnel?"

Nodding, he released his bear hug. "Catacombs."

Composing herself, she sniffled and wiped the tears from her cheeks with her flannel shirt sleeve. *Get a hold of yourself, Victoria. You saw thousands of human bones the other day. Why did this one scare the crap out of you?*

He'd read her mind. "You just weren't expecting it, that's why it scared you so much."

Nodding, she studied the skeleton arranged on the wall. The skull hung in the middle, and its bones were meticulously arranged in a circle surrounding the skull. The smaller bones formed an inner circle and the larger ones formed the outer ring.

"There are probably a lot more bones to come. Do you want to stop and take a break?"

"Don't tell me you're hungry?" she snickered.

He nodded. "Just a snack." He retrieved two bags of apple cinnamon BelVita and tossed one to her.

She took off her backpack and sat down on top of the rolling suitcase. "Fine. It might be a while before we pass through all these bones. They could stretch out for miles."

"Ah, yeah, sure, my thoughts exactly." He took off his backpack and sat on his suitcase. Ripping open the bag, he bit into the BelVita and hummed.

Sighing, she tore open her BelVita bag and bit into the sweet cracker. The apple cinnamon melted in her mouth, and she devoured all four pieces quickly. "I guess I was hungry."

"Who knows what else we'll find down here." He grabbed her empty bag and shoved it into the section of his backpack he'd designated for trash.

Opening her canteen, she gulped more water to get the BelVita crumbs off her teeth with her tongue. "Okay, I'm good to go." Standing, she put her backpack on and adjusted the padded straps on her shoulders.

Tommy stood, took a big swig of water, then mapped their last leg of the tunnel with his scanner. "Ladies first."

Shooting him a dirty look, she said, "Fine." She ducked her head under the entrance to a smaller tunnel. They walked single file through a narrow corridor. Then the corridor opened up to a large cavern, about fifteen feet wide.

"Oh, wow. It's catacombs alright," Tommy said with an appreciative tone.

They walked into the cavern and were greeted with hundreds of skulls and bones. The skulls lined the top of each pile, while the bigger bones, like the femurs, braced the wall. Behind each wall, the other bones appeared haphazardly tossed behind.

"Just like the Catacombs in Paris."

"They ran out of space under the city. The Urban Legend is true—there are catacombs outside of Paris."

Victoria retrieved her GoPro camera and attached it to her hard hat. She turned the camera on and walked slowly through the aisles of bones. Most of the bones were laid out the same. But every twenty feet or so, a few skeletons were arranged more creatively, like a work of art.

Tommy mapped the room with his gadget, then they continued through the aisles of bones.

"Where are we in relation to Disneyland?" she asked.

Tommy pulled out his iPhone. "We may not get much of a signal down here."

"I figured. One perk about cave exploring is being off the grid from cell phones and electronics.

"What the..., no way. We must be..." He hit a few buttons on his smart phone.

"What is it? Where are we?"

"We're underneath Downtown Disney."

"Oh, neat. I'm surprised you got a signal."

"I didn't. Downtown Disney's guest Wi-Fi popped up on my iPhone."

"Wi-Fi in the catacombs. Classic." I'm surprised Disney didn't discover these catacombs when they built downtown Disney."

Tommy looked up from his phone and stopped.

"Uh, I think they did." he said pointing to the brick wall abruptly blocking the path of the catacomb tunnel.

Chapter Fifteen

"Now what?" Victoria slipped off her backpack and sat on the suitcase.

Tommy grabbed his chin and rubbed it with his index finger and thumb. Studying the brick wall, he said, "Hmmm."

"What, what is it?"

Pointing, he said. "These bricks don't have mortar." he pushed one of the top ones through with his finger.

Standing up, excitement filled her. "You're right." She pushed a brick through, and it fell to the other side.

"Did you hear that? It sounds like the brick dropped really far down."

Pushing another one through, she listened to it hit the ground. "You're right. It dropped at least another story down below."

They pushed out the rest of the bricks and leaned over the edge to look down.

"Careful." Tommy grabbed her by the waist.

The head lights on their hard hats shone down into a hole. The pile of bricks accumulated on the stone floor below.

"It's not that far down, perhaps fifteen feet." Tommy studied her and gauged her reaction.

"We can climb down that. The sink hole in Florida was further down than this," she justified.

"You first, then the suit cases, and then me." He tied the heavy rope around a large rock, secured it with a knot, then tested its strength.

"How gallant of you to let me go first," she snickered.

"Would you rather untie the suitcases at the bottom or hoist them down yourself?"

"Fine." She let him tie the rope around her bottom and through her thighs, making a harness out of the rope.

Tommy held the excess rope over his shoulder and hoisted her down into the tunnel.

Wearing gloves, she held on tight to the rope and slowly descended. The light from her headlamp shone on the pile of bricks at the bottom of the vertical tunnel.

"Slow down, almost there." She kicked her foot against the wall to rappel away. Her feet hit the ground next to the brick pile.

"Are you down?" Tommy hollered.

"Yeah, I'm fine. Just give me a second." Untying the rope from her bottom, she slid her legs out of Tommy's rope contraption, then yanked on it. "I'm free. You can have the rope now."

The rope slowly ascended, then Tommy yelled, "Okay, been nice knowing you. Bye."

"Not funny. Don't you dare leave me down here alone," she warned.

"Just teasing you, my love. I'm sending the backpacks down next. But before I do, let's make sure it's not a dead end."

"Great idea." Turning, she let the light on her hard hat shine through the tunnel.

"What do you see?"

"More of the same. Just a tunnel continuing underground like before."

"Sounds promising. Walk a little further, but stay within shouting distance."

"Okay." She walked gingerly, mindful that another skeleton could be just around the corner.

"Anything?" Tommy's voice sounded fainter.

"Let me see what's around the corner."

Turning, the room opened up into a giant cavern.

She screamed.

Chapter Sixteen

"Victoria, are you okay?" Tommy descended the rope and ran to her.

"Yeah, I'm fine, they just startled me." She pointed to the bones.

Instead of bones and skulls meticulously displayed in a macabre pattern, she saw piles of bones, all neatly separated into stacks and sorted by bone type.

Tommy said, "It looks like they're still building. Or stopped and never finished."

"And the bones look so, clean. These are whiter than the others."

"I'll go back and get our stuff, assuming you're okay to continue." He arched his right eyebrow.

Nodding, she said, "Sure. I'm fine, just surprised. I'll untie the ropes from the suitcases after you lower them down."

Tommy quickly scaled back up the rope to the upper level. He lowered both backpacks and suitcases down effortlessly.

They donned their backpacks again and pulled their suitcases through the room with piles of bones. Turning the corner, they entered a narrow corridor. Walking single file, they followed the tunnel which led them to a large cavern.

"Wow." Tommy stopped and studied the room. Hundreds of bones were carefully arranged in different sections. Cubbyholes were made out of the larger femurs. Within each section, bones were meticulously placed together like works of art.

"This is freakin' cool." Smiling, she snapped a few pictures with her digital camera.

"Ever seen the Capuchin Monks in Italy?" he asked, excitedly.

Nodding, she said, "I loved, loved, loved, Rome.

126

My favorite city in the entire world. And the Capuchin Monks' meticulously displayed bones was surreal, yet morbidly spectacular."

"This reminds me of that. Much more time and thought went into this catacomb. The one in Paris tossed a lot of bones behind the walls built of skulls and femurs."

"Who did all of this? It's insane, and yet... captivating." Awestruck, she studied the creatively displayed bones.

Shrugging, he said, "Good question, I don't know. It doesn't even look that old."

"Where are we on the map?"

"Tommy checked his GPS. We're underneath Main Street USA."

"Wow, we walked that far?"

"Yes, we did. I need to map this room." He fired the scanner and let the blue beams map the room with all of the bones. While the image uploaded to his laptop, he pulled out his sketch pad and drew the area of the room with a pencil.

"I'll take some video of all of this." Retrieving her digital camera, she placed it on movie mode and walked throughout the entire room. After the video, she took more pictures, including a panoramic.

"Don't post those on Facebook," Tommy warned.

"Uh, I wasn't, just yet. But there's no one to yell at me for using the flash."

Tommy grabbed his stomach and looked at his watch. "Holy cow, it's two o'clock."

"Wow, we skipped lunch? That snack filled us up," she reckoned.

"And we've been in this room for a while. Documenting takes a long time."

"I am hungry again. Are you okay eating in here?" she asked.

Nodding, he set his backpack down and opened the suitcase with the water. He grabbed her canteen and filled it from one of the many gallons of water he'd packed.

Victoria took a blanket out of her suitcase and laid it on the floor. "An interesting place for a picnic."

"Perishables first." She opened a plastic bag of turkey and placed slices on a French baguette. Then she opened the package of goat cheese and topped the sandwiches. She handed Tommy his half. "*Bon appétit.*"

They tore into the sandwiches.

She popped some grapes into her mouth and savored the sweetness. "Huh," she said.

"What?" His eyebrow arched.

"I just noticed something." She pointed to the floor. "It's not like the dirty rock floor in the tunnel."

"No, it's polished cobblestone. And it's so clean." Tommy wiped the floor with his index finger. "You're right. This flooring looks new."

"Somebody built this recently, but why?"

Chapter Seventeen

"Break time is over. Let's keep going before dinner." Tommy stood and brushed the French bread crumbs off his jeans.

"Litter bug," she teased and packed up their late lunch.

They pulled their suitcases along and meandered through the winding rooms of the catacombs. Each display grew cooler and more creative. They stopped periodically to map the rooms and take pictures and video.

After a few hours, Victoria stopped and admitted, "That's it, I'm done for today. Can we set up camp?"

"Yes, you just read my mind. But I wanted to be manly and pretend that I wasn't tired and-"

"-Hungry?" Laughing, she slipped off her backpack and took a big swig of water from her canteen.

"When in Rome." Laughing, he sat down on his suitcase.

"Where should we set up camp?" Turning, she searched for an area without bones.

Scanning their surroundings, he pointed. "There."

"Another tunnel? How long are these catacombs?" With drooped shoulders, she sighed.

"I mean, if we sleep in the tunnel between the caverns, we don't have to worry about waking up in the middle of the night, forgetting where we are and being surprised by the bones," Tommy rationalized.

"Great point, but it's a little claustrophobic. Don't you think?"

"Pick your poison: bones or a confined space?" Tommy's head toggled back-and-forth.

"How about we sleep facing the tunnel, but stay in the big cavern?" She compromised.

"Whatever you want, dear. It's your party." He

snapped his fingers and shook his hips.

Laughing, she said, "Speaking of which." She opened her backpack and removed a second canteen.

"Why did you bring two canteens?"

Smiling, she opened the cap, took a big swig, licked her lips, and said, "Here, try this."

Tommy took the canteen and studied her quizzically.

"Bordeaux."

"Oh, I love you, Victoria." He kissed her cheek and took a big swig of wine.

"It is five o' clock." She winked, grabbed the canteen, and sipped the wine.

"My turn to cook dinner." Tommy laughed because they literally couldn't cook anything. They both knew the dangers of smoke inhalation caused by making fires in caves.

"What are you preparing for us tonight?" She retrieved the coffee cups she'd swiped from the hotel. Deciding to be couth for dinner, she poured the wine into cups.

"We'll start with brie topped with a fig sauce." He sliced the cheese, dolloped fig sauce next to the brie and handed her a plate.

Taking the plate, she cut off a piece of brie with her fork, dipped it into the fig sauce and hummed, "Mmmmm, this is so good." She sipped her red wine to accompany the poignant flavors dancing on her tongue.

Tommy dolloped his fig sauce directly on top of the brie. Then he picked it up with his fingers and tossed the goodness into his mouth. "I wonder how many archaeologists eat like this?"

"Probably none. I think the fanciest food I ever ate on a dig, before I met you, was a can of Spaghettios." Laughing, she savored the last bite of brie with fig sauce.

"Ready for the next course?" Tommy turned to his suitcase and fumbled about with its contents.

"I'm starved. All that spelunking today wore me out." She sipped her wine.

"Smoked salmon with capers, red onions, and cream cheese, coming right up." He handed her a plate.

"Wow. This is fancy, too. I can see why we had to eat the salmon tonight." Taking the plate, she bit into the savory goodness.

"Yeah, enjoy it. I'm afraid tomorrow night is Spaghettios and day-old French bread."

She poured the last of the wine.

"We drank all of that?" he asked.

"Don't worry, I have another bottle for tomorrow night." Winking, she finished her delicious salmon.

"Phew." Tommy wiped his worried brow with the back of his hand.

"Where are we in relation to the Magic Kingdom?" She sipped her wine.

Tommy pulled out his smart phone and tapped away. "Huh, we're on Disneyland Paris guest Wi-Fi. We must still be under the Magic Kingdom. Hold on, I'll try to get our exact location. Cool to think we're sleeping under Space Mountain or something."

Maybe it was the wine, but she heard music. It sounded faint at first, then it grew louder. Holding her index finger towards Tommy, she signaled for him to be quiet. She recognized that tune. *But where had she heard it?*

Before he could show her their precise location on the map of the park, a light bulb flashed in her head. Of course, she'd heard that music before.

They said in unison, "Phantom Manor. We're under the Haunted Mansion."

Chapter Eighteen

"But isn't the park closed? Why are we still hearing scary music?"

Tommy looked at his watch. "Don't laugh, but it's just before six, and the park is still open for a few more minutes."

"Wow. That's an early dinner. I feel so old." She crossed her arms and pouted her lips.

"Nonsense. It's our breed. Archaeologists, I mean. We work with the sun. We'll be up at five a.m. to continue exploring this cave."

"Okay, thanks for making me feel better." She uncrossed her arms, relieved that she wasn't an old fart, just a typical archaeologist.

"Never mind that we can't *see* the sun down here. Our bodies just know."

"Makes sense. And I guess technically, dinner isn't over until we have dessert. You did bring something sweet to nibble on? Didn't you?"

"Yes, my love." He grabbed her hand, lifted her fingers to his lips and playfully nibbled on them.

Winking, she said, "Besides that."

"What? Are you new? Of *course,* I brought something sweet—Godiva chocolate truffles."

"Mmmm, I love you!" Tearing apart the foil wrapper, she plopped the chocolate morsel into her mouth. Biting into its center, her taste buds were rewarded with chocolate goo.

"But wait, there's more." He pulled out a small bottle of white wine. "Moscato dessert wine."

"Perfect. And don't forget about the champagne. We did discover the catacombs outside of Paris."

"Oh, yeah. But let's hold off until tomorrow. One, we've had plenty to drink, and two, I have this feeling that we're on to something even bigger." He gazed at her optimistically.

"I'll drink to that. To even more discoveries tomorrow." She clinked his coffee mug filled with dessert wine.

"And to tonight." He clinked her mug with his and winked.

"Speaking of tonight and.... 'that', we should blow up our air mattress." She stood up from the blanket they'd used to picnic.

"Yes, you're right. We better set up the bed before the wine goes to our head." Standing, he set his coffee mug down on top of a skull.

"Ooohhh, you shouldn't desecrate the dead like that." She put the food away, but not before nibbling on another piece of chocolate.

"Oops, sorry, old chap. I guess I've just grown immune to all of these bones. And they all look so clean. It's like they're not even real." He pulled out the inflatable mattress and tarp.

Shaking out the blanket, she said, "You're right, they do look fake."

He unfolded the tarp and asked, "Okay, where do you want it?"

"I'm fine out here with our friends. I've gotten so used to them that they don't even bother me anymore."

"Good, I'm fine, too. It's like a party in here. Now we just need some music."

They both paused and looked up at the previous source of sound.

"Huh, it's stopped. The park is officially closed." She helped spread out the tarp.

While he unrolled the inflatable mattress across the tarp, Tommy whistled the tune from *Snow White and the Seven Dwarfs—Just whistle while you work.*

"Good one. I can't whistle, but I can sing." She

sang along to his whistling accompaniment.

Tommy placed four C batteries into the battery compartment of the mattress and turned the knob on. The mattress slowly inflated.

"What other tunes do you know?" she asked. Pulling the sheets from her suitcase, she mentally applauded herself for *borrowing* the bedding from their room. Of course, it terrified her what housekeeping would think when they came into their room to clean. She hoped the 'do not disturb' sign she'd hung on the outer doorknob would deter them from entering the room.

"Hmmm, let me think. I'll start whistling, and then we'll see if you can 'name that tune.'"

Once the mattress was inflated, she spread the fitted sheet over it. Then she topped it with a flat sheet and thermal blanket. "Okay, I should be really good at this. Growing up, my girlfriends and I loved watching Disney movies over and over again."

"My young cousins watch Disney movies when they visit Castle Garrison." Justifying how he knew the tunes, Tommy started whistling a new one. This one was slower than the first.

It took her only three notes before she sang the tune from *Cinderella*—"*A dream is a wish, your heart makes....*"

They finished the song and climbed into their portable, yet comfortable bed. He tested her with three more tunes: *Once Upon A Dream, You've Got A Friend In Me, and Let It Go.* She nailed them all.

"You're great at this." He put his arm around her, and she snuggled against his muscular chest.

"That was fun. We'll have to do that again. I think I sang myself to sleep."

"Good night, my love." He placed a chaste kiss on her lips.

"Good night, my prince."

"Good night, new friends." He referred to the thousands of bones surrounding them.

She laughed and stared at the skulls displayed in a circular pattern. The battery powered lantern partially illuminated the cavern, just enough so they could see around camp. The skulls formed a pattern of one big skull. Victoria applauded the artists for their ingenuity. Then something struck her about the skulls. She knew that many skulls looked similar, but these skulls were identical. That's why they looked so clean and less eerie than the ones they'd seen earlier, these skulls were manufactured.

Chapter Nineteen

Victoria dreamt about dwarfs. But instead of mining gems from a cave. They meticulously placed skulls and bones to form creative displays in the catacombs.

She bolted upright in bed and eyed the catacombs around her. No dwarfs. It was just a dream. She checked the time—five a.m. Waking up with the sun, just like Tommy had predicted.

Turning to Tommy, she watched his muscular body sleep next to her on the inflatable mattress. She slipped on a sweatshirt to thwart the cold cave air. Getting out of bed, she tried to move slowly so the change in the air mattress pressure wouldn't cause Tommy to sink abruptly.

Seeking a private corner to wash up with the baby wipes she'd brought, she tiptoed away in her Gator-blue thermal socks. Holding the lantern, she ventured into new territory. During her walk through the new tunnel, she noticed that the walls of the cave changed. They looked...man made, clean but authentic.

She came to a fork in the tunnel and turned to the right, shocked by what she saw. "Oh, my, God!" She covered her mouth, and the realization sank in. *Tommy has to see this.*

Running back through the tunnel, she quickly returned to camp. "Tommy, Tommy, wake up. You gotta see this." She shook his arm.

"Whoa, chill woman. What's going on?" He opened his eyes and yawned.

Damn, he sure looked cute in the morning—all sleepy, warm, and cuddly.

"Come on, you're not going to believe this." Yanking on his arm, she tried to drag him out of bed.

Rubbing his eyes, he sat up. "Okay, just...give me a

second."

"Hurry up, and bring your lock picking kit." She jumped up, excited about the possibilities of what lay behind that door.

"Can I at least have my tea first?" He stood up and pulled his jeans over his tan, muscular legs.

"No, trust me, we have to hurry. It's amazing."

"Fine." He pulled his black t-shirt over his head and put on his boots.

"Oh, yeah, I forgot my boots." She stepped into her tan Timberlands and quickly laced them up.

"This better be good," he warned.

"Oh, and before I forget." She turned to the skulls displayed on the wall.

"Another shiny object?" He shook his head.

"This might be important. I noticed it last night, but you were asleep. I'd forgotten until just now, but I think it's somehow related to what I discovered this morning." She turned his body to face the skulls.

"Okay, what am I looking at?" He stared at countless skulls and ran his fingers through his hair.

"Remember how we thought that the more recent displays looked nicer and cleaner than the first ones we saw?" She pointed to the ceiling. "The ones up a level, before the brick wall?"

"Uh, yeah, these *do* look cleaner. Maybe they bleached them or something."

"Look closer. It's not what's *different*, but what's the *same*."

"They're identical." He reached out and touched one. "They're not real skulls. I've touched many bones on my digs. These are...plastic. Fake. But why would someone place fake bones in a cave that no one knows about?"

"Now I'll show you what I discovered." She dragged him through the tunnel and turned right at the fork. A door appeared before them. This door had a sign. It read, 'Cast Members Only.'

Chapter Twenty

Tommy stared at the door with an incredulous expression. "Holy cow. So this means...?"

"Disney must be building a catacomb attraction." Victoria beamed.

"Let's break out the champagne. This is quite the discovery."

"Wait, didn't we figure out that we were directly under the Phantom Manor?"

"Yes, and we heard music, right? Or was that just the wine talking?" Tommy laughed.

"I *do* remember music. What a cool place to build a catacomb attraction, under the Haunted Mansion."

"Actually," Tommy pulled out his smart phone from his pocket and tapped on the GPS. "We're under the cemetery, next to the Haunted Mansion."

"Oh, cool." Victoria turned the handle on the door. *Click.*

"It's not locked." She pulled the door open to reveal a dark staircase.

"Guess we don't need the lock picking kit after all."

Victoria held her flashlight and climbed up the stairs. Several flights later, they emerged from a mausoleum in the cemetery adjoining the Haunted Mansion in the Magic Kingdom. The sign on the mausoleum read, 'Catacombs.'

"This is so cool. Now we can sneak into Disney without paying for tickets."

"But that would be stealing." She played her moral card.

Slumping his head, he said, "You're right, that would be dishonest."

"But hey, maybe we could exit the cave here, instead of schlepping back through the tunnel to the abandoned town."

"Yeah, but we'd have to do it late at night, or early in the morning. It would look suspicious if we climbed out of the unfinished catacombs during the day with our suitcases. Should we go now? The park doesn't open until *ten* a.m. Remember?" He chided her for arriving over an hour early to the park on their first day.

"Very funny, I remember. No, let's at least stay another day. There are still more tunnels to discover. Remember the fork in the tunnel, just after the brick wall?"

"Oh, yeah, we never went back because we got distracted by the piles of bones."

"Me and my shiny objects," she laughed.

"I love you and your distractions, look where they lead us." He pulled her close and hugged her.

Chapter Twenty-One

"Can we eat now?" Tommy asked.

Laughing she said, "Yes, dear."

They walked down the stairs, and back to their camp surrounded by *faux* skulls and bones. Victoria opened her suitcase and handed him a bag of croissants. "Here, carbs."

Grabbing the bag, he said, "Thank you. I'm starved." He pulled a croissant out of the bag and bit off a chunk. He handed her back the bag.

"Thank you." She pulled out a croissant, bit into it, and hummed, "Mmmm."

"What do we do about our camp? Should we leave it here? Or pack it and take it with us."

"Hmm, good question. I say we just take our backpacks with our lunches, water, and snacks."

"That's what I was thinking. Do you think we should leave our bed and campsite out here in the open? I mean, what if workers come down here and decide to build more catacomb displays?"

"Good point." She studied the area behind the campsite.

"What if we pack everything up, then move the suitcases out of the way, perhaps behind a pile of bones?" he asked.

"Great idea. But I hate to pack everything up if we're going to stay another night."

"As much as I loved camping with you last night...." he paused.

"I know. You're ready for a shower and a real bed. Me, too."

"We'll sneak back out after the park closes, and unless we find something major, we'll go back to the hotel room."

"Sounds like a plan. Besides, we can always come

back through the mausoleum entrance."

They packed their backpacks and suitcases, then cleaned up their campsite, leaving no trace behind. They walked back through the finished catacomb caverns and into the unfinished one with piles of fake bones. They hid the suitcases behind the big pile of skulls and continued back towards the pile of bricks they made yesterday from breaking through the wall on the upper level.

"Here it is." They turned right and followed the tunnel. "This is neat. It resembles a real cave tunnel." They ducked to accommodate the low ceiling.

"Whoa, we're too tall for this. I'm glad we didn't bring the suitcases."

After an hour of walking, she asked, "How far have we walked? And where are we now, in relation to the park?"

Tommy retrieved his iPhone from his pocket and tapped on the screen. "We're near the castle."

"Cool."

They continued down the tunnel which grew shorter and shorter. They now had to squat and walk like ducks.

"Who built this small tunnel?"

She remembered what they saw their first day in the park, when they ventured into Underground Disney. And then it hit her. "Dwarfs."

Chapter Twenty-Two

"Of course, the dwarfs. Do you remember what we saw?"

Nodding, she picked up the pace of her duck walk. After twenty more yards of squat walking, her legs muscles burned and her back ached.

An opening appeared at the end of the tunnel. Seeing the end somehow made the pain in her legs disappear. "Almost there." They came to the end of the tunnel and stopped on a ledge. It dropped three stories below them. Scaffolding surrounded the wide and deep cavern.

"They're mining the cave," Tommy said.

"But what are they mining?" she asked.

Tommy stepped onto the scaffolding to the left. He ran his fingers along a vein. Pulling out his chisel, he pecked at the wall. A red chunk of rock dropped into his hand.

"It's a ruby." He tossed it to her.

"Look at all the colors?" Victoria scanned the different veins running through the rocks. "Blue, green, red and white."

"Sapphires, emeralds, rubies and diamonds." Tommy beamed.

"It's a gem mine. A gem mine underneath Disneyland Paris." She hugged him.

"Did you bring the champagne?"

"Of course." she patted her backpack.

"Let's wait to celebrate until *after* we climb down there." Tommy pointed down to a rope ladder.

Tommy stepped down onto the first rung of the ladder and tested its weight. "It feels strong, but it was probably built for dwarfs. Let's go down one at a time."

Nodding, she said, "Good idea."

He descended down the rope ladder quickly. After stepping off the bottom rung and onto the cavern's floor, he hollered. "Okay, you're next. Just don't look down."

"I'm coming. Don't explore without me." Stepping off the scaffolding, she grabbed the rope with each hand. It was impossible to get a foothold on the rung below *without* looking down, but she kept her downward vision to merely the rungs. The thirty-foot descent went quickly, and it helped knowing that she could get off at any of the three levels of scaffolding if she needed to.

She dropped onto the floor and found Tommy standing by a mining cart. "Hey, no exploring without me, remember?"

"Sorry, my dear, shiny object, literally." He pointed to four different mining carts on a set of small train tracks. Each of the carts was labeled: Diamonds, rubies, sapphires and emeralds.

She peered into one of the carts and said, "They're empty."

"They must lock them up at night," he said.

"Duh, there must be a fortune in here."

"I'm not a geologist, but I'm surprised that all of these precious gems are in one mine."

"I just thought the same thing, too. I think the formation process is similar for each. But it must be some rare phenomenon that occurred in this rock formation to make four different kinds of precious gems."

"I'm sure their geologists have a reasonable explanation for the occurrence."

"Shhh, what's that noise?"

Holding her breath, she listened for the noise.

"It's singing."

"*Heigh, ho.*" someone sang above. The noise

echoed in the cavern. Then the sound grew louder.

She pointed up. "Dwarfs."

Seven dwarfs entered the mining cave, all singing the lyrics to the famous song from *Snow White and the Seven Dwarfs*, "*...It's off to work we go.*"

Chapter Twenty-Three

Using a sheet of plywood, Victoria and Tommy hid behind the bottom level of the scaffolding. Knotholes in the plywood gave them a protective view of the famous Disney Characters.

Carrying pickaxes on their shoulders, seven dwarfs filed in. Singing harmoniously, they swarmed about the cavern. They bustled about the four empty mine carts on a track.

One of the dwarfs held a clipboard and studied his paperwork. Flipping the pages, he barked orders in French and pointed to the empty mine cart labeled diamonds and rubies.

Gasping, she brought her hand to her throat. She recognized the dwarf from the train, the rude one who'd called them 'Stupid American tourists.' "Oh, my, God!"

"What is it?" Tommy turned to her with a quizzical expression.

The dwarf holding the clipboard must've heard her because he turned towards their direction and studied the scaffolding and plywood which they hid behind.

Victoria quickly removed her eye from the knothole, leaned back against the cave wall and held her breath.

The sound of footsteps came closer, then stopped just on the other side of the plywood. The smell of coffee and cigarette smoke wafted.

Victoria pinched her nose and grimaced in disgust.

"What is it?" One of the dwarfs asked.

"Thought I heard something. Let's get to work. Disney needs diamonds and rubies. Valentine's Day is next month," switching to English, the dwarf on the other side of the plywood ordered. His voice echoed in the opposite direction, then the sound of his footsteps grew further away.

Feeling brave, she peeked through the knothole.

The dwarfs pushed two mine carts through a tunnel on the opposite side of the cavern. Presumably this gem mine contained several caverns. Their singing resumed, echoing from the tunnel, "*Heigh ho….*"

Victoria was dying to explore further, but not today. They needed to get out of here.

"Wait, didn't seven come in? I only counted six leaving?" She wagged her index finger in the air and mentally recounted from her memory.

Tommy shrugged his shoulders and said, "Maybe one them walked through the tunnel before you got a chance to peek."

A dwarf pulled the plywood away and hollered, "What are doing down here?"

Chapter Twenty-Four

"How did you get down here? You're not supposed to be in the mine! Dwarfs only!" the dwarf pontificated while wagging his index finger to scold the truant explorers.

Standing, they held their hands in the air, surrendering to the dwarf.

"Well, we-" Tommy started to explain.

The dwarf interrupted, "-You're those stupid American tourists from the train."

"I'm Scottish, actually. We came in through the catacombs under that nearby abandoned town," Tommy explained.

"Thanks for throwing me under the bus that only *I'm* American," she whispered.

"How long have you been here? What have you seen? Did you take anything?" the dwarf fired his questions in rapid succession.

"We just got here. What's with all the precious gems?" she asked.

Tommy shot her a dirty look. *Why did you tell them we saw the gems?*

"You've seen too much! I can't let you walk out of here." The dwarf swung his pickaxe at Tommy.

With fast reflexes, Tommy grabbed the pickaxe's handle, struggled with the dwarf, then easily took possession of the pickaxe. Holding it behind his shoulder, he poised to strike the dwarf.

Surrendering, he asked, "You wouldn't hit a dwarf now, would you? That would be a douchebag move." The dwarf laughed like an evil villain.

"You're right, *I* can't hit a dwarf." Tommy winked to Victoria.

Swinging her flashlight, Victoria hit the dwarf in the head and said, "But *I* can."

Chapter Twenty-Five

"How's your sword fish?" Tommy asked.

They dined in the Blue Lagoon restaurant in the Magic Kingdom. The Blue Lagoon dining room was next to the Pirates of the Caribbean ride. With their table right next to the water, they watched tourists on the Pirates of the Caribbean ride float by on boats shouting, "*Bon appétit.*"

"It's great, complements the champagne." She raised her champagne glass and toasted his.

"What's your theory? They discovered the gem mine and built the park on top of it? Or were they just building the park and discovered the mine?" he asked.

"Great question. I imagine they're keeping it a secret. They mine the gems right here, then refine them in Underground Disney. Remember when we saw them cutting off the rock from the precious gems in Underground Disney?"

"How could I forget? I was dressed as John Smith and you as Pocahontas."

"Then they make jewelry in the gift shops and sell them."

"Pretty smart. That way they don't flood the market and drive the prices of precious gems down."

"Oh, before I forget. I got you something." Tommy pulled out a velvet box and placed it on the table in front of her.

"What is it?" she asked. The box was bigger than a ring box.

"Just open it." He urged.

She opened the box, surprised to find a rock in it, a rudimentary gift. "Oh, a rock, you shouldn't have," she snickered, her tone oozed with sarcasm.

Laughing he said, "There's a diamond inside, a souvenir from the mine below. We can refine it and

149

make it into an engagement ring."

He got down on one knee and asked, "Victoria Ventures, I love you. Will you marry me?"

"Yes," She smiled and kissed him.

"Where do you want to go for our honeymoon?"

"Hmmm? Well, given our tendency to find great things under Disney parks, what do think about Asia?"

"Tokyo, Hong Kong, or Shanghai?"

THE END

Author's note: Walter Elias Disney misspelled 'dwarves' with 'dwarfs.' When it was brought to his attention, he decided not to change it. In keeping with Walt's wishes, I'm spelling 'dwarfs' his way.

Part Three
Noah's Nickel

Noah's Nickel

AN ELEMENTS OF MYSTERY
UNDER THE MAGIC ADVENTURE

TERRI TALLEY VENTERS

Prologue

Noah steered the enormous wooden vessel as best he could. His family and animals were safe. They'd survived the Great Flood by building this enormous boat, 'Thanks be to God.'

The water receded substantially, and more land appeared on the horizon. He almost landed on Mount Ararat, but decided that he should hide his ark. He'd just tell any survivors that he landed it on Mount Ararat, if there were any others who survived the catastrophic flood.

Another mountain appeared, and he steered the ark towards it.

Noah smiled. An enormous hole appeared in the mountain—the entrance to a large cavern. He aimed the ark towards the giant hole and counted his blessings. No one would ever find his beloved ark here. The wind picked up and blew the ark straight towards the cave's entrance.

They floated into the cave. The ark's roof barely cleared the entrance. It floated in the cave for days before the water receded.

Noah and his family stepped foot on dry land for the first time in ages. He even knelt and kissed the ground. Now he'd repopulate the earth with more humans and animals. But first, he'd block the entrance to the cave so no one would ever find and destroy his precious ark.

With the water now mostly receded, Noah studied the surrounding land and compared it to the maps he'd saved. Gasping, he realized they'd drifted thousands of miles from their homeland.

He wasn't sure exactly where he was, but he knew that he was somewhere in China.

Chapter One

"Where are you taking me again?" Victoria Ventures asked her handsome fiancé, Tommy Manchester Garrison. His straight, sandy-blond hair, sea-green eyes and Scottish accent reminded her of younger Ewan McGregor.

"Why can't you just be surprised?" Tommy shook his head in frustration.

He drove the rental car from Magnolia, Kentucky to...wherever Tommy's imminent surprise took them. But ultimately, they'd catch their flight tomorrow from Louisville to Los Angeles, then on to Shanghai. They were about to scratch another Disney park off their Bucket List.

"Thanks for coming, by the way." Victoria referred to her Great-Grandmother's funeral. She'd passed peacefully in her sleep at the age of 101.

Tommy reached his hand across the center console of the rental car and squeezed Victoria's hand. With a sympathetic tone he said, "I'm sorry I never got to meet her when she was alive."

"She lived a long life. Her social life was better than mine. She'd stay up until midnight playing Spades with her neighbors." Victoria referred to Granny's favorite card game. Snapping her fingers, she added, "Her mind was still sharp as a tack."

"I'm glad we could change our flight to Los Angeles and still catch our International flight to Shanghai." With one trip, they'd planned to visit all three Disney parks in Asia—Shanghai, Hong Kong and Tokyo.

"Me, too. But I feel so guilty about going to Disneyland a few days after Granny's funeral," she sighed.

"I know. But you could use a vacation. And besides, from what you've told me about Granny, she would've wanted you to still go on this trip," Tommy rationalized.

Chuckling, she said, "You're right. She was always on the 'go.' If you said 'go' she'd grab her purse without even knowing where she was going." Pausing, she turned to Tommy and asked, "Speaking of 'go,' can you at least give me a *hint* as to where we are going?"

"Fine, I'll give you a hint. It's three-hundred cubits long and costs forty dollars a person," he said with an irritated tone.

Remembering that 'cubit' was an ancient measurement, Victoria held her arm out and studied the length from her fingertip to her elbow—one cubit. "A football game?"

"No, but a good guess. We're almost there. Now, I need you to close your eyes for a bit. The signs will give it away and ruin the surprise."

Sulking in her seat, she closed her eyes and said with an acquiescing tone, "Fine."

Tommy parked the car, helped her out and guided her to...the surprise.

"Okay, open your eyes in three, two, one," Tommy counted down.

She opened her eyes, and incredulity flooded her. She hadn't known what to expect, but it certainly wasn't this—an enormous wooden ship. Kicking herself, she should've figured out Tommy's hint—three-hundred cubits long.

"God gave Noah the dimensions for the Ark in cubits. 'And this is how you shall make it. The length of the ark shall be three-hundred cubits, its width fifty cubits, and its height thirty cubits,'" Tommy quoted Genesis 6:15.

She stared in awe at Noah's Ark.

Chapter Two

"I'll admit, the Ark Adventure was pretty cool," Victoria said from her First-Class seat on the plane headed to China. The seats laid back to form a bed. A half wall partitioned them from the rest of the passengers.

Squeezing her hand, Tommy smiled and said, "I knew you'd love it. But admit it, if I had told you where I was taking you, you would've rejected the idea."

"Oh, absolutely. When I first heard about the Ark Adventure on the news, I laughed at the undertaking and predicted it would go bankrupt as a cheesy tourist trap. I mean, one hundred million dollars to build a full-scale replica of Noah's Ark? That's insane. But they did a magnificent job. And what a boost to Kentucky's economy."

"And you liked the zip line, too." Tommy winked.

"Oh, heck yeah, I did. I'd never been on one before. I wanted to go on the one at the Alligator Farm in St. Augustine, but when I saw that it was over the alligator pit, I chickened out." She recalled her recent trip to Florida.

"They seem pretty safe. But I'm with you. I'd be the one that was riding it when it broke." Tommy shuddered at the horrific notion.

"Be careful who you tell that to. You'd have to surrender your 'man card' for being afraid," she chuckled.

Tommy reached into his pocket and retrieved a nickel. Flipping it in the air, he caught it and said, "But nothing bad ever happens to me if I carry my lucky nickel."

"What's lucky about it? Is it one of those rare, three-legged buffalo ones?" she asked, curious about her future husband.

"It's somewhat valuable, but not enough to keep locked away. I found it on the grounds of Castle Garrison, right before I saw you get off that helicopter with Lilly. I thought I was pretty damn lucky to have met you. I've carried it in my pocket ever since." Tommy kissed her cheek.

"Ah, you're so sweet." She kissed him.

"Noah must've had a lucky nickel, too. Or whatever their coins were called back then. God chose him and his family to survive the Great Flood." She smirked.

"Rumors of the ark's remains have filtered throughout the centuries, but there's no definitive proof of its existence." He arched his blond, right eyebrow with a quizzical expression.

"Except for the Bible, of course," she bantered. "I'm surprised no one has found it. I mean, the Bible even says that 'it came to rest on Mount Ararat,'" Victoria made air quotes with her fingers.

"Some rumors say that it was found, and that people flocked to take a piece of it as a souvenir and good luck talisman. Millions of believers supposedly took a piece of the ark. Thus, there was nothing left for us archaeologists to find," Tommy explained.

"Or perhaps after 'it came to rest on Mount Ararat,' it didn't stay there and floated somewhere else," she argued.

"Or maybe Noah just lied about its final resting place to keep it safe," he speculated with a shrug.

"Champagne?" An Asian flight attendant held a tray with filled champagne flutes.

"Yes, please. That'll help me sleep on this long flight." Tommy grabbed two flutes from the tray and handed one to Victoria.

Raising her flute, she said, "To Noah's nickel."

Chapter Three

"The Shanghai Disneyland Hotel! Are we staying there?" Victoria asked from the backseat of an Uber. Her tone oozed with excitement. 'Like a kid at....'

"I'm afraid not, my dear. I originally planned to book our week here because it's the most luxurious hotel in Shanghai Disneyland. But once I saw this *other* hotel, I knew I had to book it. It's perfect for my young-at-heart fiancée. Plus, it's closer to Disneyland." Tommy grinned.

Slightly disappointed, she sighed as they drove past the fancy hotel. In the distance, gigantic Tinker Toys, several stories tall, caught her attention. Pointing, she said, "Tinker Toys. That must be a ride from Toy Story, like the one in Disneyland Paris. Funny, I don't recall a Toy Story ride when I went online. Did we get a FastPass for Toy Story?" Victoria asked.

"Actually, those Tinker Toys are not *in* the park." Tommy flipped through his iPhone.

"Not in the park? Then where....?" Before she finished her question, the Uber driver pulled up to the Toy Story Hotel.

Tommy simply grinned, obviously enjoying her immense surprise.

Clutching her hand over her heart, she gasped, "Oh, Tommy. It's perfect, the Toy Story Hotel." She wrapped her arms around his neck and pulled him in for a big kiss.

"Whoa, get a room. Oh wait, you did," the Uber driver joked.

They exited the Uber and wheeled all their luggage into the hotel lobby. They were immediately transported into *Toy Story*. Decorated with oversized toys, Victoria felt like she was in Andy's room.

Children squealed in a large play area with slides built into the oversized toys.

Excited about sliding down the cool slide, she pointed and said, "Oh, let's go in there."

Tommy kissed her hand. "You and your shiny objects. Promise me you 'won't grow up.'"

Victoria stopped abruptly, and disappointment washed through her. "Ah, man." She snapped her fingers and stomped her foot like an agitated toddler not getting her way.

"What is it, my dear?" Tommy stopped next to her with a concerned expression.

Pointing to a sign, she slumped. The sign read, *Ages 2-12*.

Tommy chuckled, "We're too old. Come on, let's go see our room." He gestured towards the elevator.

"Don't we have to check-in?" Turning, she searched for the check-in desk.

"I just did, on my phone from the Uber." Tommy held up his left wrist which sported a blue magic band. "Our bands are our room keys, park tickets, and FastPasses. Plus, we can use it to charge meals and souvenirs to our room."

"Wow, how modern. I saw electric car charging stations on the drive here." She marveled at the energy efficiency of Shanghai.

They arrived at their room and entered with a scan of Tommy's magic band. The beautiful suite greeted them with framed pictures of Woody and Buzz Lightyear. A living room boasted a leather sofa, love seat and chairs facing a giant flat screen television. A small kitchenette filled the corner nook. A large bedroom with a king size bed occupied the adjoining room via sliding doors. But the most spectacular part about the room was the amazing view—Disneyland Shanghai.

Drawn to the park like a moth to a flame, Victoria walked to the sliding glass doors and opened them. Stepping out onto the balcony, she marveled at the view. "Main Street USA."

"Actually, here they call it, Mickey Avenue." Tommy pressed his warm body against hers from behind, slid his arms around her waist and kissed her neck.

Turning around, she asked, "Why am I feeling déjà vu?" She referred to their first kiss on the balcony of the Grand Floridian Hotel at Walt Disney World in Florida.

"In keeping with tradition." Tommy kissed her.

Savoring the long kiss with her soon-to-be husband, she pulled back and asked, "Now what?"

Tommy rubbed his toned abs and chuckled, "We eat."

Chapter Four

Hand in hand, Victoria and Tommy strolled leisurely in Disneytown. Inspired by the historic Route 66, the Main Street of America offered many restaurants and shops outside of the main Disneyland theme park.

"Did you make reservations?" she asked, actually getting hungry herself.

"No, I figured the day we landed, we'd want to rest and take it easy. I'm surprised I'm not jetlagged from that *long* flight across the Pacific Ocean."

A sign caught her attention, and Victoria pointed, "Blue Frog Bar & Grill."

"I like the *bar* part, but I'm not partial to eating frogs, especially blue ones." Tommy laughed.

Smacking his arm, she quipped, "They have other food." She studied the pictures posted on the menu outside the bar. "A western menu, like back in the States."

"Oh, and these creative cocktails look intriguing. Blue, yellow, green and red." He pointed at the pictures of tasty beverages.

Squinting at her Minnie Mouse watch, she scolded, "But it's not five o'clock yet."

"The five o'clock rule doesn't apply at Disney. Besides, a tasty beverage and a full belly will give us a good night's sleep." He walked into the Blue Frog Bar & Grill.

They sat at the bar. Several flat screens hung behind the bar, glaring at them. Some showed various sports games, one showed some sort of soap opera with Chinese actors and subtitles. But the last one caught her attention. It showed the North Korean Flag, Kim Jong-Un and nuclear bombs.

"Uh, oh, that can't be good." She pointed.

"I never thought of being unsafe at Disney. But I never considered that we're relatively close to North Korea. If Trump nukes those bastards, we could have a front row seat to World War Three!" Tommy shuddered.

"We're on the wrong side of the Pacific." Fear filtered through Victoria, and she quickly ordered the Blue Frog's creative version of a rum runner by simply pointing at the pretty picture on the bar menu.

"We should be far enough away from any radiation effects, assuming the strike is isolated to North Korea. But it's the aftermath that could affect us being on the Pacific Rim."

"Many hate Americans. If all hell breaks loose, let's NOT speak English," she suggested.

"Good thinking. How many languages do you know again?" he asked.

"Seven—English, French, Italian, Spanish, German, Latin and Gaelic," she boasted.

"Impressive. With your blue eyes and my blond hair, we'll pretend to be German tourists. Germans haven't pissed anybody off in seventy years." Tommy smirked.

"But if we die, at least we'll be together at the 'Happiest place on Earth.'" She leaned into him and kissed his cheek.

Ping, Ping

Both of their phones pinged in unison.

Curious, they studied the message that popped up on their phones.

Fox Breaking News: Massive amounts of plutonium stolen from North Korea.

Chapter Five

"Tron was awesome!" Victoria squealed as they exited the high tech, futuristic ride in Tomorrowland at Disneyland Shanghai.

"I can't believe you dragged me here an hour *before* Magic hour." Whining, Tommy referred to the extra hour Disneyland resort guests were granted in the park before it opened to the masses.

"You know me. I love being the first in line at Disney. Besides, that's the most popular ride. This way, we didn't have to wait in line," she reasoned.

"But we have FastPasses for this ride after lunch." He shook his head in mock frustration.

"But they only have Tron in Shanghai. The parks in America—California and Florida—don't have Tron, yet," she argued, miffed that he was cranky. Giving him the benefit of the doubt, she rationalized his jet lag attested for his foul mood.

Slumping, he apologized, "You're right. I'm sorry. No fighting allowed at the 'Happiest place on Earth.'"

"Wanna shoot some aliens?" she asked, pointing to the Buzz Lightyear ride.

"I do, but let's do that later. I thought we should prioritize the rides based on what's unique to Shanghai Disneyland. Don't get me wrong, I love Buzz Lightyear. But we can shoot aliens in the States," he rationalized.

"Smart thinking, besides, you don't want to lose to a *girl* again," she teased and playfully patted his chest muscular chest.

"Very funny, Miss Galactic Hero." Tommy referred to her uber high score at both Orlando and Paris Disney Parks.

"Hey, not many can say that they got the maximum score of 999,999." After boasting, she asked. "What rides do they have at Shanghai Disneyland?"

Tommy recited the brochure, "Six unique and unforgettable lands: Mickey Avenue, Gardens of Imagination, Fantasyland, Adventure Isle, Treasure Cove and Tomorrowland."

"Clever, some new lands, plus the classic ones, too. What rides do they have here?" she asked.

Tommy read from the Disney App on his iPhone, "Tron, Explorer Canoes, Buzz Lightyear, Soarin', Roaring Rapids, Marvel Universe, Voyage to the Crystal Grotto and a Tarzan show."

"What about the classics?" she asked.

"Of course, it wouldn't be Disney without Small World, Pirates of the Caribbean and the Haunted Mansion. In fact, we're having dinner tonight at Barbossa's Bounty."

"What's that got to do with the classics?" she asked.

"You'll see. Can't you just be surprised?" he pleaded.

"Oh, my, God! Look at the castle. It's enormous." She pointed.

"You and your 'shiny objects,'" Tommy teased.

"But you love me and my inclination towards distractions. Look where they've led us," Victoria referred to their incredible discoveries in Orlando and Paris.

"The Enchanted Storybook Castle. I read that it's the largest of all the Disney castles." He stood next to her, gaping at the enormous castle.

"I'll say." Victoria unfolded the park map. "There's even a cool ride *inside* the castle—Once Upon a Time Adventure. The Magic Mirror is a portal which transports you to Snow White's Fairy-tale world," she paraphrased.

Wanting to run to the castle, Victoria reluctantly kept their walking pace. Holding Tommy's hand, they stood in front of the gigantic Enchanted Storybook Castle. It's pink, brick façade boasted a dozen blue turrets.

Tommy turned to her and touched her cheek, "Remember the last time we saw the castles in the other parks?" he asked with his dreamy, sea-green eyes.

Recalling the happy moments, she smiled and said, "In keeping with tradition." Then she pulled him close and kissed him in the Enchanted Storybook Castle.

Chapter Six

"This is just like the one in Disneyland Paris," Victoria referred to the Voyage of the Crystal Grotto ride. A boat floated them through various Fairy tale realms with different castles including those from Beauty and the Beast, Aladdin, Mulan, Cinderella and Tangled.

"I hear there is one in California, too," Tommy said.

"I'm glad we're saving that park for last. Since it's the original park, it seems appropriate to end our Bucket List journey where the magic began." Victoria squeezed his hand and leaned against his shoulder. "Besides, I'm glad we're hitting all the Disney parks in Asia while we're here."

"You just don't want to sit on that *long* flight again," he quipped.

"Guilty. First Class was nice and all, but it took *forever* to get here." She arched her back to alleviate the cramps from jetlag. Then she pointed. "Oh look, a cave."

"You and your caves." Smiling, Tommy kissed her temple.

"But remember where caves have led us," she recalled their previous finds.

"Touché. But I don't think we'll find anything in this cave. It's manmade."

"You never know with Disney," she speculated.

The boat ride took them into a cave with a glowing grotto and an amazing display of lights.

"This Grotto ride is way cooler than the one in Paris. Probably because it's brand new."

The couple exited the boat ride singing a montage of Disney songs that they'd just heard on the ride.

Tommy stopped and studied the map, looking up to get his bearings, he pointed. "This way."

"Let me guess, we're going to eat." She guessed.

"How did you......? Never mind. Yes, my love. Of course, we're going to eat. All of those rides made me hungry."

"So does oxygen." Laughing, she heard her own stomach grumble.

They meandered into Adventureland and Victoria pointed. "Captain Jack Sparrow. Are we going on Pirates of the Caribbean?"

"After we eat. The restaurant, Barbossa's Bounty, is *in* the ride," Tommy explained.

"I hear that Johnny Depp sometimes makes surprise appearances at the various Pirates of the Caribbean rides around the world." Her tone rang with optimism.

"Wouldn't that be cool. I guess he's always promoting the latest installment of the movie franchise," Tommy reasoned.

They entered the restaurant, not crowded at five o'clock, and were promptly seated at a table next to the water. Boats carrying passengers floated by, and other tourists said, "*Bon appétit.*"

Victoria and Tommy waved back, then studied the menu.

"What an interesting menu—Smackin' Kraken Squid, Jack Sparrow's Beef Steak and Pirate's Feast," she recited the cleverly-named entrees.

"Oh, I know what I'm having." Tommy closed his menu decisively.

"Probably the same thing I'm having," she predicted.

"Let's say it together in three, two, one...."

"Lamb chops."

Laughing, they promptly ordered a bottle of red wine to accompany their imminent feast.

"What FastPasses do we have for tomorrow?" Victoria asked.

"Uhhhh." Tommy dropped his chin with a guilty expression.

"Uh, oh. Please tell me we have FastPasses for tomorrow," she scolded.

"Sorry, my love. But I didn't want to spend *every* day of our Asian vacation at Disney."

"Why not?" she asked with a perturbed tone.

"We're in Asia. There's another continent to explore," he argued.

"Let me guess," she predicted.

Nodding, he confessed, "I have a surprise for you."

Chapter Seven

"Why did we get up before dawn?" Squinting, Victoria stared into the rising sun.

"I thought a little sunrise hike would be fun. Explore the beautiful terrain, then we can have a picnic brunch. Besides, I recall you waking me up before dawn to go to Disney," he bantered.

Shooting him a dirty look, she decided to let that remark go because he was right. She changed the subject. "Our exploring trips usually end up in a cave."

"You can never say no to a good spelunking." He laughed.

"Hey, watch your language, there could be children on these trails," she teased.

"I doubt it. These trails are for experts. Besides, we're speaking English in Asia." Tommy followed behind her, using ski poles as hiking sticks on this rugged trail.

"Shouldn't we speak German? You know, in case there's an Armageddon, and Americans lose popularity." She recalled last night's conversation.

"I'm Scottish, remember?" Tommy boasted with an exaggerated, Highlander accent.

The pair continued hiking rough terrain. Victoria took the lead and veered off the main hiking trail. She meandered up the rocky slope, determined to reach the top, and hopefully, a beautiful view.

"I'm glad we brought camping supplies this time. It'll save us a trip back to the hotel *when* we find a cave," she reasoned optimistically.

"Don't you mean *if?*" He teased. "We were smart to bring supplies, even if we don't find a cave. These trails run deep into nowhere. We can hike further if we spend a night or two camping.

"'Think happy thoughts,'" she quoted Peter Pan. "We *will* find something. Perhaps some ancient Chinese artifacts from the Ming Dynasty. I have a knack for sniffing out caves. I'm the cave whisperer," she whispered.

"You're right. You do have a knack for it. I thought it was dumb luck the first time. But after the second, I think you have a rare talent. You just can't pass up cave exploring," he teased.

"I don't *always* meander into every cave I find." Victoria pursed her lips.

"Yeah, ya do. I bet you couldn't pass up a cave entrance if your life depended on it."

"Wanna bet?"

The couple climbed the hiking trail which led them up the mountain. The air grew cooler with the increased elevation. A spectacular view of the valley and the rising sun greeted them.

Tommy stood next to her and admired the beautiful view of the sun rising in the east. It warmed their faces as its rays kissed their skin. Tommy put his arm around her and hugged her close.

"Wow. This is spectacular. Now I'm not mad at you for *not* taking me to Disneyland every day of our Asian tour. I never realized how much China offered."

"There's nothing like a good, 'I told you so.' Plus, there is so much more to see. There's the Great Wall, the Forbidden City, the tomb with the soldiers-"

"-Like the one at EPCOT with the miniature terracotta soldiers?" she asked.

Dropping his head, he shook it. Then with a frustrated tone, he said, "The one in EPCOT is merely a *replica* of the original one in China."

"Uh, yeah. I knew that." Embarrassment flooded her, and she shook off her momentary lapse of intelligence. Her best friend and future cousin-in-law,

Lilly, would chalk that up to a 'blonde moment.' But with her ebony locks, Victoria had no such excuse.

"You know what?" Tommy grinned and rubbed his belly.

She gave him an agitated stare and asked, "Already?"

Not embarrassed by his insatiable need to feed every two to three hours, he grinned. "It's the perfect place for a picnic."

Chapter Eight

With an enormous sigh, Victoria slid the large backpack off her toned shoulders and rotated her arms in big circles, relishing the temporary freedom from the weight.

Tommy followed her lead and stretched his strong arms, now unburdened by the weight of his even larger backpack.

"At least the hard part is over now. It's all downhill from here, literally." She waved her arm from their perch on top of the cliff.

"My calves burn already." Tommy shook his legs to ward off the cramps.

"Rooky," she teased, then unbundled the blanket and sleeping pad rolled up and secured at the bottom of her backpack with a bungy cord. She rolled out the cushiony sleeping pad, then spread out the blanket on top.

Tommy knelt and sat on the cushion. "Great idea, it's a lot better than sitting on hard rock."

Victoria plopped down next to Tommy and said, "Our backs will thank us when we're old."

He leaned over and kissed her cheek. "Mmmm. I like that notion, growing old with you."

"Well, good, because you will." Beaming, she swigged water from her canteen.

Tommy rummaged through his backpack and retrieved a white, coated cardboard box with red Chinese letters. "We better eat this first."

She opened the box and said, "I've never eaten Chinese take-out on a hike before." Biting into a fried wonton, she hummed.

Tommy ate his first wonton in one big bite. With his mouth partially full, he shrugged and said, "Limited options here."

"It's good. But you've spoiled me with your gourmet meals on our spelunking adventures." She recalled their fancy meals in caves under Paris and Orlando.

"My favorite was Paris. I could go for some warm brie with fig sauce." He rubbed his belly.

"And smoked salmon with onions, capers, and cream cheese." She smiled at the delicious recollection.

"At least this meal has protein and carbs to fuel us on the hike." Tommy popped another wonton into his mouth.

After finishing her last ration of wontons, she removed the plastic wrapper from her fortune cookie. Breaking it in half, she retrieved the tiny piece of paper from the cookie shell. "Huh, just like in America, the fortune is written in both Chinese *and* English."

"Well, what's it say? Or is it bad luck to read your fortune aloud?" Tommy asked with impatient curiosity.

"You're thinking of wishes when you blow out birthday candles or toss coins into a fountain. Fortunes in Chinese cookies can be read aloud." She turned to him and showed him the paper.

Squinting, Tommy read the small print aloud, "Look before you leap."

"Always good advice." She rose from their picnic blanket and stretched her arms. Arching her back, she meandered to the edge of the cliff.

"Whoa, careful! You're not going to actually leap, are you?" Tommy asked with a worried tone.

"Relax, I'm just looking," she hollered without turning back to look at him. Admiring the gorgeous view, she turned her head to enjoy the panoramic view of the valley. With her head all the way to the right, she lowered her gaze to the wall of the cliff below. As the rocky cliff jettisoned out to the right, a small ledge appeared. Victoria held her hand over her eyebrows to block the shining sun still rising in the east.

"What the...."

"What is it?" Tommy stood and walked towards her.

She grabbed tiny binoculars from around her neck and placed them in front of her eyes. She focused on the face of the cliff near the ledge. "Well, I'll be damned."

"What is it?" Tommy surveyed the direction she studied.

She handed him the binoculars and pointed to a cave entrance. "I'm about to lose our bet."

Chapter Nine

"Ah, there's nothing like a good, 'I told you so.'" Tommy beamed.

"I haven't *entered* the cave yet," she retorted.

"But you will, my love." He kissed her cheek, then turned and walked back to the middle of the clearing towards their picnic paraphernalia.

"Where are you going? Don't you want to go into the cave?" she asked with a quizzical and agitated tone.

Without turning to face her, he replied, "Of course, but we'll need our gear. Especially my cave plotter."

"Oh yeah, I was ready to waltz in unprepared." She helped them pack the remains of their brunch, then rolled up the blanket and sleeping pad. After securing the rolled-up pad and blanket with a bungy cord, she squatted next to her heavy backpack. Placing her arms through the straps, she secured them, then stood with a slight wobble.

"Whoa, you got it, Victoria?" Tommy asked like a gentleman, then put his backpack on with ease.

Carrying their heavy backpacks, they hiked along the edge of the cliff and searched for an easy way down to the ledge on the same level as the cave entrance. Luckily, they found a narrow ramp which sloped down to the ledge.

"Well, this is convenient. I'd envisioned us lowering our backpacks down with ropes, then gingerly shimmying ourselves down onto that narrow ledge." She grinned, thrilled to get to her cave easier and faster.

"Hey, honey, check this out." Tommy pointed to the stone cliff wall. He ran his finger along a vertical groove.

"Oh, wow. There are dozens of these." She ran her fingers along the vertical grooves.

He rubbed his stubbled chin with his index finger and thumb, then his expression turned contemplative. "Someone's chiseled these out."

After studying the worn grooves further, Victoria said, "They chiseled these out a very long time ago. These grooves are extremely worn with rain, wind and time."

"Early man, but smart enough to use tools. They must've found that cave and needed an easier way in and out," Tommy predicted.

"Well, we're about to find out. I bet cavemen lived here," Victoria said excitedly. Adrenaline shot through her, and she couldn't get to the cave entrance fast enough. She briskly hiked along the ledge of the cliff.

"Careful, my dear. This ledge is narrow, and that heavy backpack could throw off your balance," Tommy warned.

"I'll be fine. I'm a big girl. I can take care of myself," she shouted without turning her head back.

"Well, don't come crying to me if you fall off the cliff. You don't want another 'I told you so' in the same day," he lectured.

That warranted a response. She stopped, turned around, and stuck out her tongue like a sassy child on the playground. Her stopping allowed Tommy to catch up to her.

When she turned back around, she walked further along the ledge, but now with a much slower pace. When she stepped on a wider, but thinner, section of the ledge, the rock broke away from the cliff. She fell with the loose stones and slid down the cliff. She managed to grab hold of the rock ledge and hung precariously from the cliff, hundreds of feet above the rocky terrain below.

Chapter Ten

Just as her fingers were about to slip away from the ledge, Tommy grabbed her wrists.

"I got you. Thank God I was right behind you." He squeezed her wrists.

"Oh, my, God! Tommy, can you pull me up? I know you're strong, but how strong?" Terror saturated her, and tears dropped onto her cheeks.

"I know I can pull *you* up. I'd like to think I'm strong enough to pull you up with that heavy backpack, but I'm not willing to risk your life," he reasoned.

"Tommy, I love you, but if you have to, you can let me go. There's no sense for *both* of us to die out here." She'd sacrifice her life to save his, but prayed mercifully that it wouldn't come to that.

"Never! I'd rather die *with* you, than live *without* you," Tommy cried, too. "But it means the world to me that you'd sacrifice yourself for me. Now, here's what we're going to do. I'm going to let go of your left wrist, and grab your right one. Then I want you to carefully unfasten the backpack's shoulder straps and let the backpack fall off," Tommy explained the plan.

"Smart idea. With less weight, you can pull me up." She marveled at the brilliance of her handsome and heroic fiancé.

"Ready, in three, two, one," he counted. Then he let go of her left wrist and instantly grabbed her right forearm.

With her left arm free, Victoria unfastened the strap and freed the left shoulder strap. The shifting weight pulled on her right side. But Tommy held her right arm firmly with both hands. Then she did the same thing with the right shoulder strap, and the backpack fell off her back.

The instant the backpack fell, Tommy pulled her up in one hefty swoop. Euphoria rushed through her, and she clung to Tommy and cried.

He cried along with her and held onto her tightly. Once their sobs subsided, he kissed her face a dozen times. "Oh, Victoria, if I ever lost you, I'd die inside," he cooed.

"Oh, Tommy. You saved my life. I'd never been that close to dying before. If I hadn't stopped to stick my tongue out at you, you wouldn't have been standing right next to me when the rock broke." Still crying she clung to him.

With her cheek nuzzled against his neck, she opened her eyes and saw that most of the ledge with the ramp had crumbled away. There was no way they could go back the way they came.

"Tommy, look." She pointed at the vacant side of the cliff where their ledge ramp once was, only a few moments ago.

"I guess we're not going back down that way. We'll need to find another way down through the mountain. Hopefully, our cave has a front door." Then Tommy laughed.

"What so funny?" she asked.

Shaking his head, he giggled, but in a manly way. Then his giggle turned into a big laugh.

"Tommy? What's so funny?" she asked again, more curious than annoyed that he'd laugh after almost losing her to a freak accident on the side of a cliff in China.

Tommy's laughter grew, then he bent at the waist and placed his hands on his knees to force the laugh out of his system.

"Tommy?" She shook her head, baffled by what he found so hysterical.

Unable to control his laughter, let alone speak coherently, he held up his index finger.

Puzzled, Victoria racked her brain to find the mysterious source of Tommy's overwhelming amusement. Then it struck her. Shaking her head, she said, "Oh, no. You're going to say it, aren't you?"

Chapter Eleven

With an enormous grin and giddy expression, Tommy said, "I told you so."

Laughing, she said, "I can't believe we're laughing about me almost dying."

"Our bodies are full of emotions. Laughing helps release them, just like crying does," he explained.

"Talk about a *cliff hanger*," she laughed, proud of her quit wit.

"Good one, let's explore our cave. It'd better be good, considering we almost died to get here." Tommy shuddered at the horrific notion.

Victoria stepped into the cave's entrance, not caring that Tommy was right about her insatiable curiosity.

The enormous cavern revealed itself, and the sun disappeared as the couple walked deeper into the cave.

"This place is huge. I wonder if someone lived here." She studied the long abandoned firepit in the center of the cavern.

"A whole tribe could live in here. And they probably did. Look at the soot stains in the center." Tommy pointed.

Victoria shone her flashlight around the cavern walls. "I can picture cavemen living here thousands of years ago. I envision them painting cave walls and telling tales of their great hunts."

"Your flashlight wasn't in your backpack?" Tommy asked.

"Luckily I keep an extra flashlight in my knapsack." She patted her worn, leather knapsack. "Thank goodness I had it secured across my shoulder. At least you had most of the supplies since your backpack is bigger. I feel naked without my backpack."

"Hopefully we can find it when we hike down the mountain. Tools should survive the fall," he reasoned with an optimistic tone.

Removing his oversized hiking backpack, he set it down on the stone floor and said, "Thank goodness I packed the cave plotter. Speaking of which, I'll need to plot this room."

"Oh, my, God. Tommy, look at these." Victoria shone her flashlight on the large wall in the rear of the cavern.

"Cave paintings," he said with a giddy tone, obviously excited to witness something so ancient.

"These must be thousands of years old." Victoria ran her finger along the crude drawings, marveling at the beauty in its simplicity.

Tommy touched the black rubbings on the cave wall. Then he placed his fingers to his nose and smelled the black soot. Sticking out his tongue, he tasted it. "Sppt." He spat out the soot.

"What is it?" Victoria asked.

"Manganese. Cavemen used manganese to draw cave paintings thousands of years ago," he explained.

"Why did you spit it out?" she asked.

Tommy spat again. Then wiped his tongue with his fingers. "One, it tasted nasty. And two, manganese is linked to Parkinson's Disease." He grimaced.

"Oh, here. Wash your mouth out with water." Victoria handed him her canteen.

Tommy poured water into his mouth, slushed it around like mouthwash and spat it out.

Victoria shone the flashlight on the cave paintings, studying them intensely.

The paintings depicted typical cavemen stories— men hunting huge animals with spears, and women gathering around a fire. But then the theme changed. Animals were drawn on the wall walking towards something big. Many species of animals were depicted, walking in pairs up a hill. Then water was drawn, flooding the land. The end of the cave painting depicted an enormous ship floating on top of the world.

"Does this cave painting depict what I think it does?" Tommy asked.

Victoria smiled. "Yes, this tells the story of Noah's Ark!"

Chapter Twelve

Snapping pictures, Victoria marveled at the detailed cave paintings. Incredulity flooded her. "I can't believe we have proof that Noah's Ark truly existed."

"Well, the story of Noah's Ark *is* in the Bible," Tommy said.

"I know. But this is real proof. These cavemen must've seen it. They couldn't have made this up. But how did they survive the flood? I thought the whole world was covered with water?" she asked.

"Perhaps the highest mountain peaks, like the Himalayas, the Alps and the Rockies didn't get flooded. In fact, it makes more sense that at least some of the Earth's population survived. Some humans could've survived on high enough ground," Tommy reasoned.

"But this mountain isn't *that* tall. And it isn't Mount Ararat. This cave had to be underwater during the great flood. The only people living this low after the flood must've been-"

"-Noah and his family. Oh my, God. You're brilliant." He kissed her temple.

"It makes sense. Noah landed the ark, and his family lived in this cave for a time. Then they painted this cave wall telling their story before moving on." Victoria snapped more pictures.

"Don't post those pictures on social media. Let's keep this discovery to ourselves, at least for now," Tommy warned.

"I know. I'm sure there's no signal out here, especially in a cave. Speaking of caves, don't forget to plot this one," she reminded him.

"Yes, thank you." Tommy unzipped his backpack and retrieved his cave plotter.

"Before you do that, how about we take a 'selfie' in front of the cave paintings?" she asked with a hopeful tone.

Sighing, he said, "You know I hate 'selfies?' Let's use the camera's timer and do this right." He took the digital camera from her hands, walked over to the cave's entrance and framed a great shot of the entire back wall of the cave with Victoria standing in front. Using his backpack, he placed the camera on top. Then he set the timer, jogged over to Victoria, put his arm around her, and smiled.

Click.

"I'll go check." Tommy jogged back to the camera, studied the beautiful image of him and his fiancée in front of Noah's cave painting and gave Victoria a 'thumbs up'.

"Thank you," she said, happy to get her picture with Tommy in front of Noah's cave painting.

Tommy retrieved his cave plotter from his backpack. After wiping the lens, he aimed his gadget, which resembled a police speeding scanner, towards the back wall of the cave. A blue laser beam shone on the cave walls, scanning the digital image onto the memory stick inserted into the gadget.

Yawning, she asked. "Why am I so tired?"

Tommy studied his watch. "Holy Moses. It's four o'clock."

"We skipped lunch. I'm surprised you're not starving? I guess our 'near-death experience' suppressed our appetites," she reckoned.

"Oh, I'm starving alright. So, what do you think?" He waved his hand around the cave.

Reading his mind, she said, "I think this would be the perfect place to camp tonight."

"Good, and we won't even need to pitch the tent. We can just unroll the sleeping pad in front of a camp fire. Since mine is at the bottom of the cliff, we'll have to share."

"And since you have the champagne bottle, we can celebrate our find." Grinning, she winked at Tommy.

"I'm afraid our dinner selection is rather basic— room temperature noodles." He cringed, obviously longing for his usual gourmet meals he often concocted on their cave campouts.

Shrugging, she said, "I'm lucky to be alive. Carbs are a great comfort food. Besides, I'm still insanely shocked that we'll be sleeping where Noah and his family lived once the ark landed after the Great Flood."

Chapter Thirteen

"Oh, the big, thick ones, my favorite." Victoria stared at the extra thick Chinese noodles in the white, glossy take-out box.

But Tommy's mind was in the gutter. "'That's what she said.'"

She playfully smacked his chest and laughed with a mock perturbed tone, "Thomas Manchester Garrison, shame on you."

The couple sat on Tommy's cushioned sleeping pad topped with a blanket. A fire roared a few feet in front of them. Normally they wouldn't start a fire in a cave because many early settlers died from smoke inhalation. But since the cavern was close to the cave's entrance, they'd agreed that there was sufficient ventilation. Thus, smoke inhalation wasn't a concern.

Tommy took a large helping of noodles with his chopsticks. "I'll have to admit that these thick noodles are better."

"And the sauce is amazing. What's it called?" She plopped more noodles into her mouth and hummed.

Shrugging, he said, "I have no idea. I just pointed to the pictures."

"Tommy, aren't we forgetting something?" she asked with an arched eyebrow.

"Oh, yeah. We forgot to say grace." He bowed his head, performed the sign of the cross and prayed, "'Blessed are these gifts which we are about to receive through Christ's bounty. In his name we pray. Amen.'"

"Amen." Victoria crossed herself. But guilt consumed her because the forgetful item she'd referred to was the champagne, not the blessing.

Winking, he said, "I knew what you meant. But we should remember to say the blessing before each meal. We have so much to be thankful for." He retrieved the champagne bottle from his backpack. After removing the tin foil wrapping from the cork, he carefully untwisted the wire mesh. Aiming the cork towards the cave's ceiling, he pushed his thumbs against the cork's rim.

Pop

The cork flew and hit the ceiling. Then it bounced and rolled out of sight.

"We should save that cork. It's very special," Tommy suggested.

"I'll go look for it in a minute. I don't feel like getting up just yet." Victoria leaned against Tommy's chest.

"Sorry, we don't have any cups. We'll have to drink straight from the bottle," he apologized and added, "Ladies first."

She took the bottle, raised it in the air, and toasted, "To Noah's Ark." She drank straight from the bottle, then handed it to Tommy.

Taking it, he kissed her lips and said, "To my beautiful, future wife." He took a swig.

"Ah, speaking as your future wife. We haven't really talked about the wedding details." She squeezed his hand and stared into the roaring flames.

"Whatever your heart desires, my dear. I'll marry you anytime, anyplace. Big, small, church, courthouse, cave, anywhere." He kissed her lips.

"Ah, I don't know yet. Maybe the perfect place will present itself and we'll, just know," she predicted. "But hold that thought while I try to find a place to potty." She stood.

"And while you're up-"

"-I know look for that cork." She smiled at her handsome future husband.

Grabbing her flashlight, she turned it on and shone it on the ground. She walked towards the opposite side of the cavern where she recalled the champagne cork bounced to. She realized that they spent so much time studying and documenting the cave paintings, they hadn't completely explored the cavern. She made a mental note to explore the rest of the cavern tomorrow morning. She was tired, and ready to sleep snuggled next to her handsome man.

At last, the flashlight shone on the cork which lay next to the cave wall. "Ah ha. There you are." Bending, she picked up the cork and smiled. When she stood back up, the flashlight revealed an opening in the cave wall.

"Tommy, look, it's a tunnel."

Chapter Fourteen

The morning greeted them with the sun's early rays shining through the cave's entrance.

Stretching, Victoria sat up and poked him. "Tommy, wake up."

"I'm sleeping," he mumbled and put a pillow over his head.

"Tommy, get up! Don't forget the tunnel. You promised me you'd get up with the sun since you were too tired to explore last night." Hollering, she shook his muscular shoulder.

Groaning, he sat up. "Oh, Victoria. You're killing me." He yawned, stretched, and blinked the sleep out of his eyes.

"I'll start the fire. There's not much wood left, but I think we have enough to boil water for our tea." Standing, she pulled out the matches from her knapsack and lit the fire. She placed a small pot on top of the fire and filled it with water. Then she retrieved two tea bags and added them to the pot.

"You know, loose tea leaves are better." Tommy joined her next to the fire.

"So you keep telling me. You folks from the UK are proud of your tea." She waited for the water to boil.

"And you Americans with those silly tea bags." Grimacing, Tommy shook his head.

"Oh, be quiet. At least I switched to tea from coffee since we met. I admit, I love green tea. Yes, loose tea leaves in a Twinning's tin can are better than tea bags. But tea bags are portable." She watched the water boil and anticipated the imminent caffeine infusion.

"I suppose you'll want breakfast, too." Tommy rummaged through his backpack.

"Yes, Chef Garrison. But let's eat something quick. I'm anxious to see where that tunnel leads." She removed the boiling water with two floating tea bags from the fire.

"Hopefully it leads us down and out of here," he speculated optimistically, then handed her a bag. "Here."

"What's this?" She studied the partially clear cellophane bag with piqued curiosity.

"I'm hoping it's biscuits. I found it in the gift shop of the hotel." Tommy arched his blond eyebrow.

"Tommy, oh, my, God!" Victoria clutched her hand over her heart. Her heartbeat skyrocketed as the realization filtered through her brain.

"Honey, what is it?" Tommy asked with a worried tone.

"If Noah and his family lived in this cave after the flood-"

"-And they painted the story of the ark on these cave walls." Tommy waved his hand towards the cave painting.

They stared at one another excitedly, then said in unison, "Noah's Ark might be close!"

Chapter Fifteen

"How did we not think of that before?" Tommy asked.

Victoria gulped tea directly from the pot. "I don't know. But now I'm really anxious to follow that tunnel."

"Now, before you get too excited. Remember, the ark was made of wood. It's probably rotted away," Tommy lectured.

Rolling up the sleeping pad and blanket, she secured it to the bottom of Tommy's backpack. "I know. But maybe there's some sort of remains or evidence that indicates the ark's final resting place. Didn't Noah add some sort of special coating to waterproof the ark?"

Tommy took the last sip of his tea, and put the empty pot inside his backpack. "I think so. And the cave is pretty dry. There's zero humidity in here. It's just possible..."

"Oh, crap."

"The twine is in *your* backpack, isn't it?" He read her mind.

Nodding, she snapped her fingers. Then an idea struck here. She held up the half empty cellophane bag and said, "Shortbread crumbs. We can leave a trail with these."

"Biscuits." He grinned. Tommy put out the fire, then donned his enormous backpack.

"Shall we?" she asked, excited to see where this tunnel led.

"Ladies first." He waved his hand, gesturing towards the tunnel.

Victoria walked through the tunnel's entrance, shining her flashlight to guide them. The tunnel sloped down steeply, and she had to be careful not to topple forward.

"At least we're heading down," Tommy said from behind her.

"Yeah, but this is really steep. I don't think we need the bread crumbs yet. The tunnel hasn't forked yet." Victoria reached her hand into the bag and ate another shortbread.

"Biscuits," he teased.

"Yeah, yeah."

"Uh, oh." She stopped abruptly, filled with worry.

"What's wrong?" Tommy stopped besides her. "Oh, crap."

"It's a dead end." Disappointed, she slumped.

"How the hell are we going to get out of here. It doesn't make any sense. Why is there a tunnel to nowhere?" he asked.

Turning, she said, "I guess we'll have to try to climb up that ten-foot ledge, or what's left of it."

"Wait. Victoria, look, it's not a natural rock wall. Someone placed these rocks here to keep people out." He pulled one rock from the top of the wall.

"Oh, my, God! You're right." She pulled a rock off of the wall and tossed it aside.

Excitedly, they removed enough rocks from the wall to unblock the tunnel. Then they climbed over the remaining rocks and continued through the new tunnel.

After walking a few more yards, they entered a giant cavern. The ceiling soared several hundred feet above their heads. And the length of the cavern went on for hundreds of feet.

"This cavern is enormous. The Titanic could fit in here."

"I think this was once under the ocean."

"Duh, the Great Flood," Victoria chided.

"How is the ceiling staying up? You'd think it would collapse with all the weight above it."

"Natural arches. If the arch is just right, all of the weight transfers to the walls, like in a cathedral," she explained.

"It looks like there is some kind of ship." Tommy pointed.

"I don't see any portholes. It looks really old." Victoria studied the gigantic ship.

Tommy's face lit up. "It's remarkably well preserved in this dry cave." Tommy stared in awe.

"Are you saying......? But I thought it landed on Mount Ararat."

"Maybe Mount Ararat was the first dry land the ship sighted when the flood waters receded. But apparently, it didn't land there."

"I can't even say it because it doesn't seem real." Victoria cried.

"Let's say it together. Ready in three, two, one...."

"It's Noah's Ark!"

Chapter Sixteen

"Oh, my, God!" Victoria cried tears of joy.

"Amen, pun intended." Tommy beamed like a kid at....

Nudging him playfully, she walked towards the humongous ark. Excitedly, she shone her flashlight along the broad side of the massive vessel, searching for a way in. They meandered around the bow of the ship, then were rewarded with a wooden ramp leading into the ark.

"This is exactly how the ark was depicted in my *Children's Illustrated Bible*." She recalled her childhood reading from the beautifully illustrated book.

"Me, too." Tommy rubbed the wood on the boat, obviously marveling that it was still intact and remarkably well preserved.

Walking up the ramp, she said with an incredulous tone, "I'm shocked that it's still intact."

"Noah applied some sort of ancient sealant on the ark. Viking ships remarkably survived for over a thousand years."

"But the ark is way older than Viking ships," she retorted like a smarty pants, know-it-all.

"I *know*, that." His *duh* was implied. "But this cave is extremely dry and cool which helped preserve this biblical, archaeological find."

Chuckling, she said, "The folks at the Ark Adventure nailed it. Their replica's resemblance to the real thing is incredible. The wood on the replica is new, but their design cloned the original."

"Perhaps they had the same *Children's Illustrated Bible*," he teased, then gestured towards the entrance of the ark and asked, "Shall we?"

Placing her hand into the crook of his elbow, they walked up the wide plank, two-by-two, and entered Noah's Ark.

Snapping pictures and using the Go Pro video camera, they documented the interior and exterior of the ark.

"Oh, my cave plotter! How could I forget to scan our most substantial find?" Shaking his head with frustration, he retrieved the cave plotter and scanned to his heart's content.

"I can't get over how massive this ark is. It probably really did hold two of every species of land animal." Victoria shone her flashlight around the vast interior of the ark. They meandered to the top of the ark and peered out below. Pointing, she asked, "What's that?"

A skeleton slumped against the bow of the ship.

"He's been dead along time." After examining the bones further, he asked, "Is he-?"

"-A Crusader." Victoria studied the chainmail and a white shield with a red cross.

"I feel like we're in the Indiana Jones movie, *The Last Crusade*. Only instead of the Holy Grail, this Crusader protected the ark," he marveled.

"And this one is dead, not old as dirt like the one in the movie." I guess we weren't the first to find Noah's Ark. Darn." She snapped her fingers disappointingly.

"The Crusaders discovered it, then kept the find to themselves."

"Or he never made it out of here to tell anyone."

"Poor bloke found the archaeological find of the millennia and didn't even get the credit."

"I didn't realize the Crusaders ventured into China."

"They must've taken a wrong turn at Constantinople," Tommy quipped, referring to the ancient city, now known as Istanbul, which bridges Europe and Asia.

"Now begs the question-"

"-Do we share our find with the rest of the world?"

"And how the hell do we get out of here?"

Chapter Seventeen

"How much water do we have left?" Victoria asked, then drained the rest of her canteen.

"Well, we had enough for four days, but we lost half when your backpack dropped off the cliff. So-"

"-We only have enough for today. We should head back," she finished his sentence.

"Don't you mean, forward. Remember the side of the cliff broke off. Let's try to find another way out of here." He grabbed the last two big bottles of water from his backpack and filled their canteens.

"Is this the last of the water?" She capped the canteen.

Nodding, he said, "Make it last all day, or at least until we can get to your backpack. Hopefully the water bottles didn't break and drain during the fall."

"How long did it take us to hike to this mountain yesterday?" She shook her legs to ward off the cramps from hiking the rough terrain yesterday. At least today the return hike was downhill.

"Three hours. I remember because that's about as long I can go without eating if I'm awake." Tommy calculated, then rubbed his stomach. "Speaking of which..."

"You're hungry already?"

"I just need a snack." Tommy rummaged through his backpack and retrieved two packages of Apple Cinnamon Belvita. He offered one to her.

Taking the scrumptious snack, she said, "Let's eat quickly, we need to get out of here." She sat on the same table that Noah and his family ate on during Biblical times and drank in the spectacular view of the interior of Noah's Ark.

Rumble

Terrified, she yelled, "What the hell was that?"

Rumble

"It sounds like an avalanche!"

Tommy grabbed her and said, "Quick, get under the table!"

They ducked under the table and Tommy held her protectively while shielding her head.

Rumble, rumble, rumble.

The noise grew louder and the ark shook. The roof sounded like rocks fell on top of it.

Fear ripped through her. "Tommy, I'm scared."

"All we can do is pray." They crossed themselves like good Catholics and recited the Hail Mary prayer.

Hail Mary, full of grace.
The Lord is with thee.
Blessed art thou among women,
and blessed is the fruit of thy womb, Jesus.
Holy Mary, Mother of God,
pray for us sinners,
now and at the hour of our death.
Amen.

Chapter Eighteen

They recited the prayer repeatedly. As the rumbling, shaking, and banging grew louder, so did their fears. Clinging to one another, they prayed louder and louder as tears dropped onto both of their cheeks.

Suddenly, the rumbling and shaking stopped. They're prayers were answered—they'd survived the earthquake/avalanche unscathed.

They climbed out from under the table, relieved to find the interior of the ark the same. They climbed down to the bottom level to exit from the ramp. It was gone, or at least covered in rocks and boulders. They slipped through a crack between the boulders and into the large cavern, or at least what was left of it. The cavern was filled with rocks and boulders. Sun poured through where one of the cavern walls once was.

"At least we found a way out." Tommy laughed.

Smacking him, she said, "You're terrible."

"What? Too soon? I'm an optimist." Grinning, he hugged her and asked, "Are you okay, luv?"

Studying her arms and legs, she nodded and said, "I think so." She hugged him again and cried uncontrollably. "Oh, Tommy. I really thought we were going to die."

He hugged her tightly. "Shhhh. We're okay, luv. We're okay. I thought we were going to die, too. But the thought of being buried in Noah's Ark gave me some comfort. What a perfect grave for two archaeologists," he said.

Turning, they both studied the ark. Shock filled them. The entire ark was buried intact beneath an enormous pile of rocks and boulders. If they hadn't just exited the ark, they'd never have known it was even there.

"Oh, my, God! Tommy, how did we survive that. I'm not great with physics, but I thought the force of those giant boulders falling onto the wooden ark would crush it. We should be dead."

"I know, luv. We should be. Talk about divine intervention. Our prayers were answered, literally." Tommy held her as they stared at the gigantic ark, now buried in rubble from the avalanche.

"Tommy, we literally just witnessed a miracle. We must be destined for great things," she marveled.

"Or our kids are." Smiling, he kissed her.

Chapter Nineteen

Wearing her favorite red dress, Victoria proudly climbed the castle's spiral steps with her handsome fiancé. They arrived at the Royal Banquet Hall within the Enchanted Storybook Castle. With her hand snugly tucked into the crook of Tommy's arm, she admired the beautiful stained-glass depictions of her favorite Disney Princesses—Snow White, Cinderella, Aurora, Ariel, Belle and Rapunzel.

"Reservations for two, Garrison." Tommy held up two fingers to the Chinese hostess.

After clicking on the computer, she smiled. "Welcome to the Royal Banquet Hall. Follow me please."

They passed the large buffet spread in the center of the hall. But this was better than your typical buffet, it even had a roast beef carving station. They were seated at a table for two beneath the stained-glass window depicting Snow White in the glass coffin surrounded by Seven Dwarfs and Prince Charming.

A VIP of regally attired Disney Princes and Princesses flitted about the room greeting the dining guests and posing for pictures. Eager children hugged the princesses and gleamed excitedly.

"I hope they come to our table." Victoria giggled excitedly. She felt five instead of twenty-nine.

"Heck yeah, Sleeping Beauty is hot." Tommy winked. "I wonder if she'll give *me* a hug."

"Ahem." She studied the drink menu and the vast wine selection.

Tommy quickly ordered a bottle of Dom Perignon. "Let's celebrate."

Victoria scanned the room, taking in the beautiful interior of the castle and felt like she was in a storybook. "Uh, interesting."

"What is it, my dear?" Tommy asked.

"All of the Characters are Disney Royalty, except one," she said with a quizzical tone.

Tommy turned, then his eyebrow arched with curiosity. "Huh, you're right. Captain Jack Sparrow from the Pirates of the Caribbean is out of place in the castle."

The server appeared and presented the chilled bottle of Dom Perignon for Tommy's approval.

Nodding aristocratically, Tommy gestured for the waiter to open the bottle.

The server unwrapped the foil, then twisted the wire to expose the cork. Turning towards a solid portion of the stone wall, he placed his thumb on the cork and aimed safely away from the delicate stained-glass windows.

Pop!

The cork flew against the stone wall, then fell onto the floor. The server poured two Waterford Crystal flutes, then bowed and stepped away.

Tommy held his flute above the center of the table and toasted, "To our ark."

Victoria clinked her glass to his. "Don't you mean, 'Noah's Ark?'"

"It's ours now. Noah's long dead." Tommy reached into his pocket and retrieved his lucky nickel.

"Now begs the question. What do we do now?" She pressed her lips together.

Slumping defeatedly, Tommy sighed, "If I had a nickel for every time we find something amazing, but couldn't share it with the world-"

"-You'd have a dime," she interrupted.

Tommy's face lit up like the fourth of July, obviously grasping her meaning. "You mean..."

Nodding excitedly, she said, "Why not. We hid the first two finds for the greater good. But Noah's Ark needs to be shared with the world," Victoria referred to the Fountain of Youth they discovered under the Magic Kingdom in Florida and the abundant gem mine and catacombs they found under Disneyland Paris.

With a relieved expression, Tommy wiped his brow with the back of his hand in jest and said, "Phew. I was hoping you'd say that."

"And this time, our find is not on Disney property, just buried in rubble in a mountain nearby." Relief washed through her about the less red tape they'd have to deal with.

"Now begs the next question...."

Reading his mind, she asked, "When do we tell the world?".

"Exactly. Now, don't get me wrong. I'm anxious to tell the world that we discovered Noah's Ark," he said.

"But....?"

"I'm not ready to end our vacation. This is a once in a lifetime trip. We intended to visit all three Disney Parks in Asia in one long trip. We took a month off from work. Which is-"

"-Impossible to do it once, let alone again," she finished his sentence.

"Exactly. And once we announce it to the world, our lives will be insane with the excavation," he predicted.

"Well, since no one else discovered Noah's Ark after thousands of years, then what's a few more weeks," she reasoned.

"And now the next big question...."

"Hong Kong or Tokyo?" She arched her eyebrow along with her tone of voice.

"Let's let Noah's Nickel decide." Tommy flipped the nickel into the air.

"Heads for Hong Kong, tails for Tokyo," she called.

They waited for the nickel to come down with bated breath. But instead of coming down, the rugged hand of a pirate grabbed the coin. But not just any pirate clutched the nickel, this hand belonged to Captain Jack Sparrow.

With a perfect mimic of the famous pirate, Jack slapped the nickel on the table and said, "Heads it is."

"Oh, hello," Victoria blushed.

Grabbing her hand, Jack held her fingers close to his mouth and said with an exaggerated accent, "Good evening, Mademoiselle, you are the most beautiful and enchanting woman in this room full of princesses." He kissed her hand, then gestured to all the Disney Princesses in the banquet hall.

Blushing, she let him hold her hand. His impression of Captain Jack Sparrow was perfect, even the quirky mannerisms and accent. His face, lined with wrinkles on his forehead and around his dark brown eyes, was obviously older than the rest of the male Disney characters in the room.

Something was special about this one. Disney was strict about the ages of its Cast Members assigned to character roles. No Disney Princesses were over the age of thirty. Once a Cast Member aged too much, they were assigned a different role.

She recalled her earlier conversation with Tommy at the Pirates of the Caribbean ride, the realization sank in. Gasping, she covered her mouth, shocked and speechless.

Holding his index finger to his lips, signaling for her silence, the pirate kissed her hand again, took off his hat, and bowed gracefully.

"What was that all about?" Tommy asked.

Beaming, Victoria said, "That was Johnny Depp!"

THE END

Part Four
Manganese Magic

AN ELEMENTS OF MYSTERY
UNDER THE MAGIC ADVENTURE

Manganese
Magic

TERRI TALLEY VENTERS

Prologue

Alexandria, Egypt
48 BC

"You're going to think I'm crazy." Ptolemy grabbed papyrus scrolls by the dozens.

"I never doubt you, or your premonitions, Master." Ptolemy's long-time friend and servant hastily stuffed scrolls into a cloth sack.

"I've heard of Julius Caesar and his tyrannical ambitions. He is on a warpath to conquer the world. And Egypt is in his path!"

"Yes, Master."

"The precious scrolls of the Alexandria Library are our most prized possession. My ancestor, Ptolemy I Soter, founded this library. I'll be damned if I let Caesar take it, or worse, destroy it." Ptolemy filled another cloth sack and handed it to another servant to tote to the horse-drawn cart.

"We're going to need more men," the servant suggested.

"Luckily, I have an army of loyal servants." Ptolemy smirked.

"Not to mention your fleet of merchant ships."

"Aye. That I do." Ptolemy filled another sack with precious scrolls. "I'll do whatever it takes to save these scrolls. I'll sail all the way to China if I have to."

Chapter One

"Where to?" the Uber driver asked from the curb of Hong Kong International Airport.

"Disneyland," Victoria Ventures said, just barely above a whisper.

Embarrassment flooded her for coming all the way to Hong Kong and going straight to Disneyland. She stared at her reflection in the rearview mirror. Her face, tan from spending most of her time outside on archaeological digs, now appeared flushed with shame. Her ice-blue eyes stood out, sharply contrasted by her waist-length, ebony hair. She resembled a tan Meagan Fox, or so she'd been told.

"Here is the address of the hotel." Tommy Garrison showed the driver his iPhone's screen. After the driver typed the address into his navigation system, Tommy leaned back in his seat and grabbed Victoria's hand.

"Are you going to tell me which hotel we're staying at?" Victoria asked with piqued curiosity.

Disneyland Hong Kong represented the fourth Disneyland around the world that they'd visited. After their first date at Walt Disney World in Orlando, Florida, the archaeological couple made it their mission to visit all six Disney locations around the world. Given what they'd found beneath the Orlando, Paris and Shanghai parks, they were anxious to see what great archaeological finds rested *under the magic* in Hong Kong, Tokyo, and Anaheim.

"Why can't you just be surprised?" Tommy shook his head in frustration.

"Fine." Sighing, she crossed her arms. Miffed that he wouldn't tell her, she stared at his beautiful sea-green eyes. His tan face, capped with straight, sandy-blond hair, reminded her of a younger Ewan

McGregor. Then her frustration abated. *How could she be mad at someone so handsome?*

After several crazy lane changes, the Uber arrived on Disney property. A familiar red roof and white building filled the horizon. Red cupolas protruded from the roof of this hotel inspired by the Victorian Era.

Excitedly, she pointed and said, "It looks exactly like the Grand Floridian in Walt Disney World. Is that where we're staying?" Her tone reflected her excitement.

He shook his head. "Sorry, my love. That's the Hong Kong Disneyland Hotel. I thought about booking it, but they have another hotel that's unique to Hong Kong Disneyland."

Snapping her fingers, she reasoned, "Although that hotel reminds me of our first date, you have a good point—let's stay someplace new and unique."

He squeezed her hand.

After passing the beautiful Hong Kong Disneyland Hotel, bright colors filled the horizon.

"What the...?" Victoria sat up in her seat to get a better view of this hotel. It reminded her of old Hollywood during the Golden Age of film.

"Disney's Hollywood Hotel." Tommy grinned.

"Wow! Normally I'd be mad about staying at a Hollywood themed hotel while we're in China, but this place is so cool. I feel like we're back in America." She beamed.

The Uber driver dropped them and their luggage off in front of the hotel. After a quick check-in, the bellhop, dressed like the ones from the Golden Age of Hollywood, escorted them to their suite.

Victoria briskly walked to the balcony. Slightly disappointed because she couldn't see the theme park, she marveled at the Pacific Ocean. "You booked an ocean-view room?"

Tommy walked up behind her, wrapped his arms around her slender waist and nuzzled his cheek against hers. "It's beautiful. I thought this was a nicer option. I could just stare at the sea all day. Reminds me of home at Castle Garrison."

Pointing excitedly, she said, "We can see the pool from here, too. Huh, is that a-"

"-Piano. The pool is shaped like a piano. It even has all eighty-eight black and white keys by the steps." Tommy smirked.

"We'll have to check it out later. I hope it's heated." A chill prickled her with goosebumps, and she leaned into him.

He turned her to face him, stared lovingly into her eyes, and said with his bedroom voice, "In keeping with tradition." He closed his eyes and softly kissed her lips.

Chapter Two

"Ah, that *nap* was just what I needed." Tommy winked at Victoria, referring to their afternoon delight after their shower and nap.

The jet lag from their flight from Shanghai was nowhere near as bad as the jet lag from Los Angeles to Shanghai. Crossing the Pacific Ocean, even via a Boeing 747-400, took forever.

"Thanks for taking me to the pool. When I was growing up, staying at a hotel with a pool was a special treat," Victoria referred to her humble beginnings.

After placing the hotel-provided towels and her fuchsia cinch sack on two lounge chairs overlooking the ocean, Victoria meandered to the piano-shaped pool. Entering by the steps with the piano keys, she carefully counted all eighty-eight keys.

Obviously knowing exactly what she was doing, Tommy asked, "Did they get all eighty-eight?"

After counting, using her right index finger to keep her place, she laughed.

"What's so funny?" He studied her with a perplexed expression.

"I was just thinking, these piano-key steps would drive Monk crazy because they're not an even one hundred." She referred to one of their favorite television shows they'd recently binge watched. Monk featured an OCD detective who helped solve homicide cases for the SFPD.

"Oh yeah, you're right." Tommy ogled her from head-to-toe and grinned 'like a kid at....'

"What? Why are you staring at me like I'm a big, juicy steak?" She placed her left hand on her hip and wagged her right index finger like a parent scolding a child. "Don't tell me you're hungry."

"It's just that, I think this is the first time I've ever seen you in a bikini." He smiled.

"What? No? Really? But you've seen me, ... never mind." She waved her hand at him nonchalantly.

Stepping down into the pool, she used the chrome hand rail to guide her. After a modified breast stroke, one *without* submerging her head, across the length of the piano-shaped pool, she touched the pool's cement edge.

"How's the water? Is it cold?" Tommy shouted from the other end of the pool.

"It's refreshing." She treaded water in the deep end.

"Refreshing? Or invigorating?" Tommy walked towards the deep end.

Shrugging, she said, "Just stick your big toe in."

"A real man can't just stick his toe in. It's all or nothing." He swung his arms in big circles, obviously preparing to jump right into the deep end.

After turning to ascertain no other tourists were around, she said, "If you can handle the Fountain of Youth, you can handle this." She winked.

"But that was cold," he whined.

"Big baby." Splashing him, she swam back towards the shallow end.

"Big baby, my ass." He backed up to the shrubs along the perimeter of the pool deck, then ran towards the pool. Jumping into the air, he pulled his knees to his chest and cannonballed into the deep end.

Tommy's enormous splash reached Victoria. Holding her hands over her hair in a bun, she tried to keep her recently washed hair dry.

After emerging from his cannonball, Tommy scolded, "It's not cold at all. It's heated, like a big bathtub."

"Gotcha." Winking, she splashed him, then turned back towards the garden near the pool.

Adjacent to the Hollywood Hotel, a large glass enclosure protruded from the hedges of the garden. Pointing, she asked, "Oh, what's that?"

Shaking his head in mock frustration, he asked, "Another shiny object, my dear?"

"It looks like some sort of glass atrium."

"Wanna get out and walk over there?"

"Not yet, the water is so nice and warm. I'm not ready to get cold getting out of the pool."

"Who's the big baby, now?" he teased. "Want me to get out, check my phone and see what that is?"

"Sure." With a high-pitched tone, she grinned and kept her shoulders beneath the water's surface.

Tommy, quickly got out, walked to his phone on the tiny table between their lounge chairs, then hurried back to the water. Placing his iPhone on the edge of the pool, he slid back into the warm water and shivered, "Brrr. Now I understand why you didn't want to get out. The wind from the Pacific Ocean is freezing."

"Thank you." She rewarded him with a playful smooch on his cheek. Then she slid behind him and hugged her body against his back. "Maybe this will warm you up."

"Ah, yeah. That feels awesome." Tommy tapped away on his phone. "Oh, yeah. I remember reading about this when I booked the hotel. I was planning to take you there after our nap and swim."

"What is it?" She slid around his warm body and faced him. Giving him her best, sad-eyed-puppy look, she begged, "Tell me."

"Can't you just be surprised?" For the umpteenth time this trip, he shook his head and pretended to be frustrated with her insatiable need to know everything.

Rolling her eyes, she said with a perturbed tone, "Let me guess."

"Let's just say, I could go for a drink." He grinned.

"What, you're not *starving* already?" Victoria teased.

"You know me too well. When I said, 'I could go for a drink,' I meant-"

"-You could go for a drink with your *food*." After interrupting him. Victoria playfully smacked his chest.

Chapter Three

"If it's *not* a pool bar, then why is it near the pool?" Victoria huffed as they exited the room. Tommy insisted that they change into nicer attire because their bathing suits and flip flops wouldn't cut the mustard at this place.

Offering his arm, he escorted her through the lobby. "Just because you *saw* it from the pool, doesn't make it a pool bar." Tommy stood handsomely in his cobalt-blue dress shirt with no tie. Shiny, charcoal-grey dress pants clung to his lower body, quite nicely, and accentuated his slender, toned physique. Black dress shoes and matching belt screamed metrosexual, even though he'd never admit it.

Gaping at the abundant opulence of the lobby in the Hollywood Hotel, Victoria felt relieved that Tommy insisted they change back in the room. Although she was more comfortable wearing a flannel shirt over a tank top with skinny jeans and Timberlands, she knew Tommy loved her in this Gator-blue sundress with matching strappy high-heels.

"Welcome to the Studio Lounge." Tommy gestured for her to enter the already open glass door. The late afternoon sun shone through the glass atrium. The colorful, swirly patterns on the carpet accentuated the art-deco décor of the Studio Lounge. A large bar dominated the back of the room. High-back chairs and comfy sofas provided cozy seating areas throughout the lounge.

"Please, sit wherever you wish." A Disney Cast Member waved towards the various empty seats.

"Thank you." Victoria presumed so many seats were vacant since the parks were still open. That, and it wasn't five o'clock yet. But she wasn't judging, they were on vacation, after all.

"Have a magical day." The Cast Member smiled, then greeted the next guest.

"Where would you like to sit?" Tommy studied their choices of empty tables.

"Hmmm. Probably the hardest decision I'll make all day." Victoria scanned the Studio Lounge and felt as if she'd been transported back to the Golden Age of Hollywood.

"Maybe for you, but what I'm going to *eat* will be the toughest decision I'll make today." Tommy leaned back and rubbed his slender abs.

How he kept his eight-pack abs amazed her, especially considering the amount of red meat he consumed. "Although the sofas look comfy, they all face the bar. I'd rather view the beautiful garden and the ocean."

"Excellent choice. Not that I wouldn't love getting cozy with you on a sofa, but I'd be too tempted to get carried away with you." He kissed her temple.

"We wouldn't want to risk getting kicked out of Disneyland Hong Kong, especially since we haven't even enjoyed the park yet," she rationalized. "How's this?" She gestured towards a high-top table overlooking the gardens.

"Perfect. Besides, it'll be much easier to cut into my big, juicy steak if I'm sitting at a real table. Plus, I don't trust myself with red wine on those white sofas. What were they thinking?" Tommy's tone matched his bewildered expression.

"How do you know they have steak?" Surveying the food on the tables of the few patrons, she found no evidence of steak, especially at four in the afternoon.

"I did my homework." He beamed, then pulled out a high-back bar stool for her.

"Thank ya, kind sir," she said with an over exaggerated Southern drawl.

"Good afternoon, may I offer you a tasty beverage?" Their server placed a white cocktail napkin in front of each of them.

Studying the bar menu already on the table, he asked Victoria, "How about a bottle of wine?"

"Sounds perfect." Smiling, she appreciated not having to think too much on her vacation.

"What would you recommend to go with the steak? We like heavy reds," Tommy asked the server.

"Ah, I know just the one. Would you like a glass or a bottle?" he asked.

"We'll each start with a glass, then if we like it, we'll order a bottle." Tommy closed the bar menu, then studied the food menu.

Victoria admired the beautiful and meticulously maintained gardens just outside of the glass atrium which housed the Studio Lounge. Typical Disney, every detail was immaculate.

"You know, they modeled the Studio Lounge after the original one in Hollywood. Apparently, that was *the* place to be seen. Huge movie deals were made there, and aspiring actors hoped to get discovered there," Tommy regurgitated his recollection of the website.

Both of their iPhones pinged with a notification from their Fox News app. They both stared at each other to gauge the other's reaction. Shrugging, they both nonverbally agreed to stay off the grid and enjoy their once-in-a-lifetime vacation.

Their server arrived with two glasses of red wine. "I know you'll enjoy this red. It's my favorite. At the end of the night, the manager lets the staff take home any open bottles of wine. I'll let you enjoy your wine before I take your order." He bowed, then backed away gracefully.

"To the most magical place on Earth." Victoria raised her wine glass and toasted Tommy's.

"To the most beautiful woman in the world—my fiancée." Tommy winked.

They sipped their wine, both humming because of its deliciousness.

While Victoria's head was tilted back to drink her wine from the ridiculously large glass, the television at the bar reflected in the atrium's window. The screen caught her attention, and she turned around.

Tommy obviously noticed the same breaking news story because he turned around, too.

The flat-screen television above the bar showed a map of North Korea and a picture of Kim Jong Un. The news band at the bottom of the screen read—*More plutonium stolen from North Korea.*

Chapter Four

"Chef Mickey's? I get to see Mickey Mouse for breakfast?" Victoria performed her signature happy dance in the lobby of Chef Mickey's. Mickey Mouse and Sous Chef, Donald Duck, meandered throughout the restaurant on the top floor of their hotel.

"I knew you'd like it, another reason why I picked this hotel." Tommy winked.

Chef Mickey's boasted high ceilings and an open kitchen layout. The restaurant was tastefully decorated in art deco like the studio commissaries of Hollywood's Golden Age. The walls were decorated with whimsical murals and sketches depicting dozens of Disney's favorite characters. Hidden Mickey decorations were subtly located throughout the restaurant.

They followed the hostess past the buffet of international cuisine to a table by the window which overlooked beautiful gardens and the Pacific Ocean.

Leaning close to the window, she peered down and spotted the familiar glass atrium. Pointing, she said, "Look, Tommy, it's the top of the Studio Lounge."

Peering out the window, he said, "Oh yeah, neat. And I see the piano pool, too." He pointed to the right.

After ordering two pots of tea, they quickly filled their plates from the gigantic buffet.

Sitting back down, she poured tea into both of their tea cups. Silently, Tommy passed her the honey while she passed him the sugar like they'd been married for years.

"I'm glad you picked this place. We can fuel up quickly before the park opens, then walk right in through the hotel's dedicated park entrance."

"Yet another reason I chose this place. If I wasn't in the mood for more Chinese food, I'd at least have a convenient option of bacon and eggs." Tommy dipped a slice of bacon into strawberry jelly.

"We can have a light lunch in the park to maximize our time on the rides."

Tommy shot her a dirty look before asking, "*Light* lunch?"

"Sorry, I meant, *quick* lunch at some counter service place." Victoria bit into her croissant and hummed. Closing her eyes with food-induced bliss, she said, "Mmmm, carbs and butter."

Tommy tapped his phone and gulped the rest of his tea.

"Hey, no electronics." Victoria chided, miffed that he'd ruin their meal by playing on his phone.

"Chill, woman, I'm checking our FastPasses for the day." Shaking his head, he continued tapping on the Disneyland Hong Kong app. Multitasking, he popped a heaping spoonful of scrambled eggs into his mouth.

"Oh, well, then that's okay. Just no email or work stuff. What FastPasses did you get for today?" She poured more tea for each of them.

Holding up his index finger, he finished his mouthful of food before saying, "Since we're here for a whole week, I procured FastPasses for all the popular rides. We'll get to ride everything eventually."

"Which ones are today?" She bit into some sort of wonton dish, then mentally patted herself on the back for trying local cuisine.

"Uh, hold on, I just took a screen shot of today's list so I won't have to open the app to double check the times." Tapping away, he said, "Big Grizzly Mountain Runaway Mine Cars, which resembles Big Thunder Mountain in Florida, then Space Mountain and Jungle Cruise."

"It'll be fun to compare and contrast Hong Kong Disneyland with the other three Disney parks. What else do they have here? Anything unique?"

"Yes, there are some unique rides—Rafts to Tarzan's Treehouse and Orbitron. They have some rides like what we saw in Disneyland Paris's Toy Story land, like RC Racer and the parachute drop. And of course, there are the classics—tea cups, race cars and It's a Small World."

"What, no Haunted Mansion?" She drained the last of her tea.

"Not exactly. They have a house, but it's not scary. It's called Mystic Manor. Something about Chinese culture kept them from having a house with spirits. *Ahooooo.*" Tommy made a creepy noise.

Laughing, she said, "We need to work on your scary sound effects."

"What? No Grammy?" Tommy laughed.

Admiring their view of the park, Victoria pointed and asked, "Is that the Mystic Manor? It doesn't look scary at all. It's bright and colorful."

"It's based on the famous Bradbury Mansion in Hollywood, California." Tommy signaled their server for their bill using the international hand gesture of signing something in the air.

"Bradbury Mansion? Never heard of it." She gulped the rest of her tea.

"That's because you're young." Tommy took the bill and studied it.

"What else is in Disneyland Hong Kong?" Victoria smeared cream cheese on her bagel, then topped it with smoked salmon, red onions and capers.

"There are several new attractions coming soon. Iron Man experience opens New Year's Day. It's a 3D motion simulator with Tony Stark battling aliens attacking Hong Kong."

"That sounds cool." Then she realized that they'd be in Tokyo for New Year's. Snapping her fingers, she said with a frustrated tone, "Darn, we'll just miss it. What else are we missing?"

"In 2020, they'll open a Frozen themed area that'll resemble Arundel. There's something with Moana coming in the Fantasy Gardens. And they're expanding the Marvel Experience next to Iron Man because the Marvel Comic movies are so popular. But that's not until 2023," Tommy explained.

"Well, sounds like we'll have to come back." Winking, she sat back in her chair, stuffed. Staring out the window overlooking the park, she proclaimed, "Well, I'm ready to hit the park. It's beckoning me."

Tommy paid the bill with his Disney Chase Visa to earn valuable Disney dollars. "At least we earn double Disney dollars on Disney property."

"Shouldn't we be using the Disney dollars we earned from Shanghai Disneyland?" she asked with a slightly condescending tone.

Signing the credit card receipt, he explained, "We blew through all of our Disney dollars on this hotel for a week. You know, if I wasn't paying in Chinese Renminbi, I'd think I was back in the USA, not Asia."

"Speaking of China, I wonder if we'll find anything beneath Disneyland Hong Kong."

Chapter Five

"Oh, I'm stuffed." Grabbing her belly, she slowly meandered out of Chef Mickey's where an onslaught of guests waited in the lobby.

They exited the hotel and walked to Hong Kong Disneyland, entering through the special back entrance for Disneyland resort guests.

"What do we want to ride first? The park just opened, so we probably want a popular ride first before the line gets too long." Victoria studied the map.

Tommy peered over her shoulder. "Oh, we should ride Big Grizzly Mountain Runaway Mine Cars."

"You want to ride a roller coaster right after breakfast?" Victoria shot him an evil glare.

"We'll be fine if we only ride it once. Besides, the Big Grizzly roller coaster is right there." Tommy pointed to a gigantic rock formation which resembled Big Thunder Mountain.

Walking towards Big Grizzly Mountain, Victoria squealed when she read the estimated wait time at the ride's entrance—five minutes. "I'm glad there is practically no wait, but I was secretly hoping we'd have more time for my stomach to settle."

"Relax, my dear. Besides, if you do get sick, at least you'll have a great 'I told you so.'" Tommy laughed.

Laughing, she agreed, "You're right. There's nothing like a good 'I told you so.'"

Walking up the ramp between the faux wood rails which served as a queue, Victoria marveled at the rock formation. It looked so real. Impressed, she gave the Disney Imagineers a mental nod for their authenticity. Touching it, shock filled her, "Tommy, feel this. I think it's real rock."

He touched it and said with the same surprised tone, "You're right, it *is* real, dust and all." Tommy rubbed the stone mountain's grit between his fingers.

"I reckon Disneyland decided it was easier, and *cheaper*, to incorporate the ride into the mountain rather than to blow it up and build a fake mountain."

The queue reached the top of the mountain, then descended through the middle. Tommy slowed his pace to study the stone tunnel. "Victoria, it's like a cave in here. Tiny caverns are connected with short tunnels. This must be how a bee feels in a honeycomb. I've heard about these. But this is too open. A human couldn't survive in here." Tommy rubbed his chin with his thumb and index finger. His expression signaled he was deep in thought.

"Survive in here? What are you talking about? All one needs to survive is shelter, food and water."

"Well, *now,* yeah. But not during the Ice Age."

Her hand instinctively covered her mouth as the realization sank in. "You're right. I know what you're talking about. During the Ice Age, humans survived in honeycombed caves in the mountains. But I thought those were...." Her mind failed to recall the location. "Somewhere else."

"Yes, but surely there were several of these scattered throughout the world in various mountain ranges."

"But aren't we near sea level?" She waved in the direction of the South China Sea.

"Yes, we are. I wonder what's hiding beneath Big Grizzly Runaway Mine Cars?"

Chapter Six

"Wheeeee!" Tommy screamed from the front row of Big Grizzly Mountain Runaway Mine Cars.

The ride slowed, then stopped abruptly.

"What happened?" Victoria asked. The sudden change in motion made her stomach rumble.

"Must be, 'technical difficulties,'" Tommy quipped using air quotes.

"Oh, I'm gonna be sick." Victoria jumped out of the mine car, ran to a corner and puked.

Tommy followed her. "Are you okay? I'm pretty sure we're not supposed to exit the car during the ride."

She shrugged, not caring if she was exiled from Disneyland Hong Kong. Leaning back on a different mine car off to the side, she felt the car move. "What's this? It looks like a real mine car, not like the pretty, clean ones on the ride with seats and a safety bar."

They climbed in, begging for trouble from the Cast Members.

"They must not have cameras everywhere like the Disney parks in America." Tommy presumed.

"What's this lever do?"

"Victoria, don't!" Tommy screamed.

Too late.

Victoria pulled the lever releasing the break. The mine car rolled slowly at first, then it dipped and picked up speed. It travelled down fast at a forty-five-degree angle.

"Crap, no seat belts. Hold on tight!" Victoria hollered.

After descending several hundred feet, the car came to a screeching halt.

Exiting the car, Tommy used the flashlight app on his iPhone to illuminate the dark cave. A torch rested against the rock wall. He grabbed the torch and lit it.

"Wow!"

The cavern lit up. But it wasn't just one cavern, the area was honeycombed with tiny alcoves—an underground civilization.

"So, this is how humans survived the Ice Age—they were protected in dry, underground caverns."

"Amazing. Let's check it out." The archaeological find thrilled her. And she ignored the horrible notion—*How are they going to get out of here?*

Chapter Seven

"We certainly weren't prepared for spelunking today." Victoria shrugged. "We don't even have twine to mark our path."

"Let alone, food, water and a jacket. It's cold in here." Tommy rubbed his muscular arms to ward off the chill.

"Big baby, didn't you grow up in Scotland?" Victoria refrained from rubbing her own arms to ward off the chill because she didn't want to be a hypocrite. But in her defense, she grew up in the hot and humid city of Charleston, South Carolina.

"Yeah, but I..., never mind." Dropping his head defeatedly, he waved nonchalantly.

"I have bread." She retrieved the muffins she'd swiped from the buffet at Chef Mickey's. We can use these to mark our path."

"Oh, you stole food from the buffet. I'm tellin'," he sarcastically threatened like a kid in a schoolyard.

"It was already on our table. I couldn't finish everything I got from the buffet. They would've thrown it out anyway," she justified her theft.

Tommy studied her with a guilty expression, then he grinned.

"What? Do you think we should save it to eat?"

Tommy retrieved two bagels he'd swiped from the buffet. "How about we eat *my* bagels and use *your* muffins for a crumb trail?"

Smacking his chest, she teased, "You turd."

Sporadically dropping muffin crumbs, they meandered through various short tunnels which connected tiny caverns. Most of the caverns had low ceilings. Tommy shone the torch on the ceiling and studied the dark ash. He rubbed the ash off the ceiling and tasted it. Spitting it out, he washed his tongue off with water from his bottle. "Blah."

"What is it?" she asked.

"Manganese. It's a residue from fires. I can't believe they were stupid enough to build a fire down here." He shook his head incredulously.

"The Ice Age was a long time ago. Back then, humans didn't know about the dangers of smoke inhalation." Pointing excitedly, she asked, "Oh, what's that?"

"Another shiny object, my dear?" Teasing, he referred to her easy tendency for distractions."

"Well, duh, but look, it's cave paintings." Excited, she pointed to the cave walls and jumped up and down.

"They used the manganese from the fire residue to document their time here."

Cave paintings were in many of the caverns. They wandered through and studied the various crude depictions.

Stopping periodically to snap pictures with her iPhone, she stopped and said, "They're depicting the Ice Age. Oh, my, God. We found more caves where humans survived the Ice Age."

"Not to be a party pooper, but Disneyland Hong Kong discovered these caves. Remember the mine cart that brought us down here?"

"Oh, yeah." Meandering through the caverns, she stopped at an interesting cave painting. "Tommy, come look at this. It looks like some of the humans went crazy."

Standing behind her, he studied the cave drawing. Rubbing his chin with his thumb and index finger, he said, "Huh, you're right. I'd heard that early humans who lived in caves often succumbed to 'Manganese Madness.'"

"Manganese Madness? From the manganese in the fire ash?" she asked.

"Exactly. Too much manganese exposure can lead to Parkinson's Disease. But back in the Ice Age, they didn't know what to call it."

Shuddering, she said, "Creepy."

"Hey, what are you two doing down here?" a Cast Member scolded.

Chapter Eight

Startled, Victoria jumped back and grabbed her chest as if to ward off her imminent heart attack.

"You're not supposed to be down here. How did you even get here?" The Cast Member, dressed like the others running the Big Grizzly Runaway Mine Cars, wagged his finger at them shamefully.

"I, we..." Dropping her head defeatedly, she confessed, "It was an accident. When the ride stopped, I got sick. I jumped off the ride and he followed me. I threw up, then accidentally rode...."

"Accidentally my..." The Cast Member paused to fume. Then he pontificated, "It is dangerous down here. How were you planning to get out? You need a key card to work the elevator. I should ban you from Disneyland!"

Gasping, Victoria grabbed her throat in horror. Her worst nightmare was about to come true—banned from Disneyland! Holding her hands together in prayer, she begged the Asian whose name tag read, 'Han.' "Oh, Han, please, anything but that. We didn't see a sign that read Cast Members Only." *Not that such a sign ever stopped her before.*

Sighing, Han slumped. "Fine, I won't *ban* you from Disneyland, but I will escort you out of the park for the rest of the day."

"Oh, thank you." She hugged him.

"Whoa! It's forbidden to touch the guests, except costumed characters," Han said.

"Oh, sorry." She blushed.

"How *do* we get out of here?" Tommy asked.

"There's a service elevator which will take us to the top. Follow me." Han nodded.

Following Han, they meandered back the way they came. Muffin crumbs marked their path as they trekked back through the honeycomb caverns with cave paintings.

"These caves have archaeological significance. Shouldn't Disneyland share this with the world?" Victoria asked.

"That's above my pay grade." Han held up his hands in mock surrender.

After they passed the mine car that they rode down on, they turned a corner. More mine cars rested on tracks. Artificial lighting shone on a steel, service elevator. Crates rested next to the elevator, like they were either transporting something in or out. *But what?* Hopefully Disneyland wasn't transporting precious archaeological treasures out of the Ice Age caves and selling them on the Black Market. Victoria shuddered at the horrific notion.

Tommy obviously noticed their surroundings, too. "What's that? And why does it have biohazard warnings?" Tommy asked.

Holding his hands up in surrender, Han said, "Top secret."

"Isn't that unsafe for the guests?"

"*These* crates are empty." Han easily lifted the empty crate.

Tommy shot Victoria a skeptical expression. Han emphasized *these* crates, were empty. As in, *other* crates were full.

What were they hiding down here? And why wouldn't they share these caves with the world? Her imagination ran wild with possibilities. *Was Disney planning to turn these caves into an attraction?* She'd heard rumors that Disneyland Hong Kong struggled financially, mostly because of their nearby competitor—Ocean Park Hong Kong. But what really agitated her was those empty crates. *What were they transporting?*

They followed Han into the freight elevator. However, this elevator was more like a lift. Its open structure was pulled up and down from a crane, the same one they saw just before they entered the short queue to Big Grizzly Runaway Mine Cars. With so much construction, numerous cranes were scattered throughout the park.

Han pushed a big red button, and the crane hoisted them up.

As they lifted away from the empty mine cars and wooden crates, Tommy whispered to Victoria, "I wonder if this has anything to do with that news story we heard about yesterday?"

Victoria's brain scrambled to recall. They hadn't watched the news at all yesterday. Except for that one story they saw on the news while they ate dinner at the Studio Lounge. With her photographic memory, she recalled the image and the headline. Gasping, she grabbed her throat. Tommy referred to the plutonium stolen from North Korea.

Chapter Nine

"Now, walk peacefully in front of me towards the front entrance to the park. I must ensure that you exit the park immediately." Han stomped his right booted foot, punctuating his authority.

"But we're...." Tommy started, but was quickly elbowed in the ribs by Victoria.

"Thank you, Han. We'll exit through the *front* entrance." Victoria was dying to see the front of the park. But since they'd entered by Big Grizzly Mountain using the special entrance for Disneyland's hotel guests, they missed strolling down Main Street USA and seeing the castle.

Tommy caught on quickly and winked at her, obviously appreciating her brilliance.

Taking out her park map, Victoria got her bearings and walked towards Tinkerbell's castle.

A brightly painted mansion came into view, and Victoria whispered to Tommy, "Is that Mystic Manor? It doesn't seem scary at all."

"It's not supposed to be." Tommy grabbed her hand and they leisurely strolled towards the castle.

"Pick up the pace, please," Han ordered.

They walked in front of the castle, pausing briefly to snap a quick picture. "I was hoping for a different castle." Her tone dripped with disappointment.

"They call it Tinkerbell's Castle."

"But it looks exactly like Sleeping Beauty's or Cinderella's. I can't keep them straight."

Tommy stopped in front of the castle, pulled her towards him, gazed lovingly into her eyes and said, "In keeping with tradition." Then he kissed her like they were the only ones at Disneyland Hong Kong.

Han yelled, "Hey, save it for the room."

Reluctantly, they pulled apart and walked towards a beautifully manicured Chinese garden which highlighted the front of the castle. Chinese Pagodas scattered throughout the garden where various Disney characters greeted children and the young at heart. Once past the gardens, Main Street USA beckoned them. The shops appeared identical to the other Main Street USAs.

They finally arrived at the park entrance, and Han said, "One more thing, hand me your park tickets."

Slumping, Victoria sighed with disappointment. She'd hoped Han would forget that part because she'd envisioned re-entering the park the second his back was turned.

Begrudgingly, Tommy and Victoria handed him their park tickets.

Han walked to a nearby gate attendant, then scanned their tickets on an iPad. After tapping away for a minute, he handed back their park tickets and said, "Have a magical day."

Han's sarcasm wasn't lost on Victoria. Studying the map again, she asked Tommy, "How do we get back to the hotel from here?"

With a deflated expression, Tommy turned her to face the park. Pointing, he asked, "Do you see Big Grizzly Mountain?"

She nodded.

"Do you see our hotel behind it?"

She nodded again, then studied the map. A long sidewalk hugged the exterior perimeter of the park. Determined not to let this setback sour her mood, she thought about their amazing discovery.

Pointing at the map, Tommy said, "Perhaps we can mosey over to the other hotels and check them out."

"Oh yeah, I forgot about the other two hotels. The Hong Kong Disneyland Hotel and Disney's Explorer's

Lodge. We may as well tour those while we're here. Besides, what else would we do back at the room."

Tommy winked.

Blushing, she said, "Besides that." She opened the Disneyland Hong Kong app on her iPhone and studied the other two hotels.

"Anything good?"

"Oh yes, there are tons of shops. We can definitely kill a day gawking at the hotels."

Rubbing his belly, he asked, "Any good places to-"

"-Don't tell me you're hungry already," she scolded. But then she reasoned that after a few hours of shopping, she'd be hungry, too.

Chapter Ten

"What FastPasses did you get for tomorrow?" Victoria asked. After a few hours of shopping, eating, and gawking at the other two hotels, she fixated on their day at Disneyland Hong Kong tomorrow.

"Ah, about that, I have a surprise for you." Tommy winked.

Trying to abate her anger, she bit her tongue. *How dare he not get FastPasses for the next day? Now all of the good rides will be booked up, and they'd have to wait in the standby line with the rest of the schmucks.* But "Oh," was the only word she let escape her lips.

"I'll show you in the room." He waved his magic band on the hotel door's scanner. The green light flashed, and they entered their suite.

Tommy opened his laptop and pulled up his cave plotting software.

"Caves? What's this?" Her eyebrows arched with curiosity. Now she felt bad for getting miffed about Tommy not getting FastPasses for the next day.

"About a week before we met, I had just finished a dig near here. I decided to test my new gadget which plots caves *without* going into them." Tommy beamed like a kid at....

"What's the fun in that?" Victoria quipped.

"It's really hard to discover a cave system. It's just dumb luck."

With a sarcastic tone, she counted off on her fingers, "Like the ones we found under Walt Disney World, Disneyland Paris, Disneyland Shanghai and Disneyland Hong Kong."

"Touché. But this gadget uses a seismic charge. You set off the charge on the surface, then the magical software tells you what is beneath it," Tommy explained.

"That's amazing. Why didn't you go exploring right then and there?" Her excitement built just thinking about the unexplored cave system nearby.

"Grier called me. He and Lilly pushed their wedding up to Christmas Eve. I didn't want to go, but he insisted. And since he'd bought Castle Garrison from my broke father, we have to rely on his good graces to let us continue to live there."

"The wedding! That's where we met. If you had stayed here, our lives would be completely different. It scares me to death to think about how close we were to not meeting and falling in love." A tear dropped onto her cheek because she couldn't imagine her life without Tommy.

"I know, scary huh? But look what I discovered." He pointed to the map and compared it to the map of Disneyland Hong Kong. Most of the cave system is adjacent to Disneyland Hong Kong, but part of it spurred off under Big Grizzly Runaway Mine Cars."

"There's another entrance somewhere nearby." Clapping, elation filled her because she was dying to explore more of the caves where humans survived the Ice Age.

"Let's do this—take an Uber to mainland and procure camping supplies. Then first thing tomorrow, we'll hike and search for another entrance into this vast cave system."

"I'll bring champagne." She kissed him. "I wonder what's *under the magic* this time?" she asked.

Chapter Eleven

"Are we there yet?" Victoria asked from the backseat of an Uber.

"Almost." Tommy studied the map on his iPhone.

Trying to conceal her excitement so as not to alert the Uber driver of their illegal spelunking, she squeezed Tommy's free hand.

Squeezing back, he ordered the driver, "Here, stop at this park."

"Huh, I never knew this was here." The Uber driver stopped, exited the vehicle, opened the door for Victoria, then popped open the trunk to retrieve their suitcases and backpacks.

Tapping away on his phone, Tommy gave the Uber driver a five-star rating, then tipped him enormously.

"What's with the suitcases? I'm pretty sure you can't camp overnight," the Uber driver said.

"Surveying equipment. It's just easier to tote everything in rolling suitcases." Tommy discretely winked to Victoria.

The Uber driver's phone pinged. Studying it, the driver beamed. "Whoa. With a tip like that, I'll break you into the Forbidden Kingdom."

"That won't be necessary, but your discretion is appreciated." Tommy winked.

The Uber driver drove off with an enormous smile, obviously basking in the euphoria of Tommy's $100 tip.

"A park? I'm surprised there are parks here at all. Isn't land a high commodity given China's overpopulation?"

"Yes, but this land has been owned by the Chen Dynasty for centuries. They vowed to never sell or develop this land," he explained.

"Won't we get caught? Isn't this trespassing?" Paranoid, she darted her eyes back-and-forth.

"No, it's open to the public. At least the part above the surface is." Tommy put on his backpack and rolled his suitcase through the rocky terrain.

Walking in tandem, she surveyed their surroundings—rocky hills and dirt. Disneyland Hong Kong appeared on the horizon. "They call this a park? It reminds me of the Badlands, only not as pretty."

Tommy pulled out his iPad, and studied their location compared to what his seismic cave-plotting software showed.

"I know. I think they made it open to the public so no one would trespass. It's not as fun if it's allowed."

A gust of wind blew, chilling Victoria. Rubbing her arms, she said, "Huh, that's odd."

"What?" He turned to the direction she faced.

"I thought tumbleweed blew in the wind." She pointed to several large tumbleweed balls laying on the rocky ground.

"They do." Kissing her cheek, he said, "Victoria, you're a genius!"

Beaming, she said, "I know."

They walked to the pile of tumbleweeds resting against several giant boulders.

Tommy touched the closest tumbleweed. But instead of vines and branches meshed together, these were solid and didn't move. "They're fake and secured to the boulders."

"And good fakes at that." Reaching out, she futilely attempted to move the faux tumbleweed. "It won't budge."

Tommy reached out and knocked on a boulder. An echo resonated. "This boulder is fake, too, and hollow."

"Who would make perfect replicas of tumbleweeds and boulders, then place them in the middle of nowhere?" Studying the horizon with the early morning sun rising, she found her answer.

Tommy must've, too.

Turning to one another, they said in unison, "Disneyland."

Chapter Twelve

"What are they hiding down there?" She stomped her foot.

"Whoa, careful, my love. We wouldn't want these honeycombed caverns to cave in." Tommy protectively pulled her towards him.

"Or do we?" Winking, she recalled how the Catacombs beneath Paris occasionally caved in from the weight of buildings on the surface.

With a raised right eyebrow, he admitted, "That *would* be a way in. But we wouldn't want-"

"-To damage any precious archaeological relics," she interrupted.

"Or die."

"Oh, yeah." She grimaced.

"They must've discovered another entrance and blocked it off. Since they couldn't buy the land from the Chen family, and they couldn't build on it or fill in the entrance, they disguised it. Probably in the middle of the night," he speculated.

She studied the boulder, rubbing it and knocking on it with her hands. "I don't see a hidden door."

"Since the whole thing is hollow, maybe we can just break through it. I've got my hammer and chisel," he suggested.

Laughing, she asked, "Are ya askin' or tellin'? I don't think that's what we need to do. They covered it up, but they would've wanted it accessible. There's probably a hidden lever somewhere. And if we pull it...."

"This isn't a movie. We're not standing in front of an enormous mantel and conveniently rub our hands around the edges and find a lever which opens a secret room." Tommy's tone dripped with sarcasm.

"That's precisely what I'm hoping for." Grinning, she got on her knees and studied the entire boulder and tumbleweed structure. After rubbing her hands over every surface, she tried to keep her disappointment at bay. *Maybe Tommy was right.* "Let me see that map again."

"Hold on a second." Tommy tapped away on his iPad and displayed the map that his seismic gadget thingy generated.

Kneeling in front of the illuminated iPad, she studied the beautiful honeycombed cave system beneath them. Touching the screen, she asked. "Is this where we're at?"

"Yes, I believe so."

Something caught her eye, and she said, "Mmmmm. I wonder...."

"What?"

She brushed the dirt off of her knees and studied the ground. Walking around the boulder and tumbleweed structure, she dragged her Timberland hiking boots through the dirt.

"Are you looking for a big *X* to mark the spot?" Tommy joked.

Part of a circle appeared where she'd just dragged her foot. Following it, she dragged her foot around the perimeter surrounding the structure. When the circle was nearly complete, she smiled.

With a shocked expression, he asked, "What the...?"

Beaming, Victoria gushed, "Not an X, but Mickey Mouse ears!"

Chapter Thirteen

"You can pick up your jaw now," she teased.

A metal outline of Mickey Mouse ears appeared on the ground.

Kneeling, she rubbed the cold metal ears and lifted a lever, also shaped like Mickey Mouse ears. After turning the lever, the ground rumbled. Stepping back, they marveled at the ground rotating around the boulder/tumbleweed structure on some sort of axis.

The structure remained in place, but the ground surrounding it slowly sank beneath the surface. As the ground disappeared, spiral steps formed around the structure, leading down into the earth.

"Oh, my." Tommy shook his head in disbelief.

"That was pretty freakin' cool. Like something out of an Indiana Jones movie." Thoughts of a young Harrison Ford made her smile.

Waving his hand, he gestured. "Ladies first."

Grinning, she donned her large backpack and picked up her suitcase. She couldn't walk down the stairwell fast enough.

They quickly descended into the underground cave system via the hidden spiral staircase.

"Talk about you're 'Hidden Mickey.'" Victoria referred to the numerous Mickey Mouse ears subtly incorporated into Disney property by the Imagineers.

"Good one," he complimented while descending the stairs behind her.

The stairwell ended about thirty feet down from the surface. A tunnel appeared at the foot of the stairs.

"Well, this is too easy." She pointed to the tunnel.

Tommy studied the open staircase. Sunlight poured in. "Wait a minute. What about this? I don't think we should leave it open, do you?"

Begrudgingly, she stopped and dropped her chin. Although she was eager to explore the cave, she didn't want anyone to know they were down here. "You're right."

They parked their suitcases at the entrance to the tunnel.

"Surely there is another Mickey Mouse lever to close the stairs." With her hands on her hips, she meandered around the base of the stairs.

"Well, that was easy." Tommy pointed to the cave wall near the base of the stairs. Another lever, in the shape of Mickey Mouse ears, conveniently hung where a light switch would normally be. Turning to her, he asked, "Would you like to do the honors, my dear?"

"Such a gentleman. You found it, I think the glory is yours," she acquiesced.

"He pulled out the handle, then turned it to the right. Metal clanked, and the ground vibrated. As easily as it opened, the staircase rotated up to the surface. When the sunlight disappeared, the cave's entrance closed with a loud, omniscient thud.

"Why do I feel a sense of foreboding?" she asked, a little worried that it wouldn't open again. Fear washed through her, and she shuddered at the horrific notion.

"Because we're human. Don't fret, my love. We have plenty of food and water." Tommy patted his backpack.

"You're right, besides...."

Kissing her temple, he reassured her. "We have a map of the cave on my iPad. I'm pretty sure it connects back to the cave system beneath Big Grizzly Runaway Mine Cars."

"You're right. What the worst that could happen?"

Chapter Fourteen

"Wow! This is so cool." Victoria studied the walls of the tiny caverns.

"It's just like the caves beneath the roller coaster," Tommy said nonchalantly.

Smacking his chest, she reprimanded, "Stop acting aloof. You love these, too."

Pulling their suitcases, they meandered through the caverns which served as tiny dwellings for humans during the Ice Age.

Tommy slid off his backpack and said, "I better map this cavern." He retrieved the cave scanner from his backpack and held it up like a policeman entrapping speeding drivers. Blue laser beams scanned the cavern, then a three-dimensional image appeared on his MacBook Pro laptop.

"Why are you scanning? I thought you already mapped the cave system with your seismic gadget thingy."

"'Seismic gadget thingy.' I'll be sure to tell the product's marketing department about your great advertising jingle," he quipped.

Miffed, she shot him a basilisk stare.

"Oh, come on, lighten up. But to answer your question, the 'seismic gadget thingy.'" Tommy used air quotes, "Only provides a two-dimensional image. But my scanner plots the cave three dimensionally." Holding up the laptop, he showed her the latest scanned image.

"Okay, that *is* cool. What does the crappy one reveal?" she asked.

Shaking his head in mock frustration, he tapped on his iPad and showed her the screen.

Her eyes volleyed between the laptop and the iPad. "Oh, wow. That is crappy."

"But it gets the job done. It told me there were caves to explore."

Victoria took the iPad from him, then sat on her rolling suitcase. Swiping the images, she stopped on one that intrigued her. "Huh?"

"What?"

"How much did you study these?"

"Not much, why?"

"This one is odd." Using her thumb and middle finger, she touched the screen and zoomed in on the strange image.

"What is it?"

"It seems that a section of the cave is sealed off. It resembles some man-made building beneath the ground. Here, look." She handed him the iPad.

Studying the image, he nodded and agreed. "Huh, you're right. I wonder what it is?"

"How close are we?"

"Not too far, a mile perhaps."

"I can't believe you've had these images for two years and didn't study them," she scolded.

Putting his arms around her waist, he pulled her towards him and said, "I've been a little distracted." Then he kissed her lips.

Laughing, she said, "I'm your shiny object."

He kissed her again. "Oh, yeah."

"Come on, let's go see what Disneyland Hong Kong built down here." She put on her backpack and pulled her suitcase behind her.

Turning the corner, they saw empty wooden crates, just like the ones they saw beneath the rollercoaster, biohazard warning and all.

Chapter Fifteen

"What's with these crates? What are they hiding, and why?" Rubbing his stubbled chin with his thumb and index finger, Tommy leaned over to pick up the empty crate.

Smacking his hand away, Victoria scolded, "Tommy, no! What were you thinking? Why would you touch something with a biohazard warning?"

"Oh, my, God! Thank you, my love." Stepping away from the crate, he inhaled deeply and placed his hand over his heart as if to ward off a heart attack.

"Don't mention it." She shone her flashlight on the cave walls. More wooden crates were stacked neatly against the stone wall.

Tommy studied their location on his iPad. "We should be getting close to that strange anomaly you found in the seismic map."

Turning the corner, she shone her light on something completely unexpected and gasped, "Hazmat suits?"

"What is down here? Should we turn back? This place resembles a quarantine zone."

Curious, but not enough to venture any further, she asked, "Can you see what's inside without going in?"

Tommy peered through the plastic. The radioactive warning label was stamped on cases of *something* stacked everywhere. "Oh, my, God! It's plutonium!"

"A mine? I thought plutonium was a byproduct from nuclear power plants."

"It is. They got it from somewhere and are storing it here. Plutonium is used to make bombs and nuclear weapons. Why would Disneyland have so much plutonium?"

"Isn't plutonium used in fireworks? Is Disney trying to control the plutonium supply so the firework manufacturers never run out?"

Shrugging, Tommy said, "Perhaps. I heard that Disney is the largest purchaser of explosives, even more than the United States Military."

"I don't think they're stockpiling plutonium. I think they are hiding it from terrorists."

"That makes sense. Did they find plutonium, then decide to hide it by building a new Disneyland above it? Or did they just happen to discover someone's hidden stash while they built the park and decided to hide it?"

"I don't know, but I'm not going in there. Remember, we heard *two* news stories about plutonium being stolen from North Korea."

"Let's put the hazmat suits on to protect ourselves from radiation."

They donned the suits and laughed at each other.

Tommy tapped on his iPad and studied the cave system. "There should be a tunnel right here." Tommy pointed to a rock wall.

"Bummer, it's a dead end." Victoria sighed.

"It can't be. According to the seismic map, there're more caves here, giant ones." Tommy studied the iPad, perplexed.

"Maybe there is another entrance to the giant caves. Maybe the caves don't all connect."

Tommy studied the rock wall before them. It wasn't a solid wall, it was a pile of rocks stacked up to block the tunnel.

"Victoria, isn't a natural rock wall. Someone placed these rocks here to keep people out." He pulled a rock from the top of the wall.

"Oh, my, God! You're right." She pulled a rock off the wall and tossed it aside.

Excitedly, they removed enough rocks from the wall to unblock the tunnel. Then they climbed over the remaining rocks and continued through the new tunnel.

After walking a few more yards, they entered a giant cavern. The ceiling soared a hundred feet above their heads. The length of the cavern went on forever.

"It's so dry down here. No humidity, even though we're beneath sea level. Anything could survive down here for thousands of years," Tommy speculated.

Turning a corner, they discovered a gigantic room filled with scrolls and books.

"Anything could survive down here all right, including the Alexandria Library!"

Chapter Sixteen

"How is this possible? Didn't Julius Caesar destroy the Alexandria Library?" Victoria asked, still awestruck at the incredible books and scrolls filling the room.

"Maybe that's what the Egyptians wanted the world to think," Tommy reasoned.

"You could be right. The Egyptians feared that Caesar would ransack their city."

"A reasonable assumption given his tyrannical track record."

"Instead of waiting for Caesar to steal, or worse, *destroy* the library-"

"-They moved it."

"But why China?"

"Think about your geography."

"I don't have to. Someone painted it for us." Victoria pointed to the cave wall.

"Oh, my." Tommy turned to study the crude drawing of Europe and Asia.

"This was back when they thought the world was flat. I don't see North or South America at all."

Reaching to touch it, Tommy retracted his hand from the wall. "I almost forgot about the *manganese*." Without touching the cave wall, Tommy ran his finger along the path from Alexandria to Hong Kong.

"I see it, now. Instead of fleeing into the Aegean Sea, Ptolemy sailed in the opposite direction because he knew Caesar would come from Roma." Victoria pointed to Roma on the ancient map. Then she followed the path from Alexandria to Cairo, then to the Red Sea and through the Gulf of Arden. "Once out in the open waters of the Indian Ocean, Ptolemy meandered around Indonesia and into the South China Sea, all the way to Hong Kong."

"Why do you keep saying Ptolemy? How do you know who moved the Alexandria Library?" he asked.

"Ptolemy started the library. It only makes sense that his descendant, who was probably named after him, would become the custodian of something so important."

"Great point."

"That, plus he signed his name, Ptolemy III." Smirking, she pointed to the black letters on the cave wall. "I'm dying to touch these scrolls. But I'm afraid they'll fall apart." She shuddered, worried about the fragility of these precious scrolls.

"Yeah, don't touch them. They'll need to be catalogued and moved to a museum."

"I'm dying to take a picture, but I'm afraid that my flash will fade the scrolls."

"I'll set the camera on night vision mode so we can document our find," he suggested.

"I wonder why they keep plutonium nearby?"

A familiar voice echoed behind them, "I wondered the same thing."

Chapter Seventeen

Jumping back, Victoria and Tommy turned towards the voice. They recognized him immediately. It was Han, the Cast Member from Big Grizzly Runaway Mine Cars, who'd escorted them out of the park after finding them in the cave beneath the rollercoaster. Only this time, Han yielded a Samaria sword.

Han obviously recognized the truant spelunkers from yesterday because he said, "Not you two again. Didn't I just eject you from the park yesterday? I can't believe that you came back. The nerve. How did you get so far on foot?"

"Please don't hurt us!" she begged, then knelt with her hands above her head.

Han turned to Tommy and ordered, "Down on your knees!"

Tommy knelt next to her and explained, "We entered through the secret stairwell in the Chen Dynasty's public park."

With a perplexed expression, Han asked, "How on earth did you find the other entrance? That's not for Disneyland, that's for the Chen Dynasty." Then he covered his mouth with his left hand, the one not holding the Samurai sword.

Pointing to Tommy, she said, "He discovered the cave system with a seismic gadget thingy. Then I discovered the entrance on the Chen property because that's kind of my thing."

"How much have you seen? You're not supposed to be here. I'm not supposed to be here. But when I was transporting the...." Han arched his right eyebrow. "Did you see...?"

Nodding, Tommy confessed, "We obviously didn't go *in*, just around the plutonium."

"You did more than that. You tore down the rock wall."

Wincing, she said, "We were just exploring. Please don't hurt us."

"Why are you storing plutonium here? And why so close to the Library?" Tommy asked.

"The plutonium is only stored here temporarily, until we can ship it to the park in...." Han paused.

"I assume this is the plutonium stolen from North Korea? Are you just hiding it to keep them from blowing up the rest of the world?" Tommy asked.

"Er, yeah. That's it," Han stammered.

"What are you going to do with us? We promise we won't say a thing about any of this," Victoria promised.

"What about pictures? Did you take any?" Han asked.

Victoria turned to Tommy for guidance, then lied, "No, absolutely not. We're archaeologists. We know not to take a flash photo of the Alexandria Library."

"Good to know. But it doesn't matter, because I can't possibly let you leave this cave...ever!" Han swung the sword high above his head, preparing to strike them.

But before Han swung the sword, he fell forward and collapsed on the ground.

Chapter Eighteen

After Han fell to the ground, an old man stood behind him. His long hair and beard were pure white. Wrinkles on his face confessed his ripe old age, over one-hundred. The man knelt and clutched his hand over his heart, obviously exhausted from rendering Han unconscious.

Instinctively, Victoria and Tommy rose and aided the old man.

"Oh, my, God! Are you okay? How can we help? And how can we thank you?" she asked, then helped him to lie down. She quickly grabbed her travel pillow which conveniently hung on the outside of her backpack. After placing the pillow on the hard rock floor, she cradled his head onto the pillow.

"Thank you. Your kindness towards strangers will be rewarded." The old man smiled.

"We have so many questions." Tommy offered the old man some water.

With a wise tone, the old man said, "And I have all the answers." Squeezing her hand, he tried to get up.

"Sir, I think you should rest," she suggested.

"Just help me sit up." The old man pulled himself up using Victoria's hand. He leaned against the wall and moved the pillow behind his back.

"Can we get you anything?" she asked.

Waving his hand nonchalantly, he said, "My years are almost up. Let me tell you my story, the quick version."

Victoria and Tommy quickly nodded their eagerness for the old man to tell them his tale.

"First, forgive my great-grandson. Although he is protective of our legacy, his overzealous commitment can be trying."

"Will he be okay?"

"Of course, I just used an ancient trick on a pressure point in his shoulder. He'll be up in a bit. First, let me introduce myself, I'm Master Chen of the Chen Dynasty. I'm the direct descendant of Ptolemy I Soter, the founder of the great Alexandria Library. When the grandson of Ptolemy feared Caesar would destroy our treasure, he moved the library to his fleet of merchant ships and sailed all the way to China. He discovered these caves and hid the precious library down here. He coated the scrolls with a protective sealant to keep them from disintegrating. Over the years, he protected the library and passed the responsibility down to the next generation. Over time, we bred with the locals and eventually took the Chen name. My ancestors bought the land above us and deeded the land to the Chen Dynasty Trust which holds the property in perpetuity to protect it forever. The land can never be sold or developed."

"But shouldn't these scrolls be shared with the world?" she asked.

Nodding he explained, "Not the scrolls itself, but the knowledge in them will be shared with the rest of the world. But the location of the Library must remain a secret, forever. My descendants are digitizing the library. We are close to completion and plan to announce the library's existence one day. But the time is never right. Too many wars always waging. Mankind has always been at war with themselves."

"What about the plutonium?" she asked.

Master Chen waved nonchalantly, "They don't ask about the library and I don't ask about the plutonium. But I'm told it's almost moved to a land far, far away."

"Good, because surely you've been exposed to radiation poisoning. Do you go topside ever?"

"Oh, yes. Most of the family lives in Hong Kong. We rotate the responsibility of guarding the library and copying its contents. But when the time comes for a family member to die, most of us wish to live out their remaining days down here instead of in some hospital."

"I understand. I would, too," she said.

"Now, before Han wakes up, I need you to leave and promise never to return or utter a word about the final resting place of the Alexandria Library."

Nodding, Victoria squeezed Master Chen's hand and said, "We promise. Thank you."

Chapter Nineteen

"Where are you taking me on our last night in Hong Kong? I just assumed we'd eat in Tinkerbell's castle since we usually try to eat one meal in the castle at each park." Victoria walked up the steps of the Hong Kong Disneyland Hotel. Its theme was identical to the Grand Floridian next to the Magic Kingdom in Orlando, Florida.

"I know. But surprisingly, Tinkerbell's Castle does not have a restaurant inside like the others. At least not yet," Tommy explained.

Stopping at the entrance to Walt's Café, a slight disappointment filled her. "You had me wear my best dress to a café?"

Tommy kissed her cheek. "You know I love that sexy red dress. But despite the name, Walt's Café is the only fine dining offered at Disneyland Hong Kong."

After checking in with the maître d', they were escorted to their table.

En route to their table, she noticed the Victorian theme of Walt's Café. Antique chandeliers dimly lit the restaurant. Cream-colored walls were decorated with dozens of vintage framed photographs of Walter Elias Disney. With dark mahogany moldings and brass appointments, Walt's Café resembled the restaurant in the Grand Floridian. "It reminds me of-"

"-Victoria & Alberts," Tommy finished her sentence.

The maître d' sat them at a cozy table for two overlooking the beautiful gardens. In the background was the South China Sea.

Studying their menus, they immediately decided. Simultaneously, they said, "Rack of lamb."

They quickly ordered a heavy Cabernet Sauvignon to accompany their upcoming red, gamy meat.

"Oh, my, God!" Victoria hollered loud enough for a few nearby diners to turn and shoot her disdaining scowls. Anxiety filled her because the park was now closed and their flight for Tokyo tomorrow departed before the park reopened. Now she may never get another chance to ride Pirates of the Caribbean in Disneyland Hong Kong.

"What is it, my love?" Tommy grabbed her hand and studied her with a worried expression.

Managing to lower her voice, she asked, "Pirates of the Caribbean. How could we have forgotten?"

"What about it?" Tommy breathed a sigh of relief. The way she'd hollered made him think that the sky was falling.

"We forgot to ride it. We walked right by that pirate experience thingy where the pirates takeover Adventureland, but we never went on the ride because you rushed us off to our next FastPass. Can we change our flight? Perhaps just push it back a few hours so we can go back and ride Pirates of the Caribbean. We're not going *into* Tokyo Disneyland tomorrow anyway. So, what's the rush to leave tomorrow?" Victoria rambled on like a boring lecturer.

Tommy laughed hysterically and grabbed his belly as if that would abate his inappropriate amusement.

Miffed at his lackadaisical and comical response, she chided, "This isn't funny!" She retrieved her iPhone from her cobalt-blue Louis Vuitton handbag and logged onto the airline app.

Finally winding down his laughter, he touched her hand holding the phone and guided it into his. "I'm sorry, but it's just so endearing that you love Disney so much that you think the world has ended because you missed *one* ride."

She gave him the evil eye, then sighed. "You're right. With all the problems in the world, I reckon missing *one* ride at Disneyland Hong Kong won't kill me." She dropped her phone back into her purse and drained the rest of her wine.

Tommy shook his head and grinned.

Shrugging, she finally smiled and asked, "It's not that funny, is it?"

"It's not that, well, sort of. I debated not telling you this. But that would be *too* mean." He refilled her wine goblet.

"Tell me what?" Her tone grew perturbed again.

"That you got upset over nothing."

"You're right, I did. I'm behaving like a bratty toddler who just had her favorite doll taken away. What the hell is wrong with me?" She sighed.

"No, that's not it. There is *not* a Pirates of the Caribbean ride at Disneyland Hong Kong, just that pirate experience thing we walked through."

"Are you serious? How could they *not* have a Pirates of the Caribbean ride? It's a classic. Walt must be rolling in his grave right now." She waved to one of his many vintage portraits hung on the cream-colored walls of Walt's Café.

"Or he's trying to turn in his cryogenically frozen chamber," he joked about the Urban Legend.

"So, I guess Johnny Depp won't be making a surprise appearance at Disneyland Hong Kong to promote the latest installment of the *Pirates of the Caribbean* movie franchise." She referred to their trip last week at Disneyland Shanghai where the *real* Johnny Depp, dressed as Captain Jack Sparrow, worked a Character Dining experience in the Castle. He'd kissed her hand and nonverbally pleaded her silence.

"That *was* pretty cool." Tommy cut into his rack of lamb, cooked a perfect medium rare.

"We haven't discussed the elephant in the room." She referred to their recent discoveries—the caves where humans survived the Ice Age, the stolen plutonium, and most importantly, the long-lost contents of the Alexandria Library.

"I'm thinking two out of three isn't bad." Smiling, Tommy sipped his wine.

"You just read my mind. Keep the hidden, stolen plutonium a secret, and go public with the Ice Age caves and the Alexandria Library." Victoria ate the last bite of her scrumptious rack of lamb.

"But what about our promise to Master Chen?"

"My fingers were crossed." She laughed.

"Sounds like a plan. But let's wait until-"

"-*After* Tokyo Disneyland to announce our find," she interrupted, then sipped her wine.

"We'll have a lot to announce to the public. Don't forget about Noah's Ark."

"When will we have time to visit the last Disneyland park? Although I'm anxious to see the original Disneyland in California, a part of me wants to savor it. You know, have something to look forward to," she reasoned.

Tommy's face lit up with excitement. "I have a brilliant idea. Let's have our wedding *and* honeymoon at Disneyland in California!"

Tears dropped on her cheek. "Oh, Tommy. That's perfect."

"Well, then. Now that that's settled. When would you like to marry me, my love?" Tommy asked.

Staring up at the ceiling, she contemplated their work schedules, holidays, and dates that were significant to her. Then the most important day of her life flooded to the forefront of her mind—the day she met Tommy Manchester Garrison. "December 21."

"Ah, the day we met." Taking her hand in his, Tommy leaned across the table and kissed her.

After their kiss, Victoria noticed a handsome man with dark hair, dark eyes and a trim beard wearing glasses.

He stared directly at her, held up his water goblet and smiled.

The familiarity puzzled her, but just for an instant. Then the realization sank in. She mouthed, "Are you?"

Nodding humbly, he placed his index finger to his lips to nonverbally signal her silence.

Turning back to Tommy, she asked, "Didn't you say it was a shame that we wouldn't be here for New Year's Eve because they were opening the new Iron Man experience on January 1st?"

"Yes, we just missed it by only two days. It sounds pretty cool, too." Tommy slumped his shoulders defeatedly.

"Don't they usually have celebrities at the grand opening of rides?" she asked.

"Yes. For example, they had some of the cast from Once Upon a Time at the grand opening of the new Fantasyland in Orlando. They had Tom Hanks and Tim Allen, who played Woody and Buzz Lightyear, at the Toy Story ride years ago. Why do you ask?"

Smiling, Victoria nodded her head towards the dark-haired man with glasses behind her. "Don't look now, but the *real* Iron Man is at the table next to us—Robert Downey Jr!"

THE END

Part Five
Platinum Princess

AN ELEMENTS OF MYSTERY
UNDER THE MAGIC ADVENTURE

TERRI TALLEY VENTERS

Prologue

"We love London, Daddy." Catherine, Cat for short, perched in front of Big Ben's enormous clock face. The magnificent skyline, including the London Eye, dominated their view. The dark water of the Thames meandered through the city below.

"This is so cool." Connor, Cat's twin, smiled.

"I love this age." Penelope Manchester, the twins' mother, leaned into her husband, Saint Michael the Archangel.

"I know. Five is a great age. We must enjoy every precious moment with our babies. Before we know it, they'll be teenagers with an attitude." Michael wrapped his white wings with gold tips around his wife and reincarnated soul mate.

"Daddy, isn't this where Peter Pan departed from to take Michael, Jon and Wendy to Neverland?" Cat asked.

"You don't believe such nonsense, do you? You just have Peter Pan on your mind because we saw his statue in Hyde Park today." Penelope rolled her eyes.

"Where's your belief?" Michael asked. "I'm an angel, you're a powerful witch and our twins are witches with wings. But you don't believe in Peter Pan?"

"But, I...."

"Come on kids, flap your wings. 'Second star to the right, then straight on 'til morning,'" Michael said, excitedly.

"Yippee!" the twins sang in unison. Flapping their wings, they levitated away from Big Ben.

Penelope shot Michael a puzzled glare.

Extending his massive wings, he gestured for her to embrace him and assume her usual flying position.

Penelope clung to him tightly, and the magical family flew into the night.

* * * *

The morning sun's first rays kissed their wings as they flew towards the rising sun in the east. Michael nodded to the twins, signaling them to descend.

Following his lead, the magical family flew towards the Earth's surface.

Confusion filled Penelope as they hovered a few hundred feet above the surface. "Cinderella's Castle?"

"Tokyo Disneyland." Michael grinned 'like a kid at....'

"Yippee! We're going to Disneyland." The twins fluttered down to Cinderella's Castle and landed on the balcony of the highest turret.

"Oh, but I thought you wanted to go to Neverland," Michael teased.

The twins whispered to one another, obviously consulting this magical dilemma.

Always speaking for her twin, Cat stepped forward and proclaimed, "Neverland first, then Tokyo Disneyland."

Penelope gasped, "I remember now, from the *Book of Legends*."

"Took you long enough," Michael quipped.

"Mommy, Mommy, please tell us the story," the twins begged.

Penelope explained, "Neverland is real. It was a magical island in the Pacific Ocean. But modern civilization wanted to build on it. My ancestors, who wanted to protect the island without revealing themselves, created a portal to another dimension. They moved Neverland through the portal, protecting it forever."

"Do you remember the spell?" Michael asked.

Nodding, she said, "You just have to believe and add Fairy dust."

Michael held a small vial containing indigo blue dust. "Indium works, too. When a Fairy dies, their magical form turns into crystalized Fairy dust. Scientists even thought it was a new element—indium."

Penelope took the vial, threw the dust into the air, waved her hand, and believed in Neverland.

Dust spiraled in the air, creating an indigo blue cloud—a portal.

The magical family flew through the portal. Cinderella's Castle and Tokyo Disneyland disappeared. They now hovered over a lush island. Mermaids lounged on the rocks near the shore, sunning themselves.

Beaming, Michael proclaimed, "Welcome to Neverland!"

Chapter One

"Is this safe?" Victoria Ventures asked her handsome fiancé, Tommy Garrison, before sliding into the backseat of a driverless car. She promptly fastened her seatbelt, performed the sign of the cross, and prayed for safe passage.

"I hear it's safer than humans driving cars. Humans tend to get *distracted* while driving." With a teasing tone, Tommy referred to her tendency for distraction by shiny objects. He slid in next to her, then typed the address into the car's navigation system.

Their route appeared as a blue line on the screen. The computer calculated their fare, then requested a credit card to pay for the ride from Haneda Airport to Tokyo Disneyland.

"Are we there yet?" Victoria asked.

Yawning, Tommy said, "I wish. I could use a nap."

"It's 6.30 in the morning. How can you be tired?" She smacked his chest playfully.

"Are you serious? That redeye flight from Hong Kong was brutal." He rolled his eyes.

"Amen. Are you going to tell me where we are staying?" she asked with her best beguiling smile.

Shaking his head with mock frustration, he asked, "Why can't you just be surprised?"

The car pulled out of the airport terminal and safely merged onto the highway. The wheel turned by itself, then the car accelerated.

Victoria marveled at the highly sophisticated computerized car driving them to their destination— the 'Happiest Place on Earth.' One of six to be precise.

Their trip to Tokyo Disneyland represented the fifth Disneyland park around the world. After their first date at Walt Disney World in Orlando, Florida, the archaeological couple vowed to visit all six Disney locations. They saved the original Disneyland in Anaheim, California for last. It seemed poetic to end their Bucket List journey with the park where it all began in 1955 when Walter Elias Disney wanted to build an amusement park for his young daughters.

Covering her eyes, she said, "I'm not sure I can watch this."

Tommy pushed a button, and a dark partition rose between the front and back seats, blocking their view of the empty driver's seat.

"You can open your eyes now." He prodded her arm.

"Oh, thank you. Now I feel like I'm in a tiny limousine." She sighed.

"Too bad there isn't a bar back here." Tommy surveyed the backseat of the driverless car.

"Let's turn on the television." She pointed to a flat screen.

Tommy fiddled with the buttons and turned the television on. Then he flipped through various stations until he found the BBC. "At least it's in English."

"Thank you. I need a distraction." Smiling, she waited for a quick-witted quip.

"Thanks for the set up, but I'm not touching that with a ten-foot pole." Shaking his head, he grabbed her hand, squeezed it, and placed their joined hands on his lap.

"You're a smart man, Tommy Manchester Garrison," she praised.

The BBC weather appeared with a satellite view of Earth. Dozens of hurricanes, tropical storms and monsoons appeared all around the world.

"What's with all these storms? I've never seen so many at once." She stared in horror.

"Luckily, none of them should affect our trip." Tommy squeezed her hand reassuringly.

"But it's January. Hurricane season is in the summer when the warm ocean waters fuel hurricanes." Victoria recalled her hurricane formation knowledge. Growing up in Charleston, South Carolina, she considered herself an expert on hurricanes.

Shrugging, he said, "Al Gore was right."

"You take that back!" She smacked his chest.

"Whoa! Chill woman. I'm a diehard Republican, too. But you must admit, Global Warming is a serious threat."

"There's a conspiracy theory that it's not Mother Nature generating hurricanes, monsoons and tsunamis."

"Then who? How? Why?" he asked.

"Who?—Extremists, terrorists. How?—Who knows. Why?—There's a lot of lunatics out there!"

Chapter Two

"What the....?" Victoria's mouth gaped as the magnificent hotel appeared on the horizon.

The driverless car drove closer to what she hoped were their opulent accommodations for their seven-night stay at Tokyo Disneyland.

"You got a little drool here." Tommy gently rubbed her lower lip with his thumb.

"Is that....?" She turned to him excitedly, 'like a kid at....'

"Yes. That's where we are staying—the Tokyo DisneySea Hotel Miracosta." Tommy beamed, obviously pleased that the hotel excited her.

The car pulled up to the circular driveway, printed a receipt, and popped the trunk. A bellhop, dressed like a Venetian Gondolier, promptly retrieved their luggage from the trunk.

"I feel like I'm in Tuscany, not Tokyo." Exiting the car, she stared at the magnificent hotel with a Tuscan theme.

"Good, because I believe that's the theme they were going for."

"DisneySea?" She turned to him, perplexed.

"DisneySea is the second park adjacent to Tokyo Disneyland." Tommy nodded to the other park.

They followed the bellhop with their luggage through the lobby. With minimal wait, they were checked into the Il Magnifico Suite and received their park tickets for the week.

The hotel clerk then scanned their park tickets and asked them to verify their identity with a finger pressure scan.

"Wait, why are they scanning our park tickets now?" she asked.

"Because the Hotel Miracosta is actually *in* the DisneySea Park!" Tommy grinned.

"Get out! Are you serious? That's awesome," she squealed.

They followed the bellhop who wheeled a luggage cart carrying their suitcases. They entered the amazing suite, and Tommy tipped the bellhop generously.

Victoria was immediately drawn to the private terrace. She opened the sliding glass door and stared in awe at the DisneySea park sprawled out before her eyes.

Given the early hour, the park was still closed. The breaking dawn appeared on the horizon. The rising sun's early rays peeked through the darkness, slowly lighting up the morning sky.

Tommy slid in behind her, then wrapped his arms around her tiny waist.

She leaned back into him, and they enjoyed the sunrise together. Euphoria filled her, and she sighed.

Tommy turned her to face him, looked lovingly into her eyes and said, "In keeping with tradition." He referred to their first kiss on the balcony of the Grand Floridian Resort overlooking the Magic Kingdom. Since then, he'd kissed her on the balcony of each Disneyland hotel in Paris, Shanghai and Hong Kong.

Closing her eyes, she let her handsome fiancé kiss her on the balcony of the Tokyo DisneySea Hotel Miracosta overlooking the DisneySea park.

Chapter Three

"Now what?" Victoria asked.

Grinning, Tommy rubbed his belly and said, "We eat."

"How did I know?" she quipped.

"Besides, we have time to kill before the parks open." He offered her his elbow.

Slipping her hand into the crook of his elbow, she followed him out the door and down the hall to the open elevator which greeted them with the famous song from the movie *Pinocchio,* "When You Wish Upon A Star."

He grinned with a guilty expression.

Studying him, she asked, "You already know where we're going to eat, don't you?"

Grinning, he said, "Guilty. I did my homework."

The elevator stopped on the first floor, then opened. They entered the lobby and followed the signs to the Bella Vista Lounge.

Perplexed, she asked with a judgmental tone, "Isn't it a bit early to imbibe?"

Rubbing his belly, he grinned. "Breakfast buffet."

A Cast Member escorted them to a table for two overlooking the port town of the Mediterranean Harbor, part of the DisneySea park.

She gasped, "Oh, Tommy. This is lovely. I feel like I'm in Italy. Now I'm in the mood for a cappuccino."

"Sounds great. It's way before ten," he referred to the unwritten Italian rule that only tourists drank cappuccinos after ten a.m. Real Italians switched to espresso after ten.

"I thought you were a tea man," she chided.

Gesturing to their Italian atmosphere, he teased, "'When in Rome.'" Turning to the server, he ordered in Italian. "*Due Cappuccinos, per favore.*"

The server placed two menus in front of them, then scurried off to make the cappuccinos.

"Well, I'm getting the buffet." Tommy placed his white napkin on the table.

Standing, she announced, "Me, too. I'm starved. That bag of peanuts on the plane wasn't a real breakfast."

After filling a plate with her favorite breakfast items—hash browns, scrambled eggs and cheese—she returned to her table and smothered the whole concoction with honey. "A Little Asher."

"Huh?" he asked, then shoveled a heaping spoonful of scrambled eggs into his mouth.

"Skeeters, my favorite breakfast place to eat in Gainesville, served breakfast twenty-four hours a day. The Little Asher was my favorite meal, especially at two a.m. after the bars and clubs closed."

"Any place that serves breakfast all day is worthy of my patronage. You'll have to take me there sometime. Maybe you can take me to one of your beloved Florida Gator football games." He gulped his cappuccino.

"I'd love to take you to a game in the Swamp. But Skeeters closed," she sighed, missing her beloved college town.

"Sorry to hear that, but I can cook that concoction for you anytime. Us Garrison men are fantastic chefs." He beamed with pride, then gestured to the server to bring two more cappuccinos.

"Tell me about the parks. What sort of rides do they have at Tokyo Disneyland and DisneySea?" She drained her cappuccino and relished the caffeine infusion.

"Can't you just be surprised?" he asked.

"Can you at least tell me which park we're going to first? I'm looking right at Cinderella's Castle."

"Me, too." Tommy stared at the beautiful castle in the distance. His expression turned shocked. "What the...? Did you see that?"

Gasping, she pointed. "Is that a woman floating in the air?"

"You only see a woman? You don't see the..., I can't even say it." He rubbed his eyes and studied the sky in front of them. He retrieved his iPhone and quickly snapped a picture.

"What? Tell me. I just saw a woman float down from the sky and land on the balcony of the castle." She stared, awestruck. "Now she just disappeared before my eyes."

Blinking, Tommy studied his iPhone. "Huh, the camera doesn't show the others. I wonder why only I can see them?"

"What others? What did you see?" she asked with a bewildered tone.

"I saw a family with wings. A winged man carried a woman, and two children with wings flew next to them. They landed on the balcony of the castle before they disappeared into a blue spinning cloud!"

Chapter Four

"How much time do we have until the parks open?" Victoria asked.

They exited the Bella Vista Lounge, stuffed from the breakfast buffet.

Tommy looked at his watch. "We have time to browse through the shops in the hotel."

"Shopping? Oh, I love you." She kissed his tan, stubbly cheek.

Arm in arm, they meandered the high-end shopping area at the DisneySea Hotel Tokyo Miracosta.

Several young girls walked into a store. Then several young princesses emerged from the same store. The ones which emerged donned Disney Princess dresses and tiny tiaras crowning a glittered hair bun.

"What is this place?" She walked into the store which was every little girl's dream.

Tommy read the sign, smiled and said, "The Bibbidi Bobbidi Boutique."

"This may sound crazy, but I really want to go into the park dressed like a Disney Princess." She gave him her best, 'pretty please' plea.

"Like Princess Leia in the gold bikini." Tommy winked with a perverted, yet hopeful, expression.

Annoyed, she playfully smacked his chest. "You wish. I'd forgotten that Princess Leia is now a Disney Princess since Disney purchased the Star Wars Franchise from George Lucas for only four point something *billion* dollars." She shook her head, incredulous.

"I heard they already recouped their costs."

"I'm afraid it would be too cold to wear a gold bikini at Disneyland today, but perhaps back in the room later." She winked suggestively.

"Well, in that case, go ahead, become a princess for a day." Tommy gestured for her to enter the queue already filled with dozens of little girls.

Next to the queue, racks of Disney Princess costumes beckoned her. Thumbing through her choices, she couldn't decide between Cinderella or Aurora. Frustration worried her when she couldn't find any dresses in her size.

A Cast Member, dressed in a butler's tuxedo with tails, approached her. Holding an iPad, he asked. "How old is your daughter?"

"Excuse me?" she asked.

The Cast Member studied the little girls in the queue and appeared to mentally pair them with their mothers. Then he asked, "Where is your little girl?"

"We don't have any children. I just want to be a princess today," she confessed.

The Cast Member pointed to a sign and said, "I'm sorry, Your Royal Highness."

Panicked, she grasped her throat and wanted to cry. Disappointment washed through her when she read the sign—The Bibbidi Bobbidi Boutique was only for girls ages twelve and under.

"Oh, Honey, I'm sorry." Tommy pulled her close.

"Isn't that age discrimination?" she asked with an offended tone.

"I'm afraid it is." The Cast Member turned his head to ascertain no little girls could hear him. Then he whispered, "It's for the safety of our young guests. Little girls could easily confuse one of our *real* Disney Princesses with a costumed, grown up guest."

"Oh, I see your point." With an understanding, yet disturbed nod, she realized that some pedophile could easily dress up like a Disney princess and lure unsuspecting children away like the Pied Piper.

"But just next door." The Cast Member pointed. "The jewelry store sells tiaras for lovely ladies like yourself."

"Oh, thank you." With new hope, she practically skipped out of the Bibbidi Bobbidi Boutique and studied the display window of the jewelry store.

"Oh, Tommy, look at them all." Pointing, she admired all the glistening tiaras.

Grinning, he lovingly teased, "You and your shiny objects."

Chapter Five

"I have a tiara!" Victoria sang, thrilled about her new platinum and cubic zirconium tiara. She'd kicked herself for forgetting to pack the tiara Tommy had bought her at Walt Disney World in Florida.

They strolled through the DisneySea park holding hands. Elation filled her, and she restrained her urge to skip through the park. She was afraid her new tiara would fall off. Besides, queens never skip.

A Cast Member bowed to her and said, "Your Royal Highness."

Swooning at the attention, she asked, "Where to first? We forgot to get a map, but I see some cool areas on the signs." Pointing, she read aloud, "Mysterious Island, Mermaid Lagoon, Mediterranean Harbor, Lost River Delta and Arabian Coast."

Tommy studied her and smiled.

"Let me guess. It's a surprise." She'd normally pout when Tommy withheld their destination to surprise her. But she'd either grown accustomed to his insatiable need to surprise her, or she was just so happy to be at Disneyland that she'd just enjoy every moment at the 'Happiest place on Earth' with her handsome fiancé.

"Of course, my love." He squeezed her hand and smiled more than usual.

"What? Don't tell me you're hungry again." She couldn't fathom stuffing another morsel of food down her gullet.

"Oh, dear, God, no." He shook his head. "It's the surprise. You're going to love this one the most."

"What? Another archaeological find of the Millennium? What haven't we found yet?" she asked.

They stopped at Mysterious Island and studied the faux archaeological dig sight. Gesturing towards the ride, Tommy said, "Atlantis."

"Touché. This reminds me of the movie *Mysterious Island* where they find the lost city of Atlantis and escape in Captain Nemo's Nautilus submarine before the island sank again."

"Spoiler alert," he scolded.

"What are you talking about? We watched it together," she reminded him.

"But the kiddies around may not have seen it." He gestured to several young tourists meandering about the park.

"I'm surprised that you wanted to visit the DisneySea park first. I figured that after what you thought you saw this morning at the castle, you'd want to head over to the castle at Disneyland."

"Ah, you finally brought up the elephant in the room." Tommy's expression turned bewildered, and he shook his head.

"You mean, the angel." Doubt filled her. *How could Tommy see three flying angels and she couldn't?* It was a ridiculous notion. She was an archaeologist and only believed in dinosaurs and other prehistoric creatures because she'd dug them up out of the dirt with her own hands.

"I still can't believe it. And what happened to them? They just disappeared. I saw them land on the castle balcony, then some sort of blue circle appeared in the air. I know the castle was far from the window at breakfast. But I thought I saw them fly through the round spinning cloud, then disappear."

Chapter Six

"What? We're not going on the Journey To The Center Of The Earth ride? It looks so cool." Victoria made a futile attempt to drag Tommy to the giant volcano.

"We've got FastPasses for the Journey ride later. Come on. Let's be one of the first ones on your surprise ride." Tommy studied the Disney Parks app on his iPhone. Shielding the screen from her, he memorized the path leading to the surprise destination. Holding hands, he escorted her through the Mermaid Lagoon area.

Pointing she said, "Oh, cool. Ariel's Grotto." Victoria meandered into the self-guided area and entered an underground playground. Ariel's Grotto was a life size replica of the place where Ariel kept her human treasures in the movie, *The Little Mermaid*.

Shaking his head, Tommy said, "I almost avoided this area because I knew you'd get distracted."

"I loved that movie growing up. My girlfriends from Charleston—Lilly, Britta and Chelsea—and I watched all the Disney animated films together. I still have a bunch on VHS tapes back home. In fact, my copy of *The Little Mermaid* is *extra* special." She winked suggestively.

With a perplexed expression, he asked, "How so?"

"The cover of *The Little Mermaid* video showcases King Triton's Palace. The palace is a giant gold castle with towering columns. But one of the towers contains phallic imagery."

He gently smacked her shoulder. "What? Get out! Someone drew a cartoon of some dude's junk in the castle?" he asked with a shocked tone.

"Yep. I learned in my marketing class at the University of Florida that a Disney Imagineer was laid off. Disgruntled, he painted the tip of a circumcised penis on the cover. No one noticed until it was too late."

"How could no one notice?"

"It was subtle. In fact, once I heard about it in class, I immediately went back to my apartment and searched for the phallic imagery. And there it was. Once Disney discovered the disturbing image, they pulled all the copies off the shelves. But since my mother purchased *The Little Mermaid* on the day it was released, I'm one of the lucky ones who still own a vintage copy. Maybe I'll sell it on eBay one day."

Tommy pointed, "Here, stand in front of the statue of Prince Eric and I'll take your picture."

Admiring the giant statue of Prince Eric, the one that fell from the boat in the movie, she puckered her lips and pretended to kiss Eric's cheek.

Tommy snapped away with his iPhone's camera.

"Put that one on Instagram," she ordered.

"Chill, woman." He taped away on his iPhone. "Done."

"Oh, yeah. My surprise." She gestured for Tommy to lead the way.

Walking hand-in-hand, they left the Mermaid lagoon area, and arrived at their destination.

Gesturing towards the sign, he said, "Tada."

Victoria froze. Then she covered her mouth and cried tears of joy. "Is this a real ride?"

Tommy beamed and waved his arm at her favorite childhood ride—20,000 Leagues Under The Sea.

* * * *

"That was awesome!" Victoria squealed. Elation filled her and she couldn't stop smiling.

"That was pretty cool. I'd never been on the original ride. How does it compare?" Tommy asked.

Holding up her hand, she disclosed, "Keep in mind that I was ten-years-old when I first rode 20,000 Leagues Under The Sea. The Nautilus submarine was a replica from the one in the book. The ride in Orlando was bigger and held a lot more people per vessel. You sat in front of a porthole to see into the water. This Nautilus didn't look like a submarine at all. It was simply a glass submersible which held only six people."

"I liked Captain Nemo's search for Atlantis part of the ride."

"What's with all these Atlantis references—Mysterious Island and 20,000 Leagues Under The Sea?" she asked.

"I guess a Vernian designed those rides. Jules Verne regained popularity with the movies—*Journey To The Center Of The Earth* and *Mysterious Island*."

"I recall a documentary which aired just before Disney released the animated movie—*Atlantis*."

"The one with Melissa Joan Hart from *Sabrina The Teenage Witch*?" he asked.

Shocked, she said, "Yes. But I'm not sure if I'm impressed or dis*enchanted*."

"Good one," he said, obviously appreciating her clever double entendre. "But, I'm an archaeologist, too. Discoveries like that fascinate me."

"It impressed me how they mapped the ocean floor to narrow the search for Atlantis. I remember, the experts thought modern-day Cuba was once Atlantis. Only the tops of Atlantis' mountains remained above the water," she reiterated the study's results.

"And Cuba is located in a prime shipping area for trade."

"But so is Tokyo."

"Do you think...?" He arched his right eyebrow inquisitively.

"Who knows?" She shrugged. "Perhaps we'll find Atlantis beneath Tokyo Disneyland!"

Chapter Seven

"Ready to go to the center of the Earth?" Tommy asked, then extended his elbow to escort her to the next ride.

Placing her hand in the crook of his elbow, Victoria said with an exaggerated Southern accent, "Well, thank ya, kind sir."

They walked towards the volcano which dominated the Mysterious Island area of the park. Surrounding the volcano was a dig site.

"Wow, they did a great job with this dig site. It looks so real. And I've been on enough digs to know." She marveled at its authenticity and mentally applauded the brilliance of Disney's Imagineers.

"Do you think they're hiding a real dig site in plain sight?" he asked.

Shrugging, she said, "Given our track record for finding astonishing things under the first four Disney parks we've visited, who knows what we'll find beneath DisneySea Tokyo."

After scanning their FastPasses, they walked right onto the ride and buckled their seatbelts. A narrow, silver vessel took them into the volcano, then plummeted to the center of the Earth. The vessel slowly meandered through a neon jungle illuminated with black lights. Giant mushrooms resembled the ones in the book and movie. Neon centipedes, along with other oversized bugs, crawled about the jungle. The theme turned scary as the center of the Earth grew hotter. Flames blasted throughout, and a scary monster appeared. With a narrow escape from the monster, the roller coaster ascended quickly, then shot them out of the volcano back onto the Earth's surface in Italy.

The ride slowed down as they waited in the queue to disembark.

"Seeing Italy reminded me of this great Italian restaurant in our hotel." Tommy rubbed his belly.

Smacking his chest, she teased, "Always thinking about food."

"Hell, yeah!" His *duh* was implied.

"It's too bad that the ride didn't break down like the one in Disneyland Hong Kong," she recalled.

"Yeah, that was too easy. But we never went back and finished the ride. We were too busy with our truant exploring."

Their vessel waited in a narrow tunnel. An opening caught her eye. Turning, she ascertained that no Disney Cast Members lurked nearby. Faking nausea, she said, "I think I'm going to be sick." She unbuckled her seat belt, climbed out of the silver vessel and ran to the opening.

"Victoria! What are you doing?" He climbed out of the vessel and followed her.

She hunched over, coughed, and pretended to vomit.

Tommy asked, "Are you okay? I don't think we're supposed to just hop out of the vehicle in the middle of the ride."

Grinning, she said. "I'm fine. I should move to Hollywood and become an actress. You believed my performance." She bowed. "Thank you. No applause necessary."

His expression turned relieved. "I'm glad you're okay. I forgot to remind you to take Dramamine before we rode on roller coasters."

"I did, remember? After I puked on the Big Grizzly Runaway Mine Cars at Disneyland Hong Kong, I'm motivated to take Dramamine before we enter a Disney park." She placed her palm over her stomach.

"What on Earth possessed you to hop off the ride like that?" he scolded.

"Remember the dig site in front of the volcano?" she asked excitedly.

"Yeah, I thought it looked real."

Victoria gestured towards the entrance to a cave. "I think it *is* real."

Chapter Eight

"Victoria! Oh, my, God! How did you know this was here?" Excited, Tommy kissed her cheek.

"I just happened to see it when we passed through that tunnel. I know a real cave when I see one," she boasted.

"I hate to enter a cave without supplies. But I don't want to risk coming out, getting caught and miss this opportunity to explore this cave."

"I have two big bottles of water in my cinch sack." She nodded to her fuchsia cinch sack hanging from her back.

"Me, too." Tommy patted his backpack.

"That's enough for one day," she reasoned.

"After you, my love." He gestured towards the cave's entrance.

Shining her flashlight that she conveniently brought, Victoria led them through the cave's entrance. The rock walls narrowed, and the rocky path slanted downward. They slowly descended through the tunnel. Wood beams supported the ceiling. Chisels and other tools lay haphazardly strewn about.

Victoria picked up a chisel, which felt at home in her hand, and couldn't wait to peck away at something.

Tommy picked up a walking stick and followed her through the tunnel.

"I wonder what they're excavating down here."

"I don't know. But I wish I had my cave plotting software and some twine to mark our path." He snapped his fingers disappointedly.

"Luckily, the tunnel hasn't branched off. It's hard to get lost when there is only one path," she reasoned.

After about an hour, Tommy stopped and rubbed his belly. "Honey, did you pack any snacks?"

Perturbed at his insatiable appetite, she halted and said, "Of course. I packed BelVita cinnamon crackers." She slid her cinch sack off her shoulders, reached in and grabbed a pack. Tossing it to Tommy, she quipped, "Here. I've learned to pack snacks for you since you tend to get cranky if you're not fed regularly."

Catching the BelVita package, he gushed, "I love you."

"Me or the Belvita?" she teased.

Chuckling, he said, "Good one. I love you both. Aren't you going to have any?"

"Nah, I'm still stuffed from breakfast." She rubbed her bloated belly, then opened her water bottle. Taking a swig, she was careful not to drink too much. She didn't want to have to pee in the tunnel in front of Tommy.

"Mmm, I love these things. You Americans produce the best snacks."

"What, are you sick of Scotch eggs?" she teased.

"Never, but it's a lot of work to make those. And it's not convenient to pack around. Those buggers get rather messy."

"I still have to try one. Perhaps the next time I'm in Scotland," she vowed.

"Tell you what, when we get back home, I'll make you one," he promised.

"A hardboiled egg wrapped with sausage, dipped in beaten egg and bread crumbs, then deep-fried. I hope it comes with a side of Lipitor," she referred to the medication to treat high cholesterol.

Laughing with a mouthful of crackers, he said, "Good one. You're on a roll today with your quick-witted one-liners."

While she waited for Tommy to finish his snack, she shone her flashlight through the tunnel.

Something caught her eye, and she sprinted towards it with enthusiasm.

"Another shiny object, my dear?" Tommy teased.

Gasping, she placed her hand over her racing heart. "Oh, my, God! Tommy, you've got to see this."

With a mouth full of crackers, he mumbled, "What is it?" Then he walked towards her.

She shone the flashlight on a sign carved above an entrance to another tunnel. The letters were carved in a medieval, Old English font.

He read aloud, "'Second star to the right, then straight on 'til morning.'"

Excitedly, she cried, "Directions to Neverland!"

Chapter Nine

Victoria waved her flashlight beneath the sign. "But we're underground. How are we supposed to take the 'second star to the right' if we can't see any stars?"

"You don't think these are real directions, do you?" he asked with an incredulous tone.

Shrugging, she said, "Who knows. Given our track record, it wouldn't surprise me. Let's just see where this tunnel leads." She ducked under the engraved letters and hiked through the tunnel.

Tommy followed. "But how can an island be beneath the Earth's surface?"

"Ask Jules Verne," she quipped.

"Huh, I've never considered myself a Vernian. But he did write about The Center of The Earth and Atlantis. Maybe Neverland is one of those," he speculated.

"Or maybe Disney is building another attraction and this is part of it." She continued hiking and entered a large cavern. The cavern was round with a twenty-foot-tall ceiling.

"Uh, oh." Her tone grew frantic, and she ran to the other side of the cavern. Shining her flashlight around, she panicked.

"What's wrong?" His tone rang with worry.

"It can't be! I thought we were on to something." Disappointment washed through her, and tears dropped onto her cheeks.

"Honey, what is it?" He hugged her.

Tears streamed as she cried uncontrollably. "I think it's a dead end!"

"What? It can't be." He shone his flashlight on every wall of the cavern, but there weren't any entrances to another tunnel.

"Try the ground." She shone her flashlight on the cavern floor, praying to find an entrance to another tunnel.

Tommy shone the flashlight on her and laughed.

"What can possibly be funny?" she asked with a perturbed tone.

He kept laughing, harder and harder. Then he bent at the waist and grabbed his knees. Pointing at her, he finally calmed down enough to speak. "You're still wearing your crown."

Grabbing it, she touched the platinum and cubic zirconium crown. "Oh, yeah. But why is that funny?"

He approached her with dreamy eyes and kissed her lips. Then he stepped back and said, "Because we're spelunking. You look adorable." He winked.

She wrapped her arms around his neck and looked into his dreamy, sea-green eyes. Still holding her flashlight, she shone its beam onto the cavern's ceiling. Something colorful caught her eye, and she gasped, "Tommy, look."

Tilting back, he shone his flashlight on the cave's ceiling. "Did you find another tunnel?"

"No. But there are cave paintings on the ceiling." Shining her flashlight on the colorful drawings, she beamed excitedly.

"Michelangelo was here, too." He laughed, referring to the 15th Century Renaissance artist who painted the ceiling of the Sistine Chapel at the Vatican in Rome.

Ignoring him, she studied the beautiful, colorful drawings on the cavern's ceiling. "It's a map of an island."

"Mermaid Lagoon, Pirate's Cove, Skull Island and an Indian Village with teepees and all. Is this a map of DisneySea above us?" he asked.

Gasping excitedly, she said, "It's a map of Neverland!"

Chapter Ten

"What a beautiful place." Victoria stared awestruck at the map of Neverland.

"It's a map. But how do we get there? I don't see any coordinates or reference points." Shining his flashlight onto the ceiling, Tommy frantically searched for a clue.

"Now I really want to go there. Surely there is some sort of clue. Who would go to such lengths to paint a beautiful map, if the island didn't exist?" she asked.

"Maybe it was Disney," he speculated.

"Hey! What are you two doing down here?" someone yelled.

Tommy and Victoria turned and shone their flashlights towards the direction of the voice.

A Cast Member stood wearing the uniform from the Journey To The Center Of The Earth ride. Next to him was a golf cart, its headlights shone brightly into her eyes. With a scolding tone, he yelled, "How did you get down here? You're not supposed to be here."

"I felt sick on the roller coaster. I was looking for a bathroom to vomit," Victoria lied.

"Did you walk all the way here? Bathroom my ass, you trespassed!" He stomped his foot, punctuating his authority.

"We didn't see any signs. There were no doors which read, 'Cast Members only.'" Victoria scrambled for excuses. Her worst nightmare was about to come true—getting ejected from Disneyland, *again*!

Sighing, the Cast Member said, "You're right, there are no signs. I keep telling the ride supervisor that we need to block this off. Hop in, and I'll drive you out of here."

Climbing into the back seat of the golf cart, she asked, "What is this place? Was that really a map to Neverland?"

Tommy slid in next to Victoria and placed a protective arm around her shoulder.

The Cast Member turned the golf cart around, then warned, "Hold on tight."

"Well, are you going to tell us or not?" Tommy asked.

"I'm still trying to decide if I should eject you from the park," the Cast Member scolded.

"Please, don't," she begged, holding her hands together in prayer.

Studying the truant pair from the golf cart's rearview mirror, the Cast Member acquiesced, "Fine. I won't eject you *this* time. But you must never come back to this tunnel again. We don't want tourists wandering around down here and getting lost, or worse, getting hurt. Tourists love to sue Disney and the China Land Company."

"Oh, thank you." Although it thrilled her not to get kicked out of the 'Happiest Place on Earth,' *again*, it saddened her that she couldn't continue searching for Neverland.

"Disney discovered that map when they broke ground for the park. They never found Neverland. Perhaps it was once nearby. It's like it magically disappeared into thin air." The Cast Member waived an imaginary magic wand in the air.

"What are Disney's plans for the cavern?" she asked.

"The Imagineers are working on it. They'd love to incorporate it into a ride. But's it's an hour walk to get there. And safety is an issue. The insurance company is afraid the cavern will collapse on the tourists. But for now, it's hidden away from the world."

Tommy chimed in, "'Second star to the right, then straight on 'til morning.' Those directions are rather vague, don't you think?"

"I know, right. Do you start from London like in the movie, *Peter Pan*? And what time do you leave?" the Cast Member asked.

Grinning, Victoria speculated, "Maybe you need magic to get there, and a little pixie dust."

Chapter Eleven

The Cast Member stopped the golf cart at the corridor near the exit of the Journey To The Center Of The Earth ride. He parked the golf cart, removed the key, then escorted them through a door which read, 'Cast Members Only.' The door led to a concrete stairwell. Arriving at the top, the Cast Member opened the door. Sunlight poured in, and he ushered the truant tourists out of the attraction.

Victoria and Tommy exited the ride through the door, and the warm sun beat down on their faces.

Waving, the Cast Member said, "'Have a magical day.'"

Turning to Tommy, she asked, "Now what?"

Grinning, he said, "We eat."

"I should've guessed. I'm sure you already know where we're going to eat," she speculated.

"You know me pretty well. Come on." He grabbed her hand.

Walking hand in hand, they walked in the direction of the hotel.

"We're going back to the hotel?" she asked.

"You'll thank me later." He led her back into the hotel and into the Ristorante di Canaletto.

The hostess greeted them, then escorted them out onto a beautiful terrace overlooking the Grand Canal.

"Oh, Tommy. It's beautiful. I feel like I'm in Venice instead of Tokyo."

Like a doting gentleman, he pulled out a chair for her to sit upon.

She sat in the elegant chair, then took the menu which the hostess offered.

Their server appeared and asked? "May I start you with something to drink?"

"A bottle of Chianti," Tommy ordered.

"Of course, sir." The server scurried off.

"Wow, this menu is awesome. I can't decide between pasta or wood-fired pizza." She studied the menu.

"We're here all week. We can always come back. It's right in the hotel," he reasoned.

"How about we split something?" she asked.

Shooting her a dirty look, he said defensively, "I'm hungry! I need more than half a meal."

Rolling her eyes, she said, "No, silly. I meant, we order one pizza and one pasta dish and share. That way we can try both."

With an appreciative tone, he gushed, "I love you, Victoria."

"How does the fresh tagliatelle with pancetta-porcini cream sauce sound?" She ordinarily wouldn't order something so heavy for lunch. But she had a feeling that they'd nap in the room after lunch. Plus, all this walking at Disneyland burned off calories.

"Sold, and Margherita pizza," he added. Then he set down the menu, reached across the table and grabbed her hand.

The server returned with a bottle of Chianti and two crystal wine goblets. After uncorking the bottle, the server poured Tommy a sample to taste. "Have you had a chance to study the menu?"

Tommy swirled the Chianti in his glass, sniffed it, then tasted the robust wine. Nodding his head, he signaled for the server to fill their goblets. "Yes, we'll have one tagliatelle and one pizza Margherita."

"Excellent choice, sir." The server bowed, then left.

"What are we doing tonight?" she asked, hoping he wouldn't want to *surprise* her for once.

"We haven't even had lunch yet and you're already worried about dinner?" he teased.

Laughing, she said, "Actually, that would be you—always worried about food."

"Touché."

"I meant, what activity are we doing tonight? Isn't there usually a fireworks or light show?" she asked.

"I read there is a spectacular light show at Cinderella's Castle."

"You just want to go to Cinderella's Castle because of what you thought you saw this morning," she chided.

Shrugging, he asked, "Who wouldn't want to see a family of angels?"

Chapter Twelve

"Was it just me, or was that ride scary?" Victoria asked. They exited the Jungle Cruise boat ride at Tokyo Disneyland.

"I'd have to surrender my man card if I ever admitted that I was scared. But I think the darkness made the ride more eerie." Tommy pulled her close.

Studying the dark sky above, she agreed, "You're right."

"What's that? You admit I'm right? Call the *Guinness Book Of World Records*. Tommy Manchester Garrison is right!" he hollered.

"When I heard the drums and knew the headhunters were nearby, it gave me the willies." She shuddered.

"What got me was that total dark area, then they turned the spotlight on that giant snake," he admitted.

"But it wasn't all scary. I enjoyed Pride Rock with Simba and the music from *The Lion King*," she optimized.

"Don't forget the cave with the cool light show highlighting all the different animals carved into the cave walls."

"Speaking of light show. We better hurry if we want a good spot to view the Once Upon A Time light show at the castle." He grabbed her hand and pulled her towards Cinderella's Castle.

"I thought you got FastPasses for the show. What's the rush?" she asked.

"I still want to get there early. Let's get the best seats within the FastPass area—right up front. I hear the show is phenomenal. Besides, Disney is ending this nighttime spectacular and replacing it with a new show soon."

"We still have an hour. You want to sit there for an hour? Besides, with that big breakfast and big late lunch, we skipped dinner." For the first time ever, she broached the subject of food.

"That's a first, you bring up dinner. But we don't have time to sit down and eat, especially without reservations." Stopping, he opened the Disney App on his iPhone and studied the park map for nearby food places.

Walking by a food stand, she studied the menu. A brilliant idea struck her. Pointing, she asked. "How about a giant turkey leg and a beer?"

Glancing up, he smiled at the food truck. Guests walked away gnawing on giant turkey legs and sipping large draft beers. Kissing her cheek, he said, "Oh, Victoria. You're brilliant."

Tommy promptly ordered two turkey legs and two large Kirin beers. Grabbing a bunch of napkins and their dinner, they meandered towards the castle.

"Mmmm. This is so good." Victoria sipped her giant, cold beer. She and Tommy walked towards Cinderella's Castle, gnawing on giant turkey legs.

Other tourists stared at them rudely.

"Are we being uncouth?" she asked with a worried tone.

Shrugging, he said, "Nah, this is how cavemen ate. Don't worry, my love. They're just jealous of your brilliant idea. Besides, we'll never see these people again. And since when did you give a crap about what other people think?" he asked.

"You're right, *again*," she acquiesced, then nodded as she looked up. "Perhaps it's the crown. I don't think the Queen of England would ever gnaw on a turkey leg."

"'Heavy is the head who wears the crown,'" he repeated the famous quote.

"Oh, restrooms." She pointed.

"Good idea. We better hit the head before the show." He walked towards the restrooms.

A Cast Member stood in front of the ladies' room. A yellow cone blocked the entrance. He bowed and said, "Your Royal Highness. I'm afraid we're cleaning your *throne* at the moment. But there are more *thrones* by the castle."

"Oh, thank you," she said.

They walked towards the castle.

Giggling, she turned to Tommy and laughed. "*Throne*, get it?"

"Ha, ha," he said with an unamused tone.

"You're no fun." She smacked his chest playfully, careful not to drop her turkey leg.

They found the restrooms and held each other's beer and turkey leg while they took turns using the restroom.

Exiting the restroom, she grabbed her beer and turkey leg from Tommy.

"I hope you washed your hands." He smirked.

They scanned their FastPasses at the roped-off area directly in front of the castle.

"Your Royal Highness." A Cast Member bowed, then gestured towards the front row.

"Front row seats. Awesome." Tommy grinned.

Beaming, she said, "They're treating me like royalty. This crown is *fabulous*," she sang the last word.

Tommy studied the castle pensively. Rubbing his stubbled chin with his thumb and index finger, he pointed to the top turret and said, "That's where I saw that winged family disappear."

"I still don't understand why only *you* could see the family with wings."

"What, you don't believe me?" he asked.

"If I hadn't seen the lady floating towards the castle, then disappear by the turret, I probably wouldn't believe you. But I'm just curious why *I* couldn't see the angels, too."

"Huh, maybe the rumors were true." Tommy shrugged with a surprised tone.

"What rumors?"

With a perplexed expression, he said, "That I'm descended from witches."

Chapter Thirteen

"What? Did you just say, 'witches?' This Japanese beer must be stronger than American beer," Victoria speculated.

His expression grew serious.

"Oh, my, God! You're serious." Incredulous, she stared at Tommy.

Shrugging, he said, "I'd thought it was a myth. But perhaps it's true after all. Astounding."

"Witches and wizards, as in, the kind that go to magic school in that movie?" she asked.

"You've been to Castle Garrison on the Isle of Skye, for Lilly and Grier's wedding."

Nodding, she recalled, happily. "That's where we met."

"Well, nearby, there is a Manchester family. They settled on the Isle of Skye before the Garrisons. They kept to themselves for the most part. They're family tree didn't branch too much. Manchesters married their cousins all the time. But the local villagers feared that they were witches and wizards."

"As in, villagers with torches and pitch forks?"

"Exactly. I think what terrified the locals were the Manchesters' spellbinding eyes. Most of them had one green and one blue eye. Supposedly, the forest between Manchester Manor and Castle Garrison is enchanted, even haunted."

"Your ancestors probably just told you scary stories to keep you out of the forest," she speculated.

"Well, it worked. Do you remember when I gave you a private tour of the castle?"

"Yes, that place is incredible. I love how your cousin, Grier, renovated the original tower into a private master wing."

"Do you remember the portrait gallery?" he asked.

"Oh, yeah. It had portraits of all the Earls."

"Well, one portrait was dated in the early 1600s. It was my ancestor, Sir Michael Garrison, the Earl of Garrison, who married Prudence Manchester."

"Was she a witch?"

"Prudence Manchester had one green eye and one blue eye."

Victoria tried to recall the enormous portraits. "Now I remember. She wore a beautiful violet dress. Michael and Prudence looked so happy together, so in love."

"They were, but it was short lived. I didn't tell you this before because it was so tragic. Not the kind of thing you tell someone you've just met."

Grasping her throat, she gasped, terrified of his next words. "No."

Dropping his chin, he sighed and said, "The villagers burned Prudence at the stake for witchcraft!"

"No!"

"I'm afraid so. But it gets worse."

"How could it possibly get worse?" she asked.

"Sir Michael Manchester Garrison disappeared soon after. And it gets even worse." A tear fell onto his cheek. "Their five-year-old twins, Colin and Cordelia, were orphaned."

"What about the coven? Did they have any family?"

"Oh, yes, tons. They were raised by the Manchesters until Colin was of age to be the next Earl of Garrison. Colin and Cordelia moved back into the castle. Colin went on to become the greatest Earl of Garrison. Cordelia went on to marry the first Earl of Aberdeen who was also a Manchester."

Relieved, she sighed, "Thank goodness the twins weren't harmed. Do you think the reason you could see the angels was because you have diluted magic in your blood?"

Shrugging, he winced apprehensively. "Maybe?"

"Huh? Did they ever find out what happened to Michael? Perhaps he went after the villagers who burned his wife?"

"That's one theory." His expression turned shocked. "I've been racking my brain trying to recall all the old legends."

"And?"

"This sounds asinine."

"We're way past *asinine*. Don't tell me you come from a family of bird-human hybrids."

"Close. My ancestors spun a tale that Sir Michael Manchester Garrison was in fact, Saint Michael The Archangel!"

Chapter Fourteen

Victoria remained silent for an uncomfortable amount of time. Her mind processed the angelic words—Saint Michael The Archangel. Even though she was raised Catholic and attended Catholic School on scholarship, she couldn't digest that angels and witches were real.

Tommy frantically waved his hand in front of her face. "Earth to Victoria?"

Snapping out of her incomprehensive trance, she said, "Sorry. It's a lot to take in. Perhaps Michael didn't disappear. Maybe he escorted his wife's soul to the pearly gates and stayed in heaven."

"That's the other theory. 'But wait, there's more.'" His tone resembled Billy Mays, the infomercial star.

"I'm not sure I can handle more. Do you think you could conjure another beer before telling me more about angels and witches?" she pleaded, then gulped the rest of her beer.

Dropping his chin, he said, "I wish." Jovially, he waved his hand above his head, pretended to hold a magic wand, and chanted, "Abracadabra, for my dear, I wish her another beer."

Victoria bent over, laughing hysterically. "I don't think Tinkerbell could've done any better. How much longer until the show starts? Maybe I can save your seat while you buy us another beer," she pleaded with her best 'pretty please' tone.

Dropping his head, he sighed, "Fine, you're lucky I love you."

Spotting a Cast Member pushing a cart between the roped-off FastPass area and the castle, she grabbed Tommy's arm and said, "Hold up."

"What? Now you've got me craving another beer, too."

Shocked, she pointed to the Cast Member pushing a cart with ice-cold water, soda, and *beer*. Gasping, she clutched her chest, shocked that the spell actually worked.

Tommy, obviously clueless to the coincidence, nonchalantly held up Japanese Yen and pointed at a big can of Fosters beer. After making the exchange nonverbally with the Cast Member, he handed her the giant Fosters can. "Cheers."

"Where's yours?" Winking, she smiled and gulped a generous portion, trying not to think that her hot fiancé has latent magical powers because he's descended from witches and Saint Michael The Archangel.

"Not funny." Pouting, he grabbed the beer and slurped generously.

"You don't get it, do you?" she asked.

"Huh?" he asked with a clueless expression.

"Seriously? You cast a spell to conjure a beer, then a second later a Cast Member appears selling beer." She grabbed the beer and gulped it.

Based on Tommy's reaction to her theory, he'd obviously not made the magical connection. "Nah, you think?"

Shrugging, she said, "Maybe? It could've been a coincidence, I reckon. We are at Disneyland 'where dreams really do come true.'" She sang the line from Cinderella's famous song.

Taking back the beer, he nearly drained it. Handing the can back to her for a final sip, he suggested, "We better chill on the beer. We don't want to miss the show because we have to pee."

After the last sip of beer, she grabbed her full belly and said, "Whoa, I'm stuffed. I'll sleep great tonight when the tryptophan from the turkey kicks in."

"Shhh, the show is about to start."

Chapter Fifteen

The lights dimmed, the crowd cheered, and the Once Upon A Time castle projection light show began.

Various scenes from Disney's numerous animated movies projected onto Cinderella's Castle. Music, piped though dozens of speakers strategically sprinkled around the castle, accompanied the projections.

"Cool!" Victoria beamed at the lighted castle.

Mrs. Potts and Chip from *Beauty And The Beast* appeared. Chip spoke Japanese.

Confused, she turned to Tommy with a disenchanted scowl to nonverbally file her complaint. Disney Characters speaking Japanese killed the magic.

"When in Tokyo," he teased. Then his expression grew shocked. His jaw dropped, and he pointed to the balcony of the castle. "Do you see that?"

She asked, "What? I don't see anything besides Winnie the Pooh and Piglet playing with honey and speaking Japanese."

"You really don't see it?" Pulling her close, he pointed to the balcony.

"What am I looking at?" she asked.

"Remember this morning when I saw a spinning blue cloud on the balcony of the castle?"

"I thought you saw a family of flying angels," she recalled.

"I did. I saw them flying through a blue cloud before they disappeared."

"Oh, I forgot about the blue spinning cloud. But what's that go to do with 'the price of tea in China?'" she asked,

"We're in Japan," he corrected.

Shrugging, she said, "Close enough, it's Asia."

Shaking his head to obviously ignore this tangent, he asked, "You really don't see the blue cloud?"

Studying the balcony again, she shrugged. "No, just Snow White dancing with three stacked dwarfs."

"Okay. Now, I believe." Yanking her away from their front row seats, he dragged her out of the FastPass viewing area.

"Hey! That hurts. Why are we leaving? The show isn't over. Where are you taking me? Why can't we see the rest of the show? What's so important? Did you see more angels? Is that what this is about? Can't it wait? How often do we get to watch the light show at Tokyo Disneyland? Tommy, will you please tell me where we're going?" she asked, all in one, belligerent breath.

Once they cleared the enormous crowd watching the light show, Tommy finally stopped, turned to her, and said, "Chill, woman."

"Don't say it. Please don't say it," she begged.

Tommy laughed hysterically. Then he bent at the waist, grabbed his slightly bent knees and let out a bellowing laugh.

"Are you drunk?" she asked with a perturbed tone.

He held up one index finger, signally for her to give him a minute.

"What? Are you enjoying this?"

He stopped laughing, regained his posture, then kissed her cheek. "Oh, my love. I thought you were getting better, but I was wrong. You're getting worse, but it's one of the many things I love about you."

"Tommy?"

With a wicked grin, he asked, "Can't you just be surprised?"

Chapter Sixteen

Tugging her, Tommy rushed them into the castle. Bright lights from the projection show reflected off their clothes.

"I don't think we can go into the castle during the show." She followed him hesitantly.

"Sure, we can. Cinderella's suite is an attraction." He pointed to the staircase.

The sign above the staircase read, 'Cinderella's Fairy Tale Hall.' Other tourists ascended the staircase, too.

"No line, cool." She climbed the stairs following Tommy. "I never thought about going on a ride during the light show. There's no wait."

They arrived in Cinderella's suite. Stained-glass windows featured glass slippers. Murals and mosaics covered the walls. Each work of art depicted a different scene from the animated film.

"Cool, these are like the mosaics in Cinderella's Castle at the Magic Kingdom in Florida." She stopped and snapped a few pictures with her iPhone.

They meandered to the next room—the throne room. A glass slipper rested on a cushioned stool. Dying to try it on, she walked towards the glass slipper. But something even better caught her attention—the throne.

"Tommy, look." She handed him her iPhone excitedly. "Take a picture with me on the throne. With my beautiful crown, this will make an awesome picture for Instagram."

"Later, Honey. We don't have time." He pulled her away from the throne and dragged her to the terrace.

Tears dropped onto her cheek. He'd never treated her this way before. "Tommy, what's the rush? You act like a door is about to close."

He dragged her onto the balcony and pointed. "It is, look."

Victoria didn't see anything on the balcony, just the spectacular view of the park. The crowds below stared in awe at the castle. Bright lights still projected onto the castle. "What am I looking at? The light show?"

"You really don't see it?"

"See what?" she asked.

"The same thing I saw this morning."

"Angels?"

"Not yet. But I see an indigo-blue spinning cloud right in front of me." He waved his hand in a circular motion.

Starring at the empty balcony, she said with a perplexed tone, "Huh, I don't see anything other than the lights from the show."

Tommy turned to her, stared deeply into her eyes, then asked, "Do you trust me?"

Baffled, she nodded. "Of course, I trust you."

He grabbed her hand and stepped further out onto the balcony.

Air rushed against her, and gravity pulled her forward. She felt like she was on a roller coaster. "Tommy what's happening? I feel weird, like I'm on Space Mountain with my eyes closed."

"You don't see the lights?"

"No. I don't see anything, not even the castle. Am I blind?" Terror filled her.

"Huh, we're in a blue lighted tunnel. I wonder why you can't see it." He squeezed her hand.

"Tommy, whatever it is, make it stop!" she cried with a terrified tone.

"I don't think I can," he admitted.

"Why not?"

"We're going through a portal!" he yelled.

"What the...?" Panic rushed through her. "Did you say, portal?"

"Yes, I saw the same blue spinning cloud that the family of angels jumped through this morning. When I saw it again from the light show, I needed to rush up onto the balcony before it closed," he explained.

"Make it stop!" she screamed.

"I see a light at the end of the tunnel. I think we're almost through the worm hole."

"Where is it taking us?" she asked.

"I have no idea. Just hold on tight." He hugged her protectively.

"I can see!" Pointing, she squealed with delight. An aerial view of a beautiful island appeared at the end of the tunnel. "Oh, my, God, it's beautiful!"

"It's breathtaking. I wonder what this place is? Are we on another planet? In another dimension?"

They flew through the air. The blue tunnel led them over the top of a mountain peak.

"Wait, I've seen this before." She racked her brain to recall why this island was so familiar.

As they flew over the water, mermaids lounged on rocks. A rock formation, resembling a giant skull, jettied out of the water. Old ships, circa 1700s, floated in the harbor. Indian teepees littered a clearing on a hill.

"Oh, my, God! I know this place." Excitement rushed through her. Tears of joy dropped onto her cheeks as they floated towards the beach.

"Well, are you going to tell me? Or make me guess?" He studied her, then the tropical paradise beneath them. "I think I saw this island in a movie."

"You did, but it was an animated one. This is the real thing." Her tone rang with excitement.

"Wait. Don't tell me. Mermaids, pirate ships, teepees. No, it can't be."

Grinning 'like a kid at...,' she said, "From the movie *Peter Pan*. Welcome to Neverland!"

Chapter Seventeen

"Neverland!" Victoria hollered. "Never in a million years did I ever think this place was real."

"Or that we'd travel through a portal to get here," he added.

They floated towards the island. Tall trees covered the mountain in the center of the island.

She smacked his arm and scolded, "I can't believe you blindly took us through a portal. Who knows where we could've ended up?"

"Uh, you're welcome. First of all, nothing bad can happen at Disney. And second, as long as we're together, it doesn't matter where we are."

"Ah." She kissed his cheek as they floated closer and closer to the beach.

"But you're right," he acquiesced.

She held her palm next to her ear, leaned in, and interrupted, "What's that?"

"Ha, ha. That wasn't the smartest thing to do, now that I think about it. That's the problem, I didn't think about it at all. The portal beckoned me." He grimaced.

Their pace slowed as they approached the sandy shore.

"I'm afraid to even ask, how do we get home?" Her tone rang with worry.

Holding his hands together in prayer, he said, "I'm praying that it's a roundtrip ticket." Then he performed the sign of the cross.

Just as they approached the end of the tunnel, their pace slowed.

"Look, it's the family of angels, only I don't see their wings," he said.

Pointing, she screeched, "I can see them. Can they see us?"

"I don't think so, not yet anyway."

The tunnel ended with a loud, vibrating sound.

They fell out of the tunnel and rolled onto the warm sand. After brushing the sand off their limbs, they stood.

"What the...?" A beautiful woman with long, black hair asked. She stood behind what appeared to be five-year-old twins—a boy and a girl. A tall, gorgeous man with golden curly hair stood next to the woman.

"Oh, hello." Victoria smiled.

The woman protectively placed her hands on the children's shoulders.

"It's okay, my dear. I sense these are good people." The man reassuringly placed his arm around the woman.

"How did you get here?" the woman asked.

"Through the same portal at Tokyo Disneyland that you all flew into this morning," Tommy explained.

"Are you a Disney Princess?" the little girl asked. With her golden, curly hair, she was the spitting image of her father.

Confused at first, Victoria reached for her crown and touched the faux diamonds. "Oh, no. I just wore this to Disney. Hi, my name is Victoria Ventures." She extended her hand to shake the little girl's hand.

Glancing up at her mother, the adorable little girl nonverbally sought approval to shake a stranger's hand.

Smiling down at her daughter, the woman nodded approvingly.

The little girl extended her hand, shook Victoria's and said, "It's a pleasure to meet you, Miss Ventures. My name is Catherine Manchester, but everyone calls me, Cat."

Victoria turned to Tommy to acknowledge his previous theory—that the only reason he could see the portal and the wings was because he was descended from Manchester witches!

The family of four all shared the same spellbinding eyes, one blue and one green.

Tommy extended his hand to the man's and said, "Hello, I'm Tommy Manchester Garrison from the Isle of Skye."

The man shook Tommy's hand with a firm handshake. "Ah, yes. Castle Garrison. I'm Michael Manchester, and this is my wife Penelope, our son, Connor, and you've already met Cat."

"Hi, we must be related." Penelope shook Tommy's hand, then Victoria's.

After all the handshakes, Tommy grinned and said, "Now I know why only I could see you all flying through the portal this morning."

"I thought he was hallucinating." Victoria rolled her eyes, incredulous that her fiancé was descended from witches.

"You were lucky the portal stayed open for as long as it did. We opened it, then *someone* had to go potty." Penelope's tone indicated her irritation as she shot her son a scolding stare.

"Oh, you're headed back? Why the rush?" Victoria asked, bummed that she couldn't spend more time with Tommy's distant and magical relatives.

"We're trying to get back in time for the light show. I hear it's amazing," Penelope said.

Victoria snapped her fingers with a disappointing swing. "Oh, you just missed it. It was almost over when we jumped through the portal. The rumors are true—the Once Upon A Time projection light show is phenomenal."

Snapping her fingers, Penelope sighed, "Ah, bummer."

Digesting her surroundings, Victoria asked incredulously, "Is this really Neverland?"

"Yes, it's a sanctuary for magical creatures. But when man discovered this island off the coast of Japan, they started to develop it. My ancestors created a portal to another dimension and moved Neverland, thus protecting it forever," Penelope explained.

"Uh, silly question, why is the portal at Cinderella's Castle?" Victoria asked.

"Because that's the closest Lay Line," Penelope said, nonchalantly.

"What's a Lay Line?" Victoria asked.

Tommy raised his hand like a know-it-all schoolboy, and said, "Oh, I know this one, probably because I grew up in Scotland. Lay Lines are invisible lines of energy all around the world. Magic is stronger on these lines. And where Lay Lines intersect, the energy is even stronger, like at Stonehenge."

"Very good, cousin," Penelope praised.

"So there just happens to be a Lay Line through Cinderella's Castle at Tokyo Disneyland?" Victoria asked.

"Of course not. Disney wanted their parks magical," Michael quipped.

"Uh, another silly question. How do we get back?" Tommy grimaced.

"Oh, we can leave the portal open?" Michael turned to Penelope for guidance.

With a hesitant expression, Penelope said, "Uhhhh, technically we can. But it's risky. Someone or some*thing* could also travel through the portal."

Wincing, Victoria asked, "Some*thing*? What kind of *things* are here?"

"Pirates, crocodiles, mermaids, fairies and the tribe." Penelope counted on her fingers.

"I'm okay with that. The scariest are the pirates. But we won't stay long. It's getting late." Victoria stared at Tommy to gauge his reaction.

"What about crocodiles?" Tommy asked.

"Just don't go in the water." Michael laughed.

Tommy asked, "How *do* we close the portal once we travel back through? Can I even do that? I imagine my powers are diluted with centuries of my ancestors mating with non-magical humans."

Penelope asked, "Do you have a cell phone? Text me when you get back to the castle, and I'll come and close the portal."

Nodding, Victoria retrieved her iPhone from her cinch sack. "Huh, no service here."

Tommy laughed. "What did you expect?"

Victoria shot him a dirty look, then smacked his chest. "Hey, don't be a big meanie."

"Sorry."

The ladies exchanged cell phone numbers.

"Well, it was nice to meet you. If you're not back before sunrise, we'll come back and look for you," Michael suggested.

"Daddy, can we please sleep in the castle?" Cat asked.

Michael knelt to face his daughter. "I'm sorry, sweetie. But other guests are already sleeping in the castle."

"Ah, shucks." Disappointedly, Cat snapped her fingers.

"Do we just walk back through, like how we got here?" Tommy asked.

"Yes, exactly. We'll plan on meeting you at the castle at dawn, unless we hear from you sooner," Penelope said.

"Thank you. It was nice to meet you." Victoria waved.

"Have fun." Penelope waved back.

The magical family stood in front of the portal, joined hands, jumped through, then disappeared.

Chapter Eighteen

"Now what?" Tommy asked.

"Let's go see the mermaids." Victoria grabbed his hand, and they strolled down the beach.

"Remember this spot because we have to come back here," he said.

After walking several hundred feet while admiring the pristine beach of this tropical paradise, Victoria stopped suddenly. "Uh, oh."

"What is it?" He stopped next to her.

Terror shot through her. She pointed to the reptiles sleeping on the beach. "Alligators."

"Crocodiles actually. Do you see their teeth and pointy snouts?" he corrected.

"Aren't you scared?"

"Yep." He turned and ran in the opposite direction.

Victoria jogged and passed him. "Me, too."

Tommy quickly caught up and ran beside her. They both ran as fast as they could on the beach, away from the crocodiles and back towards the portal.

Panting, she asked, "Should we look back?"

"Nah, I'd rather not know if a crocodile was about to eat me. Besides, unlike you, I like surprises."

"Touché. I've heard gators can actually run pretty fast if it suits them. But I have no idea about crocs. Too bad we can't ask Siri," she laughed through her heavy breathing.

"I think we can run faster than crocs. But just in case, I'm going to run slightly behind you so they'll eat me first." He slowed his pace slightly, and ran behind her.

"Ah, how valiant," she gushed.

They passed the blue, spinning portal and kept on running.

After a minute of World Record sprinting, he asked, "How are you doing? Are you getting tired yet?"

"Nope, but I'm dying to look back. I can't stand it much longer," she confessed.

"If you stop hearing my voice, then you'll know I'm a goner."

"Or if I hear you scream like a baby," she bantered.

"Yeah, there's that, too."

"I think I see something up ahead. There's a bunch of rocks just off the shoreline."

Laughing, he said, "You and your shiny objects."

"I can't stand it anymore." Victoria turned her head.

The crocodiles weren't anywhere near them. In fact, they hadn't moved at all.

She stopped and faced Tommy. "We're good. Those lazy reptiles probably didn't even notice us."

He stopped, bent over and placed his hands on his knees. Wheezing, he said, "That's my exercise for the day. Phew. I guess they weren't hungry enough to bother chasing us."

"Thank you for your heroic deed." She hugged him tight. Tears dropped onto her cheeks.

"I've told you this before. I'd rather die to save you than risk living without you. You're my life, my love," he sobbed.

She rewarded him with a passionate kiss. Finally pulling her lips away, she grabbed her crown and said, "I can't believe it stayed on."

Wiggling his fingers at her tiara, he teased, "It's magic."

Glancing down at his watch, she asked, "How are we doing on time?"

Rotating his wrist, he looked down and said. "We've only used an hour. But let's not wander too far away from the portal." Glancing up, he added. "There's no way in hell I'm hiking up that mountain."

"You, big baby. Want some cheese with your whine?" she teased.

"Actually, wine and cheese sound great." He rubbed his belly.

Without looking back, she teased, "Good luck with that. Besides, we just ate a huge turkey leg."

"I'll have to write Tokyo Disneyland a letter. How dare they not provide food and beverage on their ride to another dimension," he threatened sarcastically.

"Good luck with that, too." She laughed.

"Phew, I'm whooped after that marathon we just ran. We should probably steer clear of the tribe, too."

"What, you don't want to get scalped?" she teased.

Running his fingers through his gorgeous mane of sandy-blond hair, he said, "I like my hair, thank you very much."

"Me, too." She ran her fingers through his beautiful hair, then kissed him.

Rubbing his index finger and thumb against his stubbled chin, he said, "Mmmm, that leaves lost boys, fairies, mermaids and pirates."

"Maybe the mermaids are lounging on the rocks." She pointed.

"That's a great direction to head, *away* from the crocs." He grabbed her hand, and they strolled along the shore of the beautiful island paradise.

"Can mermaids be dangerous?" she asked.

"I hope not. I'm not sure about all the differences between Sirens and Mermaids, but Sirens lure ships to the rocky shores with their spellbinding singing. Then the ship crashes on the rocks, and the Sirens eat the sailors!" He shuddered.

Wincing, she said, "Remind me not to go into the water."

Chapter Nineteen

"Sirens or crocs, either one is a horrible way to die," he said.

Large boulders appeared in the water along the shore.

She studied the boulders, hoping to see a mermaid. But disappointment washed through her once she realized the boulders were vacant. Snapping her fingers, she said, "Darn, no mermaids."

"Maybe they saw us and hid underwater," he speculated.

"Or they hang out further away from the crocs," she reasoned.

The shoreline turned to the left and revealed a lagoon.

Pointing excitedly, she squealed, "Oh, cool, a lagoon."

They turned left with the shoreline and walked towards the lagoon. Something big on a rock jumped into the water and made a big splash. Several more splashes followed.

"Do you think?" she asked optimistically.

"Maybe we scared them," he reasoned.

"What if they're Sirens?"

"They can't come ashore. We'll be fine as long as we don't go into the water," he rationalized.

As they walked towards the U-shaped lagoon, more docks and ships appeared. The wooden vessels resembled those of the Eighteenth Century with their big sails and ornate caricatures at the bows of the ships.

"Wow, I feel like I'm in the movie *Pirates of the Caribbean*." She marveled at the beautiful ships.

"I don't think we'll see Captain Jack Sparrow here," he chuckled.

"I still can't believe we saw Johnny Depp at Disneyland Shanghai." She recalled their last night at the third Disney location around the world.

"I don't see any pirates around. Do you think the Sirens got them?" he asked.

"Possibly? But those ships are docked, not crashed on the rocks."

"I'm sure they could still get them. All they'd have to do is sing and lure them into the water." He shuddered with a fearful expression.

"You're paranoid."

A noise echoed across the lagoon's surface.

"Did you hear that?" Tommy asked with a paranoid tone.

Leaning her head closer to the water, she held up her palm to her ear and listened. "No, I don't hear anything."

"Huh, that's strange. It sounds like Ariel singing in *The Little Mermaid*."

Shrugging, she speculated, "Sorry, but I don't hear a thing. Maybe your magical ancestry allows you to hear it and not me."

Pointing, he picked up his pace and said, "It's getting louder. It's coming from over there."

He jogged closer to the harbor and frantically studied the rocks along the shore.

A woman's head emerged from the surface several yards offshore.

Chapter Twenty

Tommy stood near the shore, mesmerized by the Siren.

"Tommy! It's a trap!" Victoria pulled him further away from the shore, but he barely budged.

The Siren turned toward Victoria. Yellow eyes glared eerily. The Siren hissed, exposing her sharp teeth.

Tommy stood on the shore, his expression grew hypnotic. The whites of his eyes now glowed the same yellow as the Siren's eyes.

The Siren's mouth moved, but no sound resonated from her lips.

Luckily, Victoria was somehow immune to the Siren's enticement. *Perhaps because she was a girl? Did this creature wish to mate with her fiancé, breed another Siren, then eat Tommy like a female praying mantis?*

"I don't think so, bitch!" Victoria picked up a rock and hurled it at the Siren.

The Siren ducked into the water and disappeared. Ripples appeared beneath the surface, moving further away from the shore.

"Ha, take that, tramp!" she hollered, victoriously.

Tommy stood in a trance on the shore. Then he blinked and shook his head. "What happened? I feel funny."

"Oh, my, God! Tommy, a Siren hypnotized you! I saw her yellow glowing eyes and razor-sharp teeth. I think she wanted to mate with you, then *eat* you!" Tears streamed down her cheeks.

He embraced her. "How did you-"

She interrupted. "-Not get hypnotized, too? For some reason, I could see her but not *hear* her."

"Where did she go?"

"I threw a rock at her. Then she dipped underwater." Victoria pointed towards the ripples in the lagoon.

Tommy's eyes grew hypnotized again. He turned to the water and stared.

"Tommy?" Her tone grew panicked, then she turned to the water and scanned the surface.

Further out into the water, the Siren's head reappeared. Her mouth moved, but no sound emerged.

Victoria bent down, picked up another rock, and hurled it at the Siren. The rock fell short and splashed several yards in front of the Siren.

The Siren hissed again.

Panicked, Victoria threw several more rocks towards the Siren. But they all fell short of the evil creature.

The Siren's mouth moved silently.

Like a mummy, Tommy raised his arms and walked towards the water.

"Tommy, no!" Victoria pulled at him frantically, but he was too strong for her. She tried with all her might, but he walked closer and closer to the water.

A buzzing echoed from the nearby woods. The humming resembled a swarm. *A swarm of what?* The sound grew louder, but Tommy still walked towards the water.

The swarm emerged from the woods. Dozens of creatures the size of her thumb buzzed towards Tommy, then swarmed in front of his face.

"Tommy, watch out! They might sting you!" She pulled Tommy again, but he still walked slowly towards the water.

The creatures buzzed around Tommy's head. They moved so fast that Victoria couldn't make out what they were. *Bees? Wasps?*

Although she should've backed away to avoid being stung, she somehow knew that they wouldn't harm her or Tommy. These creatures, whatever they were, tried to save him.

One of the creatures flew away from the swarm and slowed its frantic flutter. *Was it injured?*

Victoria gasped because she realized what the swarm was—Fairies!

Chapter Twenty-One

Fairies tried to save Tommy!

The swarm's buzz grew so loud that Victoria had to cover her ears.

Just as Tommy's feet were about to hit the water, the injured Fairy threw gold dust into Tommy's face and chanted in Latin.

The Siren, who had since moved closer to the shore, waited patiently for her imminent coupling feast.

Tommy stopped abruptly and blinked. "What happened?"

"Oh, Tommy! I nearly lost you." She embraced him.

Hugging her back, he asked with trepidation, "Lost me? You couldn't lose me if you tried."

"A Siren sang to you. You were inches away from the water. But a swarm of fairies sprinkled gold dust on you and broke the trance," she explained in one breath.

"Fairies?"

Pointing, she said, "Look."

The fairies swarmed next to a tree. Their fluttering wings slowed. Then one-by-one, they landed on a long tree branch. The branch was at Tommy's and Victoria's eye level. The injured Fairy fluttered in front of Tommy.

Instinctively, Tommy opened his palm, and the Fairy landed on his hand. Adoringly, he said, "Hello, little one."

Gasping, Victoria cried, "Hello. You are magnificent." Turning to the rest of the Fairies, she added, "All of you."

The Fairies perched on a branch and appeared winded and sweaty from their frantic swarming. Each one was different. Their hair colors ranged from the traditional blonde, brunette, and red head to pink, teal, and purple. Each of their outfits matched the respective color of their hair.

Her gaze dropped to the tiny Fairy on Tommy's palm. Her bright-pink hair matched her pink outfit. The camisole top and short skirt resembled a figure-skater's costume.

The tiny, adorable creature studied Victoria's head and asked, "Are you a princess?"

Speechless, Victoria stuttered, "I, uh...."

Tommy finished her sentence, "Of course, she's my princess." Then with his free hand, he held Victoria's.

"Is your crown silver?" the pink Fairy asked.

"Actually, it's platinum." Victoria bowed her head so the pink Fairy could get a closer look.

"I've never met a Platinum Princess before. My name is Fuchsia," she boasted.

"Thank you for saving my life," Tommy gushed.

Remembering her manners, Victoria said, "Yes, of course, thank ya'll for saving my fiancé."

A blue Fairy said, "You're very welcome. Those Sirens are evil. We've seen many men succumb to their lure."

"When you get married, you'll be a prince." Fuchsia studied Tommy.

"Fiancé. That makes sense." A yellow Fairy beamed.

"What do you mean, 'that makes sense?'" Victoria asked.

Blushing, Fuchsia explained, "We only appear if we choose to, and only in the presence of true love."

Chapter Twenty-Two

Screams echoed from the harbor. A pirate ran towards them with his sword drawn and ready for battle.

The Fairies quickly swarmed and flew high into the trees. Poor Fuchsia struggled with her injured wing and couldn't fly away.

Instinctively, Tommy carefully held her, then gingerly placed her in the pocket of his flannel shirt. "Fuchsia, you're coming with us. You saved me. Now it is my turn to save you."

Victoria turned to Tommy and hollered, "Race ya'll to the portal."

They ran as fast as they could, yet again, on the sandy beach. Occasionally turning to ascertain the pirate's distance, they realized he hadn't gained on them. Then Victoria saw why the frantic pirate ran like his life depended on it—because it did! A crocodile chased him on the sandy beach.

Once they turned the corner, the blue spinning portal greeted them. Jumping through with ease, they traveled through the same wormhole that brought them to Neverland. The journey home seemed quicker. A light appeared at the end of the tunnel, and so did Cinderella's Castle at Tokyo Disneyland.

Victoria and Tommy floated out of the worm hole and landed gently on the same balcony they'd departed from the evening before. The dark night greeted them.

"Are you all right, Fuchsia?" Tommy peered into his pocket.

"I'm peachy. This shirt is so soft and warm. I could sleep in here." Fuchsia snuggled against Tommy's chest though the flannel shirt pocket.

"I'd better text Penelope so she can come and close the portal before something else travels through."

A scream echoed through the portal.

Tommy yelled, "Too late! Quick, move out of the way!" Tommy ordered. He grabbed her hand, then entered the throne room of the castle through the glass door.

Terrified of what else might travel through the portal, she asked, "Oh, my, God! Do you think-"

"-I hope not. Quick, text Penelope," he said.

She fired off a text to her new witch friend. *We're back, please come and close the portal. We were chased by a pirate and a crocodile.* Then she turned to Tommy and said, "Done."

A loud noise erupted from the portal, then the pirate landed on the balcony. He surveyed his surroundings, then jumped off the second story balcony. He landed on the ground unscathed, then ran through the park.

Tommy pointed to the sky and said, "Look, here they come."

Glancing up, Victoria saw Penelope floating in the air. But she couldn't see the others. "Huh, I only see Penelope."

Another loud noise erupted from the portal.

"Oh, my, God! Something else is coming through!" Victoria screamed.

Penelope presumably heard her because she wiggled her fingers at the portal and chanted in Latin.

Just in the nick of time, the portal closed.

Chapter Twenty-Three

Sighing with tremendous relief, Victoria placed her hand over her heart as if warding off a heart attack. "Oh, thank, God."

Michael instantly appeared on the balcony and said, "Why are you thanking my father?" He laughed. His wings were gone. He'd obviously retracted them so Victoria could now see him.

"Huh?" Tommy and Victoria asked in unison while exchanging bewildered expressions.

Grinning, Michael said, "In case you haven't figured it out yet, I'm Saint Michael the Archangel."

Obviously incredulous, Tommy said, "Then the legends are true."

Penelope, now released from her flying position with Michael, said, "Phew, that was close. Did anything else come through?"

"Just a pirate, but he ran off into the park," Victoria said.

Penelope hollered, "It's safe children, you can come down now."

The children instantly appeared on the balcony, too.

"How was Neverland?" Michael asked.

"Terrifying, Tommy was almost eaten by a Siren," Victoria rehashed their horrid tale.

Fuchsia spoke up, "Who's there? Are they safe? I'm scared."

"It's okay, you can come out," Tommy said with a soothing tone.

Fuchsia poked her head out of Tommy's flannel shirt pocket.

Squealing excitedly, Cat pointed and said, "Mommy, look!"

Fuchsia flew out of Tommy's pocket, hovered tentatively and surveyed her surroundings.

Cat held out her palm and said, "Hello, my name is Cat Manchester. What's your name?"

Fuchsia immediately flew to Cat as fast as her injured wing allowed. Beaming at the beautiful girl, Fuchsia landed on Cat's palm and said, "I'm Fuchsia."

"It's a pleasure to meet you, Fuchsia. You're he most beautiful Fairy I've ever seen," Cat said with perfect manners.

"Thank you. You've seen Fairies before?" Fuchsia asked.

"Of course, we have dozens in our rose garden. But you seem smaller than our Fairies. If you don't mind my asking, how old are you?" Cat asked.

"I'm twenty-five in Fairy years, but that's like five in human years," Fuchsia explained. She stared at Cat with mutual adoration.

"We picked up a passenger and saved her life. With her injured wing, she couldn't escape with the other Fairies," Tommy justified bringing Fuchsia through the portal.

Michael smiled, obviously touched by the tender moment between the child Fairy and his daughter. "I'll fix your wing. I happen to know a few things about wings." Michael winked.

The grown ups stared at one another with an obvious understanding of who Fuchsia would live with.

Michael nodded to Cat and said, "Go ahead, ask her."

Picking up on the hint, Cat smiled and asked, "Fuchsia, how would you like to come live with us?"

THE END

Epilogue

"Cheers." Tommy raised his champagne flute and toasted Victoria's.

They sat at a cozy table in Magellan's steak house. The privacy in the wine cellar offered more intimacy than the main dining room. The four-course meal provided them with their choice of soup or salad, appetizer, main dish and dessert.

Victoria studied the menu and said, "I assume you're having the steak. I think I will, too."

"Actually, I'm having the braised cheek of filet," Tommy said with a surprised tone.

"Huh," was all she could say. She couldn't fathom that *cheek* was even a food people ate.

"I've always wanted to try it." He shrugged.

"I can't believe it's our last night in Asia. The last three weeks flew by. I'm not looking forward to that *long* flight across the Pacific," she whined.

"At least we're only flying to California, that'll cut seven hours off our journey to the states." Tommy referred to her home on the east coast in Charleston, South Carolina.

"What an adventure. I can't believe we went to Neverland while we visited Tokyo Disneyland." With an incredulous tone, she sipped her champagne.

"I know, even after our track record of discovering amazing archaeological finds beneath the first four parks, never in my wildest fantasies did I ever imagine that Neverland was real."

"Or angels, witches and Fairies," she added. "Speaking of fantasies."

Winking, he said with a sexy tone, "Oh yeah?"

Smacking his hand, she laughed with a pretend perturbed tone. "Not that kind of fantasy. Remember when we were in the cave in Shanghai?"

"How could I forget, we found Noah's Ark!" His tone rang with appreciation of discovering an archaeological find of biblical significance.

"Besides that, obviously. Remember you said, you'd marry me anytime, any*where*?"

"I do," Tommy rehearsed the most important wedding line.

"Well, since we're headed to the original Disneyland in California...."

"You want to make that our honeymoon?" His tone oozed with excitement.

Nodding, she beamed and said, "I've always wanted to get married at Disney!"

Victoria studied the beautiful décor of the wine cellar at Magellan's steak house. They had one of the best tables in the restaurant. Only a few patrons were granted the privilege of dining in the wine cellar. She surveyed the other patrons, then gasped.

Sitting at the table next to them, Tommy's doppelgänger, albeit a few years older, studied Tommy with the same incredulous expression. The older Tommy's beautiful, brunette dining companion obviously noticed the striking resemblance, too.

Completely clueless, Tommy Garrison studied the menu to presumably ensure he hadn't overlooked a spectacular dish.

"Didn't you mention a new Star Wars themed area was opening in the park soon?" she asked.

Finally closing his menu, he said, "Yeah, but what's that got to do with the 'price of tea in China?'" he bantered about her prior quoted quip.

"And isn't an Obi Wan Kenobi—A Star Wars Story movie in the works?"

"Yeah, I can't wait to see it. But I'm still not connecting your dots." He studied her with a bewildered expression.

Victoria nodded to the table next to them and said, "Don't look now, but sitting at the next table is the actor who plays Obi Wan Kenobi from *Star Wars Episodes I, II and III*—Ewan McGregor!"

Part Six
Plutonium Princess

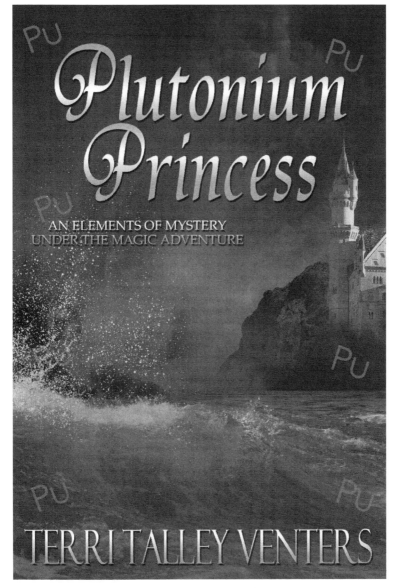

Prologue

Minerva awoke to the soothing sounds of the sea, just as she did each morning. An early riser, she thrived on the solitude of her early morning swim. She meandered through the palace as her family slumbered. Arriving at the terrace, she jettisoned herself into the peaceful serenity of the open water.

She began her routine at *mach* speed, waking up her body and mind as her lithe form cut through the water like a spear. Invigorated from the aqua sprint, she dove towards the depths of the sea.

Swimming at the bottom of the ocean, she admired the tiny seahorses with their tails wrapped around the plant branches. The sand, undisturbed, sparkled as the rays of the morning sun breached the water's surface and illuminated the ocean floor.

Minerva froze. A Great White shark swam nearby. She prayed the carnivorous creature wouldn't sense her presence. The shark appeared occupied with a bloody carcass at the surface. More sharks joined the Great White and his feeding frenzy.

A dark shadow loomed over her, blocking the sun's rays from the surface. Scared, Minerva knew the shadow's source before she verified the terrifying object above—a boat.

She swam away and headed home, wishing she'd never left the safety of Atlantis, at least what was left of it. Thousands of years ago, an earthquake opened a giant fissure in the floor of the Atlantic Ocean. Atlantis sank into the ocean floor, leaving only the tippy top of the gold palace on the bottom of the ocean. That's when the mermaids moved in and took over what little remained of Atlantis.

A wall of rope came towards Minerva. It extended from the surface to the floor with its sides angled towards her. She knew the dangers of the net because she'd witnessed it capture her fellow Atlanteans before. She retreated from the dangers of mankind's fishing net, but sensed a presence behind her. Fearful, she turned to face yet another enemy—the Great White shark!

The enormous creature swam towards Minerva, trapping her between the net and his carnivorous intentions. He lunged towards her with closed eyes, but missed. She darted away from the great beast, never taking her eyes off the predator. She realized her mistake as the ropes of the net caught her fin.

The shark retreated and avoided the net. But the net closed around Minerva, and she struggled. Then hopelessness sank in, and she stopped squirming. Tears flowed as the net lifted her up towards the surface.

Crunched together with a mixture of fish, seaweed and trash, she saw the morning sun as the net raised her out of the water and onto the wooden deck of the fishing boat.

"Captain, we've caught a mermaid!"

Chapter One

"Are you going to tell me which hotel we are staying at?" Tommy Garrison asked from the backseat of an Uber.

After landing at LAX Airport, the archaeological couple headed straight to Disneyland. This trip represented the final Disneyland park around the world. After their magical first date at Walt Disney World in Orlando, Florida, they vowed to visit all six Disneyland locations around the world—Orlando, Paris, Shanghai, Hong Kong, Tokyo and Anaheim.

Shooting him a playful glare, Victoria Ventures said, "Now you know how it feels," she referred to their reversed roles. Normally, Tommy planned their Disney trips. But this time, she planned their trip to the original Disneyland in Anaheim, California. She insisted because the main purpose of this particular trip was to plan their wedding at the 'Happiest Place on Earth.' They'd just set the date for December 21st, the anniversary of the day they met at Lilly's and Grier's wedding at Castle Garrison in Scotland's Isle of Skye.

"You're going to say it, aren't you," Tommy accurately predicted.

Laughing, she nodded and said, "Can't you just be surprised?"

Shaking his head in mock frustration, he said, "You really enjoyed that, didn't you?"

"Dern straight." She kissed his cheek.

Tommy pulled her close, then kissed her.

"Get a room. Oh wait, you did." The Uber driver laughed.

With almost a year to plan their magical wedding at Disneyland, she was thrilled to get started. She'd even perused the Disneyland wedding website during their *long* transpacific flight. There were a dozen venues to choose from. In fact, several were located at their hotel.

Their Uber driver pulled into the semi-circle driveway at the entrance to the hotel.

A bellhop, dressed in Safari attire, opened their car door and said, "Welcome, Mr. Garrison to the Grand Californian."

As Victoria and Tommy exited the car, Tommy arched his right eyebrow inquisitively and whispered, "How did they know my name?"

"I booked the suite under your name. They must be tracking your cell phone with GPS or cell tower pings and were alerted that you'd just arrived. Kinda scary, actually." She shuddered at the invasion of privacy.

They exited the Uber, and Victoria rated the driver from her phone. As she tapped away, Tommy grabbed her head and turned it towards the massive façade of the Grand Californian Hotel which resembled a large hunting lodge.

The bellhop, whose name tag read, Bob, placed their luggage onto a rolling luggage rack.

"How did you know my name, Bob?" Tommy asked.

Grinning, Bob turned, pretended to wave a magic wand in the air, and said, "Magic."

Chapter Two

"Wow!" Victoria walked into the massive lobby and gaped at the beautiful hotel. The lobby soared several stories high with exposed wooden beams in the ceiling. Large chandeliers hung over numerous cozy seating arrangements. The focal point of the lobby was the enormous hearth surrounding the warm fire place. Large boulders were stacked on both sides of the hearth which welcomed her to come and sit by the roaring fire.

Bob gestured and said, "Check in is over there, I'll be waiting here to escort you to your room."

Victoria and Tommy meandered to the check-in desk which contained beautiful wood carvings of dancing bears.

"Checking in?" The Cast Member, dressed like a Safari hunter, waved them over to his station.

Smiling, Victoria stepped forward and said, "Yes, Garrison. We booked a suite with a view of Space Mountain."

The Cast Member tapped away on the computer keyboard. "Ah, yes. Here it is." His expression turned grim. "Uh, Oh."

Fear whipped through her. "Oh, my! What's wrong?"

"Please excuse me for a moment while I get my manager." The Cast Member scurried off.

Victoria shot Tommy a worried stare.

Grabbing her hand to comfort her, he said, "Relax, my dear. We'll still get a room."

The manager appeared wearing a black suit. "Hello, Mr. and Mrs. Garrison."

Victoria blushed and confessed, "Oh, ah, we're not married, yet. In fact, we're recently engaged and planning our wedding here in December."

"Congratulations on your engagement. I'm afraid the suites with a view of Disneyland and Space Mountain are still under renovation. But I'll try to give you a free upgrade to a suite with a magnificent view of the California Adventure Park. Our hotel is located right between the two parks so we have rooms with views of both parks," the manager said.

"Oh, that sounds lovely." Victoria breathed a sigh of relief. Excitement filled her about getting a free upgrade.

The manager typed away on the keyboard for what felt like an eternity. "I swear, I'm not playing Candy Crush," the manager joked about the popular and addictive online game.

"Oh, the Arcadia Suite is available." The manager checked them in and gave them their magic bands. Then he opened a drawer and pulled out two pins with a picture of Mickey and Minnie Mouse touching noses. The top of the pins read: 'Congratulations on your engagement.' Then he beautifully scribed their names with a red sharpie. He even topped each *i* in Victoria with Mickey Mouse ears. Then he said, "Have a magical day."

Victoria turned to Tommy and smiled. "Ah."

They pinned their new buttons onto their plaid, flannel shirts and followed Bob to the elevator.

They exited the elevator on the top floor of the Grand Californian hotel. Tommy asked, "Is this a penthouse?"

Nodding enthusiastically, Bob rolled the luggage rack to the door, then gestured for Tommy to wave his magic band over the scanner.

Tommy scanned his blue magic band, and the door clicked open. He turned the knob and entered the beautiful suite.

"Welcome to the Arcadia Suite." Bob wheeled the cart into the bedroom portion of their suite and placed each of their suitcases on luggage racks in the closet. He placed their backpacks on the closet shelf, then turned to the happy couple. "Enjoy your stay."

Tommy handed him a twenty. "Thanks, Bob."

The separate bedroom boasted a king size bed with an intricately painted mural for a headboard. The hand-painted mural depicted a blossoming orange tree with the famous chipmunks, Chip and Dale, mischievously playing on the branches. Seeing the chipmunks reminded her of the handsy Cast Member dressed as the chipmunk Dale at Disneyland Paris.

The adjoining living room offered an inviting sectional sofa, an enormous flat screen television, a dining table and a wet bar. A stained-glass floor lamp with a silhouette of Thumper from the movie *Bambi* illuminated the room. But the best part of the room was the phenomenal view.

Victoria walked to the balcony and opened the sliding glass door. She walked out onto the large terrace with a breathtaking view of the California Adventure Park. The famous Mickey Mouse Ferris wheel dominated their view.

"I feel like I could just jump off the balcony and land in the park." She marveled at their close proximity to California Adventure.

Tommy stood next to her and said, "Wow. We *really* are close."

"In fact, this hotel has its own separate entrance into California Adventure," she said.

Tommy turned her away from their magnificent view of the Ferris wheel. He looked lovingly into her eyes and said, "In keeping with tradition." Then he kissed her on the balcony of the Grand Californian Hotel.

Chapter Three

"I'm starved!" Victoria announced as she exited the shower of their luxurious suite. She towel-dried her hair and mentally applauded the Bambi shower curtain, typical of Disney's attention to detail.

"Really? I'm good," Tommy shouted from the living room.

Shocked by his words, she donned the soft white robe, courtesy of the Grand Californian Hotel & Spa, and dashed to the living room because something was seriously wrong with Tommy. She found him sitting in front of the fireplace with a cup of tea and a copy of the *Los Angeles Times*. Standing in front of him, she stared at him incredulously.

Looking up, he asked, "What, my love?"

"You're kidding, right?" she asked, still shocked that she was starving before him. He needed to eat every two to three hours, if he was awake, or else he grew cranky. She could set her watch to his hunger pangs. But considering jetlag and the time difference with Asia, his stomach presumably thought it was nighttime.

Laughing, he stood and kissed her cheek. "You know me too well. Of course, I'm kidding."

Sighing with relief, she studied his expression. "You already know where we're going to eat, don't ya?"

"Obviously." His *duh* was implied. "Hurry up and get dressed, woman. I'm starved."

* * * *

The archaeological couple arrived at Storyteller's Café, conveniently located in the hotel. Exposed wooden beams and chandeliers decorated the ceiling. Silhouettes of mounted horses decorated the walls, along with large wilderness paintings.

A Cast Member immediately sat them at a cozy corner booth. Mickey Mouse, dressed like a safari hunter, waved to them with his white, oversized hands.

Victoria waved back and slid into the round corner booth. Tommy slid in next to her, and they took the menus presented by the hostess. Since it was the weekend, the Storyteller Café offered brunch from 11:30 to 2:00.

"Thank you." Victoria studied the beverage options. "So many choices—Bloody Mary, mimosa flight, raspberry champagne, Bellini-"

"-What the hell is a Bellini?" he asked.

"Prosecco sparkling wine and peach nectar. It originated in Venice," she recited.

"That's oddly specific. How did you know that?" He arched his blond right eyebrow inquisitively.

"I had one at Tokyo Disneyland, remember?" she asked.

Shaking his head, he said, "None of those girly, frou-frou drinks for me. How about a bottle of champagne?"

"What are we celebrating?" she asked.

"Being in a country where they speak English," he referred to their last three weeks in Asia. Only wanting to cross the Pacific roundtrip just once, they knocked out all three Disneyland parks in Asia in one long trip.

"Good enough for me." Closing the drink menu, she read the items offered on the brunch buffet.

Tommy did the same, then gasped, "Dear God in Heaven."

"I know. We have some tough decisions to make. Eggs benedict with Canadian bacon and hollandaise sauce, smoked salmon with capers and onions, omelet station, pork sausage, crispy bacon and French toast with maple syrup and strawberry compote," she read aloud from the menu.

"And warm bread pudding with vanilla sauce for dessert." He closed the menu.

A Cast Member arrived and asked, "Good morning, may I offer you something to drink? Non-alcoholic beverages are included with the buffet."

"We'll have a bottle of champagne," Tommy ordered.

"Excellent choice, sir. You may help yourself to the buffet." The Cast Member gestured towards the scrumptious feast.

Since she couldn't decide on just one thing, Victoria decided on a little bit of her top three choices. Dolloping small portions of eggs Benedict, smoked salmon and French toast onto her plate, she salivated over her imminent feast.

Once back at the table, the Cast Member presented them with a bottle of champagne. He showed it to Tommy, who promptly nodded his approval, then popped the cork. Pouring the bubbly goodness into two crystal flutes, the Cast Member said, "Enjoy your brunch."

"Oh, we will." Tommy lifted his flute. Then he turned to Victoria and toasted, "To us."

Clinking her flute with his, she said, "Cheers. I wonder what we'll find *Under The Magic* this time?"

Chapter Four

"Here's a great spot." Victoria pointed to a pair of cushioned lounge chairs near the beautiful pool of their hotel.

Obviously studying their options, Tommy asked, "Sun or shade?"

About to make perhaps her hardest decision of the day, she decided. "Sun, for now." Studying her normally tanned limbs, she rationalized that she could use a little more color. Besides, the January air in California chilled her.

"Great choice, my dear." He dropped the hotel-provided towels onto a pair of beige cushioned lounge chairs facing the pool with a magnificent view of California Adventure. He removed his Mickey Mouse t-shirt, exposing his muscled torso and eight-pack abs, then settled into his lounge chair.

Staring at his ripped upper body, she decided that Tommy provided a better view than the theme park. She dropped her fuchsia cinch sack onto the tiny table between the two lounge chairs. A random thought entered her mind, and she asked, "I wonder how Fuchsia is adjusting to her new home in New Orleans?" She referred to the tiny, injured Fairy they'd rescued from Neverland during their stay at Tokyo Disneyland.

"I'm sure Fuchsia and the Manchesters are doing well," Tommy referred to his distant relatives, who happened to be a witch, an archangel and their twin children with wings.

"We should invite them to the wedding," she declared. She removed her teal coverup and exposed her toned limbs, flat belly and Gator-blue bikini. They settled into the comfortable lounge chairs.

Tommy ogled her. "We should chill by the pool more often."

"Amen."

Grabbing her hand affectionately, he said, "Speaking of weddings, I'm excited to marry you at Disneyland. I wonder what wedding venues they offer?"

"I'm sure the right location will simply present itself, and we'll know." Comfortable, and slightly buzzed, she adjusted her position on the lounge chair.

"You pick the place, and I'll pick the food," he offered.

"Deal, I may have already found the venue." She tapped away on her iPad, then showed him a picture from the Disneyland wedding website. The picture showed the venue in front of Sleeping Beauty's Castle.

"Oh, wow. That'll work." He nodded wholeheartedly.

She recited, "Sleeping Beauty Castle Forecourt." In the picture, elegant chairs lined up in rows in front of Sleeping Beauty's Castle. Beautiful pink roses decorated the stage and aisles.

"Great job, hopefully we can book the castle on December 21st. But I'm just curious, what are our other choices?" he asked.

"Disneyland offers different gardens, courtyards and ballrooms for weddings. In fact, there are even a few venues at this hotel." She fiddled with the iPad and showed him the different venues on the website.

"Sleepy Beauty's Castle sounds great to me. If we're going to get married at Disneyland, better do it whole assed instead of half assed," he said jovially.

"I like the idea of you being in charge of the food," she admitted.

Tommy picked up his iPhone, tapped away, nodded appreciatively and said, "Done."

"Wow, that was quick," she marveled at his culinary efficiency.

"'That's *not* what she said,'" he joked with a wink.

"Let me guess, the food once had four legs," she quipped.

"You know me too well." He showed her a picture on his iPhone and said, "The Stardust Serenade Enchanted Duet Menu."

She admired the picture of an exquisitely plated dish with filet mignon and salmon.

He read aloud from the menu, "An artesian bread basket, creamy tomato basil soup with balsamic essence, grilled filet mignon *and* herb-roasted salmon with a cabernet shallot reduction and sauvignon blanc butter sauce. And finally, individual chocolate fondue with lots of goodies to dip."

"Sounds marvy. If I wasn't so stuffed from brunch, I'd suggest that we try it for dinner." She rubbed her bloated belly.

Tommy picked up the Los Angeles Times. Turning the pages, he arched his right eyebrow and said, "Huh."

Curious, she asked, "What is it?"

"Remember when we were in Asia and heard the news story about plutonium being stolen from North Korea?" he asked.

Holding up two fingers, she corrected, "Twice."

"Well, the Port of Los Angeles confiscated plutonium on a freighter ship from Asia."

"Huh, was someone smuggling plutonium in a new Toyota fresh off the assembly line in Japan?" she asked.

With an astonished tone, he said, "No, they found it in a huge shipment of Mickey Mouse souvenirs."

Chapter Five

"Which ride are we experiencing first, my dear." Tommy squeezed Victoria's hand as they entered the original Disneyland. With the time change from Asia, they'd gone to bed early and woke up before sunrise.

"Can't you just be surprised?" she teased.

"Now I know why you wanted to select the FastPasses this time. It's because you can't stand not knowing what ride we're going on next." He smirked.

"Care to take a guess?" she asked.

"Hmmm." He rubbed his stubbled chin with his thumb and index finger while he studied the Disneyland park sprawled out before them. "The Matterhorn?" He pointed to the iconic roller coaster.

"Great guess. We have FastPasses for the Matterhorn this afternoon." After strolling through Main Street USA, Victoria surveyed the shops lining the famous street. Admiring the balconies above the shops, she speculated which apartment Walt's brother, Roy Disney, once lived in.

"What rides do they have here?" he asked.

"All the classics—Space Mountain, Small World, Haunted Mansion and Pirates of the Caribbean. Plus a few rides unique to this park, like the Matterhorn. The Haunted Mansion here resembles a Southern plantation, instead of a creepy Victorian mansion like the one in Orlando."

"Any catacombs?" he asked, referring to their trip to Disneyland Paris where they discovered catacombs, real and fake, beneath Mystique Manor. Not to mention a gem mine filled with emeralds, rubies, sapphires and diamonds. Dwarfs and all.

"I doubt it. Catacombs are unique to Paris. During Halloween, they decorate the Haunted Mansion in a spooky, Tim Burton theme."

"Ah, like the movie *The Nightmare before Christmas*?" he asked enthusiastically.

Nodding she said, "With Jack the Pumpkin King and his ragdoll girlfriend, Sally."

Shivering, he said, "That sounds a little creepy."

"What? You're not scared, are you? Big baby," she teased.

"Ever since we met the Manchesters, and I know that witches, angels and demons are real, I'm terrified about what's really out there. Before I just thought my dad fabricated scary stories to keep me out of the woods near Castle Garrison."

"Well, if you think that's scary. Perhaps I shouldn't tell you one of Disneyland's best kept secrets," she teased.

"Well, *now* you must tell me," he said.

"When they first built Pirates of the Caribbean, Walt thought that the plastic skeletons looked too fake. So he-"

"-No!"

"Yep, he purchased real skeletons from the UCLA medical school."

"That *is* creepy. Now I've got the heebie geebies." He shivered.

"But they've since made better fakes and replaced the real ones," she said with a soothing tone.

"Ah, good to know when we ride Pirates of the Caribbean." He sighed with relief.

"Oh, wow." She stopped in front of Sleeping Beauty's Castle and admired the pink façade with blue turrets. "It's just like the one in Paris." She held up her iPhone and snapped a few pictures.

"Uh, I think you mean, the castle in Disneyland Paris is just like the original castle here in California," he corrected.

"Tomatoes, tomatoes," she chuckled.

They simultaneously surveyed the area in front of the castle where they hosted weddings.

"Is this the spot?" he asked, then placed one arm around her shoulder and pulled her close.

"I could definitely envision us getting married here." She smiled appreciatively.

"Like I said, I'll marry you anytime, anywhere." He kissed her cheek.

"This is definitely my favorite spot so far. But something nags the back of my brain."

"We'd get married in a cave if I'd let you." He smirked.

Shrugging, she said, "Maybe. But I'm waiting for that *ah-ha* moment. Then we'll just know the perfect place to get married."

"Would you like me to take your picture?" a Cast Member, holding a camera, asked.

"Sure," Tommy turned to face the Cast Member. He wrapped his arm around Victoria and pulled her close again.

Smiling for the camera, they posed for several pictures with Sleeping Beauty's Castle behind them.

"Thank you," Tommy said, then held out his magic band.

The Cast Member scanned his band and said, "Your pictures will *magically* appear on your 'My Disneyland Experience app.'" Then the Cast Member scurried off to photograph other tourists in front of the castle.

"In keeping with tradition." Tommy turned to her, stared lovingly into her eyes, then kissed her in front of Sleeping Beauty's Castle.

Chapter Six

"Are you sure you don't want to ride the Matterhorn first? There's no wait." Tommy nodded towards the iconic roller coaster, unique to the original Disneyland.

"Chill, woman," she chided, then dragged him to their first ride. This one excited her the most. She'd nearly cried when she'd read about this ride online.

A lagoon appeared before them. Yellow submarines floated sporadically throughout the lagoon.

Pausing, he said, "Ah, now I get it. 20,000 Leagues Under The Sea."

"Actually, it's Finding Nemo Submarine Voyage." She walked into the Stand-By entrance, thrilled that the wait time was only five minutes.

"Yellow Submarines? Not the Nautilus? I wonder if Disney recognizes the irony," he referred to the famous Beatles song, *Yellow Submarine,* which supposedly symbolized smoking a joint.

"I think Disney knows everything. But I wish they would have kept my favorite, classic ride." She pouted, only slightly disappointed.

"I guess with the popularity of the movies *Finding Nemo* and *Finding Dory,* Disney refurbished the ride for the kiddos," he speculated.

"Oh, we're practically the first ones in line." Smiling, she walked up the ramp, stepped into the rear of the yellow submarine and walked down several steps.

"All the way down, Miss." The Cast Member gestured towards the interior bow of the submarine.

Excitedly, she walked to the front and sat on the round stool in front of a porthole. Characters from Ray's fish school hovered above the coral reef. The projections were exactly like the movie, but the neon-painted Coral Reef resembled the real thing.

The submarine closed its doors, then a Cast Member recited the rules.

Chuckling, she felt like he read the rules specifically to her. Especially the part, "*Stay seated with your seatbelts fastened!*" Twice in Asia, she'd exited the ride before it ended, then trespassed and explored real cave tunnels.

The submarine floated through the coral reef. Music piped into the ride which coordinated with the various scenes from the animated film. By the end of the ride, Victoria felt as if she'd watched a condensed version of *Finding Nemo*.

Tommy nudged her and grinned. "That was neat. I feel like a five-year-old. But now all those songs are stuck in my head."

"'Mine, mine, mine,'" she quoted the famous line of the seagulls from the movie *Finding Nemo*. "But don't worry, you'll forget all the songs from *Finding Nemo* after we ride It's A Small World."

Rolling his eyes, he said, "Oh, dear, God."

"I wonder what Jules Verne would think about this?" Her tone rang with curiosity.

"He must be rolling in his grave," he speculated.

"Do you really think Jules Verne was right?" she asked.

"About...?" He arched his right eyebrow.

"All of it. The Center of the Earth, Mysterious Island, Atlantis...."

Shrugging, he justified, "All the Vernians believe," he referred to fans of Jules Verne, "but no one has ever found anything. But based on what we've found under the first five Disney parks, I'll believe anything."

Chapter Seven

"Is it just me, or was the Matterhorn slow?" Victoria asked as she disembarked from the ride.

"No, it's not just you; and yes, that was the faster track." Tommy referred to the two separate tracks of the Matterhorn with different intensity levels. Grabbing her hand, he led her through the exit queue.

Smiling, she said, "But it was still neat."

"Space Mountain was faster than that," he said with a disenchanted tone.

"It's cool that this Space Mountain had two passengers per row instead of one like the rides in Orlando and Paris."

"Was that the last FastPass for today?" he asked.

"Yes." She nodded.

"Come on, follow me." He guided her away from the Matterhorn.

"Where are we going? I thought I was in charge of the rides," she asked, slightly annoyed that he tried to take charge.

"Chill, woman. Besides, you said that *I* could be in charge of the food," he reminded her.

"Oh, yeah. You always make the best food choices," she easily acquiesced and eagerly anticipated their next meal.

He led her up a ramp, and they meandered through the metal queueing bars until they stood in front of an empty electric track.

Shooting him a puzzled stare, she asked, "We're going on the monorail?"

"Yes, it'll take us straight to California Adventure." He gestured in the direction of the adjacent theme park.

The monorail pulled into the station, slowed, then stopped. Its doors opened, and they entered.

"Too bad we can't sit up front anymore." He snapped his fingers disappointedly.

"Oh, I never even knew that sitting up front was once a thing." She arched her right eyebrow inquisitively.

Waving his arms to the front of the monorail, he pointed and explained, "Do you see those empty seats in front of the driver?"

The front of the monorail offered leather seats in front of the glass windshield. "Oh yeah. That would be neat. Why did they stop letting people ride up front?" she asked as they boarded the monorail.

Sitting on the seat, he dropped his head with a saddened expression.

"Uh, oh." She sympathetically placed her hand over her heart.

Nodding somberly, he said, "People died in the front when a monorail crashed with another monorail, even the driver."

"How sad?" She mourned the tragedy.

The monorail picked up speed and glided quietly above Disneyland. As it meandered above the theme park, it provided a great aerial overview of the original Disneyland.

Staring out the window and trying not think about dying on the monorail, she said, "This is neat."

"I think we rode everything today, and it's only 3 o'clock."

Glancing up, she mentally recalled the list of rides, then agreed, "I think we rode everything with the exception of Toon Town which is more for kiddies."

"Great job, my dear. It's difficult to ride every ride at Disneyland in one day," he slowly clapped with a congratulatory nod.

"It helped that this park is really small compared to the Magic Kingdom in Florida. Everything here is so close together." She marveled at her own efficiency.

"And the time of year helps, too. I imagine the second week of January is one of the least crowded times at Disney, especially during the week."

"And this weather is perfect. It's January, but it's sunny and not cold, just a slight breeze. It feels like fall in Charleston," she reminisced.

"Definitely not like the brutal winters in Scotland. *Brrr.*" Tommy shivered.

The monorail picked up speed and headed towards California Adventure.

She chuckled, then shook her head incredulously.

"What's so funny?" he asked.

Grinning, she said, "I think the monorail is going faster than the Matterhorn."

Chapter Eight

"Why do I feel like I've been here before?" Victoria asked.

"Because that's the view from our balcony." He pointed towards their hotel.

They exited the monorail and entered California Adventure.

"I wasn't planning on visiting this park this afternoon. We don't have any FastPasses. What should we do first?" She studied the park map to get her bearings.

Smiling, he grabbed his belly and said, "We eat."

"Of course." Her *duh* was implied.

Taking the map from her, he studied the restaurant guide. Running his finger along the colorful map, he pointed and said, "Ah, here it is. The restaurant is on the Pacific Wharf."

"Huh? I thought the Pacific Wharf was in San Francisco," she said with a perplexed tone.

"The real one is. California Adventure includes areas unique to California, like Napa, Sonoma and the Pacific Wharf."

"I could really go for some wine tasting." She grinned mischievously.

"And I could go for some wine drinking!" He grabbed her hand and guided her through the park.

"Are you going to tell me where we are going?" she asked.

"Chill, woman. Don't make me say it." He shook his head with mock frustration.

"Come on. It's one of the many things you love about me," she referred to her insatiable need to know everything.

"Of course, my dear." He kissed the top of her hand, still held by his, and said, "Mwah."

They walked through the main street filled with souvenir shops including the 'Five and Dime.' Victoria silently chuckled because the over-priced store probably didn't sell anything for a dime, except perhaps two nickels or ten pennies. The path of shops ended at a pedestrian round-a-bout surrounding a beautiful fountain.

Distracted by a shiny object, Victoria pulled Tommy towards a bronze statue of Walt and Mickey Mouse. The plaque read, 'Story Tellers'. After snapping a selfie, Victoria immediately posted the photo on Instagram.

They meandered around the fountain and passed The Grizzly Peak water rapid ride, Mater's Junkyard Jamboree. Then Tommy stopped in front of a building resembling a Californian winery. Terra cotta tiles capped a peachy pink, two-story building. She felt as if she was in Napa Valley. "Is this it?"

"*Voila!* The Alfresco Tasting Terrace," he announced their dining destination.

"But it's not five o'clock yet," she quipped.

"That rule does not apply at Disney." He held up two fingers to the Cast Member at the hostess stand and said, "Two please."

The Cast Member grabbed two menus and said, "Follow me, please." She guided them up a flight of stairs and out onto the open terrace offering alfresco dining. Tables were filled with tourists sampling wine and enjoying appetizers, small plates and flatbreads.

The food obviously caught Tommy's attention because he scrutinized each occupied table as they passed.

The hostess escorted them to a table for two which provided a breathtaking view of Radiator Springs. "Best seat in the house." She placed two menus on their table and said, "*Bon appétit.*"

Taking a seat in the chair Tommy had pulled out for her, Victoria said with an exaggerated Southern accent, "Well, thank ya kind sir."

Ignoring the menu, she marveled at the beautiful view of Radiator Springs. She felt as if she was in the movie, *Cars.* "Isn't this view amazing?"

Without looking up from his menu, he referred to the food, "Oh yeah, everything looks awesome."

Shooting him a mock perturbed expression, she asked, "Tommy Manchester Garrison, do you ever think about anything besides food?"

Grabbing her hands from across the table, he squeezed them, looked lustfully into her eyes and said in his bedroom voice, "Oh, yeah!"

Chapter Nine

"Good afternoon, may I start you off with some wine? We have an excellent wine tasting flight and a collection of Disney family wines made in California's wine region."

Briefly taking his eyes away from the food menu, Tommy studied the extensive wine list. Something obviously stood out. Decisively, he ordered, "Silver Oak, Napa Valley."

"Excellent choice, sir. You have exquisite taste." The Cast Member bowed, then scurried off to fetch the wine.

Curious, Victoria studied the wine menu, shocked that Tommy just ordered a $200 bottle of wine. Although they were now both *uber* rich because of the silver mine Victoria discovered beneath Castle Garrison two years ago, her humble beginnings often drove her frugal tendencies. "Holy shit, Batman!"

With a nonchalant shrug, he justified, "At least we're earning double Disney dollars while we're in the park."

Returning her attention to the food menu, she studied their choices, "Oh, we *have* to share the charcuterie and cheeseboard." Anticipating his reaction, she mentally prepared herself for his imminent protest.

Like clockwork, Tommy retaliated with a basilisk stare. "What, are you new? You know that I hate to share food. Besides, the Charcuterie and cheese board looks pretty small." He nodded at a nearby table.

"It's just an appetizer. I thought we could share that, then each get our own flatbread."

"Argh, fine. That's probably a good idea because I'm sure you don't want the flatbread I want. Sausage and arugula probably won't appeal to you because it has green stuff in it," Tommy referred to her abhorrence of vegetables.

"Hey, sundried tomato flatbread with pesto and mozzarella has green stuff on it," she bantered.

"Pesto does not count as a vegetable," he scolded.

"Humph." She crossed her arms and pouted.

The Cast Member appeared and presented Tommy a bottle of Silver Oak, Napa Valley. Tommy nodded his approval, and the Cast Member uncorked the wine and poured Tommy a sample to taste.

He swirled the wine glass, watched the wine's legs slowly descend the bulbous glass interior, and sniffed the aroma before finally tasting. Nodding his approval again, Tommy said, "Wow. That's up there with the best wine I've ever tasted."

The Cast Member poured Victoria's and Tommy's glasses, then asked, "Would you like to place a food order?"

Tommy couldn't order the charcuterie and flatbreads fast enough. After the Cast Member scurried off, Tommy asked, "What rides do they have here?"

She waved her arm towards their view. "There's a new area called Cars Land which is obviously themed from the animated film, *Cars*."

"*Cars* one, two, *and* three," he referred to the most recent installments of the movie franchise.

Their charcuterie and cheese board arrived in record time. Various pepperonis, salamis and cheeses were neatly displayed on a butcher block in the shape of Mickey Mouse ears. Honey, nuts and dried fruit occupied the middle, and bread crostini formed the ears.

Tommy made a tiny sandwich with crostini, a slice of salami, parmesan and a dollop of honey.

Victoria chose to eat her items separately. Taking a bite of cheese, she hummed. "Mmmmm. This is so good."

With food still in his mouth, he asked, "What other rides are here?"

"Most of the rides are unique to this park. Except Soarin', we rode that one in EPCOT on our first date," she referred to their first date at Walt Disney World.

"We saw the Mickey Mouse Ferris wheel and that giant roller coaster from our balcony. I hope the Incredicoaster goes faster than the Matterhorn," he quipped.

She recited the ride description from memory, "It goes from zero to fifty-five miles an hour in four seconds. It's also the third longest steel roller coaster in the United States and eighth longest in the world."

"Awesome, but maybe we should wait until our flatbreads settle." Turning, he smiled as the Cast Member placed their flatbreads in front of them. "Speaking of which."

"*Bon appétit*," the Cast Member said.

"This looks delicious." She admired her flatbread.

"More wine?" Tommy picked up the bottle of Silver Oak.

"Duh." Picking up the flatbread, she took a bite. Mozzarella cheese, topped with sundried tomatoes and pesto, slid into her mouth. "Oh, my, God. This is so good," she said with a mouthful of food.

Tommy closed his eyes in food-induced bliss. "Hmmm. Mine is awesome, too. Even the green stuff. I would never think to put arugula on pizza, but it pairs nicely with the sausage."

"You'll have to make it sometime, on *your* half." She sipped her delicious wine and decided it was worth the hefty price.

"The food is distracting you. What other rides do they have here?" He corralled her tangential thoughts.

"They have Toy Story Midway Mania, like the one at Hollywood Studios in Florida," she referred to the three-dimensional carnival game where the riders shoot at various targets to score points.

"I love that ride. Shooting stuff is always fun, but my hand always hurts after rapidly yanking that string trigger." He rubbed his right hand preemptively.

"They have a bunch of stuff I've never heard of. And they completely revamped an old ride, and I think you'll love it," she speculated.

"What makes you say that?" He arched his right eyebrow inquisitively.

"Because you loved the movies, especially the sound tracks." She grinned playfully, knowing it would drive him nuts if she left him wondering.

"You're not going to tell me, are you?" He shrugged defeatedly.

"Nope. There's a cool parade with Disney Pixar characters." Her mind corralled the rest of the rides she'd read about on the Disneyland app. Then disappointment settled in and must've shown on her face.

"What's wrong?" he asked, intuitively.

"I don't think any of the rides here have the potential for hidden caves." She pouted.

Shrugging, he said with a reassuring tone, "Relax, my dear, maybe the entrance to a cave will just *open up*."

Chapter Ten

"Wheee!" Victoria squealed as the Incredicoaster came to an end.

Exiting the roller coaster, Tommy squeezed her hand and sang, "That was awesome!"

"I love how they themed the roller coaster after the animated film—*The Incredibles*."

"Those dark tunnels they added to the roller coaster were so cool," he said excitedly.

"I love how they projected the characters from the movie onto the curved walls of those dark tunnels. Mr. Incredible, Elastagirl, Violet, Dash and Jack Jack were right there in our faces." She held the open palm of her hand in front of her face.

"I'm glad we did Toy Story Midway Mania before the roller coaster. I'd rather keep all that wonderful food and wine in my belly," he said.

Quickly studying the map, she mentally planned their route from the Incredicoaster to Tommy's surprise ride. She couldn't wait to ride this and see Tommy's expression when they got there. Pointing, she said, "This way."

Shaking his hand, he said, "How does your hand not hurt after yanking that trigger repeatedly on the Toy Story ride?"

"I don't do the practice round. I save my arm strength until the end when you can rack up big points on those plates. That's how I get to the five-thousand-point plates. I'm surprised you didn't notice that I wasn't pulling the trigger at first," she said with a surprised tone.

"Huh, that's actually a great idea." Shaking his head with frustration, he added, "You didn't practice and you still beat me."

After exiting the Incredicoaster, they meandered through Cars Land. Race cars at Radiator Springs whizzed by on a nearby track.

Pointing, she said, "We have FastPasses for Radiator Springs tomorrow."

"Looks like fun." He grinned.

They walked past Luigi's Rollickin' Roadsters and Tuck and Rolls's Drive 'Em Buggies.

They turned the corner, and a tall tower dominated their view. Victoria stopped in front of the surprise ride and stared up at the massive, thirteen-story structure. "Tada!" she sang, then turned to Tommy to gauge his reaction.

"Oh, my, God, I love you," he said, elatedly, without taking his eyes off the ride.

"Me or Guardians of the Galaxy?" she chuckled.

"Both." He kissed her cheek and squeezed her hand appreciatively.

They walked through the Stand-By entrance. "Only twenty minutes. That's not so bad," she said.

They slowly meandered with the crowd through a museum of The Collector's collection. Oddities from the galaxy filled the room and gave them something to look at. Eighties music from the movie's soundtrack played in the queue.

Tommy studied the oddities occupying glass cases. "This is so cool. I'm glad we didn't have FastPasses for this ride." He pointed towards the FastPass entrance which went directly onto the ride, bypassing the cool museum. "The FastPass riders don't get to see all this cool stuff."

The twenty-minute wait, more like ten, flew by. Rocket the Raccoon gave them instructions in a holding room. Their mission was to breakout the Guardians of the Galaxy.

Finally in the boarding room, Tommy studied the large service elevator they were about to board. With a whisper, he asked, "Why is this familiar?"

"Think about it," she hinted.

His eyes lit up, he'd obviously made the connection. "Ah, yes, the Tower of Terror," he referred to the ride in Hollywood Studios in Orlando, Florida.

They boarded the elevator with seats and buckled their seatbelts. Then the music started, and everyone in the elevator sang, *Hooked On A Feeling*. The elevator went up and down sporadically and opened up on different floors. At each level, different characters were projected in front of them as the passengers freed the Guardians of the Galaxy.

"That was awesome!" Tommy grinned 'like a kid at...'

They exited the ride, which corralled them into the gift shop, and perused the Guardians of the Galaxy souvenirs. "I know, right? I hear that there are six different versions, each with a different song and different projections. You can ride it six times and get a whole new experience each time."

He arched his right eyebrow and asked, "Are you up for it? The wait isn't that long. We've got time to kill before the Pixar Parade."

"Absolutely, but let's get some t-shirts, the one you're wearing is old and ratty," she chastised.

"Hey, I love this t-shirt. It's worn in. But I can always get another one." Shrugging, he acquiesced.

They purchased their t-shirts and the soundtracks to both movies—*Guardians of the Galaxy-Volumes 1 & 2*.

Exiting the gift shop. Victoria checked the Disneyland app on her iPhone. She tapped on 'my photos' and a picture of her and Tommy smiling on the ride appeared. Puzzled, she asked, "Did you wave your magic band on the scanner beneath our picture when we exited the ride?"

"No, sorry, I forgot. Want me to go back? But it's probably too late. They only give you about thirty seconds to scan your magic band beneath your picture," he sighed.

"No need, the picture *magically* appeared on our Disneyland app." She showed him their picture on the Guardians of the Galaxy ride. Puzzled, she wondered how Disney knew they were there.

"Huh." He shrugged.

"How did they know? We didn't use our magic bands because we didn't have FastPasses." Puzzled, she racked her brain to figure out how this was even possible.

Holding up his blue magic band, he speculated, "The magic bands must have some sort of GPS tracking our precise location in the park."

"But how did they know to send this exact picture to our app versus some other tourist?" she asked, feeling violated for this invasion of privacy.

"Magic." He laughed.

Then a creepy thought filled her. "Facial recognition."

"That's scary." He grimaced.

Laughing off the eerie notion, she said, "Remind me never to go into hiding at Disneyland."

Chapter Eleven

"Oh, I think I'm going to be sick." Victoria ran to a trash can and vomited.

"I told you to take another Dramamine," he said with his best, 'I told you so' tone.

Wiping her mouth with a tissue, she scolded, "Whose bright idea was it to ride Guardians of the Galaxy six times in a row?"

"I didn't have to twist your arm. Are you okay?" Tommy retrieved a stick of Juicy Fruit gum from the side of his backpack and handed it to her.

"Thank you." Quickly unwrapping the gum, she popped the juicy goodness into her mouth, rapidly chewing to get that God-awful vomit taste out of her mouth.

"I happen to have a vested interest in the taste of your mouth." He kissed her cheek.

"I actually feel better." Checking her watch, she said, "We better find a good place to watch the parade."

He pointed to a nearby park bench conveniently located next to the temporary queuing ropes being erected by Cast Members. "How about you save our seats on the bench, and I'll grab us a turkey leg and a beer."

"Sounds marvy." She kissed his cheek, then sat on the bench and plopped her fuchsia cinch sack next to her to save Tommy's seat.

While he scurried off to procure dinner, she marveled at the beauty of the park at dusk. Lights on the Ferris wheel and streetlights turned on. Cast Members pushed carts of glow-in-the-dark gadgets for tourists to play with during the imminent parade. Children walked by swinging their recently acquired, *Star Wars* light sabers.

Little girls, dressed as Cinderella, Belle, Aurora and Rapunzel walked by. Their tiny tiaras topped the glittered buns on each of their heads. Victoria touched her crown—the one Tommy had bought her in Tokyo Disneyland. For the first time ever, she thought about having children. Tommy would make a wonderful father. She looked forward to bringing their children to Disneyland.

Spotting Tommy carrying two beers and a giant turkey leg, she said, "That was fast."

Tommy handed her a beer and sat down next to her. "Cheers." He toasted his plastic beer cup with hers.

"Cheers, what a great way to watch a parade." She sipped her beer and hummed. "Mmm."

Tommy yawned. "I'm exhausted."

"We're still on Asia time. I say we head back to the hotel after this." She nodded to their nearby hotel.

"But it's so *far* away," he whined sarcastically.

She sipped her beer again. "What kind of beer is this? It's hoppy, I like it."

"Does it really matter? It's some local IPA." He sipped his beer, placed the cup on the bench and tore off a piece of turkey. He offered her the first piece.

"Thank you. I'm glad you only got one turkey leg because I'm actually not that hungry," she confessed.

"Me neither, but I knew I would be soon. I'm sure you'd appreciate not having a starving, cranky butt on your hands during the parade." He smirked.

The lights dimmed, and music played. Victoria whispered, "Shhh, the parade is about to start."

The Pixar Logo Lightbulb led the parade. The theme song from the animated film *Toy Story, You Got A Friend In Me*, piped through the sound system. Next, the characters from *Monster's Inc.*—Sullivan, Mike Wazowski and Roz—rolled around on wheeled contraptions. Next, the Incredibles stars—Mr. Incredible, Elasta Girl and Frozone—rolled on contraptions which resembled a cross between a flying saucer and a Segway. The characters from *Inside Out*—Joy and Sadness—passed by waving on a float. Then Nemo and Dory floated by, followed by the giant sea turtle, Crush, and his abundant offspring. The caterpillar from *It's A Bug's Life* rolled by, followed by ants swinging on floats. The melody from Cindy Lauper's famous song, *Girls Just Wanna Have Fun* played. But they changed the lyrics to "Bugs Just Wanna Have Fun."

"I wonder how much Disney paid Cindy Lauper to butcher her song?" Victoria asked.

"I'd accept a lifetime annual pass to all of the Disneyland Parks worldwide," he confessed.

Next were the characters from *Up*—the old man Carl, the scout Russell, Doug the dog and a tinker toy version of Kevin, the female rare bird.

Bringing up the rear of the parade were all of the favorite characters from *Toy Story*. The green army men marched with precise synchronization, followed by the green, three-eyed aliens from the claw machine at Pizza Planet. A float with the rest of Andy's toys, starring Buzz and Woody, finished the spectacular parade.

* * * *

"What a magical day." She sighed as they exited the park. Luckily, their hotel was just a quick walk away.

Ping
Ping

375

After exchanging quizzical expressions, they silently acquiesced one another to check their phones.

Fox Breaking News—Scientists predict the 'Big One' is imminent in California. Intense seismic activity along the entire San Andreas fault could even break the western part of the state away from the Continental United States.

Chapter Twelve

Rumble

Victoria and Tommy shot up in bed the next morning.

"What the hell is that noise?" she asked.

"Thunder?" He stared at her with a bewildered expression.

Peering through the window, the early morning sun greeted them. "There's not a cloud in the sky."

Nodding down, he said, "It sounds like it is coming from the ground."

The fire alarm blared, and they covered their ears.

Donning their hotel-provided white robes and slippers, they exited their room, then walked down several flights of stairs to the lobby. Droves of people exited the hotel.

"What's going on?" Tommy asked.

"Earthquake," a Cast Member said nonchalantly.

"Oh, my God! What do we do?" Victoria asked with a terrified tone. She'd never experienced an earthquake before.

"Just stand outside away from buildings." The Cast Member's tone was calm, like earthquakes were a normal occurrence. Apparently, they were in California.

Tommy and Victoria walked away from the hotel. The hotel pool was a safe distance away.

Rumble. Rumble. Rumble.

A huge crack in the Earth appeared. It started near the pool and continued away from them towards Disneyland.

As quick as it started, the rumbling stopped. Fortunately, the crack never reached the 'Happiest place on Earth.'

"Look at the pool. The water drained away." Tommy pointed.

"I thought the Earth was solid. Where did the water go?" Victoria asked.

Tommy rubbed his chin with his thumb and index finger. "Well, actually, some people believe that the Earth is hollow inside, once you get through the outer crust."

"Who believes that?" she asked with a condescending tone.

"Vernians believe that the Earth is hollow and that there is another world within the surface world."

"My geology is rusty, but that sounds like a load of...." Victoria crossed her arms.

The empty pool revealed a giant crack, at least ten feet wide.

"Why don't we find out?" Tommy pointed.

Her curiosity overruled her common sense. "We have our rock-climbing gear back in the room. I'd just thought that we'd use it to go up, not down."

He studied the crowd of hotel guests walking away. "Looks like everyone is going back into the hotel. The earthquake must be over."

An hour later, they returned to the empty pool, fully equipped to see what lay beneath the Earth's crust.

Tommy shined his flashlight into the large crevasse. "It's a straight drop to another level. I'll go first." Tommy secured the rope, then tested its strength. He rappelled down into the hole about two hundred feet.

"Come on down, there's something shiny down here," Tommy shouted.

You don't need to tell me twice. Victoria couldn't rappel herself down fast enough.

Tommy greeted her at the lower level of the large crack.

"That was fun. Now, where's my shiny object?" Her jaw dropped. The walls sparkled. "Is that white gold?"

"No, it's rhodium. It's eight times more valuable than gold and nearly five-hundred times more valuable than silver. It's used to coat gold in jewelry to make it shinier. They call it rhodium flashing."

"How do you know so much about rhodium?" she asked.

"After you discovered the silver mine beneath Castle Garrison, I did tons of research on precious metals."

"Nerd," she teased.

"That's not what you called me last night." Tommy winked suggestively.

"Touché." She smiled at the happy recollection of their nocturnal activities.

"In fact, Guinness awarded Paul McCartney a rhodium album. Since he sold a gazillion albums, he deserved something more than just gold and platinum albums."

"Google much?" she teased.

Ignoring her quip, he said, "I wonder if Disney knows that there is a fortune in rhodium beneath their theme parks."

"I hope they own the mineral rights, too." She recalled the gem mine they discovered beneath Disneyland Paris.

Tommy retrieved a chisel from his backpack and broke off a piece. "For early retirement."

"You can't steal that!" she scolded with a smack on his knuckles.

Ignoring her, Tommy broke off several more chunks of rhodium.

Rumble!

"I thought the earthquake was over. I hope your chiseling *slash* stealing didn't cause another earthquake." Fear flew through Victoria.

The walls around them trembled. They clung to each other, terrified.

"Aftershocks?" he asked.

"This feels worse than the first one."

The floor beneath them cracked open, and they slid down, and down, and down, thousands of feet.

Chapter Thirteen

They landed on some sort of island with ancient temples on the mountain. Miniature moons glowed brightly and illuminated the island and its surrounding waters.

"Looks like Jules Verne was right. The Earth *is* hollow." Tommy surveyed their new surroundings with an awestruck expression.

"Are we in the center of the Earth?" she asked.

"Perhaps not in the exact center, but somewhere inside." They walked along the shore of a sandy beach. Palm trees swayed with a gentle breeze. Not a sun, but some sort of blue light illuminated the island paradise.

"Reminds me of Neverland," she referred to their recent discovery, via portal, in Tokyo Disneyland.

"Hopefully, there are no Sirens here." Tommy shuddered, obviously recalling his near-death experience in Neverland when a Siren hypnotized him with a spellbinding song and nearly lured him into the water. Luckily, a swarm of Fairies saved him with pixie dust.

"This place feels soothing, like nothing bad could happen here." Strolling along the shore, she admired the temples on top of the mountain. "Huh?"

"What is it, love?" he asked.

Pointing she said, "Look at the top of the temple. It stops abruptly, like part of its top was sliced off."

"Yeah, you're right. I wonder what happened? I don't see anyone here." He surveyed their surroundings.

"They might be hiding, or sleeping. It was early in the morning when the earthquake struck," she speculated.

"If anyone is even down here at all. How did this place even get down here? And how can it sustain itself?" he asked.

Walking towards a red, lush tropical flower, she touched the petal. "I don't know, but somehow it does, the plants and trees are thriving." She gestured towards the green and colorful plants hugging the mountain.

Something shimmered in the sky, and Tommy turned his head to study its origin. He jogged in the opposite direction of the mountain.

"Tommy, wait! What is it?" she asked, jogging to catch up to him.

Stopping abruptly, they stared in awe at some sort of blue, glowing force field.

The force field curved up and formed a dome over the island.

With a marveling tone, he said, "I think we're in some sort of protective bubble or dome."

"What? A dome?" she asked, incredulous.

"Yeah, check it out." He waved his hand up over his head, gesturing at the blue shimmering force field which capped the island.

"Huh, it's like the force field provides the light source. What is it?" she asked.

"Ancient Alien technology," he speculated.

"What's that orange and black stuff on the other side?" Just outside the protective walls of the force field, orange lava flowed. Plates of flat stone floated along the lava, like rafts on a river.

"What the...?" He marveled at the lava.

"We're in a bubble floating on a rock in a lava river in the middle of the Earth. How did this even get down here? And don't get me started on how the hell we're going to get out of here." She shuddered at the horrific notion.

Hugging her, he said, "At least we're alive and together. I guess there could be worse places to be stuck."

"How did we even break through the force field?" She held her hand up to the shimmering, blue glowing wall of the dome.

"Don't touch it!" he hollered.

"I won't. It's like we're on a tiny planet." She marveled at their surroundings.

"Maybe a small planet crashed into Earth," he speculated.

"Or maybe during an earthquake, the Earth opened up and swallowed the entire island." Her mind was onto something, but she wasn't sure what.

"An island sinking into the Earth?" he asked.

With a perturbed tone, she asked, "What wrong with that theory?"

"Nothing. I think you're onto something?" He rubbed his stubbled chin with his thumb and index finger.

"What do you mean?"

"Think about all the theories about islands sinking into the Earth," he said.

"Mmmm." She stared at the top of the mountain, and the answer was on the tip of her tongue.

"Victoria, come on, you're over thinking this. I can only think of *one* island." He prodded.

"No. It can't be," she said with an astonishing tone.

"It's gotta be." He shrugged.

"I can't even say it." She shook her head, astonished.

"Let's say it together in three, two, one..." he counted down.

"We're in Atlantis!"

Chapter Fourteen

"Wow! I can't believe we discovered Atlantis." A thrill shot through her, and elation filled her heart with joy.

Shaking his head incredulously, Tommy said, "It's surreal."

"How did it get down here?" she asked. Turning, she studied the palace on top of a mountain. Its golden columns rose to the top of the protective bubble.

"Well, the legend says it sank into the ocean. I'd always interpreted that to mean a giant tsunami flooded the island and it stayed underwater permanently," he explained.

"Well, it sank alright, just not to the bottom of the ocean. Perhaps it got down here the same we did—an earthquake opened a giant fissure in the Earth, and the island sank through it."

"But how do you explain the giant, protective bubble around Atlantis." He waved his arm towards the shimmering force field.

"Magic." She waved an imaginary wand. Since she'd recently learned of Tommy's latent magical powers, she was now a true believer of the magical world.

Winking, he said, "Good one."

"But it could be some sort of Ancient Alien technology," she referred to his conspiracy theory that Ancient Aliens once roamed the Earth.

Grinning excitedly, he said, "Now we're talking. But even you must admit, it makes sense. Ancient Aliens were once here. They harnessed some strange new energy source that protected Atlantis just before the Earth swallowed her whole."

Fear shot through her, and she gasped.

"What's wrong, love?" he asked, staring into her eyes with deep concern.

"What if the Ancient Aliens are still here?" Terror shot through her, and she shuddered.

"'That's highly illogical, Jim,'" Tommy quoted Spock from *Star Trek*.

"I'd forgotten that you were a 'Trekkie,'" she referred to the coined term describing avid *Star Trek* fans. "But, why not? The plants survived." Victoria waved to the luscious vegetation surrounding them in this tropical paradise.

Studding their surroundings, he obviously contemplated the notion. "Huh."

Inhaling deeply, she said, "Since we're breathing down here, there must be oxygen."

Inhaling too, he agreed, "You're right. Why didn't it dawn on me before now?"

"It's okay, you're entitled to a *blond* moment." She ran her fingers through his golden locks.

Crackle, crackle.

Turning abruptly, she studied the nearby trees. "Did you here that?"

Standing in front of her protectively, he said, "I sure did."

Crackle, crackle.

Turning in the opposite direction, she studied the shrubs.

Crackle, crackle.

Turning ninety degrees, she stared at yet another noisy area of shrubs and she clung to him. "Tommy, I'm scared."

"I know." He held her protectively.

"What should we do?" Her tone echoed with fear.

"Don't make any sudden movements. Whatever it is, they have us surrounded. There is no point in running," he rationalized.

"Should we hold up our hands?" she whispered.

"No, if it is an animal, it might interpret our intended surrender as an act of aggression," he rationalized.

"Good point, should we stay still? Should we get on our knees and bow?" she asked.

"I think we should stay perfectly still, in case it's a T-rex," he warned, barely moving his lips.

With that, she remained silent, quickly remembering that some predators see by motion, not sight.

All they could do now was pray!

Chapter Fifteen

Hail Mary, full of grace. The Lord is with thee. Blessed art thou among women, and blessed is the fruit of thy womb, Jesus. Holy Mary, Mother of God, pray for us sinners, now and at the hour of our death. Amen.

Silently praying, Victoria repeated the prayer over and over again. She knew Tommy prayed, too. Recalling how their prayers were answered when an avalanche nearly killed them after they discovered Noah's Ark near Disneyland Shanghai, she embraced a sense of peace. If she was about to die, at least she was with her beloved, Tommy. And she had to admit, if they were going to die, being forever interred in Atlantis sounded epic. Then she realized that no one even knew they were in Atlantis. Her mother, and social media, knew she was at Disneyland in California. Everyone would presume them victims of the earthquake.

The crackling noises stopped, and her curiosity finally allowed her to open her eyes. Dozens of humanoid creatures surrounded them, but they didn't carry weapons. Their heights ranged from eight to ten feet. Their skin was alabaster white, like they'd never seen the sun before. Which they probably hadn't considering that they lived beneath the Earth's surface. Their platinum blond hair hung in long braids to their waists. Their eyes glowed the same shade of blue as the force field. They appeared to be equally curious about them. Humans don't exactly fall into Atlantis every day.

"Who is this Mary you hail?" A humanoid asked, stepping forward to study them more closely.

Victoria and Tommy turned to one another and exchanged shocked expressions. Then they shrugged simultaneously.

"You speak, English?" Tommy asked, his tone oozed with incomprehension.

"Yes, we know all the languages in the Universe," the humanoid boasted.

"You can read our minds?" she asked.

"Yes, that is how we knew you were more scared of us than we were of you. We know all of the Gods in the Universe, but we've never heard of Mary." The humanoid stared with a perplexed expression.

"You've obviously been down here for more than two thousand years," Tommy speculated.

"How did you know?" the humanoid asked.

"Because Christianity is only two thousand years old. Mary is the mother of Jesus Christ, the son of God," Tommy explained.

"Ah, that is why it is not in our knowledge base," the humanoid said.

"How long have you been down here?" she asked.

"Thousands of years. Come, we will take you to our princess. She will be most curious about you." The humanoid turned and gestured towards the palace.

Chapter Sixteen

"My name is Tommy Garrison and this is my future wife, Victoria Ventures." Tommy stood and held out his hand to shake the humanoid's.

The humanoid stepped forward and held out his hand, but didn't touch Tommy's. Then he said, "Greetings, my name is Ketko. Forgive me, I'm not sure what to do with your hand."

Tommy grabbed it and shook it. "This is the custom on Earth."

"Ah, in Atlantis, we greet one another like this." Ketko held his fingers together, then separated the middle and ring fingers.

Tommy held his hand out and mimicked Ketko's fingers.

"'Live long and prosper,'" Ketko unknowingly quoted Spock from *Star Trek*.

Grinning, Tommy said, "'Live long and prosper.'" Then just knowing what to do, Tommy linked fingers with Ketko between the gaps of their middle and ring fingers. "Just like Spock on *Star Trek*."

"What is this, *Star Trek*?" Ketko asked.

"Never mind." Tommy shook his head.

Victoria greeted Ketko and the other Atlanteans with the Vulcan sign, quote and handshake.

"How far is it to the palace?" she asked.

"Several miles," Ketko said.

"We have to hike up that mountain?" Tommy asked.

Ketko grinned and said, "Only if you wish, but that would take hours. You can ride with me." Ketko gestured behind him, revealing a horseless chariot which magically hovered off the ground.

"Cool." Tommy grinned, then gestured for Victoria to step into the flying machine.

With part amazement and trepidation, she gingerly stepped into the golden contraption with intricately carved letters and symbols. "Tommy, look. Is this what I think it is?"

Immediately recognizing the ancient language, Tommy gasped. "It's Ancient Sumerian!"

"Of course, Ancient Sumerian. It makes perfect sense. One of the oldest civilizations which dates back before the Ancient Egyptians." Awestruck, Victoria studied the ancient carvings on the flying, golden chariot.

Ketko climbed aboard and pushed a few buttons which resembled precious gems.

Pointing to the gems, she asked, "Are those real?" Perplexed that something so valuable was used to control a flying chariot.

Ketko smiled and said, "Of course. We're beneath the Earth's surface. The heat and pressure forge these beauties in abundance."

"How do you, uh, er, retrieve them?" Tommy asked.

"We have a machine which can withstand the heat and pressure. I'll have to show you. Think of it as a giant claw that seeps through the force field and grabs whatever we wish without jeopardizing the integrity of the shield," Ketko explained.

The chariot hummed to life, rose higher above the ground, then sped towards the palace. The other chariots followed behind.

"When did you arrive on Earth?" Victoria asked.

"I'll let the princess explain everything." Ketko waved his hand nonchalantly.

"What else do you grab beneath the surface?" Tommy asked.

Ketko said, "Diamonds, rubies, emeralds, sapphires, and, if we time it just right, plutonium."

Chapter Seventeen

"Hold up, did you just say, plutonium?" Tommy asked with a shocked tone. Then he turned to gauge Victoria's reaction.

Immediately thinking of all the stolen plutonium recently reported in the news, Victoria comprehended the significance. "Why do you collect plutonium? Isn't it dangerous?"

"Yes, that's why we use it. It was the princess's idea. We explode the plutonium just beneath the fault lines of the Earth's crust. Our hope is that one day, we can open a crack large enough to raise Atlantis back to the surface."

Victoria and Tommy studied one another. Then she said, "That's how we got down here to begin with. During an earthquake in Southern California, a giant crack opened in the Earth's crust. We climbed down into it to explore. Then another quake hit and opened up the fissure. We slid through, miraculously unscathed, then fell into Atlantis."

"Yes, that part of the world has an enormous fault line, that's why we keep exploding the plutonium each time we pass under the San Andreas Fault," Keto said.

Victoria and Tommy exchanged perplexed expressions, then Tommy asked, "What do you mean, pass beneath the San Andreas Fault?"

"Think of the Earth's crust as a hard, outer shell. Beneath the crust is a partially liquid center. Molten lava flows beneath the surface. Since we sank just below the crust through a fissure, we've been floating in this bubble and flowing around the world beneath the surface. We thought it was random at first. But after studying it over the years, our scholars recognized a pattern."

"How often do you explode the plutonium?" she asked.

"We use the plutonium whenever we're beneath either a volcano or a fault line," Ketko said.

Victoria immediately thought of Pompei which erupted in 79 AD along the Amalfi Coast of Italy, killing thousands by covering them in lava and volcanic ash. "Volcano? I thought that was a natural occurrence? It was you! Do you realize how many humans you've destroyed over the millennia?"

Ketko shrugged. "I just follow orders from the princess. But that's why they call her the 'Plutonium Princess!'"

Plutonium Princess? Victoria shuddered at the strange title, then anger bubbled inside. *How dare the princess kill humans?* She couldn't wait to meet this princess. More questions swam through her mind. *Was she in charge? Shouldn't there be a King or Queen of Atlantis?* As much as she wanted to give this Plutonium Princess a piece of her mind, she realized that she'd better be nice. Hers and Tommy's fates rested in her hands. If they were stuck in Atlantis forever, then she'd better not piss off its ruler!

The beautiful golden palace shimmered at the top of the mountain. Intricately carved columns touched the top of the of shimmering force field. Lush tropical plants below resembled a rain forest.

They arrived at the palace, and the chariot slowed as it lowered and hovered just off the ground.

Stepping off the chariot and onto the ground, Victoria and Tommy marveled at the beautiful architecture of the palace. Two large columns, carved in hieroglyphs, depicted the Sumerians', Atlanteans' or possibly Vulcans' journey here from outer space.

"It's beautiful. It reminds me of the Egyptian temples in Africa only even more magnificent." They walked through the entrance and into the temple with more engraved columns. Between each column were globes of various sizes which resembled different planets. The ceiling rose several stories above her head. But instead of a roof, the ceiling boasted all of the stars. She felt as if she were looking up at the heavens instead of the ceiling of an Atlantean temple beneath the Earth's crust.

They continued walking down the long aisle of the palace. At the far end was an altar and three thrones.

An epiphany struck her. They were in the most beautiful place *in* the world, literally and figuratively. She knew now more than ever. *This is perfect.* "Tommy, are you thinking what I'm thinking?" She studied his expression.

He gazed in awe at their beautiful surroundings. "Uh, huh."

"What do you think?" she asked with a hopeful tone.

"It's perfect in every way imaginable," he gushed.

Euphoric, she smiled and said, "I always knew the perfect place to marry you would magically appear and we would know without a doubt."

They hugged one another and said in unison, "We're getting married in Atlantis!"

Chapter Eighteen

Trumpets blared and the soldiers and citizens of Atlantis knelt reverently.

Following their lead, Victoria and Tommy knelt, too.

"What's going on?" Tommy whispered.

Shrugging, she presumed, "This must be the Plutonium Princess."

Trumpets blared again, then a man donning a white toga said, "Her Royal Highness, Princess Eve, the acting ruler of Atlantis."

Victoria's theory was correct—the Plutonium Princess was the acting ruler. Presumably, the King or Queen were too old to rule effectively.

A beautiful woman appeared. Her platinum, blonde locks hung in perfect curls to her ankles. Her porcelain complexion showed no signs of aging. Her bright blue eyes sparkled. Precious gems hung from her elfin ears. She wore a purple toga and strappy sandals. Standing nearly nine-feet-tall, her regal stature left no doubt who was in charge of Atlantis.

With a gesture, Princess Eve said, "Rise my fellow Atlanteans." She sat on her throne, surveyed her audience, and immediately spotted the humans.

Victoria made eye contact with the princess and smiled.

With a curious expression the princess waved them towards her. "What do have we here? I've never seen a human before."

Victoria curtsied and Tommy bowed.

"Come here. Let me get a good look at you," the Platinum Princess commanded.

Victoria and Tommy walked towards the throne and stopped just before the steps.

"How did you get here?" Princess Eve asked.

"An earthquake opened a fissure in the Earth's crust and we fell down here," Tommy explained.

"Yes, the earthquake. It's a shame the opening wasn't big enough for Atlantis to rise again. Tell me what the Earth is like now. The continent was breaking apart the last time an Atlantean saw the surface."

"Which continent?" Victoria asked.

"The only one of course, Pangea." Princess Eve laughed at the silly question. She gestured towards a globe of a planet. The globe showed land clumped together in the middle. The other two-thirds was water.

"Which planet is that?" Victoria asked.

"Why it's Earth, obviously," Princess Eve said with a condescending tone.

"Wow," Tommy exclaimed. "Now it's split up into seven different continents."

"Can you show me? Someone, get this human a papyrus and quill," Princess Eve ordered.

A soldier promptly handed Tommy a scroll and ink quill.

Tommy quickly drew a crude map of all seven continents and handed the scroll to a guard who walked the map up to the princess.

Princess Eve studied the scroll with a curious expression. "Thank you. This will help us determine the best places to explode the plutonium."

"If you don't mind me saying, you're killing thousands of humans each time you cause an earthquake." Victoria pleaded.

"Thousands of humans? How many humans populate the planet?" she asked with a shocked tone.

"Billions," Tommy said.

"Dear God. That won't do. I need to kill more humans. Overpopulation is what destroyed our planet. Too many Atlanteans exhausted all of our natural resources. Just a few of my ancestors fled our planet eons ago and settled on Earth. We need to cause more earthquakes so we can get back to the surface and stop the Earth from overpopulation."

"What if there was another way?" Tommy asked.

Perplexed, Victoria turned to Tommy.

"Magic." Tommy waved an imaginary magic wand.

"You know of sorcery?" Princess Eve asked.

"Yes, my Manchester cousins are witches and wizards. They once created a portal to move Neverland to another dimension. Surely, they can create a portal to transport Atlantis back to the surface," he suggested a more humane solution.

"Interesting. Can they transport us back to where we once were?" Princess Eve asked.

"Can you show me where Atlantis was before it sank?" Tommy pointed to the globe.

The princess walked down the steps and towards the globe of Earth. "We settled on a tiny island in the middle of the ocean. It was the only part of the planet not connected to Pangea. We weren't sure what was out there and we wanted to remain hidden until we could safely explore our new planet. She compared it to the new map Tommy had drawn on the papyrus, then pointed. "Atlantis was right about here."

Victoria and Tommy turned to one another and nonverbally acknowledged their prior theory. The Princess pointed to modern-day Cuba.

"Cuba. That's what it is called now. In fact, part of Atlantis remains underwater. I've heard tales from my Manchester cousins that after Atlantis sank, only the tippy top of the golden palace remained on the ocean floor. Then the mermaids moved in."

"Interesting. When we knew Atlantis was about to sink, we created a force field to protect the island. In the process, the tippy top of the palace was pinched off and left behind. Have you been to this, underwater Atlantis?"

"No, but some of my ancestors have," Tommy said.

"How do we contact your magical family to create a portal to raise Atlantis back to the surface?" Princess Eve asked.

Tommy bowed his head and said, "We pray."

Chapter Nineteen

Princess Eve studied Tommy with piqued curiosity. Then her expression changed from curiosity, to desire.

Victoria knew the look all too well. Tommy's gorgeousness turned the heads of many females, and males.

The eyes of Her Royal Highness dilated, then smoldered. They reminded Victoria of Tommy's bedroom eyes.

Princess Eve must've sensed Victoria's glare. She turned to her and ogled her up and down with a jealous expression. Then her gaze turned to Tommy again with the same adoration as before. Her expression grew pensive, then contemplative as if her mind brainstormed a shocking idea.

Fear ripped through Victoria, and she clung to Tommy protectively.

"Honey, what's wrong?" Tommy asked while pulling her close.

Victoria began to voice her fears, but was interrupted by Princess Eve's horrific command.

"Guards, take this female human to the dungeon!" Princess Eve pointed at Victoria.

The guards, armed with ten-foot long spears, approached Victoria aggressively.

Victoria clung to Tommy like scotch tape, and the guards literally had to peel her off him.

Tommy vehemently protested, "What are you doing? Please don't take her, take me instead!"

"But taking you to the dungeon instead would defeat the purpose." Princess Eve descended the steps from the throne and eyed Tommy with a lustful expression.

"What purpose?" Tommy asked.

The guards finally broke the connection between Victoria and Tommy and escorted her struggling form back down the long aisle of the grand palace of Atlantis. "Tommy! Help me!" She turned back towards the front of the throne room with a horrific notion of her beloved and the Princess of Atlantis.

Princess Eve stared into Tommy's eyes, obviously mesmerizing him. "Oh, my love. We will make beautiful babies together. Our children will unite our worlds and our species. Then once we rise to the surface, we can rule both worlds together."

Victoria screamed, "Noooooooo!"

Chapter Twenty

The Atlantean guards dragged Victoria kicking and screaming, literally, down several flights of circular stairs. At the end of the stairs, a long narrow tunnel with dimly lit, blue glowing lights dissected two rows of cells. The dark, damp corridor reminded her of the cells depicted in Medieval Times.

They tossed her into a cell with iron bars and locked her in. Fearful of being trapped down here forever while Tommy played house with the acting ruler of Atlantis, Victoria felt determined to find a way out of here. With no windows, she focused on the iron bars themselves. Grabbing the cold metal, she rattled the bars. "Help! Get me out of here!"

Met with silent defeat, she cowered into the back corner, hugged her knees, rocked back-and-forth and wailed uncontrollably. She couldn't believe how abruptly her life changed for the worse. An hour ago, she and her beloved Tommy discovered Atlantis and their wedding venue. Now she was locked in a dungeon for the rest of her life while Tommy would soon mate with the evil Plutonium Princess!

"It's no use. I'm afraid that you're trapped down here forever, too," the voice of a saddened female echoed from the cell next door.

Startled, Victoria said, "I thought I was alone down here."

"I'm Princess Sarah, the rightful heir of Atlantis. What did you do to my evil twin sister, Princess Eve?" Sarah asked.

"I'm human. My gorgeous fiancé and I basically fell into Atlantis, and the evil Plutonium Princess Eve imprisoned me so she can mate with my man!" Victoria cried.

"Oh, I'm sorry. Are my parents, the King and Queen of Atlantis, still alive?" Sarah asked with a hopeful tone.

"Yes, but just barely. They are frail and appear to be spellbound by Princess Eve," Victoria said.

"Oh, blessed be to God. All I do now is pray that I will be rescued and restored to my rightful place as heir to the Atlantean throne. In fact, I will pray now. Will you pray with me?" Princess Sarah asked.

"Of course." Victoria clenched the Crucifix from around her neck and recited the Hail Mary prayer. Recalling how their prayers were answered in the past, more specifically at Noah's Ark, she intended to pray until she either died of dehydration or was rescued. Then another recollection of prayer flitted into her consciousness. St. Michael the Archangel once told her and Tommy, "If you ever need any help, just say my prayer."

With a renewed sense of hope, Victoria recited the prayer to St. Michael the Archangel.

"'Saint Michael the Archangel, defend us in battle; be our protection against the wickedness and snares of the devil, May God rebuke him, we humbly pray: and do thou, O Prince of the heavenly host, by the power of God, thrust into hell Satan, and all the evil spirits who prowl about the world seeking the ruin of souls. Amen.'"

Chapter Twenty-One

The sound of flapping wings resonated throughout the dungeon. St. Michael's angelic form magically appeared before Victoria. His white wings with gold tips spanned six feet. His golden curly locks framed a youthful, cherub face. His spellbinding eyes—one blue and one green—sparkled with amazement.

With a bewildered expression, he turned to her and asked, "You again? I find you in the strangest places."

Standing upright, she grabbed the bars with bliss and said, "Thank God you're here! Pun intended."

Laughing, Michael waved his hand over the locked gate, and the cell door magically opened.

Victoria ran out and couldn't hug Michael fast enough. She squeezed his muscular frame and silently appreciated his perfect physique. "Thank you." Tears of relief dropped onto her cheeks.

"What happened? How did you even get down here? And where is Tommy?" Michael fired his questions in rapid succession.

"There was an earthquake in California. A giant fissure opened up, and Tommy and I explored it. Then an aftershock struck and we fell into Atlantis. The Plutonium Princess intends to raise Atlantis and destroy the planet. She locked me in this dungeon and plans to mate with Tommy to unite the species," she summarized in one breath.

"That's why my father sunk Atlantis in the first place. The Atlanteans invaded Earth and planned to drain it of its natural resources. Princess Eve sounds like a raving sociopath. We need to get rid of her for good. Let me call my wife." Michael closed his eyes.

Victoria expected Michael to pull out his cell phone and call Penelope Manchester. But instead, he kept his eyes closed and obviously communicated with his magical wife telepathically. After several nods, he opened his eyes and said, "She's coming and bringing backup."

One by one, dozens of Manchester witches and wizards appeared in the now cramped dungeon.

"Thank ya'll for coming to save us," Victoria sighed with an appreciative tone.

An Elder wizard said, "The sinking of Atlantis has been documented in our archives. This evil princess must be destroyed!"

Chapter Twenty-Two

The Manchesters held hands and the oldest Elder recited, "*Eo Ire Itum*, throne room of Atlantis." With this magical travelling spell, all of the Manchesters were instantly transported to the throne room.

Dozens of Manchester witches and wizards magically appeared in front of the Plutonium Princess. Victoria kept her distance in the back and prayed this sudden distraction would camouflage her presence.

"Ah, you must be here to raise my beloved Atlantis." The Princess smiled devilishly.

The Manchester Coven bowed to Her Royal Highness. While concocting their plan of attack, they'd decided to bow respectfully to avert suspicion.

"Yes, we are," an Elder said.

"But where's St. Michael the Archangel?" the Princess asked.

Grinning, Penelope said, "My husband prefers to fly."

The sound of flapping wings resonated throughout the palace. Everyone turned to see St. Michael the Archangel fly into the temple, then land at the base of the stone steps leading up to the thrones.

Bowing to Princess Eve, Michael said, "Your Royal Highness."

"Rise, St. Michael. I am Princess Eve, ruler of Atlantis. Our human visitor claims you can help us raise Atlantis back to the surface." The Princess gestured towards Tommy.

"Yes, we plan to raise Atlantis," Michael said.

Princess Eve stood regally in front of her throne and said, "Thank you all for coming. I've been looking forward to this day for a very long time. Is this all of you?"

Penelope said, "No, about half. The rest are on the other end to create the portal by Cuba. Are you ready?"

"Yes." Princess Eve nodded eagerly.

The Manchesters wiggled their fingers towards the Princess.

"Wait, what's this?" the Princess asked with a fearful expression.

"Direct orders from the man upstairs. You must account for your evil actions," Michael chastised.

Blue bolts of light ignited from all of the Manchesters' fingers. Dozens of lightning bolts struck the evil princess, and she incinerated into a pile of ash, vanquished for all eternity.

"Yippee!" the Atlanteans cheered in unison. The loss of their princess was obviously welcomed.

Victoria ran into Tommy's arms and cried. "Oh, Tommy. I was so scared in the dungeon."

"What the hell happened?" he asked.

"I prayed to St. Michael the Archangel, and he appeared as promised. Then he called his wife."

A hush fell over the crowd and the Atlanteans bowed to their ancient King and Queen. The rulers now stood fraily in front of their thrones. The King of Atlantis addressed his subjects, "Rise my people. We've been living in torment with the tyrant who cursed us into submission to her evil rule. Now that the Plutonium Princes is vanquished, thanks to the Manchesters, we may now live in peace and hope for a humane way to rise to the Earth's surface once again." A tear dropped onto his cheek.

"It's okay, my love. A true leader will emerge since we have no heir," the Queen said soothingly.

Victoria spoke up, "Actually, you have an heir. I met Princess Sarah in the dungeon. Sarah said her younger twin, Eve, was so jealous of her that she imprisoned Sarah in the dungeon in secret and told everyone that the true heir died tragically in her arms before her body mysteriously disappeared."

"Mother? Father?" A frail form emerged from the dungeon. Her once platinum locks were dingy with neglect. Her dirty skin reeked from infrequent sanitation. But her former beauty was still evident in her beautiful, blue eyes and warm smile.

"Oh, my precious Princess Sarah!" The King and Queen hugged their daughter with great love and affection.

The kingdom of Atlantis hoorayed the joyous reunion and the return of the rightful heir.

"Oh, we almost forgot," Victoria piped up.

St. Michael asked the King, Queen and Princess, "Your Majesties, if we raise Atlantis, do you swear to God that you will respect the Human Race?"

"Of course," the Royal Family nodded vehemently.

"Father, do I have your permission to raise Atlantis?" Michael asked. Then he smiled reassuringly. "Let's raise Atlantis!"

The Manchesters held hands and recited Latin words. Atlantis rumbled, then traveled through a blue wormhole.

Victoria felt like she was on a roller coaster. Holding Tommy's hand, she watched Atlantis, still protected by its shimmering blue force field, travel through the glowing blue tunnel.

Water appeared at the end of the tunnel. With a loud splash, Atlantis landed on the surface of the Atlantic Ocean near Cuba.

Chapter Twenty-Three

Eleven months later
Atlantis

Victoria walked down the aisle of the grand temple in Atlantis. Her white wedding dress had a modest lace front, but the back was sheer, save for the silk buttons. An intricate lace cape served as a train. Her platinum and diamond tiara capped her ebony locks piled in curls on top of her head. The Garrison rubies, borrowed from Lilly, adorned her neck.

Victoria's father, handsome in his tuxedo with tails, escorted her down the long aisle. Tommy stood at the altar with his cousin Grier as his best man. Lilly, Grier's wife and Victoria's matron of honor, had just walked down the aisle in her cobalt-blue, full-length taffeta dress. She now stood at the altar with her other bridesmaids—Chelsea and Britta. The flower girl, Cat Manchester, stood next to her brother and ring bearer, Connor. Fuchsia the Fairy, perched upon Cat's shoulder, smiled sweetly.

Garrisons, Manchesters, Atlanteans and select Charlestonians filled the enormous temple of Atlantis. Victoria processed to the altar and was greeted by her mother's warm smile. Next to the altar, Princess Sarah, now fully recovered and restored to her former glory, sat on her throne which had been temporarily moved to the side for the wedding ceremony. The ancient King and Queen sat on either side of the princess. After Victoria's father gave her away to Tommy, Victoria bowed to the royal family.

St. Michael the Archangel, wearing a white toga, stood in front of the altar with his giant wings fully extended.

"Dearly Beloved."

THE END

Terri Talley Venters,
Author of *Carbon Copy, Tin Roof, Silver Lining,
Luke's Lithium, Copper Cauldron, Cobalt Cauldron,
Calcium Cauldron, Chromium Cauldron, Zirconium
Cauldron, Sulfur Springs, Europium Gem Mine,
Noah's Nickel, Manganese Magic, Platinum Princess,
Plutonium Princess, Iron Curtains, Body Of Gold &
Elements Of Mystery*

Terri received her Bachelor's degree in Accounting, and Master's degree in Taxation from the University of Florida. She is a licensed CPA and a Second Degree Black Belt in Taekwondo. She lives on The St. Johns River in Florida, with her husband, Garrison, and their two sons.

For more information about Terri's books, please visit her website www.ElementsOfMystery.com.

Terri is the daughter of Leslie S. Talley, author of *Make Old Bones, Bred In The Bone, The Closer The Bone & The Bonnie, Bonnie Bone*. For more information about Leslie's *Cozy* murder mysteries, please visit her website www.MakeOldBones.com

Excerpts from

Elements Of Mystery- A collection of 118 short stories titled after each element in the Periodic Table

12
Mg
[Ne]3s^2

Magnesium

Premise for novella
Europium Gem Mine

"We must be getting close, I see *magnesium* veins in the rock walls." Victoria led her boyfriend and colleague through a cave system outside of Paris, France.

"Let's be careful, we don't want to ignite this mine." Tommy's straight, sandy blond hair framed his handsome, green-eyed face.

"We're fine, we're using battery powered lights, not gasoline lanterns." Victoria pointed to the light on her headband covering her long black hair.

They came to a mining tunnel and stared incredulously at the low height.

"Why would they make such short tunnels? We're going to have to crawl through on our hands and knees," Tommy complained.

"I thought you liked me on my knees." Teasing, Victoria winked.

"You owe me a back rub later for making me hunch over like Quasimodo to get down here." Tommy smiled suggestively at Victoria, recalling prior rub downs and where they often led. Tommy stared into Victoria's ice-blue eyes and couldn't think of anywhere else he'd rather be—in a cave exploring with his beautiful girlfriend and fellow archaeologist.

They crawled through the shaft for a hundred yards. Just as Victoria felt claustrophobic, the tunnel opened up into a large cavern. Victoria stood upright and brushed the debris off her toned limbs.

Scaffolding and ladders went from the floor to the fifty-foot ceiling. Someone mined this cave, recently.

Tommy shined his flashlight along the cavern walls. Light bounced off the cave's treasure with tiny prisms.

"Are those?" Victoria asked.

"Diamonds." Tommy finished her sentence. He retrieved a small chisel from his excavation kit and tapped the rock surrounding the precious gem. A diamond as big as his fist dropped into his eager hands.

"Incredible, look at all of them. The diamonds I can see in this cavern alone must be worth a billion Euros," Victoria said with an incredulous tone.

"I never knew such an abundant supply existed, let alone in France," Tommy said.

"I wonder who owns all of this. They must be hoarding them to avoid flooding the market and deflating the price of diamonds," Victoria said.

"You know, I think I know who owns this, assuming the land owners above also own the mineral rights. Look at what is located directly above us." Tommy handed Victoria his iPhone which displayed Google maps.

"We're right below Disneyland Paris!"

"I feel bad for stealing from a mouse. But this will fund our digs for the rest of our lives." Tommy pocketed the diamond.

"Shhh, I hear something." Victoria ducked behind a mining cart and hid from the intruders. She grabbed Tommy's strong bicep and yanked him down beside her.

"Oh, crap! Who are these men? They look like... No, they can't be." Tommy's chiseled jaw dropped to the floor, along with Victoria's.

They stared incredulously as a group of miners entered the gem mine. Their short stature and bearded faces looked familiar. They sang a catchy tune as they started their work shift.

"They're dwarfs," Tommy said, without taking his eyes off the unique workers before him.

"This explains the short height of the mining tunnels and scaffolding. They look just like..."

"I know, only there's more than seven working here today," Tommy said.

The dutiful dwarfs began their shift. They grabbed their pickaxes to mine diamonds and precious gems out of the rocks beneath Disneyland Paris.

They sang the familiar song in unison "*Hi Ho....*"

Author's note: Walter Elias Disney misspelled 'dwarves' with 'dwarfs.' When it was brought to his attention, he decided not to change it. In keeping with Walt's wishes, I'm spelling 'dwarfs' his way.

16
S
[Ne]3s²3p⁴

Sulfur

Premise for Novella
Sulfur Springs

"Thanks for traveling across the Atlantic Ocean to join me on this excavation, Tommy." Victoria Ventures hugged her ruggedly handsome colleague.

"When a beautiful woman calls and asks me to leave the harsh winter in Scotland to play in the dirt with her in sunny Florida, I take the first flight out of Edinburgh." Tommy Garrison grinned.

"You came at the best time, we finally cut through all the bureaucratic red tape. Now we can get our hands dirty," Victoria said.

"How did you find this place?" Tommy asked.

"A condo developer demolished an old hotel near Disney World. When they dug up the old foundation, they found an entrance to a cave," Victoria said.

"Just a cave? I thought you mentioned an excavation every archaeologist dreams about," Tommy asked.

"I promise you, Tommy, it will be! I haven't told you the best part yet, come on." Victoria winked.

They traversed the cave system for over an hour, covering the distance of almost four miles. They barely spoke as they hiked through the vast tunnel system. Victoria's excellent physical condition made it easy to keep up the intense pace. Her excitement to show Tommy her discovery motivated her to practically run to the discovery of a lifetime.

"I'm glad you marked the path with twine. If I got lost, I'd never find my way out again," Tommy said.

"I've walked this tunnel so many times I don't even need the twine anymore. But it's smart to have, just in case," she said.

"Like the guy who killed the Minotaur in Crete. Didn't he use twine to find his way back out of the labyrinth?" Tommy asked.

"I forgot how nerdy you are." Victoria laughed, poking fun of her college boyfriend.

"Yuk! Did something die down here? It smells like rotten eggs." Tommy pinched his nose to mitigate the foul smell.

"We're getting close now. You're smelling the *sulfur* commonly found in hot spring water," Victoria explained.

"This reminds me of how they discovered the ancient Roman baths, in Bath, England. During the Victorian era, hot water leaked into someone's basement. They started digging and uncovered the archaeological find of the century," Tommy said.

"Sorry I'm walking so fast, but I'm anxious to see the look on your face when you see what I found," Victoria said.

"You mean, what your *team* found," Tommy corrected.

"What I'm about to show you hasn't been seen by anyone, at least no one still living. I've been in a holding pattern waiting for you to arrive. I need a diving partner, and no one will take the risk. The cave dead ends into a hot spring," Victoria said.

"Sounds fascinating, but I imagine the fear of diving in uncharted hot springs sounds intimidating," Tommy reasoned.

"It's not exactly undiscovered. In fact, someone discovered it thousands of years ago. They left markings. Ancient Egyptians discovered it before the Spanish did five hundred years ago.

"Okay, now you just gave me the biggest hard on. Did you say Ancient Egyptians were here?" Tommy asked.

"Yes, but I'm not an expert in hieroglyphics, that's one of the reasons I called you. I merely possess basic knowledge, and I don't recognize much," Victoria said.

"No one has ever found evidence of Ancient Egyptians in the New World. But we studied Egyptian hieroglyphs together in graduate school. I'm surprised you're so rusty. I recall feeling furious when you earned an 'A' when I got stuck with a 'B+.'" Tommy pouted.

"Do you regret turning down your fellowship at Harvard to be with your father in Scotland after his heart attack?" Victoria asked.

"Not as much as I regret not staying in the States to be with you." Tommy's heart ached for the missed opportunity with his college sweetheart.

"You're here with me now." Victoria blushed bashfully.

"If the Spanish found this cave in the 1500s, why haven't we heard anything about the discovery?" Tommy asked.

"I think I know why this place is still a secret. Look here. Our predecessors left warnings." Victoria shined a light on the cave wall a few yards away from the start of the hot springs. She and Tommy stared at the engravings.

"Don't feel bad for not recognizing the hieroglyphics, they're not Ancient Egyptian," he said.

"What are they?" she asked.

"Something older, Sumerian perhaps?"

"The one below it is written in Spanish." She translated:

Do not touch the water, or you will watch
everyone you love die
--Ponce De Leon

"Come on, we're almost there," Victoria said. Grabbing Tommy's hand, she led him to the start of the hot springs. She pulled out her lighter and ignited incense to mask the pungent smell of *sulfur*. She shined her flashlight on the control box for the recently installed lights. Placing her finger beneath the switch, she looked at Tommy.

"Ready? 3, 2, 1." She pressed the switch, and the lights shone brightly on the hot, *sulfur* springs. A layer of steam hovered several inches above the milky water.

"Oh my God, the only thing stopping me from diving in is Ponce De Leon's warning," Tommy said.

"I have a confession to make." Victoria dropped her chin.

"No, please don't tell me you risked your life by touching the water?" Tommy asked.

"Only by accident. The other day I tripped and stumbled. My hand automatically reacted by going down to brace my fall. It accidentally landed in the water." Victoria held her right hand up to show Tommy.

Tommy gently took her hand in his and examined it. He enjoyed the intimate moment of caressing Victoria's hand. He ran the tips of his fingers over her soft skin as he admired her youthful hand. He instinctively pulled her hand to his lips and kissed it.

"Your hand is as beautiful as I remember. It's like you never dug in the dirt in your life." Tommy still held her hand, and his strong feelings for Victoria came rushing back, filling his heart with love again.

"I know. That's just it, until the other day, my right hand looked as rugged and aged as my left. Here, look." She held her left hand next to her right to allow Tommy to compare the astounding difference between the two.

Tommy studied her hands and jerked his head back, shocked at the sight before him. While Victoria's right hand appeared youthful and unblemished, her left resembled his own—wrinkled, rugged, and covered with tiny scars from digging in the dirt for a living.

"When I noticed the change, I initially thought it healed from the medicinal powers of the hot, *sulfur* spring water. But then I did an experiment, and I realized this is something much more," she said.

"Victoria, no, what are you saying? It can't be?" Tommy asked.

"My cat is eighteen years old and ready to be put to sleep, but I can't muster the courage to say goodbye," Victoria said.

"You still have that calico cat from college, Cali?" Tommy asked.

"Yes, I brought her down here, carried her in one of those papoose things mothers use to tote their infants around. I submerged her in the water for only a second, and now she's as good as new," she said.

Tommy stared at Victoria incredulously. His eyes bulged as the shock settled in. "Do you mean you've discovered..."

"The Fountain of Youth."

25
Mn
[Ar]4s²3d⁵

Manganese

Premise for novella
Noah's Nickel

"I'm not used to seeing the sun on our dates." Squinting her eyes, Victoria Ventures teased her boyfriend, Tommy Garrison.

"I know. I thought a little hike in the mountains would be nice. Get some fresh air, have a picnic, and make love on a blanket." Tommy winked.

"Our exploring trips usually end up in a cave."

"You can never say no to a good spelunking."

"Hey, watch your language, there could be children on these trails."

"I doubt it. These trails are for experts."

"And I don't *always* meander into every cave I find." Victoria pursed her lips.

"Yeah, ya do. I bet you couldn't pass up a cave entrance if your life depended on it."

"Wanna bet?"

The couple climbed the hiking trail which led them up into the mountain. The air grew cooler with the increased elevation. The spectacular view of the valley below greeted them.

"Isn't this the mountain from the Bible where…"

"Yes, it is." Tommy nodded.

"Cool. Glad I paid attention in Sunday school. Uh, oh." Victoria stopped and stared at the mountain wall near the ledge.

"What is it?"

"I'm about to lose our bet." She pointed to a cave entrance.

"Ah, there's nothing like a good, 'I told you so.'" Tommy beamed.

Victoria stepped into the cave's entrance, not caring that Tommy was right about her insatiable curiosity.

The enormous cavern revealed itself, and the sun disappeared as the couple walked deeper into the cave.

"This place is huge. I wonder if someone lived here."

"A whole tribe could live in here. And they probably did. Look at the soot stains in the center. I bet whoever lived here built their fire right here." Tommy pointed to the cave's floor.

Victoria shined her flashlight around the cavern walls. "I can picture cavemen living here thousands of years ago."

"You brought a flashlight on a day hike?" Tommy asked.

Victoria glanced down, a tad ashamed of her nerdiness.

"You brought your archaeology tools, too. Didn't you?"

"Occupational hazard." Victoria referred to their joint passion and careers as archaeologists.

"Oh, my, God. Tommy, look at these." Victoria shone her flashlight on the large back wall of the cavern.

"Cave paintings."

"These must be thousands of years old."

Tommy touched the black rubbings on the cave wall. Then he placed his fingers to his nose and smelled the black soot. Sticking out his tongue, he tasted it. "Sppt." He spat out the soot.

"What is it?" Victoria asked.

"*Manganese*. Cavemen used *manganese* to draw cave paintings thousands of years ago."

"Why did you spit it out?"

"One, it tasted nasty. And two, *manganese* is linked to Parkinson's disease."

"Oh, here. Wash your mouth out with water." Victoria handed him her water canteen.

Tommy poured water into his mouth, slushed it around like mouthwash, then spat it out.

Victoria shone the flashlight on the cave paintings, studying them intensely.

The paintings depicted typical cavemen stories—men hunting huge animals with spears, and women gathering around a fire. But then the theme changed. Animals were drawn on the wall walking towards something big. Many species of animals were depicted, walking in pairs up a hill. Then water was drawn, flooding the land. The end of the cave painting depicted an enormous ship floating on top of the world.

"Does this cave painting depict what I think it does?" Tommy asked.

Victoria smiled. "Yes, this tells the story of Noah's Ark."

45
Rh
[Kr]5s¹4d⁸

Rhodium

Premise for novella
Plutonium Princess

"Oh, what a magical day!" Victoria held Tommy's hand as they exited Disneyland in Anaheim, California.

"Every day with you is magical, no matter where we are." Tommy squeezed Victoria's hand and kissed her cheek.

They leisurely strolled back to the Disneyland Hotel, just a quick walk from the Magic Kingdom and California Adventure theme parks. Bright stars glittered the beautiful night sky.

Rumble

"What the hell is that noise?"

"Thunder?"

"There's not a cloud in the sky." Tommy looked up.

"It sounds like it is coming from the ground."

Droves of people exited the hotel from the lobby.

"What's going on?" Tommy asked.

"Earthquake," a Disneyland Hotel employee said.

"Oh, my God! What do we do?" Victoria asked.

"Just stand outside away from buildings." The employee's tone was calm, like earthquakes were a normal occurrence.

Tommy and Victoria walked away from the tall hotel. The hotel pool was a safe distance away.

Rumble. Rumble. Rumble.

A huge crack in the earth appeared. It started in the pool and continued away from them towards the Magic Kingdom.

As quick as it started, the rumbling stopped and, fortunately, the crack never reached the 'Happiest place on earth.'

"Look at the pool. The water drained away." Tommy pointed.

"Where did the water go? I thought the earth was solid." Victoria asked.

Tommy scratched his chin with his thumb and index finger. "Well, actually, there are some that believe the earth is hollow inside, once you get through the outer crust."

"Who believes that?"

"Vernians."

"Who?"

"Fans of Jules Verne, the author of *20,000 Leagues Under the Sea, Journey To The Center Of The Earth, From The Earth To The Moon, Mysterious Island, Around The World In 180 Days,* and more.

"You mean, like the movie *Journey To The Center Of The Earth* with Brendan Frasier?"

"Which is based on the book. In the book, Jules Verne believed that the earth was hollow and that there is another world beneath the surface."

"My geology is rusty, but that sounds like a load of...." Victoria crossed her arms.

The pool water, now gone, revealed a giant crack, at least ten-feet wide.

"Why don't we find out?" Tommy pointed.

Her curiosity overruled her common sense. "We have our rock climbing gear back in the room. I just thought we'd use it to go up, not down."

"Looks like everyone is going back into the hotel. The earthquake must be over."

Thirty minutes later, they returned to the empty pool, fully equipped to see what lay beneath the Earth's crust.

Tommy shone his flashlight into the large crevasse. "It's a straight drop to another level. I'll go first." Tommy secured the rope, then tested its strength. He rappelled down into the hole about two hundred feet. "Come on down, there's something cool down here," Tommy shouted.

You don't need to tell me twice. Victoria couldn't rappel herself down fast enough.

"That was fun. What's so cool?" Her jaw dropped. The walls sparkled. "Is that white gold?"

"No, it's *rhodium*. It's eight times more valuable than gold and 450 times more valuable than silver. It's used to coat gold jewelry to make it shinier. They call it a *rhodium* flashing."

"How do you know so much about *rhodium*?" she asked.

"Remember when we discovered the silver mine beneath Castle Garrison? I did tons of research on precious metals."

"Nerd."

"That's not what you called me last night." Tommy winked.

"Touché."

"In fact, Guinness awarded Paul McCartney a *rhodium* album. Since he sold a gazillion albums, he deserved something more than just gold and platinum albums."

"Google much?" she teased.

Ignoring her quip, he said, "I wonder if Disney knows that there is a fortune in *rhodium* underneath their theme parks."

"I hope they own the mineral rights, too."

Tommy retrieved his chisel from his backpack and broke off a piece. "For early retirement."

"You can't steal that?"

Ignoring her, Tommy broke off several more chunks of *rhodium.*

Rumble!

"I thought the quake was over. I hope your chiseling and stealing didn't cause another quake." Fear flew through Victoria.

The walls around them trembled. They clung to each other, terrified.

"After shocks?"

"This feels worse than the first one."

The floor beneath them cracked open and they slid down, and down, and down, thousands of feet.

They landed on some sort of island with temples everywhere. Miniature moons glowed brightly and illuminated the island and its surrounding waters.

"Looks like Jules Verne was right. The Earth *is* hollow."

"Are we in the center of the Earth?"

"No only that, we're in Atlantis!"

49
In
[Kr]5s²4d¹⁰5p¹

Indium

Premise for novella
Platinum Princess

"We love London, Daddy." Catherine, Cat for short, stood in front of Big Ben, perched in front of the clock's enormous face. The magnificent skyline, including the London Eye, dominated their view. The dark water of the Thames meandered below.

"This is so cool." Connor, Cat's twin, smiled.

"I love this age." Penelope, the twins' mother, leaned into her husband, St. Michael the Archangel.

"I know. Six is a great age. We must enjoy every precious moment with our babies. Before we know it, they'll be teenagers with attitude." Michael wrapped his white wings with gold tips around his wife and soul mate.

"Daddy, isn't this where Peter Pan departed from to take Michael, Jon, and Wendy to Neverland?" Cat asked.

"You don't believe such nonsense, do you? You just have Peter Pan on your mind because we just saw his statue in Hyde Park." Penelope shook her head.

"Where's your belief?" Michael asked. "I'm an angel, you're a powerful witch, and our twins are witches with wings. But you don't believe in Peter Pan?"

"But, I...."

"Come on kids, flap your wings. 'Second star to the right, then straight on 'til morning.'"

"Yippee!" the twins sang in unison. Flapping their tiny wings, they levitated away from Big Ben.

Penelope shot Michael a puzzled glare.

Extending his massive wings, he gestured for her to come into his embrace to assume her usual flying position. Penelope embraced him.

The magical family flew into the night.

* * * *

The morning sun's first light touched their wings as they flew towards the rising sun in the east. Michael nodded to the twins, signaling them to descend.

Following his lead, the magical family flew towards the earth's surface.

Confusion filled Penelope as they hovered a few hundred feet above the surface.

"Cinderella's Castle?"

"Tokyo Disneyland."

"Yippee! We're going to Disneyland." The twins fluttered down to Cinderella's Castle and landed on the fake balcony on the highest turret.

"Oh, but I thought you wanted to go to Neverland," Michael teased.

The twins whispered to one another, obviously consulting this magical dilemma.

Always speaking for her twin, Cat stepped forward. "Neverland first, then Tokyo Disneyland."

Penelope gasped, "I remember now, from the *Book of Legends*."

"Took ya long enough," Michael quipped.

"Mommy, Mommy, tell us the story," the twins begged.

Penelope explained, "Neverland is real. It was a magical island in the Pacific Ocean. But modern civilization, and the Japanese, wanted to build on it. My ancestors, who wanted to protect the island without revealing themselves, created a portal. They moved Neverland through the portal, protecting it forever."

"Do you remember the spell?" Michael asked.

Nodding she said, "You just have to believe, and add Fairy dust."

Michael held a small vial with indigo blue dust. "*Indium* works, too. When a Fairy dies, their magical form turns into what scientists thought was a new element. *Indium* is simply crystalized Fairy dust."

Penelope took the vial, threw the dust in the air, waved her hand, and believed.

Dust spiraled in the air, creating an indigo blue cloud—a portal.

The magical family flew through the portal. Cinderella's Castle and Tokyo Disneyland disappeared. They now hovered over a lush island. Mermaids lounged on the rocks near the shore, sunning themselves.

"Welcome to Neverland!"

59
Pr
[Xe]6s²4f³

Praseodymium

Premise for Novella
Manganese Magic

"I'm stuffed." Grabbing her belly, Victoria stood from the table in the Enchanted Garden Restaurant in the Hong Kong Disneyland Hotel.

The character dining starred Snow White and Dopey who meandered through the dining room speaking with each guest. The elegant, Victorian themed dining room reminded Victoria of the Crystal Palace Restaurant at the Magic Kingdom in Florida.

"An American breakfast. Thank you, Victoria, for eating here. I'm sick of Chinese food." Tommy paid the bill with Chinese Renminbi.

"If you didn't just pay with funny money, I'd never know that I was in Hong Kong. What a breakfast spread—eggs, bacon, sausage, ham, fruit, pastries, and the signature mouse ear shaped waffles and pancakes."

"Don't forget the dim sum." Tommy laughed.

They exited the hotel and walked to Hong Kong Disneyland.

"What do we want to ride first? The park just opened, so we probably want a popular ride first before the line gets too long." Victoria studied the map.

Tommy peered over her shoulder. "Oh, we should ride Big Grizzly Mountain Runaway Mine Cars."

"You want to ride a roller coaster right after breakfast?" Victoria shot him an evil glare.

"We'll be fine if we only ride it once." Tommy extended his arm, and they strolled through Main Street USA.

* * * *

"WHEEEE!" Tommy screamed from the Big Grizzly Mountain Runaway Mine Car. The roller coaster resembled Big Thunder Mountain in the Magic Kingdom in Florida.

The ride stopped suddenly.

"What happened?"

"'Technical difficulties.'" Tommy quipped using air quotes.

"Oh, I'm gonna be sick." Victoria jumped out of the mine car, ran to a corner, and puked.

Tommy followed her. "Are you okay? I'm pretty sure we're not supposed to exit the car during the ride."

She shrugged, not caring if she was exiled from Hong Kong Disneyland. Leaning back on a different mine car off to the side, she felt the car move. "What's this? It looks like a real mine car, not like the pretty, clean ones on the ride with seats and a safety bar."

They climbed in, begging for trouble from the Cast Members.

"They must not have cameras everywhere like in America." Tommy presumed.

"What's this lever do?"

"Victoria, don't!" Tommy screamed.

Too late.

Victoria pulled the lever releasing the brake. The mine car rolled slowly at first, then it dipped and picked up speed. It was going down fast at a forty-five-degree angle.

"Crap, no seat belts. Hold on tight!" Victoria hollered.

After descending several hundred feet, the car came to a screeching halt.

Exiting the car, Tommy used the flashlight app on his iPhone to illuminate the dark cave. A torch rested against the rock wall. He lit the torch with the *praseodymium* torch striker.

"Wow!"

The cavern lit up. But it wasn't just one cavern, the area was honeycombed with tiny alcoves—an underground civilization.

"I've heard about these. It's how humans survived the ice age—they were protected in dry underground caverns."

"Amazing. Let's check it out."

The archaeological find thrilled her. And she ignored the horrible notion—*How are we going to get out of here?*

"It's so dry down here. No humidity, even though we're beneath sea level. Anything could survive down here for thousands of years," Tommy speculated.

Turning a corner, they discovered a gigantic room filled with scrolls and books.

"Anything could survive down here alright, including the Alexandria Library!"

94
Pu
[Rn]7s²5f⁶

Plutonium

Premise for novella
Noah's Nickel

"What a magical day." Victoria held Tommy's hand while they walked back to the Toy Story Hotel after a wonderful day at Shanghai Disneyland.

"Too bad we didn't get to every ride. The park just opened a few months ago, so it was really crowded."

"I think Disney is always crowded, regardless of how new it is," she said.

"You're right, my love." Kissing her hand, he smiled.

"What FastPasses did you get for tomorrow?" she asked.

"Ah, about that, I have a surprise for you." Tommy winked.

Trying to abate her anger, she bit her tongue. *How dare he not get FastPasses for the next day? Now all of the good rides will be booked up, and they'd have to wait in the standby line with the rest of the schmucks.* But "oh," was the only word she let escape her lips.

"I'll show ya in the room." He waved his magic band on the hotel door, the green light turned on and they entered their suite.

Tommy opened his laptop and pulled up his cave plotting software.

"Caves? What's this?" Her eyebrows arched with curiosity. Now she felt bad for getting miffed about Tommy not booking FastPasses for the next day.

"About a week before we met, I had just finished a dig near here. I decided to test my new gadget that plots caves without going into them." Tommy beamed like a kid at....

"What's the fun in that?" Victoria quipped.

"It's really hard to discover a cave system. It's just dumb luck."

"Like the one we found under Walt Disney World or Disneyland Paris." Her tone grew sarcastic.

"Exactly, both times were just dumb luck. But this gadget uses a seismic charge. You set off the charge on the surface, and the magical software tells you what is beneath the surface," Tommy explained.

"That is amazing. Why didn't you go exploring right then and there?" Her excitement bubbled just thinking of the unexplored cave system nearby.

"Grier called me. He and Lilly pushed their wedding up to Christmas Eve. I didn't want to go, but he insisted. And since he bought Castle Garrison from my broke father, we have to rely on his good graces to let us continue to live there."

"The wedding! That's where we met. If you had stayed here...? Our lives would be completely different. It scares me to think of how close we were to not meeting and falling in love." A tear dropped on her cheek because she couldn't imagine her life without Tommy Garrison.

"I know, scary huh? But look what I discovered." He pointed to the map and compared it to the map of Shanghai Disneyland.

"Part of the cave system goes right under the park. I wonder what's 'under the magic' this time?" she asked.

* * * *

The next morning, armed with camping gear and supplies for a few days, they entered the cave system a few miles away from Shanghai Disneyland.

Tommy opened his laptop and studied the cave system. "There should be a tunnel right here." Tommy pointed to a rock wall.

"Bummer, it's a dead end." Victoria sighed.

"It can't be. According to the seismic map, there are more caves here, giant ones." Tommy studied the laptop, perplexed.

"Maybe there is another entrance to the giant caves. Maybe the caves don't all connect."

Tommy studied the rock wall before them. It wasn't a solid wall, it was a pile of rocks stacked up to block the tunnel.

"Victoria, it's not a natural rock wall. Someone placed these rocks here to keep people out." He pulled one rock from the top of the wall.

"Oh, my, God! You're right." She pulled a rock off the wall and tossed it aside.

Excitedly, they removed enough rocks from the wall to unblock the tunnel. Then they climbed over the remaining rocks and continued through the new tunnel.

After walking a few more yards, they entered a giant cavern. The ceiling soared several hundred feet above their heads. The length of the cavern went on for at least a thousand feet.

"This cavern is enormous. The Titanic could fit in here."

"I think this was once under the ocean, many millennia ago."

"We're in a cave that was once underwater." Victoria shook her head, incredulous.

"How is the ceiling staying up? You'd think it'd collapse with all the weight above it."

"Natural arches. If the arch is just right, all of the weight gets transferred to the walls, like in a cathedral."

"It looks like there is some kind of ship." Tommy pointed.

"I don't see any portholes. It looks really old." Victoria studied the gigantic ship.

Tommy's face lit up. "It's remarkably well preserved in this dry cave. Now I know what they're really hiding. I imagine that religious zealots would start World War Three if this discovery went public." Tommy stared in awe.

"Are you saying.....? But I though it landed on Mount Ararat."

"Maybe Mount Ararat was the first dry land the ship sighted when the flood waters receded. But apparently, it didn't land there."

"I can't even say it because it doesn't seem real," Victoria cried.

"Let's say it together. Ready in three, two, one...."

"Noah's Ark!"